Deborah

Deborah

by Colette Davenat

translated by Anne Carter

William Morrow & Company, Inc.
New York 1973

Printed in the United States of America

Davenat, Colette.
 Deborah.

 CONTENTS: [1] The springtime of love.
 I. Title.
PZ4.D2456De3 [PQ2664.A878]   843'.9'14   73-1673
ISBN 0-688-00171-8 (v. 1)

Per molto variare la natura è bella

A favourite aphorism of Queen Elizabeth I

Deborah

PART ONE
Chartley

I

London, 1586.

The girl went swiftly through the Great Court. Her small feet, shod in softest leather, seemed to glide noiselessly over the stones as she passed, a black velvet shadow paying no heed to the nocturnal sounds about her. A light wind touched her cheek, bringing a faint scent of woodbine, while from the privy garden came a muffled clamour of frogs. Somewhere a nightingale was singing, accompanied by the low, rippling murmur of the river close at hand, beyond the high, brick walls, its garbage-laden waters lapping at the frontage of Whitehall.

Pausing at a small doorway, the girl knocked three times, distinctly. The door opened and a tall serving man appeared in the aperture. With a few whispered words, the girl passed through and, taking the candle he held out to her, began to climb a narrow stairway. At the first landing, two guards in steel breastplates sat astride a bench throwing dice. One got to his feet and, seeing who it was, made haste to draw back the tapestry masking the entrance to a broad corridor, devoid of all furnishing, in which the only sign of life came from the glimmer of the candle flame reflected in the beeswaxed surface of the fine, inlaid wooden floor.

At the far end a woman stood waiting, a small woman dressed in grey who scurried forward, mouselike, to meet the girl, gave her a silent greeting and, retracing her steps, selected a key from the bunch hanging at her waist and inserted it in a lock.

The room into which the door opened was not large but it was bathed in a soft light and furnished with a luxury in striking contrast to the austerity of the passage outside. The walls and ceiling were panelled in pale oak that glowed a warm gold in the candlelight. The feeling of warmth and intimacy was enhanced by the rich Persian rug spread on the floor of black and white marble tiles and the curtains of jonquil satin framing the tall latticed windows. There was little actual furniture beyond a single silver-inlaid chest placed opposite the hearth and a scattering of some half-dozen heavily carved stools.

The girl glanced questioningly at the serving woman.

"You must be patient a while, Mistress Deborah. So Mrs Tucker bid me tell you. Her Majesty being not yet returned."

The woman bobbed a curtsy and left the room. Deborah slipped off her cloak and sat down.

She was feeling slightly sick, as if a heavy weight had settled on her stomach, very much, in fact, as she had felt as a child after secretly devouring a whole pot of plum jam stolen from the stillroom. Well, it looked as though the plums were coming home to roost today! She gave a little shrug, crossed and uncrossed her fingers, muttered a brief prayer then forced herself to take a deep breath, and repeated the process. . . . She could feel her nerves getting the better of her. What did the Queen want? It must be a matter of some importance – great importance even! Her aunt's manner that morning had been flustered and that, the Lord knew, was unlike her! Could this, by any chance, be the moment both of them had dreamed of for so long now? Had it come at last, an end to this waiting which, it seemed to Deborah suddenly, had been going on for an eternity?

She had been born seventeen years earlier, at the village of Hatfield. Her mother? It was all she could do to recall a wistful, almost childish smile, framed in a cloud of golden curls. Her father, then? The devil fly away with him! Him, she had never known at all. Yet it must have been from him that she had got her dark red hair, a rich and glowing chestnut, her high heart and the pride which could not fail to set her apart from her condition. "A lord, as sure as sure!" Mrs Tucker was wont to say, complacently admiring her niece's beautiful and unusually well-shaped white hands. But whoever he had been, whether gentleman or common rogue, Rose Mason, Deborah's mother, had carried the secret with her to the grave.

Rose was the younger daughter of the Hatfield farrier, a girl whose fragile beauty and quiet, sober bearing seemed in no way to mark her out for a tragic destiny. Yet, at the age of sixteen, she had suddenly vanished without trace. A search had been organized, men with hay rakes and pitchforks had scoured the countryside, even venturing into the patch of swampy ground said locally to be the haunt of ghosts and evil spirits, but their efforts were in vain and they went home and barred their doors, while the unhappy family

4

were left to mourn their daughter's loss and attribute it to the work-ings of witchcraft. They thought so still when Rose returned some time later, on a December night, as white as the snow which lay on the fields and meeting all their questions with the same, stubborn silence. All the same when, six months later, she was brought to bed of a fine girl, the facts could not be denied. Strange tales were told, to be sure, of the goings-on at witches' Sabbaths but who had ever heard tell of anyone being got with child that way?

Who, then, was the guilty party? The smith stormed and threatened and pleaded, but to no avail. Rose said never a word and little by little people grew accustomed to the little fatherless child. She was a pretty creature and her mother called her Deborah, though why such a strange, outlandish-sounding name, rather than Jane, or Mary or Bess like anyone else, none could say.

The farrier laughed and accused her of getting ideas above her station. "Hast heard the preacher call our Queen 'the new Deborah', and wilt thou call thy bastard brat the same?"

Then, five years later, Rose pined and died. The Masons' elder daughter, Jane, came and fetched Deborah away from the village, once and for all.

To the little girl, what followed was a complete and almost miraculous transformation of her whole world. A child's memory is blessedly short and her tears soon dried at the sight of the palaces to which her aunt, like a fairy godmother out of a story, whisked her off: Whitehall, Richmond, Hampton Court, handsome buildings, brilliant with lights, set in fairytale parks peopled with elegant beings in scented, silken garments. How could she have any regrets for the dark cottages with their smoke-blackened beams, squatting amid ploughed fields, or for the cast-off clothing which had been all the orphan child had known until then? How could she have dreamed of these wonderful, soft, floating, brightly-coloured clothes, chosen not for warmth and durability but for the simple pleasure of the moment? And to this paradise her aunt had the right of admission! Heavens, what an important person Aunt Jane must be!

In sober truth, Jane Tucker's position was humble enough and Deborah very quickly learned to know how great was the gulf that divided her from one of the fine ladies she admired as she sat perched, with her small legs dangling, on the wall of the kitchen court.

"Oh, Aunt! Tell me, please, how it was you came to Whitehall?"

"You are very young, child. It takes me back a long way . . . Very well, then. Do you remember the big house at Hatfield?"

Oh yes, Deborah remembered that. A great red-brick manor, its peace broken now and then by the coming and going of horses' hooves, with a small, enclosed garden full of marigolds and forget-me-nots where, last spring, she and her mother had crept in secretly one day to plunder the blossoms.

"Well, I was about three times as old as you are now when your grandfather obtained a post for me in Her Majesty's service. Oh, she was still only a princess in those days, of course, and a most unhappy one at that, poor child! Her sister, Queen Mary of evil memory, kept her virtually a prisoner – but there, you wouldn't understand. . . . At all events, Her Majesty was very lonely, all hedged about with spies, and she was good enough to notice me."

As she spoke the words, Jane Tucker's ample, black-clad bosom swelled with pride.

"What happened then, Aunt?" Deborah crammed her small fist into her mouth, breathlessly awaiting the sequel.

"From that moment, I have never left her. I slept on a truckle bed in her room, I dressed her and combed her beautiful hair, so fine and silky it might have been spun gold. And she would talk to me . . . oh, the things she'd tell me. She was a clever one was my princess, she knew at once that I should not betray her. Well, things went on this way for two years and then one day . . ."

"What happened, Aunt?"

"Patience, child. Don't you hurry me. Let me think . . ." Jane Tucker's eyes were half-closed and her voice was dreamy. "In 1558 it was, in November, the seventeenth to be precise. It was a grey, gusty afternoon but my princess never heeded that. No, she sat herself down under an oak tree, calm as you please, with her nose in a book – because there's no one can compare with her for a scholar, you know— So there we were, she reading away and me blowing on my fingers to get warm and thinking of a nice cosy fireside, when up gallops a great crowd of gentlemen, all swarming round us and going down on their knees to my lady and telling her that she is queen. They'd come straight from St James's with the news. Mary had died that very morning! Gentle Jesus, how we all rejoiced! We packed our traps and a week later we were away to London."

"And then?"

"Then? My goodness, I went on working hard! I've worked hard all my life, you know. And then I married my Tucker and, five years

6

ago, the very year that you were born, Her Majesty made me her chief tire-woman. God bless her, such an honour! And now – well, here you are, child."

The girl gave a start as the distant sound of a door shutting broke in on her thoughts.

She sprang up and crossed quickly to the door, not that by which she had entered but another, on the other side of the room, which gave directly on to the Queen's withdrawing chamber. She listened, her ear pressed to the wood . . . soft, padding footsteps hardly disturbed the silence. A servant probably, most assuredly not Her Majesty who was justly renowned for her tempestuous entrances.

Deborah sighed and moved to the window. A night owl called and she turned away with a little shiver to resume her seat but paused instead before a delicate Venetian mirror set in a circular frame of chased silver, staring abstractedly at the image it reflected. Her gaze was idle, quite without vanity, seeking merely the reassurance of a familiar face. There had been, as yet, no young man to tell her that she was beautiful and to awaken her from a child's unselfconsciousness. She knew, of course, that she was pretty but she had no idea of the effect on men's minds of that exquisite oval face with its pearly complexion and the glance of those blue-green eyes, full of unspoken promises of a passionate nature lurking behind the modest screen of silken lashes. Added to this was a straight, wilful little nose, a mass of copper curls and wide, characterful mouth whose full, ripe contours added a touch of sensuality in oddly attractive contrast to the classical regularity of the other features.

Summoning up a faint grin, the girl turned her back on her reflection and began to walk up and down the room. She was frowning slightly and fiddled nervously with her lace cuffs as she walked. She told herself that she would willingly have parted with her garnet bracelet, though it was a pretty trinket, heaven knew, and one that she was fond of, only to know what was in the Queen's mind. Waiting was becoming a torment. She sighed again and sat down.

One, two, three . . . if she could count up to a hundred before that wretched owl hooted again, then all would be well. Superstition? No, just a little trick she had which had brought good luck before now.

Sixty-six, sixty-seven . . .

Deborah jumped to her feet. An imperious tap of heels in the

7

distance, the sound of an oath uttered in a strong, ringing voice. Merciful heavens! The Queen!

She gabbled breathlessly through the remainder of her charm: ninety-eight . . . ninety-nine . . .

The door opened.

Mistress Tucker sailed in, massive and dignified, dressed as always in black, a great gold chain winking on her bosom. She bestowed a brief peck on her niece's cheek and then stood back and looked at her with an air of satisfaction at odds with her somewhat stern and forbidding features.

"Well, child," she said quietly, "it is time."

"Oh, Aunt, tell me quickly . . ."

"Hush, now! What will the Queen think to see you in such a flutter? Yes, the time has come, at last! You are to set forth the day after tomorrow."

"Set forth?" Oh Lord, you looked forward to it for so long and then, when the moment came at last, you hardly knew if it were joy or terror that made your breath stop suddenly! Deborah's knees gave way beneath her and she sank on to the stool. "What is my mission, Aunt?"

"It is not for me, child, to speak of that. Her Grace will tell you herself soon enough. Now, listen to me, for we have not long." She laid her hand firmly on her niece's shoulder. "This is your opportunity, Deborah. Make the most of it. As my poor Tucker used to say, God rest him, the Lord helps those that help themselves!"

Nervous as she was, Deborah had to bite back a smile. Now that he was dead, Uncle Tucker had become an amazingly convenient husband. Such pearls of wisdom as were put into his mouth! Yet what had he ever done when he was alive, poor man, beyond ogling anything in petticoats and drinking himself into a stupor behind his wife's back?

"Don't worry, Aunt," she said, rising and kissing her aunt impulsively. "I shan't let you down."

"I hope so indeed, lass. Think of the pickle I shall be in if you fail! I have fought hard for you, you know . . . Oh, to be sure, I have nagged you often enough, but once more will do no harm, now least of all, but when I brought you from Hatfield I knew right away that you were different. How did I know? We ordinary folk, we have our instincts. And so all my ambitions centred on you, child as you were. For myself, the post I held then, and hold still, was the highest I could aspire to, but you . . . You, with your pretty ways and your

8

quickness! You were never made to be a waiting woman. Oh, I laid my plans carefully. I said to myself, 'Jane,' I said, 'there's only one person in this world of ours can help us, and that's the Queen!' Remember how I brought you into her presence, slowly at first, and induced her to take an interest in you? Dear Lord, such patience I had! And then, one fine day, the miracle happens! The Queen has made up her mind at last ..."

Miracle indeed! There was no other word for it.

Deborah saw herself at the age of ten, leaving Whitehall for a discreet house in Fleet Street, the pleasant quiet street leading off the Strand. Away from her aunt, away from the spacious galleries of the palace, through which she had trotted eagerly, clinging to Mistress Tucker's ample skirts. Gone was the shouting, jostling crowd of serving lads whose games she had shared! She had found herself transformed overnight into a young lady with servants to wait on her and grave tutors to instruct her. And so a new life had begun for her, bounded by her studies and preserved from all external distractions by tall heaps of books and reverend, white-bearded scholars.

They had taught her everything. She had been so ignorant, but, oh, so very eager to learn. The rudiments of knowledge to begin with, followed by more advanced education in the arts and sciences, languages, ancient and modern, history and, above all, the new study of geography which appealed so strongly to the girl's adventurous mind that her enthusiasm made even the Queen smile on the occasions of Deborah's infrequent visits to Whitehall. And later, still more exciting, there had been lessons in horsemanship, in the handling of weapons, dancing and, much less enjoyable, in deportment. Oh, what this last had cost her in effort and correction! "Curtsy! Sit! Walk . . . No, no, Miss Deborah! That is not the way! Strive for an easy, graceful bearing! Once again ..." And then the laughter, politely hidden behind the fan, and the special voice, the slight air of distance to be adopted when addressing servants and a host of other little details which had taken so long to learn and yet which came to her now as naturally as breathing. So much hard work had gone into making her what she was today, and what ... As though divining her thoughts, Mistress Tucker broke in on them:

"Well, well, child, what a long way we have come, to be sure! Lord, who'd have thought a Mason's by-blow would ever come to be a secret agent of the Queen!"

"Let's not count our chickens! It might bring bad luck!"

"And how may that be to count our chickens, pray? When it was for this very thing that her Grace has had you educated, as lavishly as a princess, for the past seven years, and at her own cost? Wasn't it to make you hers, body and soul, to be her eyes and ears wherever she might send you?"

Secret agents, a secret service organization wholly outside the normal workings of the law and controlled directly by the Queen herself. Its personnel, a mystery. Anonymity was the very essence of their service. Of what, precisely, was the nature of that service, Deborah was still largely ignorant . . . she thought in vague terms of information . . . espionage, but great had been her joy and pride that it was for this the Queen had destined her. It was a much more exciting life than those around her, something of a game with a delicious spice of adventure added, but it was also a position of trust, offering limitless opportunities to be of use – indispensable even – both to her benefactress and to England. Who would not envy her? Nevertheless, to allow one's imagination to run riot and to come face to face with the facts were two very different things and, Deborah finally admitted it to herself, she was horribly afraid.

"Yes, of course," she concurred meekly, in answer to Mistress Tucker's last remark. "But – oh, how can I explain? So much responsibility all at once, Aunt, makes me afraid. And the thought that in a few moments . . ."

"Tush! Enough of this foolishness! This childish fear will pass. I know you. You have more courage and coolness in your little finger than all these court dolls put together. Come, it is time to go. No, wait . . ."

She cast a critical eye over Deborah's appearance, smoothing the dark cloth of her plain, schoolgirlish gown which rose modestly above the proud, young breasts and lightly moulding the slender waist fell in still pleats to the ground.

"You'll do," she said. "That plain dress could not be better. Our good Lady is an accomplished flirt, God knows, but nothing irritates her more in other women. And we must not put her out of humour. . . . Oh, but you're so pale! When she likes a bright complexion!"

Deborah ran to the mirror and pinched her cheeks energetically, then paused to push back a straying curl beneath her cap.

"There – is that better?" she asked anxiously, her face suddenly crimsoned.

Mistress Tucker condescended to smile. "Yes. Now you look like a harvest apple!"

She drew her niece close and gave her a hug which was unusually demonstrative for her.

"This is the moment, child. God be with you! Do not disappoint me."

A passage . . . then another room where the light of many candles threw huge shadows on the gilded and coffered plaster ceiling. The biggest of the shadows moved and turned.

With moist palms and trembling knees, Deborah sank into an irreproachable curtsy. She was in the presence of the Queen.

II

"Ah, there you are, child! God's death, Tucker, unpin me or I faint!"

Deft, competent Mrs Tucker was already silently at work, aided by three of the Queen's maids of honour.

But the mission . . . what of her mission? The word beat in her head like the wingbeats of a flock of startled sparrows.

Stop!

Deborah knew she must take hold of herself. It was absurd to allow herself to panic, like a nervous servant girl, and quite unworthy of a future secret agent. She strove to turn her mind to other things and escape from the vicious circle of unanswerable questions. Her bent head lifted imperceptibly.

Heavens, what an age her aunt was taking to undress the Queen! Deborah's eye made a respectful note of the exquisite splendours now being shed, from the wide French farthingale to the quantities of pearls, diamonds and rubies scintillating like so many precious tear-drops against the gold brocade. There were more pearls, more diamonds encircling the Queen's neck, wrists and waist, more rubies . . . Deborah blinked and let her gaze travel upwards to the face stiffly framed in all this reliquary magnificence: a long, spare face, pale in spite of the paint which liberally reddened the cheek-bones, drawn into lines about the thin mouth and marked faintly by the plucked brows, delicately arched. The girl smothered a small sigh. Her Grace had aged a good deal in recent years. Little remained of her fine complexion and her wonderful red-gold hair, hidden now beneath that flaming wig. To be sure, she was fifty-three – and what signified a wrinkle more or less? She was as tireless as ever: first in the chase, last to be still dancing, astounding and mystifying every court in Europe by her wit and her prodigious energy.

Deborah's heart swelled and she gave another sigh, of pride, this time, in her Queen. Was there ever such a Queen, or would there ever be another such? She was no pampered princess whose succession had been a foregone conclusion. No, every step to her throne had been climbed in trepidation, fearing for her life. Like Deborah, she had borne the stigma of bastardy, put upon her by the papists who refused to recognize the legality of her father's marriage to Anne Boleyn. Thence, too, had sprung the troubles which beset her girlhood, a terrible experience, according to Aunt Tucker who should surely know better than anyone. While still no more than a child, her Grace had been compelled to learn dissimulation, to pick her way through a maze of intrigue, the potential tool of every conflicting interest. She had looked on — as often as not through prison bars or what was very little removed from them — while three reigns ran their course, the two last, those of her brother and her bigoted Catholic sister Mary, mercifully short. God, in his wisdom, had seen to that! Then, at twenty-five, she had become queen. Elizabeth of England! Oh, not the England of today, but a poor and hungry enough place by comparison. But she was not afraid of hard work and she had rolled up her sleeves and set herself to rule. The outcome was a great and prosperous nation that was the wonder and the envy of the continent. How was it done? By a compound of intelligence and love: intelligence amounting to genius and limitless funds of love, for it was in this that Her Majesty differed from so many rulers. She lived for her people and in her people. She loved them and they worshipped her, and indeed, she had done everything in her power to win their love.

Deborah's eyes grew moist as she thought of the long, lumbering progresses, the royal procession winding its way like a jewelled snake through the countryside and herself perched up beside her aunt on a hard wooden seat on one of the baggage carts, a little girl half-hidden among the chests and baskets. They stopped at every town and village on the road and everywhere was like a holiday. Coachmen cracked their whips and the crowd cheered. There were splendid ceremonies at which the Queen, encrusted with jewels, sat to receive the homage of the local notables and then, suddenly, without warning, she would be transformed into a laughing, mischievous creature, clapping her white hands and joking broadly with the crowd with easy familiarity and a real kindness which was not the least part of her charm. Privilege indeed to serve such a mistress.

But the mission . . . *her* mission! Once again the words danced a jig in the girl's head.

"Now, child, we are alone."

Hard, beringed fingers pinched her chin, tilting it imperiously.

13

Gold brocade and maids of honour alike were gone. There remained a pair of very blue eyes, bright and almost unbearably piercing.

"Hm! Bright eyes, sweet mouth, firm chin . . . well, very well. Add to that your tutors' good report of your wit – God's death, we shall make something of you, Deborah Mason! Ha, ha! Ambitious, too, by all accounts!" The Queen smiled. "That suits me. I have not spent money on your education, a great deal of money, to put you to the kind of humdrum business that might be undertaken by any one of my agents. That would be a criminal waste and waste, let me tell you, is a cardinal sin! No, in rearing you at my charge, I looked farther, and higher." Abruptly, the Queen released her grip on Deborah's chin and began to pace up and down before the girl's rapt eyes.

"Even as a child, you had quality. Quality! Not to be confused, my dear, with such everyday qualities as industry, courage, patriotism, in all of which our countrymen excel. True quality is something quite different and not, alas, to be often encountered in those of low degree. You either have it or you have not – a God-given something which ever raises its happy possessor above the common run. But to return to yourself. I was tempted to undertake your education as a kind of insurance for the future. A well-bred young woman, able to insinuate herself into any company, here or abroad, to pry out intrigues in the making to my good profit could have many uses. There were, of course, certain risks involved, which in general I prefer to avoid, but the years would seem to have justified them. Now you have learning and that, with the gift I have already mentioned and an appearance of considerable . . . charm, let us say, should enable you, should I so desire it, to compete with any daughter of our noblest families but without the attendant disadvantage of family obligations. You will owe your advancement to myself alone, and during my good pleasure. For you owe everything to me, child, and do not forget it!"

The Queen came to a halt in front of Deborah. "What, but for your Queen, would be your present state? It is not hard to imagine. An ignorant, baseborn serving wench, to be robbed of her maidenhead by the first lusty lad. Whereas do but fulfil my hopes . . . But all depends on yourself, on your actions and your wit. It is too soon to think of the future. For the present, you will continue to pass for an orphan of good birth living, according to your parents' will, in your own household in Fleet Street. The story is a good

14

one, the people there are used to you and our good Tucker in the role of the old family friend plays her part well. How old are you now?"

"Seventeen, Your Majesty. Two weeks since."

"Seventeen! Good God, I have forgotten what it is to be seventeen!" Pressing her hand briefly to her temple, the Queen continued rapidly: "You are young, but never mind. Experience is soon gained. And your very youth may be an asset. Who would suspect that smooth face and clear gaze? Very well, now is your chance to prove yourself. You will set out the day after tomorrow for Staffordshire, for Chartley, where our cousin, the Queen of Scots, at present resides. You are aware, I think, of her practices against us . . ."

Here the Queen broke off and, crossing to a desk took out a letter which she perused attentively. To Deborah, it seemed as if a peal of bells had begun to ring in her heart.

Pride had driven out nervousness. She was drunk with excitement, too exalted even to feel the cramps which had seized her thighs from being obliged to remain for so long on her knees. First, the Queen's praise, of more worth than all the fabulous jewels of the Americas; the rich promise which her words contained and now a mission to the realm's most celebrated prisoner, Mary Stuart herself!

Determined not to be caught at a loss, Deborah ran over in her mind, at speed, the story of Elizabeth's past troubled relations with the Scottish Queen. It was nearly twenty years now since Mary had arrived in England, a fugitive from her own lords and under strong suspicion of having stained her dainty fingers with the blood of her second husband, the murdered Lord Darnley. Nearly twenty years during which Her Majesty had harboured this Scotswoman who brought with her nothing but trouble. How different they were, the Queen and her cousin Mary! The one so dedicated, devoted to the cause of the reformed religion and to her people, the other so impulsive and capricious, a woman first and a queen second, and more than all this – a papist! Yet between them lay the one, inconvenient link of common descent from King Henry VII from which Mary traced her claim to the English throne. A fine return she had made to Her Grace for her hospitality! She was for ever engaged in some conspiracy, acting as a magnet for Catholic gentlemen and disaffected subjects. And so far, it seemed, no remedy had been found for her incorrigible mischief-making beyond a change of residence and stricter governors. No loyal Englishmen but in his heart could provide a better and a surer answer! But the Queen would not hear of it.

If her mission was to Mary, then it was weighty indeed. The girl found herself shivering with something more than excitement. Gracious God! If the honour was great, then so too was the peril! Would she be equal to it?

With a rustle of silken underskirts, the Queen returned, the letter in her hand.

"Here, child. Take his letter and keep it safely. No one must know of it. No one, do you understand?"

Obediently, Deborah loosened the top of her gown and tucked the paper away invisibly between flesh and fabric.

"You will give that letter into Queen Mary's own hand," the Queen continued. "Into hers and no other! It is unsealed. You will learn the contents by heart so that you may destroy the paper at need. You are thinking, perhaps —" Elizabeth's voice hardened slightly. "Your mission appears to you a simple one. It is not so. If it were, I should not have selected you. Any courier could have done the business. There may be some unpleasant surprises awaiting you on your journey – commencing with my own intelligence service which must on no account get wind of this. You must deal with that in your own way. Above all, do not get into trouble. Chartley itself is a nest of papists still, in spite of all that we can do. One way or another, they may hear of this and seek to intercept the message and its bearer. In that event, you may bid farewell to your own ambitions, for even supposing they should spare your life I should not forget your stupidity."

Deborah sprang hotly to her feet, court etiquette forgotten.

"Your Grace need have no fears! I would die before I prove unworthy —"

The Queen smiled. "Peace, child! I am not to be interrupted. Yet your words gladden my heart since they prove both your courage and my judgement. Be on your guard. May God go with you and . . ." the thin lips tightened, "whatever may be the answer, let me hear it with all speed. It will be brief. A simple yes or no. Therefore, as the possibility of any indiscretion is ruled out, I think it best that two should know of it. Sir Amyas Paulet, our cousin's governor at Chartley, is an honest man. Tell him and he will convey word to us here."

Elizabeth paused again before concluding: "John Strong shall go with you. Further instructions will be given you by your aunt, with

16

a modest purse to defray the cost of your journey. See that you do not waste it. And remember: no one but the Queen of Scots must see that letter. No one! Now go. England and your Queen will know how to show their gratitude if you serve us well."

The interview was at an end.

Deborah's lips brushed the white hand held out to her and she curtsied herself out backwards in due form.

She was half-way across the court when the sound of a horse whinnying came clearly through the darkness.

John Strong, she thought, with the horses. Poor man, he must be tired of waiting. She quickened her step in the direction of King Street, full of happy anticipation at the news she had for her faithful servitor. But John Strong was much more than a servant to Deborah. Ever since her arrival, as a very little girl, at the house in Fleet Street, she had turned to him in all her troubles and childish disappointments. He had been her friend and companion, someone to giggle and play with when she could escape from her books and her teachers. Big, clumsy, grinning John had been there, like a great, faithful dog, yet with something of the father about him too, and the only person, apart from Mrs Tucker herself, to share the secret. Deborah thought of country John's fluently expressed dislike of London and guessed how happy he would be.

Absorbed in the prospects which were opening before her, she did not notice the dark figure lurking under the wall by the corner just ahead. Suddenly, the figure moved. A dagger pricked her side and a gruff voice murmured in her ear: "Keep quiet, mistress, and no harm will come to you. There's somebody would like a few words with you, that's all."

Before Deborah could recover from her surprise, rough hands had gripped her arms and hustled her into a coach which stood waiting in the entrance to a side street, conveniently hidden behind an outcrop of the wall. She found herself seated between two men. Neither spoke but the man on her right rapped on the panel as a signal to the invisible coachman and the vehicle began to move.

Receiving no answers to her furious questions, Deborah fell silent at last. Where were they taking her? As far as she could judge in the almost total absence of light, these men were gentlemen. She caught the glimmer of white ruffs, heard the rustle of silk. The coach, too, was luxurious. What did it all mean? Tears of rage started to her eyes. This was something to be proud of indeed! She had let herself be snapped up like a gnat between the hands! What a fool! She was conscious of the letter, scratchy against the skin under her dress, and wondered what the Queen would say. Supposing, that was, that she was going to live to hear it. Deborah gritted her teeth. It was no good thinking along those lines! Only a cool head could help her now!

The horses' hooves rang on stone flags and the coach stopped with a jerk. Deborah was hurried out by her captors and caught a brief glimpse of an imposing façade of tall, glazed windows, flaring torches and carved stonework. A door opened and, still guarded by her captors, Deborah mounted a short flight of steps and entered.

Inside was a spacious hall adorned in the most stately fashion with tall pilasters between which hung Flemish tapestries alternating with plain hangings of dull red cloth. In the centre stood a magnificent table inlaid with patterns of ivory and a variety of carved and metal-studded chests were ranged about the walls. The whole spoke of a cultivated taste backed by a long purse, and Deborah found herself drawing some comfort from the fact. It was not easy to imagine dirty goings-on in such surroundings.

A great staircase displaying tier upon tier of round-cheeked cherubs carved in the solid oak of the balusters rose massively from one side of the hall. From underneath its heavy shade there now appeared a black-liveried manservant who came towards her with the words: "Follow me, Mistress, if you please."

The tone was respectful enough, but the words were undoubtedly a command, and Deborah obeyed. There seemed nothing else to do. Besides, curiosity was beginning to get the better of her fears.

They passed through a series of antechambers, all wrapped in heavy silence, and halted at last before a modest doorway. A discreet tap and then the door swung open on oiled hinges. At a sign from the servant, Deborah stepped inside.

The person seated behind the great desk at the far end of the dimly-lit room was writing. He laid down his pen.

"Come in, Mistress. Come in."

He looked up as he spoke, and the candlelight fell on a stern face surmounted by a skull-cap and framed by a short, pointed beard of a pepper and salt colour. It was a face that Deborah had seen before, once or twice, briefly at the palace. Sir Francis Walsingham.

She forced herself forward, struggling with amazement. The close air of the room seemed to have become suddenly unbreathable.

Who was she that this all-powerful person, the Queen's Principal Secretary of State, member of the Privy Council and shadowy head of a secret service rumoured to be so efficient that not a word uttered within the realm escaped its notice, should send for her? What had all these things to do with her? Unless . . . Deborah's stomach contracted at the thought, very cold and explicit, of what precisely he might want.

For the moment, however, Walsingham's manner was benevolent as he dismissed the servant and addressed himself to Deborah, standing rigidly on the other side of his table.

"Please accept my sincere regrets for the somewhat rough and ready means I was forced to employ in bringing you here. It was" – he spread out his fingers in a conciliatory gesture – "a necessary precaution. My information is that you are a young woman of some intelligence and my own time is precious, so I will come straight to the point." He glanced at the stack of papers before him and went on: "You are called Deborah Mason, the daughter of Rose Mason and of father unknown, niece of the Queen's Grace's tire-woman, Jane Tucker . . ."

This was a statement, not a question. No answer was expected. The penetrating eyes were bent on her.

"Hmm. My information appears to be correct, Mistress Mason. You are a pretty child and no doubt ambitious behind those modestly drooping lashes. Join us and I'll engage to satisfy your ambitions."

"I am overcome by your honour's kindness but I do not understand . . ."

He interrupted her, smiling. "Then you are about to understand. I know that you are to some extent honoured by Her Grace's confidence and perform some slight services for her. This is what I propose. Keep me informed of these and you shall have no cause to complain of my generosity."

Deborah took a step forward. She found that her hands were trembling and thrust them quickly into the folds of her skirt.

"Do you think that I will betray my mistress!"

Sir Francis clicked his tongue indulgently. "Betrayal is a big word, my dear, and only goes to show how inexperienced you are. I know of no one with a better claim to love and serve her Majesty than myself, and yet . . ." He paused. "You see, Mistress Deborah, her Majesty is sometimes . . . how shall I put it? Impulsive? There are matters in which I may assist her better if I am informed beforehand of her intentions. There is no harm in it. Quite the reverse, in fact! Especially as you may be well assured that I shall hear of it sooner or later in any event. You will not be betraying a trust, you see." He smiled again. "So, you agree?"

"I am sorry I must disappoint you, sir . . ."

"What nonsense is this?"

Walsingham's lean fingers beat a tattoo on the desk in time to the anxious thudding of the girl's heart.

"Let us be quite frank. What hopes have you of the Queen? To speak bluntly, you lack birth, rank, fortune – everything but beauty. Yet beauty may be found on any street corner and, you may believe an old man, it will not take you far without address. Come, now! Surely you'd like to be established, have a place in society? I can give it to you, and soon, whereas her Majesty – well, no doubt you know how it pains her to undo her purse strings. While even should she do so, you will not despise a secondary source of income, eh, my young friend? Not when your conscience tells you that you are serving your country doubly thereby? For I repeat what I have already said: the Queen and I have one thing at heart, the good of England. Are you convinced now?"

Deborah put all the firmness she could muster into her reply.

"I do not doubt that you mean well, sir. And I beg you not to take offence at my refusal. But you must understand I serve the Queen and it is not for me to divulge what she has seen fit to conceal."

Walsingham rose. The friendliness of his manner hitherto vanished abruptly and his expression was icy.

"Let me advise you to think well, girl. If you are fool enough to reject my offer, I have other means to overcome your obstinacy. I can be a useful protector or a dangerous enemy. The choice is yours." He dropped back into his chair and added in a more normal tone: "Good God, are you going to let these childish scruples stand in the way of your whole future? This course of yours is ill-considered, Mistress Deborah, nor is it wise."

Up went Deborah's small chin defiantly. The anger which had been building up in her from the beginning of the interview overflowed suddenly, driving out all fear or moderation. Her eyes met his almost challengingly.

"Nothing will make me change my mind, sir. I owe too much to Her Grace's kindness to be bought now by another!"

"Little fool! You will be sorry!" Walsingham hissed through his teeth. "One last word. I shall not speak of this meeting. I counsel you strongly to be equally silent." A sneer crossed his features.

"Eager as I am sure you are to report this conversation, you know that if the Queen learned that I had unmasked you all your credit with her would be gone."

He rang the bell.

"Herbert and Jones will escort Mistress Mason to her house," he told the servant who appeared in answer to his summons.

Deborah curtsied briefly but Walsingham did not return the courtesy. He was frowning, his eyes fixed on the wall before him.

It was not until some minutes after the girl had left that he rose and, going to a handsome cypress wood chest with a silver lock, mounted on a stand, felt for something inside. When he returned to his desk, he held a sheet of paper in his hand. He scribbled a few lines, then, smiling unpleasantly, reread what he had written. Still holding the document he had just signed in one hand, he rose once more and left the room in his turn, by way of a small door cunningly concealed in the panelling behind his chair.

By the time Deborah reached the Fleet, the silent, shuttered buildings were beginning to emerge faintly through the pale, barely flushed mistiness of dawn.

Disregarding the hand extended to assist her, she sprang out of the coach without a word of farewell and darted across the tiny courtyard and up the four steps to the door.

Her mind was whirling in panic. There was no time to lose. She must saddle a horse and ride at once to Whitehall and warn her aunt! In her haste she almost fell over the large figure sitting slumped on a joint stool just inside the door. John Strong! She had completely forgotten him until that moment!

"John!" she cried, shaking him. "What are you doing there?"

He shook himself and rubbed his eyes, yawning bearlike, and sprang to his feet.

"Mistress Deb! I've waited these two hours and more. There's nothing wrong, is there? The fellow made no mistake?"

"Fellow? What fellow?"

John scratched his head.

"Eh, I don't know! Some serving fellow. I was waiting in King Street, in the usual place, when along comes this chap and says as how you'll come home later, and that I'm not to wait. That was right, wasn't it, Mistress Deb?"

He was looking at her in sudden worry, but Deborah was no longer listening.

Walsingham, it seemed, had thought of everything, even to sending a message to John Strong. Oddly enough, it was this thought which jerked her mind back to sense again. Heavens, what a fool she was! To tell the truth meant to say good-bye to her mission, and to any future mission! She knew the Queen well enough to be sure that there would be no forgiveness for one who, however involuntarily, had brought one of Elizabeth's plans to nought. And what would become of her then? Deborah felt her senses swim. If the Queen disowned her, all she could hope for was a servant's place, to be a tirewoman like her aunt! With nothing to look forward to but a pompous and self-satisfied old age, a hanger-on on the fringe of the great world, dressed in a black stuff gown and spending her days brushing and inventorying beautiful things with no hope of ever possessing them for herself! Was that what she wanted? Surely she was worth something more than that? What use were her studies, her vaunted intelligence and the beauty which even Walsingham had praised? He was right. She had better say nothing. The Queen would never know. As for Walsingham – the Secretary's words, filled with subtle menace, re-echoed in her mind but she shrugged them away. The realization of how much she had to lose had served to strengthen her grip on the present. He was powerful, certainly, but would he have the audacity to attack one whom the Queen herself protected? Surely not! He had merely been trying to frighten her like a child who is shown the rod. Well, she was not going to be frightened.

She smiled reassuringly at John Strong who was still gazing at her open-mouthed, bewildered by her silence.

"It's all right, John. There's nothing to worry about. But —" She put her hand coaxingly on his arm. "But, dear John, you won't – will you – tell my aunt? I – I felt like walking home tonight, that was all. But you know what she is. She would never understand and it would mean trouble for both of us."

"Walked home! You went walking about the streets at night all by yourself! With every kind of villainy abroad! Miss Deb! Are you out to make an end of yourself? No, I'll not give you away. But you must promise me you'll not be up to such tricks again."

"No, John. I promise." Deborah could not help laughing at his horrified expression. "Now, listen to what I have to tell you. In two days, we shall be off!"

III

Early on the morning of July 10th, 1586, two travellers left London and took the road to the north-west.

The elder, mounted on a stout chestnut cob, was a burly man of an age nearer to forty than thirty with a placid full moon of a face framed in a thatch of red hair. His suit of sober russet and the plain silver button which adorned his bonnet gave him the look of a respectable merchant travelling on business. His companion was a slender youth who appeared slighter still by contrast with that huge frame. He wore a doublet of soft grey velvet slashed to reveal the fine white linen shirt and foaming lace beneath. Matching trunk hose disappeared into a pair of well-made boots of palest cordovan pressed close to the mare's silky flanks. The rakish tilt of his felt hat left one half of his face in shadow.

They rode in silence, keeping their eyes on the road which from a broad expanse of ruts and puddles nearly fifty feet wide dwindled in places to a dusty track sunk between high, overgrown banks. Occupied with the progress of their horses, the two had little attention to spare for the landscape, yet for all that, the prospect was a fair one. The morning sun shone gladly on the English countryside, still sparkling under a heavy dew. On either side fields of ripening wheat and barley rippled lazily, the sea of pale gold broken here and there by the darker shape of an orchard. Next, they came suddenly on a village, nestling among pastures, the cottage gardens rampant with roses and honeysuckle which scaled the walls and rioted among the thatch, clothing in glory the poverty which too often lay beneath.

The women stood on their doorsteps, arms akimbo, in their russet petticoats and linen caps and stared curiously at the travellers while at their feet a grubby brood of children broke into shrill hoots of laughter.

There was plenty of other traffic on the road. They met many horsemen like themselves, a pedlar with his pack on foot, a tinker with his cart, hay wains everywhere and other wagons, sometimes singly, sometimes in strings of half a dozen or more. Once or twice

23

a group of gentlemen on horseback appeared, surrounding a horse litter in which travelled some noble dame and once, at a crossroads, there was the reassuring sight of a thieving rogue hanged in chains from the branch of an elm tree.

They changed horses at the first of the post-houses which lay at intervals of ten miles or so along the route, enabling the traveller pressed for time to hire a fresh mount and a boy whose task was to return the animal to its stable from the next stage. In this way it was possible to cover distances of between sixty and eighty miles a day, far more than could have been accomplished by a rider sparing his own horse. The cost, admittedly, was exorbitant, twopence half-penny per horse for every mile but in an emergency the time saved was worth the expense.

As they dismounted, the innkeeper came hurrying to meet them, hat in hand. The elder traveller produced a handful of coins.

"Here, my good fellow. Take these and make haste!"

In a very few moments, a lad appeared, leading three horses. At a sign from the innkeeper, he sprang into the saddle while his customers followed suit.

"In God's name, John, let us hurry," the younger traveller muttered impatiently. "We must be at Chartley tomorrow."

Deborah flung herself down on her bed with a great sigh of relief. Her muscles ached and she felt as sore as she had done as a little girl after one of Mrs Tucker's whippings.

Her hat and boots lay with her doublet and hose on the floor. Naked but for her shirt, she relaxed with her hands behind her head, enjoying the feel of cool sheets and the prospect of a few hours' rest in this quiet room. She understood now why it was that English inns were praised so highly that men claimed their equal was not to be found anywhere on the Continent. Her eyes roamed idly about the room, seeing the floorboards gleaming softly in the candlelight, the starched curtains at the window and the small table close by where a welcome meal awaited her attention: a roast capon with a salad and a dish of eels, a bowl of late wood strawberries and cream, to be washed down by a flask of Spanish wine, the whole laid out on a spotless white cloth. The down-filled mattress, too, was almost equal to her own in London – not that she had ever appreciated that one as she did her inn bed tonight.

She stretched herself luxuriously, giving an involuntary groan as her forgotten aches and pains caught her once more, and began to hum a little tune to herself for sheer happiness.

This was the life! No one to tell her what to do, no aunt, no tutors to obey. Not that she was such a monster of ingratitude as to forget all that she owed to them, but it was wonderful to shake off the dust of her books and be free, free to laugh and sing, even to sneeze if she liked, without constant reminders of good manners, free to indulge herself with this delicious supper . . . as a special treat, of course, she told herself, remembering guiltily the Queen's dislike of unnecessary extravagance. Free, above all, to conduct her own affairs and take the first steps towards that still vague yet glorious future which hovered so enticingly just out of reach.

Still with a song on her lips, Deborah flung back the clothes and, slipping out of bed, wandered barefoot over to the table. She was very hungry.

The eels had disappeared entirely and a large hole had been made in the capon by the time she nibbled her way through the last few strawberries and, draining her glass in a toast to herself, yawned her way back into bed and fell instantly asleep.

She woke abruptly to the sound of urgent hammering on her door.

"Mistress Deb! It's me – John Strong!"

Fumbling in the dark for her trunk hose, Deborah dragged them on and then went quickly to the door.

John Strong lurched towards her, moonlight falling on his battered face and his torn and battered clothes. One arm hung limp while the other clutched it to his side and his face was twisted with pain.

Deborah shut the door behind him and drew the bolt. Not until she had got a candle burning did she turn back to John.

"What happened?" she asked crisply.

"Begging your pardon, Mistress Deb, but happen you'd take a look at this arm o' mine? A parcel of damned rakehells below sought to quarrel with me. I accounted for two of them but the third got me, damn his eyes."

"Sit down." Deborah regarded him without much sympathy. How often had she impressed upon him that they were on no account to draw attention to themselves. She scrutinized the shoulder briefly and said: "I think you've put it out. I'll do what I can but you'll be sore for a day or two. Of all the idiotic things to do."

She rummaged in her saddlebag and found a linen towel which she began viciously tearing into strips.

25

"Tweren't my doing, Miss Deb," John said pathetically. "I was set down quiet in the tap-room minding my business and supping a quart of ale like, when up steps these three fighting cocks and picks a fight with me, a-purpose it might have been."

An icy trickle seemed to run down Deborah's back at his words, as though an alarm had sounded inside her. She reminded herself that John Strong was a peaceable fellow, not given to quarrelling. Her carefree mood of the evening was shattered and she asked herself if this were a deliberate move on someone's part to separate her from her servant. But who could know of her presence here in this inn? Walsingham's agents? Or Mary Stuart's? Unless, after all, the affair was merely a piece of drunken mischief . . . And yet . . .

She saw that big John was watching her with the hurt, anxious look of a dog who has been beaten for some reason he does not understand, so she gripped his good arm reassuringly and said in a softened tone:

"Never mind, old friend. What is done is done. Now let me see what I can do for that shoulder. And call me at five tomorrow. I think we shall be wise to leave here at dawn."

They were well past Coventry now, riding through a country of bare fields dotted with big, isolated trees. Now and then the gaunt arms of some riven giant added to the desolation of the scene. The road stretched ahead, a faint, twisting track, half-overgrown with bushes, to disappear at last into the murky shadows of a wood. No living soul was in sight. Rooks wheeled overhead and occasional rabbits scattered at their approach, but otherwise the land lay under a heavy, grey stillness which presaged a coming storm.

Deborah urged her horse forward. Her hand strayed continually and as if unconsciously to her doublet into the lining of which was sewn the precious letter from the Queen. All her thoughts now were centred on reaching Chartley and being rid of it.

With a growing sense of unease, she kept her eyes fixed on the approaching thickets. London was full of dreadful tales of robbery on the highways. The countryside was infested with thieves and vagabonds. They formed a kind of realm within the realm, subject to their own laws and owning their own lords, some of them rumoured to be sons of good families. Their profession was an old one, it might even be called a vocation, and it had its own martyrs and heroes, but then every trade had its hazards and the risks of this were few compared to the opportunities. On the unguarded roads was a constant traffic of plump citizens with plumper purses. What then if the gibbet waited at the end of the road? No prospect of capture was allowed to blunt the edge of their daring and ingenuity. Some innkeepers were even said to be hand in glove with the thieves and the hostler who came forward so readily to unstrap your saddle-bags, the chamberlain deftly stowing them in your chamber, even the tapster with his innocent inquiries as to your destination might well be preparing the bird for the morrow's plucking. Rumour had it that there were those merchants and wealthy yeomen who, tired of these incessant depredations, settled for a kind of annual insurance of twenty-five shillings paid to the Upright Men, as they were called, which purchased them protection. Such an encouragement to evildoers was wrong, of course, but for those who could afford it it was better than the loss of life and property.

Other people formed the habit of always travelling in groups or well-armed, like Deborah and John. Now big John was handicapped by his injured shoulder and Deborah strongly doubted if he were in any state to live up to Mrs Tucker's parting assurance that he would be worth three or four men in a crisis. She glanced at him a little anxiously.

He was riding slightly in front, his large figure hunched awkwardly in the saddle. A certain rigidity in the set of his shoulders, as well as his unaccustomed taciturnity, enabled her to guess what he was suffering from their present speed on this stony, uneven track. He probably needed all his energy to keep up a steady pace.

Their guide, the son of the innkeeper with whom they had changed horses last, was whistling gaily as the little cavalcade passed under the shadow of the wood. The horses had slowed down of their own accord, thrusting aside the long grass and overhanging shoots that barred their way. One of them whinnied suddenly and immediately, as if in answer, the wood exploded into thunderous noise. Deborah saw the boy in front throw up his arms and slip sideways, like a puppet unstrung, to lie in a crumpled heap on the ground. It had all lasted no more than a few seconds. Before the other two had time to realize what had happened, five men had stepped silently out of the trees with muskets at the ready.

"Softly, my masters," said he who seemed to be their leader, a great, fierce-looking lout who stood straddling the middle of the road ahead. "Don't be hasty now. These fine fellows mean you no harm. They want nothing but the pleasure of your company – and a mite of gold to drink your health. So no tricks, eh? Down with you, and sharpish, before —"

A loud report interrupted his words. One of their attackers pitched forward and lay still. John Strong had taken advantage of the momentary diversion caused by the leader's speech to snatch one of the pistols from his saddle holsters and fire.

"Quick, Mistress Deb!" he yelled. "In God's name, fly! Don't mind me. I'll do my best to hold them off!"

In that moment of confusion, Deborah clapped spurs to her horse. Big John was right. Whatever it cost her to leave him to his fate, the Queen's service came first. Savagely rowelled, the mare leapt forward, only to be brought to a wrenching halt almost at once when one burly fellow jumped for the bridle and hung on, dragging at the tender mouth. Quick as a flash, the girl had pulled out her own pistol, cocked it and fired. The noise, by this time, was deafening, a babel of shouts, curses and the screams of terrified horses. The ball struck the man full in the chest and he fell back while in the same instant, with the ghastly precision of a dance, John Strong also collapsed.

Tears pricked at Deborah's eyelids but she had no leisure to indulge her grief for even as she fought to control her panic-stricken mount she felt herself seized round the waist. Cold steel pressed against her neck and foul breath was on her cheek. "Don't move, for your life!"

Rough hands dragged her from the saddle and she found herself standing in the road with three men around her. Her heart turned over at the animal lust in their eyes. Hurriedly pulling out her purse, she flung it at their feet. Anything rather than feel their hands on her.

"What have you done with my servant?" she demanded in a voice that shook more than she liked.

"That's the least of your worries, my lass," the leader growled.

"Do we mill her, then?" asked the smallest of the gang eagerly. He was a pock-marked individual with a ferocious squint.

"Ye maundering ass! Ain't yer never 'eard of orders? It's up to us to make 'er ladyship talk first. An' between you an' me, my bully boys, there ain't no special hurry about that neither. Be a pity to let this dainty go to waste." He leered horribly at Deborah. "You owe me two good men, my beauty, and I'm going to see you pay." He chuckled lewdly and was echoed freely by his men.

Deborah shrank back as they advanced on her. Her cap had fallen off in the struggle and her hair spilled in a dark golden cloud about her shoulders, broken by the sheen of silken skin where shirt and doublet had been rent and torn. Her eyes bright with anger and with fear, her lovely mouth quivering, she was tempting enough to bring a light of bestial desire into the reddened eyes of the three men around her.

She screamed once, in terror, as one of the brutes reached out and grabbed her by the hair, forcing her backwards over his knee. The fabric over her breasts parted with a ripping sound and then the man was fumbling with his free hand at the points of her hose. The other two looked on, licking their lips and encouraging their confederate with a stream of foul jokes and obscene promises of what each meant to do when his turn came. Half-mad with shame and horror, Deborah fought as in a nightmare, kicking and scratching, her supple body writhing away from the clutching, prurient hands, but even as she did so she knew that her resistance was only stimulating the creature's lusts and wearing out her own strength. Then her boot caught in a projecting root and she overbalanced and fell heavily, taking the man with her.

The squinting man bent over her, pinning her arms to the ground.

"Here you are. I'll make it easy for you," he offered with his greasy giggle.

Deborah screamed again, seeing the leaves close about her like a green cage. There was a thundering in her head. She was going to be trampled . . . That was her last thought before losing consciousness.

Deborah opened her eyes cautiously and shut them again at once with a long, shuddering sob. A pair of very black eyes was regarding her intently and remembered horror overcame her once again.

"There's nothing to be afraid of now." The voice spoke in cultured tones very far removed from the rough accents of the men who had waylaid her. Becoming aware of this suddenly, Deborah burst into a flood of tears.

"Hush now, sweeting. Comfort yourself. It's all over, on my oath it is. Here – drink this."

She opened her eyes. She was sitting on the grass, her back supported against a tree and the strange man was bending over her, a flask in his hand. She took it shakily and drank with gratitude. The liquor slid down her throat and set fire to her stomach. Deborah leaned over, coughing and spluttering.

"Don't be afraid," the stranger went on. "That scum will not trouble you again. I was riding this way in company with my servants when we heard sounds of a fight. I am glad that I was in time." A faint smile curved his lips. "By now, I imagine, your late assailants are settling their score with Satan."

Deborah summoned up a wan smile in return.

"How can I thank you? But for you —"

"Not at all," the gentleman interrupted her politely. "It was the least I could do. Oblige me by putting the whole matter out of your mind. It is I who should thank you for the chance to display myself in the role of knight errant." He laughed, with a reassuring warmth and spontaneity that went straight to Deborah's heart. She sat up and began to look more attentively at her rescuer.

Up to then, she had been aware of no more than providence in the shape of a human being with a smile and a comforting voice. Now she saw that he was a tall man, unusually tall, with the body of an athlete elegantly attired in a cloak of wine-coloured velvet braided with gold. She was conscious of a dark face and springing black hair curling in impudent profusion from under the white hat clasped at the brim by a claw of rubies, and found herself gazing into a bold, high-bred countenance marked by the dominant traits of firmness and sensuality. With its strong cheekbones, faintly aquiline nose, masterful jaw and the gleam of white teeth between lips whose fine moulding was accentuated by the short, dark beard, it was like no other face that Deborah had ever seen, at Whitehall or anywhere else. No woman could have remained for long insensible to the powerful aura of attraction emanating from the stranger, a charm derived in part from a strong will and extreme masculinity, in part from some indefinable quality of sheer, heathenish enjoyment in the man. Deborah found herself blushing violently as her heightened awareness of the man before her made her suddenly conscious of her own rent doublet. A hasty glance showed her that someone – he? – had made shift to fasten the burst points and the colour in her face deepened to a ripe scarlet as the implications flooded over her. When she recalled how he had found her, she was ready to die of shame.

"Well, I'm glad to see that you are feeling better."

It appeared that none of these reflections had been lost on the gentleman who was smiling at her with a good deal of amusement.

"Oh! Please – my horse is over there." Deborah pointed rather

30

unsteadily to her mare. "If you will bring me my saddlebags I . . ." Her voice tailed off somewhat lamely.

He fetched the bags without a word. Rummaging feverishly inside, Deborah brought out the spare shirt she had brought to wear at Chartley. Then, just as she was about to pull off her doublet, her heart stood still. The letter! She felt the garment cautiously. Thank God! It was still there, sewn into the lining. A furtive glance at the stranger showed her that he had politely turned his back and had not witnessed this manœuvre. Abandoning all thought of removing the doublet, Deborah simply pulled the shirt on over the top: it strained at the seams and she must look ridiculous but no matter. At least she was covered. This done, she dragged a comb through her tangled hair and tied it back with a ribbon she carried in her bag and felt better, almost her old self again.

The gentleman sat on a fallen log and surveyed her coolly.

"Now, perhaps, you will tell me what brought you adventuring into these perilous groves."

"My home is in Coventry, sir," said Deborah, improvising wildly. "I was on my way to visit relatives a few miles from here, escorted by my servant, when these robbers fell upon us." Tears sprang to her eyes. "They have killed him," she finished piteously.

"A manservant?" He got up. "Do you recall whereabouts he fell? He may be only wounded."

Deborah ran ahead of him into the thicket, telling herself that her wits seemed to have gone begging since her faint. Was it possible that poor John Strong was still alive?

They found him lying by the side of the road, half-hidden in the long grass. He was flat on his back and there was a large red stain on his jerkin just below the shoulder. His face was very pale and his eyes were closed but he was breathing. Deborah went down on her knees, followed by her companion whose swift, efficient hands unfastened the jerkin and began expertly probing the wound.

"Your friend was lucky," he said at last. "The ball caused no more than a flesh wound. But he seems badly concussed." He was deftly refastening John's jerkin as he spoke. Then, rising, he went on: "My house is close by. With your permission, we will carry your servant thither. He shall be cared for according to his needs and I will see that you are provided with a sufficient escort to continue your journey. My men will be back soon. They have merely gone to alert the watch. We will be off as soon as they return."

Deborah looked up at him, her lovely face glowing with

31

gratitude. "I owe you so much already . . . I hate to impose on you any more. If it were anyone but John Strong – but indeed, I am very grateful. I hope it is not too much trouble . . ."

"Not in the least. If it were, I should not have offered. Now suppose you stop talking to me about gratitude and tell me what gentleman would not have done as much to serve you, sweetheart?"

His hands were on her shoulders, drawing her close, his eyes searching hers.

Deborah abandoned herself joyfully, filled with a delicious sense of trust and relaxation. The velvet cloak under her cheek had a nice manly smell of leather, horses and ambergris. The horrors of the day faded from her mind and with them her fatigue and her fear. He tightened his hold and she felt the strong, tender pressure of his arms about her shoulders and the hard, muscular thighs touching her own. Her head swam and a hot wave rushed over her. Her body trembled. Abruptly, with a disconcerting suddenness, he released her, deposited a brief kiss on her forehead and stepped back.

"Forgive me, sweetheart." Deborah stared at him, uncomprehending. He gave a short, bitter laugh. "Faith, I am no better than those other brutes!"

Still she did not understand. Why was he asking her forgiveness? Yet, faced with that masked, almost hostile expression, she dared not question him. Instead, she began to wander rather uncertainly along the track. He fell into step beside her.

"Tell me, did the villains rob you at all?"

Deborah started.

"Oh, good God! I was forgetting! They took my purse. And then there was the boy who was our guide, he —"

"Do not trouble yourself about him. He is dead."

He turned and strode back the way he had come. Deborah, following, saw him bend down and approached unwillingly. The three robbers lay in pools of blood. Moved by a sudden wave of hatred, she stepped forward under the shadow of the trees and stared down at them with a kind of savage satisfaction. The devil damn the base dogs . . . But the stranger's voice broke in on her curse.

He was on his feet again. In one hand he held Deborah's purse, while the other was thrusting a sheet of paper towards her.

"A pretty tale you told me! I'll take my oath on it you never saw Coventry!"

"What do you mean? Why should you think —?" She was very pale.

32

For answer he held out the paper. "Here. Read this. One of them had it in his pocket."

Deborah took it and saw the signature: Walsingham! The paper shook in her hand but she forced herself to be calm and read it. It contained directions concerning the road with detailed descriptions of herself and John Strong. The bearer was ordered to take the manservant dead or alive and the girl unharmed so that she could be delivered for questioning. At the bottom of the page was the address to which she was to be taken.

So her fears of the night before had not been groundless! Neither this ambush nor the affair at the inn had been the result of pure chance. She understood now why it was that their attackers had failed to kill her, although they had had plenty of opportunities to do so during the scuffle in the road. Fortunately, the minutely worked out plan had failed to take account of one thing: the nature of the beasts who were to carry it out which had made them waste precious minutes. But for that, where would she be now? In some cellar somewhere, being put to the question, most probably, to be quietly eliminated once she was of no further use to her captors. It was with a certain feeling of triumph that Deborah tore the paper across and across. She had won this bout! She still had the letter. Now her next task was to deal skilfully with this stranger.

She glanced at him sideways under her long lashes. He was watching her, evidently waiting for her explanation. Well, he should have one.

"Sir," she said, with just the touch of dignity she hoped would be needed to discourage further inquiry, "the true facts of this business are not mine to tell. But whatever ideas this letter may have given you, please believe me when I say that, on my honour, I have done nothing to be ashamed of." She opened her fingers and let the fragments of Walsingham's letter flutter to the ground.

He made her a mocking bow.

"How can I insist? Keep your secret, child. It is no concern of mine. I confess I was merely curious. You may not be aware that the agents of our worthy Secretary are usually employed after bigger game than waylaying young girls."

Deborah was silent. There was a pause, broken at last by her.

"Your servants are long in coming, sir." She smiled hesitantly. "You will think me very rude, perhaps, but my poor John —"

"Not at all." His moustache twitched a little. "You are perfectly right, fair mystery. There is a tavern at the other end of the wood. I

33

dare say the rogues have seized the chance of a draught of ale. I will go in search of them. Will you come?"

"I'd rather wait. John . . ."

"As you wish. But keep your weapon within reach. I'll not be long." He was in the saddle before he had finished speaking. Deborah went up to him and laid her hand on the horse's neck.

"Thank you again for your kindness. I shall never forget." Her voice broke a little. "Do, I beg of you, do all you can for my servant. He is a good man."

"Have no fear. As for your gratitude —" The rest of his words were lost in a cloud of dust.

His white hat showed for a moment against the dark green of the trees, then, in a moment, even that was gone. Deborah was alone.

Without wasting a moment, she picked up her saddlebags and threw them over the mare's back. As soon as she had made them fast, she led the animal over to where John Strong lay, still unconscious, and thrust her purse gently inside his jerkin.

"God be with you, John," she murmured. "I have to leave you." Then, choking back a sob, she hoisted herself on to the mare's back, dug in her heels and set off determinedly in the other direction.

It was an hour later that the host of the small wayside tavern belonging to the village of Blackfields beheld a youthful rider tearing hell for leather down the road towards his hostelry. He had been set upon by thieves, the youth explained, slithering breathlessly to the ground. His business was urgent, however, and he needed a fresh mount and a guide as soon as both could be got. The landlord, who had seen the glint of gold in that soft, girlish hand, made haste to oblige.

So it was that, after swallowing a slice of beef and a pot of ale, the rider departed again at full speed for the north.

IV

God was on her side. There could be no doubt about that. Such brilliant moonlight was certainly a gift from heaven and her guide, too, young as he was, knew his business. The two together enabled Deborah to reach Chartley that same evening.

The village, as they walked their horses into it, proved to be a small clearing in the prevailing dark blanket of woodland, a few tiny fields hacked out inch by inch from the forest, hedged in with quickthorn, among which rose an assortment of untidy, thatched cottages. The whole place seemed to be asleep.

Deborah turned to her companion, a lad of about thirteen or so whose ginger hair, light hazel eyes and thin cheeks gave him an odd resemblance to one of the lean cats that prowled about the stables at Whitehall.

"Do you know 'The Queen Bess'? I was told it was a thriving inn, although I can't imagine where it gets its custom from in these parts."

The boy raised his arm and pointed. "It's that way. On the Sheffield road. And there's good custom hereabouts, make no mistake. Travellers going between Coventry and Sheffield, as well as people with business at the great houses round here. There are plenty of those on account of the hunting, you see. And now, since the Queen of Scots has been here, trade is brisker than it ever was. Over there" – he nodded in the direction he meant – "that's where they've mewed her up, although the house really belongs to our lord of Essex."

Deborah looked quickly in the direction he had indicated. Through the trees, at some distance from the village, she thought that she could discern the battlemented roof of a great house.

So this was where she was, here in this rural solitude, a prisoner within those silent walls, the woman whose name was hated throughout the realm. Nor was it in England alone that the name of Mary Stuart had become a byword for trouble. She seemed to have been born for nothing else. Queen of Scotland at a week old, Queen

35

of France at eighteen, only to be widowed a year later and politely shown the door by her formidable mother-in-law Catherine de Medici, sent back from the most luxurious court in Europe to the mists and discomfort of her native Scotland. Nor, once there, had her problems been slow to multiply. There was the uneasy situation between Protestants and Catholics, with Mary not so devoted to her mass as to leave a kingdom for it, but still frequently irritated by the arrogant assumptions of her Protestant subjects. Then she had made the grave mistake of bypassing her cousin Elizabeth's advice in her choice of a husband and what must she do but take up with Lord Darnley, a brainless stripling of whom she tired almost as soon as she had wedded him, whereupon she had committed the unforgivable sin of falling for that "glorious, rash and hazardous young man", the Earl of Bothwell! After Darnley's murder, she had married him in the teeth of her subjects' opposition, despite the fact that he was being openly accused of her husband's death, but that marriage, too, had been short-lived. A month later, Bothwell was a fugitive and Mary a prisoner. Before the year was out had come the escape from Loch Leven Castle and the flight to England. How old was she then? Twenty-six? And now she was well into her forties . . .

"Is that why you are here?"

Her young guide's shrewd question pulled Deborah from her reflections.

"I?" Her smile was disarming. "By no means. Tomorrow I must be on my way to Sheffield. But it is late. We must make haste to the inn. A good meal would do neither of us any harm."

They rode on in silence, the boy's mind probably dwelling on the promised supper while Deborah digested the moral to be learned from his remark. Avoid giving rise to undue curiosity, watch every word and every action, act quite naturally . . . in theory she knew it all by heart. In practice, it appeared that it was easier said than done.

They passed the last cottages of the village and the road stretched before them, a long, pale ribbon ending abruptly at the first bend in the dark wall of the trees.

"This is it."

The boy reined in his mount and Deborah followed suit. It was a relief, after so many miles of riding through a blank and unfamiliar countryside, to find herself back again in something approaching civilization.

36

To their right stood a substantial house built in the old style, of stone, with a long roof of rose-coloured tiles, broken midway along its length by a tall, projecting gable end. All the windows in the creepered front were shuttered fast and the magnificent oak door had been secured for the night.

"Seems as if they're all asleep," the boy offered, not without hope.

Dismounting, Deborah tossed the reins to him to hold and made for the doorway with its swinging sign. A series of resounding thumps on the great iron knocker soon brought an answering sound of bolts being withdrawn.

The man who stood in the opening, wheezing blearily upon the world while with one hand he maintained the fustian breeches across his ample paunch, had evidently been woken out of his first sleep and was in no very good humour in consequence.

"Now then, now then! There's no call to go waking honest folks out their beds with that racket at this hour of night. Besides, the house is full."

Ignoring him, Deborah stepped quickly inside, before the man could gather his wits together to prevent her.

"This is the house of Mistress Goodgraves?" she asked imperatively.

The man nodded, speechlessly, and Deborah, assuming she had to deal with some boorish serving man, went on: "Then go and fetch her, my good fellow. I can promise you that your mistress will not blame you for getting her out of her bed."

Red-faced, the man said, spluttering: "I am Thomas Goodgraves. Anything you have to say to my mother may as well be said to me!"

It seemed that she had offended him. Repressing a giggle, Deborah studied the unappealing figure before her. He must have been somewhere about thirty years old, a barrel-shaped individual with a fleshy face in which, half hidden by the rolls of fat, were a pair of curdled, shifty eyes and small, pursed lips which he moistened continually with the tip of his tongue.

Careful, however, to hide her disgust, she summoned up a friendly smile and, taking a folded paper from her pouch, held it out to him.

"In that case, Master Goodgraves, perhaps you will be good enough to carry this to your mother . . . in the Queen's name," she added as an afterthought.

The effect was miraculous.

37

Thomas's flabby face was contorted into an obsequious grimace and he departed, bowing lavishly, taking a candle with him.

In a part of England still largely papist in feeling, Mrs Goodgraves was known in London as a sound Protestant. She had not failed to profit from it, either, and her son Thomas had acquired the contract, from Sir Amyas Paulet, Mary Stuart's keeper, to supply beer to her household. A useful appointment, as Mrs Tucker had remarked as she gave her niece the Queen's instructions, and one that ought not to be neglected.

A door creaked and candlelight, warm and living, pushed back the darkness, revealing a large woman with a shawl bundled over her shift and wisps of grey hair escaping from her nightcap.

"Mistress Mason? I am Dorothy Goodgraves, an it please you." She dropped a curtsy as she spoke, her sharp eyes studying the girl. "How can I serve you?"

"I thank you, Mistress Goodgraves. What I need most is a bed for myself and supper and lodging for my horse and guide. And if you could find something for me to eat I should be grateful, for I have eaten nothing since this morning, and I am very hungry."

Mother and son set to at once and in a very short time there appeared on the table, as if by magic, a fine ham, bread, cheese and a syrup of quinces, while Thomas came labouring up the cellar steps with a flask of wine.

Deborah made a hearty meal while the landlady hovered around her, visibly bursting with curiosity, and Thomas stood by the wall, following her every movement with his eyes. At length, swallowing a last draught of wine, the girl pushed back her stool and prepared to enlighten them.

"Her Grace has entrusted me with a confidential message for Sir Amyas Paulet and it is my wish to enter the house without attracting attention. Can you arrange this?"

"Nothing easier," said the old woman promptly. "I could have lent you the dress of a serving maid and sent you with my son when he takes in the fresh barrels of beer." She shook her head dolefully. "But as luck will have it, Sir Amyas is from home. He left yesterday for the chase with the Papist woman. They went to Tixall House."

Deborah frowned.

"In that case, I will wait," she declared, concealing her disappointment. "I hope he will not be long." She made a little face. "I shall have to keep my presence secret until his return."

Mistress Goodgraves and her son whispered together for a moment.

"There may be a remedy, an you like it, mistress. I have a niece much about your age, that dwells in Sheffield and has not visited here these many years. We might pass you off as her and that way no one would suspect you. And you can never be too careful with the way things are nowadays. If you only knew, Mistress Mason, what a nest of spies this village has become ever since that Scotswoman has been here!"

"Yes," thought Deborah uncharitably, "and I'm very sure, you old harridan, that every one of them makes use of your house as a base!" She found Mrs Goodgraves's air of pious horror oddly irritating. However, she kept her thoughts to herself and answered cheerfully: "That seems to me an excellent notion, Mistress Goodgraves, and one I shall be very glad to take up!" She laid some coins on the table before her. "Let these cover your expenses. And you may be sure the Queen will hear of your loyalty."

Thomas had remained a silent but deeply interested audience to this exchange.

"The Queen Bess" was a hostelry famous all the way from Coventry to Sheffield for the excellence of its cooking and the comfort of its beds.

One entered directly into the big, cosy, welcoming common room with its carved beams which occupied almost the entire ground floor of the place. The walls were gay with frescoes depicting various hunting scenes, an innovation of which the widow Goodgraves was not a little proud, and justly so, since this fashion for painted walls was still very much a London one and not often seen so far north as this, where folk were more inclined to stick to their traditional whitewash.

Opposite the great hearth where a little dog trod tirelessly round and round in his treadmill cage to turn the spit there stood a great trestle board, groaning under the array of good food spread upon it. There were fat hams, pink and succulent, gilded pies, rich, roasted capons, several kinds of fish with their accompanying sauces, smoked or stuffed, whole haunches of roast boar and venison; food of every kind to make the traveller's mouth water. The rest of the furniture consisted of an assortment of settles and joint stools ranged about the trestle tables with their pewter jugs and tankards.

39

On the afternoon in question, a trio of youngish gentlemen were seated at the principal table, deep in low-voiced conversation. They broke off as a pretty girl entered, bringing a heavily loaded tray.

"Aha! The landlady's adorable niece! And what have you got for us, sweetheart?" cried one, a tall, sandy-haired person with a pleasant face and twinkling eyes.

"Clary wine, my lord, which I hope will prove to your liking," the girl answered with a smile as she served them.

"By the faith, as fair-spoken as she is lovely, eh, David?" He dug his elbow in the ribs of the young man beside him whose delicately handsome face, outlined by a fringe of golden beard, had remained fixed on the girl ever since her entry.

She was dressed, in the manner of prosperous countrywomen, in a rich and comely fashion: a red taffeta kirtle well tucked up over a clean, white petticoat, a green silk stomacher outlining her neat waist with a partlet of linen above. The laced cap on her coppery hair was held in place by a single gold pin and framed the sweetest little face the young man had ever seen.

The red-haired man laughed again. "Here, say, old chap! Wake up! You're devilish castaway today. Or are you ravished by a pair of green eyes?"

"Oh, for God's sake, William!" the one called David muttered pettishly. "Can't you be serious for a moment?"

They were interrupted just then by the arrival of a fourth man. He had evidently overheard the last remarks for his long, sallow face bore an expression of reproof.

"My lords, my lords," he said, with a strong foreign accent, laying one lined hand on the table. "We are here to discuss matters of more moment than the attractions of a serving wench."

The girl's face crimsoned and she turned on her heel. David made a move to follow her but the third man of the original trio, the one who had not yet spoken, put a hand on his sleeve to restrain him.

"My dear friend, do you forget the object of this meeting? Perez is right. The cause we have at heart is too sacred to allow of even a few minutes' distraction." His voice was vibrant with sincerity.

"I'm sorry, Anthony. It is true – I was behaving like an ass."

Yet even as he said it, his gaze wandered involuntarily to the door behind which the girl had disappeared.

Meanwhile, William had refilled their glasses with the ruby wine. They drank it down and resumed their conversation.

Every now and then, as they talked, one or the other would look

40

up and glance about him nervously, but the chamber drowsed easily in the afternoon warmth. It was the quiet time of day before the evening rush and the only other occupant of the room was an elderly traveller quietly drinking a pot of ale in a corner, half hidden in the wreaths of smoke from his pipe. Then came a clatter of boots on the flagged floor and two sergeants tramped in, talking loudly. Anthony tossed a silver coin on to the table and the four men left in silence.

Merciful heavens, Deborah thought, it was certainly an exhausting business being Mrs Goodgraves's niece! All day, and the day before, she had worked like a slave, tramping up and down the dark, slippery cellar steps with jugs of cool beer from the wood or laden with dusty bottles that must be handled as if they were made of priceless crystal, shuttling back and forth between the kitchen and the common room bringing dishes of meat and clearing tables, doing her best to satisfy each customer according to his degree, as explained by Mistress Goodgraves who, she was sure, must be finding the whole thing highly amusing.

It was getting dark and to escape for a moment from the blazing heat of the fire and her hostess's incessant chatter Deborah slipped out of the kitchen door.

At the back of the inn, at the far end of the courtyard formed by the angle of the stables and the bakehouse, lay an attractive pleasaunce, its neat, sanded paths bordered with lavender and rosemary, with kitchen garden and orchard beyond, running close up to where the forest began.

Deborah made straight for one of the small arbours, twined with musk roses and sweetbriar, and sinking down on to the low, wooden bench kicked off her shoes with a heartfelt sigh of relief. Her feet ached unbearably. She wondered how much longer Sir Amyas Paulet was going to keep her kicking her heels in this place and when, if ever, she would meet the Queen of Scots. Slowly, out of habit, she repeated the Queen's message over again in her mind.

It was some time later that she looked up suddenly. A man was standing at the entrance to the arbour, one hand resting on the wooden framework, quietly watching her. It was, Deborah saw with some surprise, one of the three young gallants who had been in the common room earlier that afternoon. She was about to spring to her feet when he forestalled her, saying urgently:

"Stay, Mistress, if you will . . . only for a moment. I was looking for you." He stammered a little with embarrassment as he continued: "My friend was unmannerly. I would not have you think that I —"

If the truth were told, Deborah had too many other, more important things on her mind to have even remembered the incident but faced with the appeal in the melting blue eyes fixed so earnestly upon her she bit back the tart response which sprang to her lips.

Instead, she answered politely: "It was nothing, my lord. A trifle not worth your trouble."

He took a step forward into the arbour.

"Then, perhaps . . . may I sit with you for a moment? Let me introduce myself." He bowed. "I am Lord Ashbury."

Half-rising, Deborah said: "Deborah Mason, at your lordship's service."

They sat side by side on the narrow bench and a somewhat embarrassed silence followed. Lord Ashbury was clearly racking his brains for a suitable beginning to a conversation, in which he received no help from Deborah, who now found herself in something of a quandary.

She had been well taught and in any gathering of august personages no fault could have been found with her manners. But her elderly preceptors had totally omitted to instruct her in the proper way for a girl to respond to an attempt at a flirtation. The handsome boy beside her, the moonlight filtering through the leaves and scattering bright leaf-shapes over the two within the arbour, the soft, whispering solitude which enclosed them, all combined to bring an unfamiliar constriction to her throat. She was vaguely aware that she ought to break the spell and leave him there, and yet she stayed.

"I'd no idea that Mrs Goodgraves possessed such a charming niece," he said at last. "Do you stay here long?"

"Oh, no. Only for a short visit. My parents sent me to help my aunt for a few days, but I must go at the end of the week."

"So I shall not see you again?" He laid hold of her hand and clasped it between both his own. "Do you know your beauty haunts me? Ever since I first saw you, this afternoon, I have been unable to get you out of my mind . . ."

Deborah had withdrawn her hand and risen, gathering her skirts about her.

"It is late, my lord. Excuse me. I must go in."

He, too, had risen.

42

"So soon? . . . Oh, please —" He made a move as if to keep her but let his arm fall. "Have I offended you? I was clumsy, perhaps, or do you think me overbold? I swear to you I do not fall in love with every pretty girl I see. But there is something about you, something priceless, some witchcraft which has made me lose my head." His voice grew very gentle as he added: "Yet you have nothing to fear from me, my dear. Are you still angry with me?"

"How could I be? You are forgiven." She smiled. "And now, my lord, I must go."

"When can I see you again? Now that we are friends, you cannot deny me that?"

Deborah hesitated, but she thought of the days ahead with no one but old Mrs Goodgraves for company and her resolution wavered. Lord Ashbury's compliments, this last passionate declaration and the wholly new and pleasurable sensations it aroused were, it had to be admitted, by no means unwelcome.

"Another night . . . perhaps," she murmured with unconscious coquetry.

"Tomorrow? At this hour? Oh, do say yes!" he urged impetuously.

And, with a sense of doing something pleasantly foolish, Deborah agreed.

This was the fourth time they had met by moonlight. For two nights, now, they had talked together endlessly, as young people will, and although each was aware of things the other had held back, still they had, in that short space of time, come to know one another very well.

David had discovered, with a good deal of surprise, that Deborah possessed a quick intelligence, considerable education and a cultivated mind which shone through everything she said. They were not the attributes he had expected to find in an innkeeper's niece and they hinted at a mystery which both attracted and intrigued him and in no way lessened his first, instinctive liking. He had tried to question her about her family and her life but she had eluded him skilfully and he had not liked to press the point.

He had said little enough about his own affairs. He was twenty-three, his mother and father were both dead and he lived mostly with an aunt. Beyond that, his confidences were limited to matters of sport and of books.

Deborah, on her side, asked for nothing more. What was this boy's life to her? She would probably never set eyes on him again. What mattered was now, this present moment with its novel, bewitching sensation of being alone with a young, a very charming young man evidently head over ears in love. It was easy to sink into a blissful dream, listening to him telling her that she was beauty's self, that her complexion put the budding rose to shame and in her eyes the deep blue sea mingled with the clear green of a mountain spring. How could her heart help but beat faster as she looked at his face and saw that, from a child, she had become a woman with intoxicating powers?

She would have recoiled from the practised advances of an experienced man of the world but David's very artlessness and obvious inexperience worked in his favour. As she sat with her small hands held fast in his warm, tender clasp, her eyes on the fine, slightly wistful features in their frame of fair hair, worn rather long, just brushing the lace collar, she melted insensibly.

Now and then, as they talked, David would break off what he was saying and sit staring into the night with shoulders bowed as if under the weight of an intolerable secret.

Moonlight lay, milk white, on the sleeping earth. All was still, with the deep, breathing silence of a world gorged with sunshine and now abandoned to sleep beneath a sky of spangled black velvet. From the woods and fields around came rich scents of earth and moss and mown hay, creeping into the arbour along with the smell of herbs and the spicy fragrance of musk roses.

It was during one such pause that Deborah, turning to David, suddenly found their lips very close. His first kiss had a timid fervour, his closed mouth soft on hers; then, made bold by the touch of young flesh that did not shrink away, his tongue probed the moist lips and their breath mingled. Soon he was smothering her throat with kisses, murmuring broken words of love, and, little by little, the touch of her smooth skin, the feel of her body pressed against his and her hands caressing his neck made him lose all control. His hands undid a ribbon here, put aside a kerchief there, tore open the thin shift to cradle the round, white breasts while his eyes sought imploringly for the answer hidden behind her closed lids . . .

"Deborah! Deborah! Are you there?"

A voice was calling in the dark and footsteps crunched on the gravel.

44

David sprang to his feet while Deborah, her face flaming, dragged her dress to rights. The grinning face of Thomas loomed into view, leering at the pair of them as if to make quite clear that he was well aware of what he had interrupted.

"It grows late, girl," he said smugly. "Your aunt would not have you out of doors at this hour. In with you now. His lordship will excuse you." This last was spoken with an exaggerated bow to David who picked up his hat and, bowing in his turn to Deborah, quickly left the arbour.

Deborah stalked back through the garden, quivering with nervous rage and mortification. It was bad enough to have been discovered by this bumpkin, but that he should dare to give her orders before David passed all bounds. Unable to contain her anger, she stopped in her tracks and swung round on him.

"By what right do you spy on me?" she demanded hotly. "Mind your own business! I do not pay you for this, I think!"

"Why, as to that, if you'd have folk take you for my cousin you must needs let me care for your honour. Ours is a respectable family, I'll have you know."

"The devil fly away with you, then!"

"Now then, my girl. There's no call to take that tone with me – unless, maybe, you were wishful to have ended that little scene on your back. Because if so, well, you've only to say the word, my dear, and we'll soon find a cure for that!"

He let out a shout of laughter and as Deborah recoiled from him with a little scream, his hand shot out and grabbed her by the shoulder. Sick with disgust, Deborah spat deliberately in his face and then, wrenching herself free, sped like an arrow for the house.

Thomas did not attempt to follow her but stood thoughtfully wiping his beard, his eyes on the slim, flying form.

"I'll be paid for that, you trollop," he said softly at last. "A kiss for old Thomas'd have come cheaper in the end." With that he turned and made his way swiftly towards the stables.

He reappeared a few minutes later, leading a horse by the bridle. Making his way cautiously through the orchard he came to the road, mounted and was soon lost among the trees.

V

The brewer's men had loaded the full barrels of ale. Thomas cracked his whip and the thong coiled back on itself like a spring before it shot out to flick the broad hindquarters of the two powerful dapple grey horses harnessed in front. The dray moved forward.

Deborah sat beside Thomas who, apparently regretting his conduct of the previous night, was all smiles and showing a clumsy, bear-like eagerness to please. Tight-lipped and unbending, she sat in stiff silence, ignoring his broad attempts at humour. His repentance might be real or feigned: she did not greatly care. Certainly she was not obliged to go out of her way to be agreeable. A few hours more and she would be on her way back to London and could forget all about the Goodgraves, mother and son. Mary Stuart had returned from Tixall the night before. Deborah had heard the news on waking and was on her way to apply to Sir Amyas Paulet for an audience with his prisoner.

The heavily laden dray creaked and groaned with every bend in the road. Thoroughly jolted, half-blinded by dust and sunshine, they emerged at last into the broad avenue leading up to the house. Great trees met in an archway overhead making a cool shade into which the sunlight fell intermittently like showers of sparks. As they drew up, a sergeant and five men emerged from a stone gate-house.

"Ho there, Tom, lad! Get down, you fat rogue and let's be having you. State secrets stuffed up your breeches, I shouldn't wonder, eh?" The sergeant roared with laughter at his own wit.

The ritual was evidently a familiar business. Thomas descended, smiling, and held out his arms while the guards patted his clothes, turned out his pockets and the lining of his hat and tapped the heels of his boots, all in an atmosphere of good-natured cheerfulness and banter. Naturally the search was a formality. Thomas was known to them but none the less orders were orders and must be carried out without regard to persons.

The conduct of the house was based, in fact, on the practice at Tutbury where Mary Stuart's confinement had been at its strictest and whence she had been transferred, some six months since, to Chartley. Here she could enjoy pleasanter surroundings and, of late, some excursions beyond the house but in other respects there had been no relaxation for, if her prison was changed, her gaoler remained the same. Sir Amyas Paulet was a rigid puritan and a man of unyielding efficiency. A twenty-four-hour guard was maintained on the park and no unauthorized entry was permitted. As at Tutbury, the distribution of alms to the poor of the neighbourhood had been suspended. The Queen's people were no longer allowed to move freely about the district. Parcels, letters, books and correspondence of every description were strictly censored, to the sole end of preventing any communication between the captive and the outside world. All this, Deborah knew from the Goodgraves who had explained it with great thoroughness.

"Well, well, my pretty one! And what may you be doing here?" The sergeant had abandoned Thomas and was standing looking up at Deborah. "Hop off that box, like a good girl. You can keep us company while your sweetheart unloads his beer. By the pox, friend Thomas, you do yourself proud! A morsel fit for a king – and light as a feather with it!' He had his arm round Deborah and swung her gallantly to the ground.

In an instant she had slipped from his grasp and produced a folded paper from her pinafore.

"Be good enough, sergeant, to take this letter to Sir Amyas Paulet," she said curtly.

The sergeant's face went from red to purple. His hand went out automatically to take the paper and purple became deathly white as he recognized the royal seal. At last, emerging from his daze, he shook himself like a dog and snapped an order. One of the guards who had been bemused witnesses of the little scene made off running towards the house.

The door closed behind the man who had escorted her. Deborah gave a tiny shiver. The room struck chill and dark as a tomb after the warm, bright greenery outside. She moved forward uncertainly, with a disagreeable sense of shrinking moment by moment as she did so. Ahead of her stretched an endless perspective of grey flagstones between high walls pierced by narrow windows, walls so high that you had almost to crane your neck to catch a sight of the ceiling: not a tapestry on the walls nor a rug on the floor, not even so much as a stick of furniture; nothing but this dismal bareness ... No, there was one thing, there, above the monumental fireplace: a portrait. The fresh, painted colours seemed to draw unto themselves all the daylight in the room. Deborah's glance clung to it.

It was the portrait of a lordly young man whose large eyes looked meditatively, yet not without a touch of mischief, from a pale, fine-drawn face. He was bareheaded and the painter had succeeded in catching the silky richness of the chestnut hair combed back from his face.

A panelled door to the left of the fireplace opened silently and a man came in.

He could not have offered a greater contrast to the man in the portrait. His face was set in stiff, unbending lines and he was dressed from head to foot in sombre black.

One glance was enough to inform Deborah of the identities of these two. The attractive person on the wall could only be the owner of the house, the Earl of Essex. The newcomer's name could easily be guessed by his reputation. She stepped forward.

"Sir Amyas Paulet?"

The man eyed her coldly, ignoring both the question and the curtsy which accompanied it.

"How may I serve Her Majesty? I am instructed to place myself at your disposal and I shall do all in my power to carry out Her Grace's wishes, although," and here the eye regarding Deborah grew colder than ever, "I fail to perceive what function a serving wench may have to perform."

"As to that, I believe Her Majesty is the best judge, Sir Amyas," Deborah retorted, stung by his disdainful tone. "I come from London. This" – she indicated her homespun skirt – 'is merely a disguise and —"

With a gesture, Paulet swept away the rest of her speech. "Very well, Mistress Mason. Let us not digress from the subject of your business here. What do you want?"

Swallowing her annoyance, Deborah said: "I carry a letter from the Queen which I am to deliver into Queen Mary's own hand. May I have an audience today, if possible? I would rather not linger at Chartley."

"There should be no difficulty in that." Paulet permitted himself a grim smile. "Her Grace delights in fresh company and she has had little enough of it since her arrival at Chartley. I have seen to that. Wait here. It may be that she will receive you at once."

He was back in a moment.

"You may go up. A guard will go with you."

"I thank you. There is one thing which I must ask you before I go. It is of the utmost importance. The Queen desires that no one shall know the precise reason for my being here."

Sir Amyas Paulet smiled faintly. "You may rest assured, Mistress Mason. I regard this charge as sacred. No word escapes these walls without my express sanction."

Deborah followed her guide, her quick eyes taking in every detail of her surroundings: a stately staircase rising to the dimness of a lofty, vaulted roof; many passages; the swish of a silken curtain and all at once a setting fit for a queen: tables, chests and cabinets of precious woods, carved and inlaid, Flemish tapestries, a profusion of ornaments, vessels and figurines of silver and silver gilt. Eastern carpets of the finest quality lay on the floors and stands of tall wax candles blazed everywhere even in broad daylight.

They passed through a succession of rooms and came at last into a small chamber filled, like the rest, with a rich and padded silence. Seated in an armed chair, a woman bent over her embroidery. She set her work aside and, at a sign from her guide, Deborah sank into a deep curtsy. She felt suddenly breathless.

She had heard so much about this queen, so many tales of her pride and wickedness, her numerous love affairs, her legendary beauty. Now, looking up, she saw an ageing woman with a plump, unhealthy face, an obvious wig and a heavy, unyouthful figure clothed in enveloping black.

The footsteps of the guard retreated. They were alone.

"Well, child? What is it?"

The cool, musical voice restored Deborah's presence of mind. Slipping her hand into the bosom of her dress, she brought out the Queen's letter.

"So please Your Grace, I bring you a letter."

"I know. Our gracious cousin. Only her messenger would receive the gallant Paulet's blessing. Let me have it."

She sat for a moment, weighing the letter in her hand, pensively. "Do you know the contents? Then, tell me, child. My eyes are not good and we shall save time."

" 'Madam —' " Deborah cleared her throat and then began again, more firmly: " 'Madam, Grant, we pray you out of our

49

concern for your welfare, with no longer delay, that which will at once put an end to your confinement and to my own deep anxieties on your behalf.

" 'Leave off forthwith to dabble in those matters which may well prove fatal to you and put not your faith in unreal temptations which must infallibly bring you to grief. Trust rather in our friendship.

" 'The bearer of this has our confidence and may therefore be safely entrusted with a verbal answer which, it is our dearest hope, may remove all doubts from the mind and heart of your loving sister, Elizabeth.' "

Deborah finished and Mary Stuart sat in silence, a remote and enigmatic smile on her lips. At last she seemed to remember the girl before her.

"Tell your mistress," she said, drawing herself up proudly, "that I thank her for her loving kindness and her gracious counsel. And give her my answer: that a Queen of Scots does not submit to instruction." She paused, and when she spoke again her voice was gentler and more friendly. "There, you are a good child, and young for our sister's service. Take this for your pains. God go with you."

She smiled and the smile lit up her tired face so that, for an instant, Deborah felt touched by an ineffable grace. But the moment passed, the light died and Mary Stuart returned calmly to her embroidery. The interview was over.

After leaving Deborah at the gate, Thomas had driven round the house and brought the dray up to the cellar entrance where, with the aid of various menials, the barrels were unloaded.

Yet even after the wagon was empty, Thomas seemed in no hurry to quit the cellars. He remained sitting astride a cask, his eyes fixed on a low doorway in the wall. Eventually, this swung open slowly and Mary Stuart's cellarer stood before him. At once, Thomas sprang to his feet and, drawing the bung from the cask on which he has been sitting, removed a wooden flask from the interior. This he handed to the cellarer who thrust it quickly under his coat, at the same time giving Thomas a second flask identical to the first. Both men made their way to where the empty barrels stood awaiting collection. They opened one and slipped the new flask inside, securing it by means of pegs which had been prepared in advance. Their movements were precise and economical, as if this were something they had done many times before.

The cellarer departed with scarcely a word exchanged. The servants came back to help Thomas load the empty casks and when this had been done he resumed his seat on the dray, whistling cheerfully.

In a few moments, Deborah reappeared and they made their way back to the inn.

VI

Deborah sat on the edge of her bed, pulling on her boots. A brand new riding dress lay on the nearby chest and she thought that Mistress Goodgraves had been inspired to choose that beautiful green stuff to replace her old, torn doublet. It had, to be sure, been somewhat expensive but she could manage, with the little extra which her aunt had given her before she set out, and the colour went perfectly with her red hair. Up to this point she had made a habit of dressing with a restrained elegance that was almost severe and, beyond that, had paid little attention to her appearance. Now, the matter seemed to have acquired a much greater importance. She found herself all of a sudden desperately anxious to do justice to the newly discovered beauty of which David had made her aware. My goodness, she thought, it's fun to be pretty!

She stretched herself and sighed pleasurably, blinking away a vision of David. This was no time to be thinking of young men. A fresh horse stood waiting in the stable and in two days she would be in London – before the Queen. Her eyes brightened and she gazed, without seeing it, at the branch of the lime tree across the window. The Queen would be pleased. No doubt of that. In spite of everything, the letter had reached its destination safely and Paulet must by now have sent the answer to London by the usual messenger, thus avoiding any suspicious inquiry. Deborah had given him the scrap of paper bearing the single word 'no', according to her Majesty's instructions. Of course, it was not the answer Elizabeth had hoped for but – and here Deborah gave the faintest shrug – after all she was a messenger, not an ambassador, and that task she had carried out admirably. Perhaps, now, the Queen would have another mission for her? Now that the danger was safely past, she felt bold enough for anything and fully confident of success. She grinned a little complacently as she remembered how she had eluded Walsingham and had then given her convenient, but rather too inquisitive, rescuer the slip.

The smile faded from her lips with the recollection of the

stranger's firm, enigmatic countenance and her heart beat a little faster. Suddenly she longed to see him again. But how? Who was he? She knew nothing about him, not even his name. The boot dropped from her hands and her fingers began idly stroking the bed-cover . . . unless . . . Of course, that was it! John Strong would know. Poor John, if only . . .

A timid knock on the door interrupted this somewhat melancholy train of ideas. A servant girl came in.

"I've brought a message for you, Mistress." Her eyes studied Deborah's dress intelligently. "Are you leaving, Mistress?"

"Never you mind. Give me the message."

"Well, you know his young lordship as comes to the house now and then? Lord Ashbury, he is. He was here this morning when you were out with Master Thomas, asking for you. He was ever so disappointed not to find you. 'Betty,' he said to me. 'I must see her. It's important. I'll be waiting at ten o'clock at the end of the orchard. You tell her that, and don't you forget,' he says. And he gave me a penny. That's all, Mistress."

She had delivered herself of her errand, like a schoolgirl reciting a lesson, and now stood hovering from one foot to the other, as though on the point of flight. Deborah tossed her a coin.

"That for yourself, child, and my thanks."

Betty bobbed a curtsy and withdrew, leaving Deborah to pace the room in some perturbation.

Dear David. He wanted to see her. What a pity it could not be managed. She had to leave – Deborah paused suddenly, her small nose wrinkled in a frown. Why had he not written to her? Why send a servant? It was not very polite, to say the least. Especially after what had already passed between them. She coloured hotly at the memory of his kisses. But perhaps that was it! Perhaps he took her for a loose woman and was treating her as such! Instantly, tenderness was swallowed up in anger. A silly, rustic creature and fair game, was that how he saw her? Oh, how could she have been so stupid! To have let him think . . . She must have been out of her mind! Falling like a ninny for the first man who smiled at her, she, who thought herself so smart and intelligent! It was enough to make a cat laugh! Deborah's eyes filled with tears. He was probably hoping to meet her tonight just so that he could tumble her in the hay like – like any Southwark harlot, to be whistled up as the fancy took him!

Seizing hold of the hairbrush that lay on the chest, a pretty brush with a chased silver handle, she hurled it violently against the opposite wall. Very well! She would go. She would go and tell him just what she thought of him. Did it mean putting off her journey? It was already late in the day and no more than a few hours would be lost if she left Chartley first thing in the morning. But live with this biting shame she would not . . .

Hurriedly finishing dressing, she went downstairs to tell Mistress Goodgraves of her change of plan.

No moon . . . no stars . . . only masses of inky-black clouds.

Deborah, moving very cautiously, had left the garden and could feel the long grass of the orchard underfoot. Feeling every step, her hands stretched out in front of her, eyes wide open to catch every glimmer of light through the confusing trunks of the apple trees, she was conscious of a considerable drop in the heat of her rage. Naturally, she had no intention of repeating her folly, or even listening to David's blandishments but, after all, perhaps he was not entirely to blame. Perhaps he had indeed lost his head, as he had told her. It was for her to make it clear to him, very calmly, that she had recovered hers and that he was not dealing with a shameless wanton. A smile of pure enjoyment lit her face as she pictured the scene: his passionate approach halted by her with a dignified gesture that should hold just enough of outraged modesty to bring him to his knees, imploring her forgiveness. All in all, this little affair with David would be a pleasant memory to carry back with her to London.

Her step quickened. Suddenly, now, she was in haste to find him. It was so dark, so quiet . . . Why on earth had he appointed this lonely spot for their meeting? To avoid further interruptions by Thomas, probably. There was a rustle in the nut trees alongside her and she thought that she could make out a standing figure.

"David," she called softly. "Here I am."

The figure rose up in front of her, broad and squat. She uttered a cry of fright and swung round, only to bump into two more figures cutting off her retreat.

In no time at all, she was gagged and bound, carried off like a parcel and dumped unceremoniously across the crupper of a horse which waited in the road close by the inn wall.

Her field of vision was limited to a riding boot, glimmering faintly a few inches from her face. It was a good boot, made of soft leather with a silver spur, and certainly belonged to someone of a very different condition from the horrible Thomas. In which case, how did the innkeeper fit into all this?

She had known, as soon as she had set eyes on him there, with his evil grin, that he had laid a trap for her and the first thought that came to her mind was that he had recruited some ruffians of the neighbourhood to help him carry her off in order that he could have his nasty will of her. But Thomas seemed to have disappeared and these men gave no impression of being engaged in a drunken frolic. What then?

At that point, the horses turned aside among the trees, proceeding in single file with a confident lack of hesitation which suggested a familiarity with every tree and bush. From time to time, Deborah's captor would bend down obligingly and, without speaking, put aside twigs and branches that were in danger of hitting her. Far from reassuring her, this courtesy only served, curiously, to increase her alarm. There was something sinister about this ordered march which reminded her forcibly and unpleasantly of a ride to execution. How much longer? When would she know? And meanwhile, she was beginning to suffer the most agonizing cramp.

Then, abruptly, the rustle of foliage ceased and there was only blackness. By twisting her neck, Deborah was able to make out the shape of a small manor house. They traversed a gentle, grassy slope and crossed over an almost dry moat. The horses stopped of their own accord and Deborah's captor dismounted, then lifted her down and hoisted her over his shoulder. There was a narrow door in the wall and through this he went into a damp-smelling passage which led to a steep stair.

Suddenly, she was set on her feet and stood looking round her in alarm.

She was standing in a cellar illumined by smoky torches, a cellar without casks, bottles or hams but which featured a long table cluttered with papers and surrounded by a litter of stools and benches. Two men stood in a corner warming their hands at the embers of a fire. They had their backs to her. Not far from them, a group of men in riding dress were talking eagerly. Gentlemen. Deborah felt herself begin to breathe more freely. If she had not to do with either Thomas or Walsingham's henchmen she felt that the danger must be less pressing. She was mistaken, as she was soon to find out.

One of the men approached and, drawing a dagger from his belt, he swiftly cut through her bonds and removed the gag from her mouth. Their eyes met and, to her amazement, Deborah recognized David's friend, the red-headed man from the inn.

"Perhaps, sir," she said, rubbing her hurt wrists, "you will be good enough to explain what this means? There must be some mistake . . . Surely you know me?" She caught him by the sleeve. "I am Mistress Goodgraves's niece and I do not understand —"

The man removed his arm from her grip, unsmiling. He showed no trace of surprise, warmth or friendliness, only a gravity which chilled her to the heart.

"Enough of this playacting," he said. "You are no kin to the Goodgraves. We know that. You were sent from London to spy on us. You may as well admit it. It will save time."

"What do you mean? I tell you, I do not understand. And who are you, sir, to treat me thus?"

He raised his eyebrows at that.

"Sir William Dalridge — as you very well know, I am sure. You play the innocent very cleverly, my dear, but let me warn you, that little game will get you nowhere. It is too late for your winning smiles. You have lost, so take my advice and do not make matters worse for yourself. Why did Walsingham send you to Chartley?"

"Sir Francis Walsingham? What has a poor girl like me to do with such great men as he? Good God! This is absurd!" She gave a nervous, unconvincing little laugh. "First your men behave in this indescribable fashion and now you make these fantastic accusations against me! You cannot make them stand — and in any case, I do not see how my actions are any concern of yours. I must ask you —"

But the man continued in an expressionless voice, disregarding Deborah's fierce retort: "Do you deny that this very morning you had an interview with Paulet, our Queen's gaoler?"

God in heaven! Deborah felt as if the ceiling had descended on her head. "Our Queen" could only mean Scottish Mary — which meant that this house was a nest of papists!

"Ah, you are beginning to realize that we know all about your movements," the gentleman pursued, with some satisfaction, seeing her face suddenly white.

"My lord," she said, holding out her hands imploringly. "You are making a terrible mistake. I swear to God that I am not in Walsingham's pay. As for your secrets, whatever they be, I know nothing of them."

"Then what were you doing at Chartley?" His voice had softened slightly, as though influenced by the ring of undoubted sincerity in hers.

"Nothing that has any bearing on Walsingham's affairs. You must believe that."

"Then how do you explain your visit to the house?"

One of the men standing huddled over the fire looked up and spoke to Dalridge. He had a strong Spanish accent, Deborah noticed.

"My dear sir," he said with a touch of irony. "You are wasting your breath, if you will allow me to say so. Believe me, nothing was ever gained by being over-gentle. In my country, we know something of methods of interrogation and, with your permission, I should like to take over the questioning. You will get nowhere by bandying words. There is but one way to soften the girl up."

"Very well, my dear Perez. No doubt you will prove more adept than myself. I confess that I have little talent and less liking for such pastimes."

With a slight bow to Dalridge, Perez came and took up his station before the horrified Deborah.

"Now, girl. Talk, or it will be the worse for you." His voice rang through the cellar like the crack of a whip.

Deborah glanced frantically about her but her eyes encountered only a cold hostility. Dalridge had rejoined the group of gentlemen and was watching with a detached expression as though, having resigned his task to this unpleasant foreigner, the matter had ceased to concern him. For a moment, it crossed her mind to run to him and tell him everything, but what good would that do? Elizabeth or Walsingham: to these men it was all one. A long shudder of loathing ran through her. The fate which the papists meted out to agents of the crown was well known. The curs would kill her. Well, if that were so, she would rather die with her head held high! She drew herself up.

"I have nothing more to add," she said resolutely, forcing herself to meet the man's eye despite the fear she felt.

"Very well. The choice is yours." He smiled evilly, a gloating expression on his sallow face. "I know of a number of ways to make you more talkative. Basilio, come here!"

The man who had been standing next to him at the fire came over and stationed himself behind Deborah. He was a giant of a man with narrow eyes, bald as an egg and naked to the waist, a red woollen scarf tied round his middle. At a sign from his master, he

57

seized both the girl's arms and twisted them roughly behind her back. She screamed aloud and struggled frenziedly to free herself, but Basilio's calves might have been made of iron for all the impression her kicks made on him.

Perez, meanwhile, had strolled over to the fire and picked up a poker which he thrust into the glowing embers to heat. As he supervised this operation with loving care, he rolled his eyes sideways from time to time to observe the effect on his victim. She was standing very still, her hair tumbled about a face as white as chalk, and her screams had ceased. All her strength had abandoned her and but for Basilio's big hands she would have fallen. Trembling in every limb, she watched with a fascinated horror every movement the Spaniard made.

At last, he stepped back, holding aloft the red-hot iron, and advanced on her.

"Now, little heretic," he said smoothly. "I am going to put the sign of the cross on that soft, white breast of yours. I dislike beauty. It is the imprint of the devil. And so I shall labour to reduce yours to a more modest condition. And should this iron prove insufficient . . ." He gave a hollow laugh. "Por Dios, what use are those deceitful eyes, that impertinent tongue save to blaspheme against your creator? Better for your soul to have them out. But before I have done with you, I promise you, you will talk."

He had hold of Deborah's collar and pulled sharply. At the same time a shriek rang through the underground vaults.

No, no! Oh God, no! Not that! Let it not be that! Mad with terror, Deborah shrank back against Basilio. No, not that! Death, rather. A quick death she could bear, but not this hideous torment, her delicate flesh seared by this demon! Her courage was not equal to this. She would tell them everything . . . everything they wanted to know, even things that were not true, if only they would make him stop. Let them kill her, kill her quickly . . . There was a sound of rending cloth. Deborah's lips moved.

Simultaneously, swift footsteps descended the stairs. A man appeared, a whirlwind of grey velvet and fair hair. In four strides he had reached Perez and, thrusting him aside with one sweep of his hand, had snatched Deborah from Basilio's grasp and was holding her in his arms, carrying her gently to a bench where she lay, sobbing convulsively, while he rounded on the others who had been speechless witnesses of this tempestuous arrival.

"My lords! What is this? Can I believe my eyes? What is this girl doing here, and how dare you treat her so?" Receiving no answer to this, he went on hotly: "You, William. Explain, if you please."

"How do you come to be here, David? I thought you to be on the road to London to meet Anthony?"

"As I left Chartley I ran into Roger. I gathered that you had laid hands on a spy of Walsingham's and I thought best to return here and make sure that all was – but, 'sblood! what do I find but this disgusting —"

"You are mistaken, David. Look at this girl. She is the spy."

"*She!* It is not possible. You're lying!" David said furiously. "You are —"

"David, my dear friend, listen to me, instead of saying things you will come to regret. It is hard to believe, I know, but we have proof. She comes from London and is no more kin to the Goodgraves than you or I. It was a convenient excuse to spy on us. Furthermore, she was at the house yesterday in conference with Amyas Paulet, for more than two hours! All this we know from Thomas Goodgraves who is loyal to us and has no part in his mother's trickery. What more would you have?"

"No," David said again. "It is impossible. How does she answer these charges?"

"She will say nothing."

Before William could prevent him, David was bending over the still sobbing Deborah and gripping her hard by the shoulders.

"Speak, Deborah! Speak, I implore you! It is all a mistake . . ."

"Wait," William said to him. "You have not heard all yet." His eyes on the younger man, he added heavily: "Although, God knows, it is what I would rather spare you. But I can see that nothing else will convince you. Can you think of any better weapons than a studied innocence allied to surpassing beauty? I am quite sure this girl had orders to try her wiles on you in the hope that you would fall an easy victim."

"It is a lie!"

Deborah sprang up, the tears still streaming down her cheeks, and spoke to David who had recoiled, his face livid.

"My lord, you cannot trust this man! You know me better than that —"

"Yes," David said slowly. "And that's just it, you see. I do know you better, and I am beginning to understand, I am afraid. Your manners, your education are all those of a person of standing not of a country wench. It surprised me before, but now I understand. You

59

took me for a fool, but now the game is up." With a look of infinite scorn, he put on his hat and turned away from her. "I leave you to your judges. And you, sirs, forgive my misguided —"

"No! For pity's sake, my lord! Do not desert me now!"

Deborah had flung herself after him and was clinging to his sleeve.

"I will tell you – only you. In God's name, a few minutes . . ."

David hesitated, glancing about him at the threatening circle of men gathered about the girl, at William, and then at Perez, deep in whispered conclave with Basilio, his thin lips twisted into a diabolical grimace.

"Very well," he said. "I assume that you have no objection, my lords? By granting the girl's request you will be spared a disagreeable interlude and her confession cannot be other than of service. One quarter of an hour, no more and she is yours again."

They were alone. The young man stood, one hand resting on the table.

"Well?" he said coldly. "I am all ears. Let us hear what fresh tale you have to offer."

"I can't imagine anyone who has had to do with that beast Perez being in any state to tell tales," Deborah flashed back bitterly. "No, David. I will hide nothing from you. Besides, how should that serve me? I am not guilty and I will prove it to you."

He stiffened perceptibly and she added quickly: "You promised to hear me. Listen, then." Without pausing to draw breath, she told him everything – everything except for the contents of the letter which no one would expect her to know and which she would not reveal.

"If that is so, then I do not see how we can accuse you," he said weakly, when she had finished. "But —"

"Oh, David!" she said softly, standing very close to him. "I can feel that you are not sure whether to believe me, and you are not sure because of – because of those wicked things your friend said earlier. Forget them, I beg of you. Why should I try to deceive you? Your friends will kill me anyway. I know that. I knew nothing about you. I agreed to meet you because I liked you, that was all. Look at me." Her face was very close to his, her eyes sparkling with tears. She was pale, trembling and very lovely. "I am a virgin. You are the first man, I swear by my hopes of salvation, who has ever held me in his arms like that. I ask you, could I have feigned the joy I felt, the —" In her eagerness, she had forgotten the words she had used later to describe her conduct to herself. Her voice shook with her sincerity and, little by little, it found its way through David's mask of indifference until he was drinking in her every word. She laid her hand on his.

"Remember, David. Oh, in God's name, remember! If it had not been for you, I should have left Chartley long before. But I was a fool. I could not bear to go away and leave you thinking ill of me and so —"

"What is this?"

He was questioning her, seemed at last to wish to hear her explanations. Perhaps, after all, all was not lost. He might still help her. She glimpsed at last a ray of light in this abominable evening and, with faint hope beating in her heart, she began to tell him of Thomas's plot.

"The filthy rogue!" he exclaimed with real revulsion when she had told him all, apparently forgetting that the man was on his side. He held Deborah's hand in his. "To use my name to – oh, my dear, forgive me! Yes, I believe you. Indeed, I don't think I ever stopped believing you. But William's words made me mad. To think that I could ever suppose you guilty of such black treachery after — What an ingrate I am! Can you forgive me?" He was holding her close to him when suddenly his arms dropped and his face changed as a new thought struck him. "Oh Christ! How am I to get you out of this? At this of all moments!" He sat for a moment in thought before continuing: "Dalridge, Perez and the rest will not spare you. The very fact that you were sent by the bastard will be enough for them. God! What are we to do?" He paced up and down before Deborah who sat in the grip of a fresh wave of anguish. "Unless . . . Anthony Babington! He is a good man, and a fair one. There may be a chance . . . But I shall need some kind of proof to make Anthony listen to me, or with our present business . . ." His voice changed slightly as he went on rather fast: "He will send me to the devil! Think hard, Deborah. Is there nothing – no letter, nothing?"

"No," Deborah stammered. "I can't think of anything. All I had was the letters for Sir Amyas Paulet and Queen Mary, nothing else . . ."

"This is absurd. It would be too stupid that they should kill you and there be nothing I can do! I have not been one of their company for long, you see, and for all their friendship, they do not yet trust me implicitly. Come, think again. Perhaps there is some small thing you have forgotten. For God's sake, try! Your life hangs on it!" His hands were on her shoulders and he was shaking her fiercely, as if he could force her to remember. "Try!"

There was a metallic clatter on the cellar floor. David bent and picked up the tiny purse which had fallen from Deborah's pocket.

"Is this yours?"

Deborah uttered an exclamation of surprise.

"Yes. Oh, yes! Oh, what a fool I am! That purse had completely slipped my mind." She thrust at David's hand. "No. Keep it, David. Look at the clasp. There. Do you see the initials on it? M and S."

Bewildered, he did as she asked. "Yes, but —"

She interrupted him triumphantly. "It was a present from the – from Queen Mary. She gave it to me. Well? What do you say? Oh, David, dear David! Surely it is exactly what you need to convince your friend?"

David's fingers tightened on the purse. "Our Lady be praised! Now I am sure Anthony will listen to me. That is the main thing, you know. After that, we can easily check your story with the Queen herself."

"But how? None can enter the house save —"

"Never you mind. We have a trick or two more than our friend Walsingham knows of. Babington will have the confirmation we need and you will be saved." His arms went round her. "Now I must call William." He kissed her tenderly once more and let her go. "Trust me, my darling. No harm can come to you while I am here."

VII

So it was true, the thing that had been rumoured in London. In defiance of the Queen's edict, mass was still celebrated in England.

With head bowed and eyelids lowered, Deborah risked a glance about her and encountered a flock of cloaks and gowns above which hovered an air of pious meditation.

All these papists and herself the only Protestant among them! It was the world turned upside-down indeed, for in the whole of England there remained only a bare handful of these recusants. Oh, why couldn't they have joined the reformed Church like everyone else? It would have made everything so much simpler and she would not have been where she was today, trembling like a hen about to have its neck wrung. Why?

It had all begun in 1531, with King Henry's failure to obtain the papal annulment of his marriage to his first wife, Catherine of Aragon which would enable him to marry Elizabeth's mother, the charming Anne Boleyn: whereupon he had broken with Rome and declared himself head of the Church of England. There was to be no more foreign interference in so personal and private a matter as religion. Naturally, there were those who were not best pleased: the monasteries for one, when their goods were confiscated. But there is no pleasing everyone and plenty of others were delighted with the distribution of church property. Then, with Henry's son, Edward VI, had come the Book of Common Prayer and reform was an established fact. Yet even facts may be reversed and the accession of Edward's sister Mary Tudor had brought back the papists who had not been slow in taking bloody revenge for the harsh treatment they had been subjected to in the reigns of Henry and Edward. Then, after that, had come Elizabeth, admirable Elizabeth who, wiser and more diplomatic than her predecessors, had succeeded not only in re-establishing the Protestant religion but at the same time bringing about a national unity, except in a few isolated instances. Yet now Mary Stuart with her plots and schemes, having got herself driven out of Scotland, was busy fanning these isolated sparks into a roaring conflagration, bringing a new wave of conspiracies, arrests and bloodshed.

A bell rang and a ripple ran through the congregation as all those present bowed forward on their knees, leaving Deborah a clear view ahead.

In the front row, kneeling before a bench padded with red velvet, she could see Sir William Dalridge, David and a number of other gentlemen, including those who had been present during her interrogation. Behind them were Perez, the giant Basilio and a group of men in black. Farther off to the right and looking very small beside a vast carved oak chair was a young woman with a small child on either hand seated demurely on cushions. She was praying earnestly. Her fair hair was covered by a veil and every now and then she would hug her cloak of plum-coloured silk trimmed with fox fur more closely round her, with a little shiver as if she were cold. Right at the back, servants and farm labourers knelt on the bare stone floor.

The chapel was ablaze with light from the many stands of candles whose flames struck a rich glow from hangings and woodwork. Pictures gleamed in the alcoves, soft tones of gold and red, blue, green and yellow, revealing marvellous haloed figures. Away to the right, beneath a kind of domed canopy of pale blue satin, stood the statue of a woman wearing a sweet, fixed smile, her deep blue robe falling to marble feet that trod a blossoming carpet of flowers. Goodness, the luxury and wealth of it all! Deborah could hardly believe her eyes, so different was it from the simpler form of worship to which she was accustomed: the plain, whitewashed walls, the simple altar table and the Prayer Book, with an absence of all church ornaments and candles, except, of course, at Christmas. And yet, she saw with amazement, forgetting her own troubles for a moment in a burning curiosity, none of these people seemed in the least distracted by the magnificence around them.

The priest, in an embroidered cope, officiated before an altar covered with rich cloths and laden with jewelled vessels. Between him and his assistant, a young boy in a white surplice, a kind of mystic ritual dance took place, punctuated by solemn stretches of Latin.

Startled, Deborah realized that her right-hand neighbour was tugging at her sleeve. Understanding, she knelt likewise.

Now what was she to do, she wondered. Should she pray? No, for surely any prayer uttered in such a place would qualify as blasphemy. Yet if ever she had needed divine aid it was now. She shivered. It was bitterly cold in the underground chapel and she was desperately short of sleep. At an order from the red-headed man, they had taken her to a room with a hard bed in it for a few hours but no sooner had she escaped from this nightmare world than it seemed a servant was shaking her awake again with an invitation to attend the mass which was about to begin. Situated as she was, Deborah could scarcely refuse and so she had followed the man through a maze of passages and rat-haunted stairways leading down to the nethermost parts of the house.

She sighed. Well, she was awake now, whether she liked it or not, and much as she longed to sink back into the safe haven of sleep, she had better make the best of it. Now was her chance to do some hard thinking about how she was to escape from this hornet's nest. To begin with, where was she? Not far from Chartley, so much was certain, but how did that help her? The house was evidently closely guarded and her room as secure as any prison cell with its barred window and double-locked door. She heard a cough behind her and remembered that the servant who had fetched her was still at her shoulder. She was being narrowly watched. For the present, at any rate, she would have to abandon all hope of flight. There remained the man Babington, so Deborah concentrated on him. Who was he? Their leader, it seemed. But would he be more kindly disposed towards her than Dalridge or the unspeakable Perez? Was poor David, in his eagerness to help, perhaps taking the wish for the fact? While as for his assertion that Babington was in communication with Mary Stuart — the risks seemed quite insurmountable. But then, what was at the root of these men's behaviour and of the aura of secrecy with which they had surrounded themselves? She recalled various words and phrases uttered by David and Dalridge and all at once everything fell into place in her mind. With a gasp, she understood. This was no mere assembly of disaffected persons but the very hub and centre of a conspiracy. Panic almost overwhelmed her at the thought and it took all her resolution not to leap up from her place and trample her way out of the chapel full of worshippers. Common sense kept her where she was. Where could she go? Her only hope was to trust in David. Her eyes sought his fair head and she derived some comfort from the thought that the others would not harm her while he was there. Heaven be praised, he seemed very much in love, she thought: what Aunt Tucker's little maid, Margery, an acknowledged expert in the matter, would have called "head over ears". And therein lay her one advantage, Deborah decided cold-bloodedly. Her horrible experiences of the previous night, coupled with her present deadly danger, had effectively quenched whatever passing fondness had drawn her to David. She no longer viewed their encounters in the arbour through any romantic haze. If she had been stupid enough to put off her journey for his sake, it was a piece of girlish vanity that was likely to cost her dearly. Not that she could ever say so to him, or not without a strong risk of cooling his chivalrous ardour.

The bell rang again. It was the end of the mass. The congregation shuffled. The candles were blown out. Little by little, greyness settled once more upon the gildings.

Deborah waited patiently for her watchdog to make a move.

"Mistress Mason?"

A soft voice was speaking. Deborah looked up and saw the young, fair-haired lady at the end of the row, holding a cherubic child on either hand.

"I am Lady Dalridge. My husband tells me that you have become our" – she gave an embarrassed little smile, "our somewhat involuntary guest. Perhaps," and here her eyes took in Deborah's dishevelled appearance, "perhaps you will not object to make free of my wardrobe? I believe that we are much of a size."

"I thank your ladyship with all my heart. I must confess I should be glad to change my clothes, if it is not putting you to too much trouble."

There was another quick smile that lit up the pretty but tired-looking face and was gone almost at once.

"Come with me."

The manservant followed hard on their heels.

For every woman, young or old, pretty or plain, a new dress is a powerful tonic. Problems retreat from the new image in the mirror, wrinkles and lines disappear as if by magic, the brow clears and the sulky pout gives way to a charming smile to match the dress. It is a new lease of life, an infallible token of success which never fails.

Deborah, at seventeen, with all her new-born self-awareness, was no exception to the rule. Freshly clad in a gown of violet-coloured silk damask, cut low and square across the bosom, with her hair

66

smooth and shining, she felt ready for anything. At the meal which she was invited to share with her hosts, stuffed carp, venison, boiled fowl, asparagus and preserves vanished from her plate in rapid succession.

She was the only person present who did justice to it. The rest picked half-heartedly at their food and the conversation drooped, in spite of all Lady Dalridge's efforts to revive it. David, who had been placed at the opposite end of the table, seemed abstracted and only roused himself from his thoughts to send her, now and then, a would-be reassuring smile. No one else took any notice of her at all. They handed her a napkin or a finger-bowl when occasion demanded with a silent, unsmiling courtesy calculated to remind her that her presence at their board was on sufferance merely and that the reasons for it had not been forgotten. A plague on them, then! The golden sunshine fell freely through the open windows, the sugared cherries melted in her mouth, the wine was good and her dress pretty. What more need she ask? Babington's arrival would solve everything. She had only to look into David's warmly admiring eyes to be sure of that.

The afternoon stretched out interminably, penned between the four walls of her room. Pacing up and down between the bed and the window, starting at every sound, turning over in her mind the prospects of a future which seemed to grow more ominous with every passing moment was, Deborah found, extremely wearing on the nerves.

As the mist gathered over the woods, muffling them in dank, grey vapour, and darkness crept slowly into her prison, all the good, hopeful thoughts which she had been cherishing evaporated, one by one, along with her fleeting pleasure in her dress and the heartening effects of sack, leaving nothing but the persistent, creeping dread which she had been fighting off all day.

Supper was a dismal meal. Lady Dalridge looked up at every sound from outside, only to relapse again into a gloomy silence. The men muttered among themselves and seemed preoccupied. The tension seemed to have spread even to the servants who brought in the various courses with all the gaiety of mutes attendant on a funeral.

Even Deborah had lost interest in what she ate. She disposed of a squab without so much as tasting it as it went down, purely for something to do, and after that occupied herself in nervously rolling her bread into pellets. Her glass remained untouched.

As she was preparing to return to her room, escorted, as ever, by her inseparable guard, David paused at her elbow.

"I thought best not to come to you," he said in a rapid undertone. "Anthony is late and we are all very worried. Wiser not to draw attention to you." He squeezed her arm. "Don't be afraid, my dearest, all will be well."

These hopeful words, however, were belied by the anxious expression on his face.

The night was calm and through the squared panes faint moonlight glimmered on a world of shadows. Uphill from the house, the woods began, standing like some brooding watcher on the crest of the rise, blotting out the view. From time to time, an owl cried. Nearer at hand, the fields spread close up to the house, a patchwork of blue-grey and silver, making the room fragrant with the promise of the harvest to come. Frogs croaked in the moat. It was a perfect summer night, warm, scented and peaceful.

Deborah jumped suddenly. Someone was scratching furtively at the door. David. She ran to open it and stood staring speechlessly.

It was not David but a gentleman with a white beard whom she remembered having seen at supper, sitting on the left of the lady of the house. He pushed past her with a decisive air and shut the door behind him with care.

"I am Lord Trockton. Do you wish to leave the house?"

"But —"

"No buts. Yes or no? We have not much time."

Deborah shook her head bewilderedly. "I don't understand. Surely you are a friend of Sir William Dalridge? Why should you —"

"It is quite simple. I have a great affection for Lord Ashbury. You appear to me, Mistress Mason, to have made altogether too strong an impression on him. David is young, impressionable . . . I cannot allow a woman to interfere with the plans which we have made for him. I prefer to take upon myself the responsibility for your escape before his infatuation leads him to commit some folly. Do I make myself clear? Does that satisfy you?" He spoke with some impatience. "Make up your mind, then. A horse is saddled for you at the postern gate. But we must act quickly. I have lured your guard away for the moment but he will return at any second and then it will be too late. The choice is yours: remain here or go free."

Still Deborah hesitated. The old gentleman did not inspire her with much confidence. On the other hand, what he had to say seemed plausible enough and the patience of the rest would not endure indefinitely. If Babington delayed much longer, David would not be able to restrain them. She had a vision of Perez, waiting in the cellar, and made up her mind.

"I am in your hands, my lord. Only give me a moment to change my dress."

The room was in a corner turret. They passed along a narrow passage ending in a landing from which a miniature spiral staircase descended. At a sign from Trockton, Deborah started down it. Their two shadows loomed in front of her, enormously magnified, in the twisting light from the candle. Behind her, she could hear the heavy thud of the man's boots. Her fears grew as she found herself descending farther into the bowels of the house. Was the stranger to be trusted? Was this a fresh trap to ensure that she should vanish without trace? She was on the verge of turning back when they arrived at the ground floor. A low door swung silently on its hinges and a square of darkness showed in the wall. Lord Trockton's hand was on Deborah's shoulder, thrusting her out. As she crossed the threshold, she stifled a cry and made to draw back as a man emerged from the blackness around, blocking her path. Sweet heavens! It was the guard, the same man who had been watching her chamber door. She turned in terror and was in time to see the look of complicity on Lord Trockton's face. So, he had lied to her. It was a plot. These ideas chased one another through her brain. Before they could make a move to stop her, she had doubled back, pushed past the man behind her and plunged blindly down the nearest passage. Twisting and turning through a maze of passages, she pelted onward, driven by fear and by her slowly-gaining pursuers.

Panting for breath, she burst into the great hall, empty at that time, and clutched at the nearest piece of furniture, knowing that she could not go on. There was a roaring in her ears and a steel vice was gripping her rib cage. Her heart was pounding.

"The wench will have the whole house about our ears, John. Kill her." Lord Trockton's voice came to her too late. At the same instant there was a faint hiss in the air and a stabbing pain in her thigh. She screamed and fell.

Slamming door, oaths, feet moving about the stone floor, lights reeling and swaying against the massive, beamed ceiling, a crowd of sleepy faces bending over her, Sir William Dalridge's ruddy curls among them, a flurry of questions, and then David's startled voice and his arms round her.

"Deborah! Deborah, are you all right? Oh, my God, what has happened? She is hurt. In the name of heaven, William, let Lady Dalridge be sent for. I beg of you. She will know .. . ."

"Oh, be quiet," Dalridge said roughly. Bending down, he picked up the dagger which lay beside Deborah and ran his finger thoughtfully along the blade. "It is nothing . . . a scratch, merely. No cause to throw a fit. No, what interests me a great deal more is how the girl comes to be here and not in her chamber. There is some mystery here. Give me a hand to lay her on this settle."

When this had been done, he addressed himself to Deborah.

"Very well, Mistress Mason. I am listening."

Stretched out on the settle, her head on a cushion which David had slipped beneath it, Deborah raised one eyelid cautiously. The blood was hammering in her temples and there was a searing pain in her thigh but she had all her wits about her. She caught sight of Lord Trockton standing some way off, gently stroking his moustache. He was eyeing her challengingly. She must do something, think of something, quickly. Admit that she had been trying to escape? She might as well sign her own death warrant. But then she remembered that it was equally impossible for Trockton to divulge what he had planned. So it would be one lie against another. Better get her blow in first.

"Sir," she said, choosing her words with care. "I appeal to your justice. A few minutes since, Lord Trockton there came to fetch me from my chamber. I went with him, suspecting nothing, thinking it was by your order. How could I have guessed that one of your friends would be so far lost to all sense of honour as to murder a defenceless girl beneath your roof?"

The words, throbbing with indignation, burst like a thunderclap in the hall. Every head was turned to Lord Trockton. Dalridge, clearly a good deal perturbed at this turn of events, stood gazing uncertainly from the quivering Deborah to the silent Trockton and back again.

Suddenly, with a little gasp, the girl pointed to where a bright red stain was spreading rapidly.

"Would it be abusing your hospitality to ask that my hurt be attended to? Or am I to bleed to death like a pig? It would simplify things, I agree. Especially as you clearly find it easier to condemn the innocent than to give a fair judgement against one of your own people."

Suddenly, she was choking with rage, all her sensible resolutions flown to the winds. She had had all she could stand of these canting papists with their arrogant assumption of their right to stand in judgement. Pox take them, she would tell them – she had done with crawling and whining to them, she —

But before she could speak, sounds of a scuffle broke out at the foot of the stairs. Two men were locked in combat, black doublet with white.

Deborah's hand went to her mouth. Oh God! It was David – David and Lord Trockton. The older man was struggling to break the grip of the younger man's hands on his throat. At a sign from Dalridge, four men sprang forward to part them but David shook them off savagely. His clothes were torn, his young face pale as death, and snarling with rage he drew his sword and advanced on Lord Trockton once more.

"David, my boy! Don't do it! Listen to me! I did it for your sake, for all our sakes . . . this girl . . ." The rest of what he had to say, his desperate supplications were lost in the clatter of hooves that rang out in the courtyard. Lord Trockton was forgotten as everyone, with one accord, turned to face the door. It was thrown open and a man in riding dress came in. He was not very tall and rather slightly than powerfully made, his face was unremarkable and his brown hair, swept back, brushed the collar of his grey cloak.

He tossed the cloak to a servant and took in the scene before him in one rapid glance.

"Lord Trockton! David! What is this?" He spread his arms wide in a gesture of reconciliation. "Whatever the cause, I pray you, set aside your quarrel. Today is a great day!" His hand went to the breast of his doublet. "I have here her Majesty's answer. It is as we hoped." A light shone in his eyes, endowing his unremarkable face with a singular beauty, a look at once noble and intrepid.

"My friends," he went on, in an exalted tone. "My brothers, I need you all. If there are any differences between you, I implore you, in the name of our sainted Queen, forget them, and be friends. For we are about to fight for our Mother Church and now more than ever, we must be united to conquer."

An outburst of spontaneous applause greeted this speech. People

71

craned to shake him by the hand and slap him on the back and from every part of the room voices were raised in eager and excited questioning. The noise that greeted him was indescribable as everyone there present rejoiced with a wild, delusive optimism in the prospect of success.

Slowly, David had sheathed his sword and, turning his back on Lord Trockton, he thrust his way through the group of men surrounding the newcomer and laid a hand hesitantly on his arm.

"Anthony. My dear friend, I am sorry if what I did just now seemed strange to you. But I must speak with you urgently. This lady . . ."

"Lady? What lady? What the devil —" He broke off, following David's pointing hand. Deborah had been hidden from him until then by the press of people around him and he started at the sight of her.

"Who is this person? What is she doing here?"

"Anthony!" David's voice was pleading. "Whatever they may tell you, I will vouch for her. May I speak to you alone?"

Babington frowned. "What does this mean? I find you threatening Trockton with a drawn sword and now this girl . . . on whose behalf you seem to be acting the knight errant. I had thought better of you, David. I don't like it, let me tell you, and it could not have come at a worse moment. We'll talk of it later, you and I." He raised his voice a little. "Gentlemen, give me your attention. Let us not waste our strength in talk. Deeds call us! Follow me, all of you. The time is ripe, but first, I must be sure that each man knows exactly what it is he has to do."

A murrain on the man, he had been right. The wound, now that it had been washed and dressed by Lady Dalridge, had emerged as nothing more than a long scratch, more spectacular than serious. "A few days' rest and it will be quite better," Lady Dalridge had pronounced. Heaven grant that she was right, thought Deborah, and that the patient would be permitted to live to enjoy them!

She had been taken to a small room leading off the hall and there, for the past three hours, she had been gnawing her finger-nails. What would Babington decide? Would he simply eliminate her or would he set her free? Free? She gave a twisted grin. After the things they had not scrupled to say in front of her, she could scarcely be fool enough to hope that they would let her go. No, she could see only one end to her problem, an easy, straightforward end that made her flesh creep.

She cocked her head to listen. The house was alive with movement. Doors creaked. Oaths and impatient commands rang from the lofty walls and filtered through the dark red curtain across the door. Every few moments, purposeful steps sounded in the hall, to be followed in a little while by the clatter of furious hoofbeats over the bridge and dying away into the night.

Deborah shifted slightly and bit back a cry of pain. It was too stupid. In all this coming and going she might have found her chance to escape, and to warn the Queen. Yet here she was, tied helplessly to her bed. She gave a mirthless laugh. Warn the Queen? Poor fool that she was! A fine time for heroism, this was. No doubt this conspiracy would be like every other rising, of whatever kind, and as easily suppressed. Her Majesty was well able to manage without any assistance from Deborah. She had Walsingham for that. While she . . . Tears started to Deborah's eyes. Oh, dear, merciful God, teach David what to say!

"There is no other way. Believe me, David, this is the best course . . ."

Babington swept into the room with David at his heels, and came to a halt in front of Deborah.

"Mistress Mason, my name is Anthony Babington. Lord Ashbury has told me about your unhappy plight. We must have a talk, you and I."

Taking comfort from the fact that he did not sound altogether unfriendly, Deborah met his eyes squarely.

"Then I am sure you must be aware that I have been guilty of nothing wrong. I trust in your sense of what is right."

Waving away the stool which David had brought forward for him, Babington continued to stand looking at her. He went on: "As it happens, I am in a position to corroborate your account of yourself. I have heard from our gracious Queen that she did in fact receive a secret message from your lady the day before yesterday. No," he went on, seeing the look on Deborah's face, "do not rejoice too soon. Although we now have proof that you do not belong to Walsingham, the fact remains that you were sent by Elizabeth. That being so, you will understand that it is impossible for us to set you at liberty. You could easily identify this house and those in it and I cannot imagine that your feelings towards them are sufficiently cordial to prevent you from passing on the information to our enemies." He smiled, but without any trace of amusement. "My friends here agree with me and in their view you should be silenced once and for all." Deborah's fingers tightened on the settle where she lay. But Babington had not finished.

"For my own part, I will not stain the sacred cause I serve with murder if it may be avoided. This, therefore, is what I propose."

With damp palms and an odd lump in her throat, Deborah waited for what he would say.

"My home at Lichfield is not many miles from here. I shall escort you there before returning to London and you will remain with my wife until my return. On one condition. You must swear an oath on the Gospels to make no attempt to escape and never to reveal to any-one that you have been here, or anything of what you have seen."

Deborah almost gasped aloud with relief. Tears stood in her eyes.

"Oh, sir! How can I ever thank you? Lord Ashbury was right to praise you as he did. By your goodness, you have wiped out all the anguish I have endured in this house." For a moment her voice was choked by a sob. "Let us not talk of that. I shall remember nothing, sir, but the memory of your kindness to me."

White-faced, she hoisted herself up, despite the pain of the stiffening wound in her leg, and held out a hand which shook a little.

"I swear before God that I will never betray your trust."

"I thank you, Mistress Mason." He was watching her closely, pulling at his short beard. "I think I may trust your word. There is an honesty about your looks not often found in one so young and so . . . attractive. I ought to warn you, in any case, that should you break your word you would not enjoy your ill-won freedom for very long. However, I think I may safely promise you that your confine-ment will be of short duration. God willing," he crossed himself, "it will be over very soon and to His greater glory. But I nearly for-got —" His hand went to his doublet and he held out to her the purse which Mary Stuart had given her. "Permit me to return this precious gift. You owe your life to it, and to our friend here." He nodded towards the crimson-faced David. "You have there a most eloquent and impassioned defending counsel."

He smiled, a quick, boyish smile which made him suddenly very much younger, more vulnerable and closer. Then, abruptly breaking the spell which had descended for a moment on the room, he became the brisk commander once again.

"Very well. Let us be off. David, you take Mistress Mason up with you. I must apologize," he added, with a polite inclination of his head towards Deborah, "for the shortness of time which makes it impossible to convey you by litter. I am afraid the journey will be an uncomfortable one for you. You will have to forgive me."

Very carefully and tenderly, David bent and lifted the girl in his arms. For a moment their heads touched, red hair and gold, then they were following Anthony Babington into the hall.

VIII

Deborah sat down on a clump of moss and laid the bunch of corn-flowers, poppies and wild oats which she had been gathering in the meadow below, down by her side. The little copse where she was sitting sloped gently towards the house and if she looked to her left she could see the bright rooftops and plastered walls, pierced by tall, latticed windows. Stretching away from the house and forming a perfect foil to it, were the gardens that were Lady Babington's pride. Here were no pompous avenues, cluttered with statuary in wood and stone and with fantastic figures cut out in clipped juniper and box. Instead, a broad, green lawn liberally strewn with daisies was bounded on either side by an apparent confusion of covert walks and pleached alleys, just now heavy with the scent of the lime trees in flower. Instead of the fashionable knots and geometrical designs laid out in coloured earths, the flowers were allowed to grow in all their natural beauty: pinks and gillyflowers, sweet williams, pansies and French marigolds, lilies and roses glowed in vivid shades of red, white, blue and yellow at the foot of tall, green hedges and between the trees of apple and pear, quince, peach, apricot and cornelian. To the enchanted visitor it gave the illusion of a picture, at the same time restful and sumptuous, composed by no human artist but by the hand of nature herself.

The forest formed an almost complete circle about the manor. To the westward only, an opening in the prevailing green showed where the road ran that linked Lichfield to Chartley.

It was along this road that Deborah had come, a fortnight before, in the first grey light of dawn, riding with Anthony Babington and David. It had been a cruel journey. She had need of all her will-power to keep her precarious seat on the pillion behind David, clinging with both arms round his waist. The jolting had reopened her wound, there was an anvil beating in her head and she could barely keep her eyes open for tiredness.

She had woken, with no very clear idea of how she came there, in bed between cool, lavender-smelling sheets with the sun falling on her face and on the chamber door and the clear, piping voice of a youthful maidservant in her ears.

"Good day to you, Mistress. I hope you have slept well." The child bobbed a shaky curtsy. "I am Nan, if you please, and I am here to serve you."

Deborah smiled at the freckled, snub-nosed face that gazed at her so seriously from under a neat, white cap.

"Thank you, Nan. Tell me, what time is it?"

"Just gone noon by the church clock, Mistress."

"Noon! Good God, how came it so late? Oh, I should – Run, child, and tell Sir Anthony that I shall be ready in a quarter of an hour at most."

"Sir Anthony's gone, Mistress, long since. And my Lord Ashbury with him. I'll tell my lady."

She sped away and Deborah threw back the quilt. The next instant she had dropped back on her pillows with a sharp cry. She had forgotten all about her injured leg but the leg itself had all too swiftly put her in mind of it. Deborah told herself firmly that she must try again, must make the effort, or what would Lady Babington think of her? Eyes smarting, fingers twisted hard into the bedclothes, she was making clumsy but heroic attempts to rise when the door opened again and a young woman entered.

"Please, Mistress Mason, you must be sensible!" She came forward quietly and, drawing up the covers again with gentle firmness, laid one hand on Deborah's forehead.

"I am Lady Babington. My husband has told me all about you, so there will be plenty of time for us to get to know each other better. For today, you must be sensible. Hush, now. Do as I say and I promise you that by the end of the week you will be on your feet again. For the present, you require a fresh dressing for your wound and a little food if you can take it, and then another rest."

Under Lady Babington's unremitting care, Deborah had made a rapid recovery. The quiet atmosphere of Lichfield had been a powerful anodyne for her abraded nerves but, more than anything, the unobtrusive kindness of the mistress of the house had helped to bring her back to health.

Jane Babington was twenty-four years old and by no means a beauty, which she knew. Her figure was short and inclined to be dumpy, her hair a pale mouse, her nose too strong for her face and her movements ungraceful. Yet there was something grave and charming about her expression which held the attention. You had only to pause and examine that high, generous brow, to meet the straightforward gaze of those intelligent and perceptive grey eyes to feel instinctively the nobility and goodness underlying that plain exterior.

Deborah had never met any woman quite like her. Her knowledge of her own sex was limited to her domineering aunt, the gossiping maidservants over whom she ruled and to those brilliant, butterfly creatures encountered from time to time in the antechambers of the various royal palaces. Jane was a revelation, and she loved her immediately, spontaneously and impulsively, despite the curious circumstances which had brought them together. Now, to her great joy, Jane, who at first had shown a slight reserve, seemed to be able, in a way, to return her friendship.

Wisely, neither of them introduced the subject of religion or mentioned the names of Elizabeth or Mary Stuart. By a kind of tacit accord they avoided any topic which could break the pleasant harmony which was growing between them.

For all the friendly welcome she was given, Deborah had been conscious, those first few days, that she was being watched continually. Lady Babington had even gone to the trouble of mentioning casually that Lichfield was surrounded by a high wall which was guarded night and day. Evidently, her word had been accepted only with some reservations, but for that her hosts were scarcely to be blamed. They knew nothing of her, after all.

In all fairness, under any other circumstances she would undoubtedly have felt no scruples about making her escape by any means that offered. Surely an oath extracted under duress had never been regarded as binding? But there was Anthony Babington: a rebel, yes, but also a man of honour worthy of respect, whose generosity had made a deep impression on her. If she were to betray him, who had gone to the trouble of saving her, had trusted her and, young as she was, had judged her capable of maintaining her word, how could she ever look herself in the face again? And Jane – how could she repay Jane's care and friendship in such a way?

She was permitted a greater freedom now. She could go for short walks through the meadows and even venture a little way into the woods, endeavouring on her return to amuse Jane with the account of her ramblings. For Jane, try to hide it as she would, was clearly enduring agonies of anxiety. More and more often, Deborah would find her huddled in her chair, white-faced, her eyes reddened with crying, her hands clutching her needlework while her eyes stared blankly into space. In the evenings, she would leap up every time they heard a horseman anywhere near the house. Always, it would be a messenger on a foaming horse who delivered a letter or a verbal message and was off again almost at once. Once or twice these brought a smile to Jane's pallid lips, but more often they only made her look more unhappy than ever and Deborah was almost physically aware of the effort it cost her to resume their interrupted conversation.

Deborah was not without her own worries, although of a rather different kind. In the beginning, she had had only one idea in her head, and that was to escape, but as the days passed she knew, if she were honest with herself, that she was no longer in quite such haste to be away. Life at Lichfield was very pleasant: she met with nothing but kindness, her every need was catered for and the company congenial. She was at no one's beck and call, had no responsibilities and nothing was expected of her in return for her keep, nothing except to wait. But wait for what? There lay the fly in the ointment of this unexpected holiday. Deborah's plans for the future could no longer be said to include the prospect of a gratifying audience with the Queen. A torrent of abuse, one of her Grace's devastatingly frank and shattering tirades, followed by a swift return to an ignominious oblivion, that was all that lay ahead for her now. For how was she to explain her disappearance and, seeing that she had given her word not to reveal the truth, what could she say that would not look as though she had arrived empty-handed? She could probably make up a convincing story, her fertile imagination was equal to that, but although it might explain her delay it would not excuse it. The great ones of this world were notoriously not interested in anything not directly to their advantage, as they were known never to forget a failure, however undeserved. Oh God! Deborah cudgelled her brains until her head ached but in the end could only leave it to time, the Babingtons and her aunt between them, to anyone in fact but herself, to arrange matters. After all, it was their fault, not hers.

Sighing, she shook off such gloomy thoughts and began to sort the wild flowers lying, a heap of red and blue, in her lap. She had arranged them in a bunch and was looking about for something to tie them with when the sound of hoofbeats made her look up. A horse was trotting towards her over the grass, its rider waving eagerly. It was David.

The flowers were scattered on the ground as Deborah sprang

forward to meet him. Dear David! At last she would hear the news and would be able to thank him properly for all that he had done for her. She had not realized at the time what it must have cost him to risk losing the confidence of his friends as he had done, and all for her!

"Sweetheart! My dear one, how good it is to see you again!"

Swinging himself down from his horse, the young man seized both Deborah's hands in his and stood looking at her fondly. In her simple damask dress, figured with forget-me-nots, with her eyes sparkling like clear water and bits of moss and blades of grass caught in her loose hair, she looked as fresh and rosy as some woodland nymph.

"David!" She gave a little, happy trill of laughter. "What a relief to see you safe and sound. I was so anxious for you! Sir Anthony —?"

"Was with me, but he has already left. I must join him in a moment but you know I could not leave Lichfield without seeing you, even if only for a few minutes, Deborah."

She studied his face. It looked thinner, drawn and tired, and his eyes were restless.

"What is it, David?" she asked quietly. "What has happened to you?" Her fingers clenched impulsively on his arm. "You do not belong with these men. Your friendship for Sir Anthony – that I can understand, but the others – they are ravening wolves, and murderers! Please, David, listen to me! Leave plots to those whose nature they are. Go back to your books."

She was almost sobbing in her desperate anxiety to help him. Ignoring the resistance in his face, she went on urgently: "I do not know what you are planning but, do not be angry with me for saying so, you cannot fight the Queen!"

"Deborah!"

"No! You cannot fight her. Oh, David, I am not saying this to hurt you." She gazed at him earnestly. "I promised myself not to talk politics with you, to say nothing of my Queen or yours, but it is for your good, can't you understand? The Queen is too strong, too powerful and too clever. What can you and Babington, Dalridge, Trockton and the rest, do to her? You will be a hunted fugitive at best. Is that what you want? You are not such a fool, I know. For heaven's sake then, give it up, while there is still time. Break with these men. You have nothing in common with them. No good will come of this, I can feel it!"

He had stepped back from her quietly.

"And what of my honour, Deborah? Do you think me a base coward to desert my friends at the very moment they have most need of me? It is true I am no lover of violence. Risks hold no attraction for me." A bleak smile crossed his face. "How well you know me. I am a man of peace, made to live in some retired spot like this, loving my wife and dreaming of the moon . . . but unfortunately duty does not always follow one's private wishes. I am a loyal Catholic and so my duty is to Queen Mary. I should not deserve to call myself a gentleman, my dear, if I failed to act according to my principles." He sighed and tilted Deborah's chin with one finger.

"Now, don't look so grief-stricken. It may be for the best, after all. Tell me, are you happy here?"

Deborah held back her tears.

"Oh, yes," she said. "Lady Babington is wonderful. In fact, I wanted to thank you for all you have done for me. I —"

"It was nothing. Deborah, I — It is likely that very soon now you will be free. Anthony told me to say to you —" He spoke with something of an effort. "To say to you that should you hear no news in two weeks from now, you are to leave. Lady Babington knows and she will not prevent you." He read the mute question in Deborah's eyes and forestalled it quickly. "Now, my heart, I must say goodbye."

"So soon?"

Without answering, he had cupped his hands about her lovely face and was staring down into it with a passionate intensity, as if he wanted to engrave every line of it in his memory and when he did speak it was in a voice vibrant with tenderness.

"I love you, Deborah. What happened in the arbour was no mere flirtation on my part but a feeling I carry with me night and day. I do not know when, if ever, we shall meet again in this world, my darling, but I wanted you to know that."

He kissed her hungrily, like a starving man, raining kisses on her face and neck as she lay in his arms. Then, at last, he thrust her from him, mounted his horse and rode away without a backward look.

Deborah made her way slowly back to the house. Once or twice, as she went, she wiped away a tear.

Crossing the garden, she made her way into the house by a side door and went straight to the small room with the yellow silk hangings where Lady Babington was in the habit of sitting in the afternoons to read or work.

She was there now, very pale and distraught, and for the first time Deborah saw her crying.

"Jane! What is it?"

Deborah ran to her friend's side. "I have just seen Lord Ashbury. He told me that Sir Anthony was here. Oh, what has happened to upset you so?"

The other girl made no reply, too shaken by her sobs to answer.

"Jane —" Deborah said, clasping her hands comfortingly. "Ever since I have been here, I have seen you growing daily more anxious. I would not intrude, and the fact that there are things on which we do not think alike made it difficult for me to ask you, but don't you think it might help now if you were to tell me a little of what is worrying you? You must know it is my friendship for you that makes me say this, and nothing else. So tell me, my dear."

Jane looked up and hesitated, her reddened eyes fixed on Deborah's, before she spoke.

"Anthony has gone back to London . . . to Walsingham."

"What? Is he mad?" Deborah exclaimed, stupefied. "Oh, Jane, I'm sorry! Forgive me. It slipped out. I don't understand —"

"I thought the same as you," Jane said sadly. "I did my best to dissuade him, you may be sure, but to no avail. He means to find out for himself if he is suspected, as he thinks. He might as well run his head into a noose." She was silent for a moment, then burst out: "Oh, Deborah, it is terrible! I am sure something dreadful is going to happen. The last time he was here, on the nineteenth of July, the day you came, Anthony seemed so optimistic, so certain of success. I had never seen him so confident. But today, although he is so brave, he was depressed, almost in a state of terror! I feel in my heart that I shall never see him again alive."

"Jane, calm yourself. You are letting your imagination run away with you. They may detain him, question him perhaps, but as for thinking —"

"That is because you do not know everything, dear." Jane fell silent for a moment, then she sighed. "You are right. This secret has been on my mind for too long, and now that all seems lost, perhaps there is little to be gained by keeping it to myself. I may as well tell you, since I have got so far. I can trust you, I know. You are too generous to rejoice in my sorrow."

Deborah bent and kissed her, without speaking.

"My husband was seven years old," Jane began, "when Queen Mary came to Carlisle, after the defeat at Langside, a penniless fugitive from her own people. The tale of her sufferings and the feeling of English Catholics towards one whom – forgive me, Deborah – they regarded as their rightful queen made a deep impression on him. His devotion only increased as he grew up and because he is a brave and loyal person he dreamed of nothing but performing gallant deeds in Queen Mary's service, to set her free from her ignoble captivity. Then we were married, and for a little while we were very happy. I was too happy, perhaps, selfishly so. But Anthony did not forget."

Jane fumbled in the little tapestry-work bag at her waist for a handkerchief and dabbed at her eyes. She sighed again.

"Well, about a year ago, one of her Grace's agents – for she has many friends: she has a way of winning hearts, you know, here, and in Scotland, in Paris, Rome, Madrid, and she maintains a constant correspondence with them. One of these people came to see Anthony. Lichfield is not far from Chartley and there was a plan afoot to gain support among the gentlemen of the neighbourhood to organize the Queen's escape. Everything was ready two months since and my husband was only waiting for Queen Mary to give the word. It came – but now he seems to have lost all faith in the plan, as if his will were paralysed. I think he suspects treachery and fears the worst. So you see," Jane finished dolefully, "I have good reason to fear. If he is taken, he cannot hope for pardon."

Deborah was silent. To think that she had imagined she was dealing with a small affair of no importance! What a blind fool she had been! How could these men believe themselves a match for Elizabeth? How could they think to betray their queen for the sake of a foreign princess who had never brought anything but trouble? How many young men had already gone to their deaths on her account, and how many more would suffer yet, Deborah asked herself in anguish, thinking of Babington and David. She might hate the thing they planned to do with all her heart, yet the thought of what awaited them if they failed wrung her heart. Still she said nothing, torn between the feelings of friendship she had developed for the two conspirators and her own fierce pride and loyalty to Elizabeth, and her belief that the Queen was invincible.

Aware that none of the thoughts jostling one another so furiously in her mind were likely to be of much comfort to poor Jane, Deborah sought desperately for the right thing to say.

83

"Dear Jane," she said gently at last. "You know that my own loyalties will not let me approve of what Sir Anthony is planning. Yet it has always seemed to me a very good and wonderful thing for anyone to devote themselves wholeheartedly to an ideal, whatever it might be, and you should be proud of him, instead of tormenting yourself like this. Why must you look always on the dark side? It may be, and I hope so with all my heart, for your sake and for his, that all these plots may come to nothing and no one any the wiser. It is a thing which has happened often enough in history, isn't it? So take heart and do not cry."

Lady Babington rose and put her arms round the other girl.

"Thank you, Deborah," she said unsteadily. "I was not mistaken. You have been very kind and tactful in an extremely awkward situation. I shall not forget it."

She went over to the window, pausing automatically to straighten a crooked fold in a curtain, and then stood leaning her forehead on the cross bar and staring out abstractedly. She was breathing normally once more and her hands had stopped shaking.

"There is one thing I still don't understand," Deborah remarked suddenly. "And that is how on earth Queen Mary is able to communicate with the outside world. You have never met Sir Amyas Paulet, my dear. I have. He is a real fiend. Not a pin could leave the house without his knowing."

Jane looked round.

"It seems incredible, doesn't it? It's such an ingenious trick that no one would ever think of it. Who, I ask you, would ever think to look inside a barrel full of beer?"

"A beer barrel!"

"Yes. Amazing, isn't it?" Jane said, misunderstanding Deborah's astonished exclamation. "And to make doubly sure, the waggoner who carries the beer to the house is on our side. He is paid as well, naturally, and with every delivery he takes and brings back a wooden flask containing the messages concealed inside one of the barrels. Why, what is the matter?"

"Just that I know the man you are speaking of. He is a vile creature: it was he who sold me to Sir William Dalridge! I am surprised that your husband should trust him. He would be capable of anything."

"Yet he has served us very faithfully so far. Do you judge him harshly because he did you a wrong?"

84

She was looking worried again and Deborah blamed herself for reawakening her fears. She forced a smile.

"I expect you are right. We are all inclined to judge people as we find them and in the present instance it is not easy to be objective."

Yet as she spoke she had a vision of Thomas, with his small, greedy eyes, and a shiver ran up her spine. Poor Jane. She took her arm.

"Let's go out in the garden and pick some roses. That will cheer you up."

IX

Several days went by but no messenger appeared to bring news. Lichfield basked in utter quiet.

Then, one morning – it was the tenth of August, a day Deborah was to remember all her life – she was sitting late in her chamber, perched on the window-seat, idly brushing her hair. She was dressed only in a linen shift belonging, like everything else she had to wear, to Lady Babington, for her own luggage had been left behind at the inn at Chartley and she had arrived at Lichfield with nothing but what she stood up in, her torn and bloodstained riding-dress, fit only to be thrown away. Instantly, Jane had made her free of her own wardrobe and although the skirts came half-way up her calves and the bodices hung on her some passable results had been achieved with the aid of Nan and a few ribbons and ties, and what a joy it was to feel clean and fresh once more! It was good for the morale as well.

Suddenly, as her eye roamed vaguely over the piece of country before her, now known to her in every smallest detail, it was caught by a dark speck emerging from the forest on to the white, dusty road. The speck grew rapidly and soon resolved itself into the figure of a man on horseback. Soon Deborah could make out a broad-brimmed dark hat and flying cloak. She leaned farther out. The man was riding at a furious gallop, bending low over his horse's neck but however much she peered she could not tell his identity. She was certain, at least, that it was neither David nor Anthony Babington. By now, the rider had reached the drive that skirted the garden when, abruptly, without slackening pace, he swung his horse aside and cut straight across the mown grass.

Deborah jumped up, dropping her hairbrush. Jane's precious turf! There must be something serious the matter for the stranger to behave so unceremoniously. She strained her ears and heard the shrill voice of a servant, the banging of the front door, the sound of a second door being slammed shut and then nothing more.

Without a moment's hesitation, Deborah snatched up the green and white dress that lay on the bed and scrambled into it. She was still tying the points as she flew down the stairs.

In the hall she paused to listen. Muffled sounds of conversation seemed to be coming from Sir Anthony's cabinet. Deborah tiptoed across and laid her ear to the crack.

"Jane, my dear, I beg you, be sensible," a voice was saying urgently.

"No, Kit. It's no good. I'll not go." That was Jane's voice.

" 'Sdeath, woman, must you be so obstinate? I tell you there is not a moment to lose."

Where in the name of goodness had she heard those warm and vibrant tones before. And what did it mean? Unable to master her curiosity any longer, Deborah opened the door.

Lady Babington was standing in the centre of the room, her face deathly pale. Her hair was coming down and there was a button missing from her gown, which was badly awry.

Deborah stood in the doorway, petrified. Never, not even first thing in the morning, had she ever seen this woman looking anything but neat and impeccably dressed.

"Jane!" she uttered at last.

Jane came a few steps forward and looked at her with eyes in which all life seemed to have been extinguished.

"Queen Mary was arrested the day before yesterday, during a hunting expedition at Tixall," she said tonelessly. "Her two secretaries were apprehended also, and all her correspondence has been seized. It is all over. We are betrayed."

Deborah could only gasp at her speechlessly.

"The hunt is up for all those involved in the plot," poor Jane went on. "Walsingham's men may be here at any moment. Lord Belstone came to warn me, but I can't possibly go. Anthony" – her voice broke a little – "Anthony may yet need me. I shall not leave Lichfield. Oh dear —" She gave a small, heartbreaking smile. "I'm sorry, Deb dearest, I am behaving very badly. I don't think you know Lord Belstone, a very good friend of ours. Kit, let me present Mistress Mason to you."

The tall man who, at Deborah's entrance, had turned away in evident annoyance and was now apparently lost in contemplation of the bookshelves, turned round quickly. Deborah had a lightning vision of a pair of very black eyes that stared at her with amazement, a dark face and sardonic mouth, and was struck dumb. Her legs almost gave way beneath her. Oh yes, she knew him all right. He was the man she had last seen in the woods near Coventry.

He was bowing, with a touch of irony.

"I think I have already had that pleasure." Then he went on, almost at once: "Jane, we are wasting time. It is madness for you to remain here. Anthony will keep away, if only to avoid incriminating you. Besides, he must know that Lichfield will be watched."

"No, Kit. Please say no more. It is very generous of you and I am deeply grateful. For you to risk compromising yourself for our sake, when your beliefs are so very different, shows real friendship." She sighed. "Indeed, it is at times such as these that one finds out who are one's friends. But my mind is made up. Even if Anthony dare not come here, he may try to send a message . . . and without him, what do I care what becomes of me?" She clasped her two hands together convulsively, then extended them to Lord Belstone. "For God's sake, go now, Kit. I should hate myself for ever if I involved you in this dreadful business."

Belstone looked at her.

"Very well, Jane. It is for you to judge. I shall not insist. I will try to get news of Anthony and will let you know of it by one of my people should I hear anything." He put his arm round her affectionately. "Gilford is not far off if you should need me. Do not hesitate to call on me to serve you."

He bowed and, picking up his hat from the chest where he had dropped it, placed it over his black curls. In doing so, he caught sight of Deborah, still standing where she had been all this time, with her back against the table.

"I wish, Mistress Mason, I had leisure to pursue the conversation we began the other day," he remarked, and grinned at her wolfishly. "You left me, alas, still panting for more."

"Kit!"

The exclamation made him break off before he could say more.

"Kit, I have thought of something. There is a way in which you can serve me. Take Deborah with you. She has no business here."

Turning to the blushing Deborah, Jane continued: "You have kept your word nobly, my dear, but now I release you from it. Go with Lord Belstone. He will set you on the road for London. I know you well enough now to be sure that you will say nothing which might harm my husband. Besides, they will surely have his letters by now."

Deborah ran to Jane and put both arms round her.

"How can you think for a moment that I would leave you now?" she reproached her.

Jane's eyes filled. "Thank you, Deborah dearest. It shows your own real goodness that you should want to stay. I have not forgotten how you came to be here. But please do as I ask. Kit, I trust her to you."

Before Deborah could open her mouth to object, the door burst open and a man staggered into the room. He was bareheaded and haggard-eyed, covered with mud and dust from his boots to his black velvet doublet and dishevelled grey hair. Deborah, facing him, took one look and put her hand to her lips to choke back the cry.

Three quick strides took him to where Jane was standing.

"Fly, lady! All is discovered!" he cried chokingly. "There is a traitor in our midst! I was not able to reach Anthony but my first thought was to warn you."

"I am touched by your devotion, my lord, but I have already heard from Lord Belstone of the misfortune that has befallen."

"What's this? Lord Belstone here?" the other broke in violently, suddenly becoming aware of the presence of other people in the room. "Do you know, ma'am, with whom you are dealing? This man is a friend of the Earl of Essex, one of the scourges of our faith – perhaps one of those who even now are hounding us with their pursuit! Ask him where he got his information! Ask him!"

"My dear Trockton, I shall be only too happy to oblige. Out of regard for our hostess, I am even willing to overlook your deplorable manners. To one of your outlook the concept of loyalty to one's friends, even when one differs from them, is no doubt inconceivable."

"My lord!" Trockton's hand went to his sword, and Jane stepped quickly between the two men.

"I think, my lord, that these late terrible events must have turned your brain. How dare you behave so to me, in Anthony's house, when at this very moment perhaps —" Her voice failed her.

Lord Trockton hung his head.

"You are right and I am a boor. Forgive me. And you too, Lord Belstone. I am not in my right mind."

Belstone bowed coldly and took Jane's hand.

"Good-bye, Jane, my dear. Come, then, Mistress Mason . . . Now, where the devil —?" His searching glance found out Deborah, white-faced, shrinking back into the window embrasure. "What's the matter with you?"

The words were drowned by a roar from Lord Trockton, who had followed his look, and now sprang forward to grasp Deborah's arm in a grip of steel.

"Ha, you jade! So I find you at last!"

"My lord! This is the second time you have forgotten yourself beneath my roof! Let Mistress Mason go, this instant! I am responsible for my guests and I will not tolerate this behaviour of yours much longer. Let her go, I say!" Jane darted forward, trembling with anger.

"Pox on't! The slut has imposed on you with her innocent airs. But it is she, she who has betrayed us! To that I will swear by my hopes of salvation."

He had not released his grip on Deborah, who was squirming frantically in his hold.

"You see now," he said, "where our weakness has brought us. She should have been killed. Anthony was too lenient, but I know where my duty lies."

"You don't know what you are saying! Mistress Mason has not left my side. She cannot possibly have done the thing you charge her with. Enough! I order you to let her go!"

"Allow me, Jane." Lord Belstone had come up behind her. "I think it is time I took a hand. I do not know, my lord, what prompts you to this fury and to be honest, I do not greatly care. However, Lady Babington has entrusted this young woman to my care and I will not suffer her to be molested. I ask you to let her go."

The older man turned purple.

"Do you have the impudence to command me? It is too much!" Casting Deborah roughly from him, he drew his sword. "You will answer to me for that, and forthwith!"

"Put up your blade, man! At least spare Lady Babington a sordid quarrel!"

There was a brief pause and then Lord Belstone gave a tiny shrug.

"Very well. If that is what you wish," he said, and drew in his turn.

The two men faced one another, rapier and dagger at the ready. Jane had stepped back silently, knowing that no woman could interfere between them now, and was praying quietly.

Deborah stood beside her, her back to the wall, mechanically rubbing her bruised wrist as she followed the progress of the fight with anxious eyes.

Lord Belstone fought in a relaxed style, not troubling to do more than remain on the defensive, parrying his adversary's blows with his dagger with a careless ease, as if the combat were beneath him. Trockton, on the other hand, laid about him wildly, but he was already weary and rage made his hands shake. Suddenly, as he lunged, his foot slipped, he tripped against a stool and almost fell.

"This place and time are ill-chosen, my lord," Belstone observed. "Shall we not let the matter rest there? I am at your disposal on whatever day you choose to name."

Trockton's suffused face twisted into a snarl of pure hate. "Heretical cur! Are you afraid? Come on, then! By God, I mean to kill you!"

The fight was resumed.

Lord Belstone had lost his indolence and was fighting seriously now. The blades crossed and sparkled in the bright morning sun with a lively clash of steel. The two faces gleamed with sweat and the older man's breath was coming in harsh gasps. Jane and Deborah held theirs. Trockton skidded suddenly and left an opening. There was a shiver of white lightning about his arm and the sword fell from his suddenly slackened grasp, clattering on the floor. He stared for a moment in apparent incredulity as the blood dripped from his torn sleeve, then his eyes rolled and he fainted.

"Don't be alarmed. I barely scratched him. My apologies, but blood-letting was the only way to cool his fever."

Lord Belstone wiped his sword carefully, restored it and his dagger to their sheaths, then he stepped up to the wounded man and, gently putting Jane aside, lifted Trockton in his arms as easily as if he had been a baby.

"Just be good enough to show me the way, my dear," he said as he moved towards the door. "Oh, and if I were you, I'd get rid of him as soon as you can. He'll come round before very long. Bandage his arm for him, make him a posset and then send him packing, with one of your own servants to go with him if necessary. Let him take his threats and fantasies elsewhere. They could well do you harm if he stays here."

Deborah pulled out a stool and sat down on it heavily. Her limbs felt like water. What a morning!

She was still trying to pull her ideas together when Jane returned, with Lord Belstone at her heels.

"Well, Deb, I think you'll agree now that it's best for you to go?"

Deborah stood up. "But Jane —"

"No, dear." The other girl took her arm affectionately. "We must face facts. Your presence here can only make matters worse. Suppose Walsingham's men were to find you here? What would they assume? And if our own friends found you here at this desperate moment, they would not spare you. And next time we should not have Lord Belstone to intervene. Look at Lord Trockton. He is an honourable and high-minded man, yet in his present mood he would certainly not have hesitated to kill you. Would you make me more unhappy than I am by the knowledge that I am putting you in danger?" She hugged Deborah warmly. "Thank you for your friendship, my love. I shall always remember it with gratitude. But now you must leave us." She turned to Lord Belstone. "Kit, my dear, can you wait a few more minutes? Mistress Mason is not dressed for a journey. We shall not be very long."

Bravely holding back her tears, she hurried Deborah out of the room.

When the moment of separation came, both women felt it deeply. The feeling that had grown up between them, against all probability, was too real and too strong for it to be otherwise. Lord Belstone, sensing their distress, deliberately cut short the farewells.

Riding for the last time down the long avenue of Lichfield, Deborah turned and looked back with a heavy heart. Who, seeing that gracious dwelling set in its smiling frame of quiet trees and flowery meadows, would have guessed at the tragic tale of blood and tears that lay hidden within its walls?

Sighing, she took a firmer hold on her reins and spurred her horse forward to catch up with her companion.

"I ask your pardon, my lord. In the agitation of the moment, I failed to express my gratitude. This is the second time that you have saved my life."

"Think nothing of it," he said lightly. "It was my pleasure." He brought his horse to a walk. "Tell me, what are your plans?"

"To return to London by the swiftest way."

"Then, if it suits you, we will lie tonight at my house at Gilford. If you set out tomorrow at dawn — No, do not thank me. You will be spared a night at an inn, and its attendant inconveniences. Only" – he raised an eyebrow at her, mockingly – "if you have any thoughts of tipping me the double, I'd take it kindly if you'd warn me first."

Blushing scarlet, Deborah changed the subject hastily.

"I dared not ask you before Jane, but I have been very anxious about my servant. How is he?"

"John Strong? Of course, now that I think of it, it falls out very well. He can go with you." He caught sight of Deborah's astonished face and laughed. "Yes, he is still with me. You shall see him very soon."

"What? Why has he not returned to London?"

"His wound was graver than I thought. We had him in bed nigh on three weeks. He has been worrying himself about you. You've a good fellow there. If he weren't so devoted to his fair mistress, I'd gladly take him on myself."

"I am ashamed, my lord. As if it were not enough to impose my servant on you, now I am trespassing on your hospitality myself."

"Enough of talk. Here is the forest and we must waste no more time. But I look forward to hearing more at supper. You intrigue me, did you know? So young and so mysterious. My curiosity is aroused, and I warn you, I mean to have it satisfied."

The last words were thrown lightly over his shoulder as he set spurs to his horse, with Deborah following suit.

Lady Babington stood on the steps and watched the riders out of sight. When their moving figures had shrunk to nothing, she stirred and giving herself a little shake, as if to rid herself of a heavy burden, she went indoors.

X

The manor of Gilford lay on the borders of Northamptonshire. Lord Belstone's elder brother, the marquis of that name, had inherited the title on the death of their father, and with it the fortune and the vast estates, spread over some of England's richest farming and sporting country. Since neither he, nor his sprightly spouse, Penelope, were greatly addicted to country pursuits and much preferred the pleasures of the court and the comfort of Gilford House, their splendid riverside mansion in the Strand, they were rarely to be found at Gilford. "Ruralizing, dear souls, is an excellent tonic in small doses," was the marquis's simpering dictum.

In fact, they never came there without a boisterous party of guests to keep them company and preceded by unbelievable amounts of baggage and innumerable servants. They played games on the broad terraces, danced on the fine inlaid floor of the great chamber into the small hours, and if they ventured far from the house it was not in order to commune with nature but in pursuance of yet another scheme of pleasuring. Then the whole cavalcade would be off again to enjoy the same distractions in a different house, without ever according a single glance at the beautiful countryside around them.

The marquis had no objection, therefore, to yielding up to his brother the hunting lodge which their late father had built near the limits of the estate, and where, in his lifetime, he had enjoyed the sport of the nearby chase. Lord Belstone, while retaining its intimate character, had enlarged the place and transformed it gradually into a pleasant country retreat. Unlike the marquis, he was fond of rural life, not afraid of a touch of solitude and passionately devoted to the chase. Consequently, whenever his eventful life allowed, he would hasten to Gilford.

The house stood in a mossy hollow in the woods, backed by tall elms and hazel coppice. It was a timber-framed building, dark oak and warm, red brick, with a roof of biscuit-coloured tiles. Joined to it at the rear was a stable block housing nearly a dozen magnificent saddle horses.

94

Deborah and Lord Belstone came there in the late afternoon after a swift and uneventful journey, for both of them were excellent horsemen.

Their arrival was the signal for a frenzied greeting from four great yellow hounds who surged about their master, slavering affectionately, while a couple of grooms emerged from the stable yard and took charge of the horses.

"Down Ajax! Down Nero! How are you, my beauties? You need not be afraid, Mistress. They are as gentle as lambs. Take no notice of them. 'Fore God, they won't eat you!" Laughing, he cuffed the effusive creatures cheerfully out of the way and they went on into the house, the dogs snuffling at their heels.

The hall was a big, cool, rectangular chamber rising all the way to the massive beams of the roof. Round it, on three sides, ran a wooden gallery, no doubt giving access to the upper rooms, which was reached by a staircase from the hall where they stood. The gallery rail and balusters were all heavily carved with an intricate pattern of flowers and vine leaves. Deborah gazed about her, smiling with pleasure.

"Oh, what a lovely room! It makes one feel so welcome!"

The floor was yellow sandstone to which incessant care had imparted the gloss of marble and it was warmed here and there by several very fine bearskin rugs. The furniture was simple but good and the plain, whitewashed walls adorned with a variety of trophies of the chase. Above the wide hearth hung two magnificent hunting horns, collector's items both, one bound with silver, the other of carved ivory. Facing Deborah where she stood was a big, full-length portrait of a martial young gentleman whose features bore a startling resemblance to her host's, although the fashion of his yellow doublet and the soft velvet bonnet worn tilted over one eye combined with the darkness of the paint to show that the picture had been painted many years before.

"My late father, the Marquis of Gilford," Lord Belstone said. "I imagine you would like to rest?" He raised his voice in a shout of: "Margaret! Where are you?"

"Thank you, I should —" Deborah was beginning when she was brought up short by the entrance of a tiny little old woman who trotted breathlessly through a door at the far end of the hall, a huge bunch of keys clinking musically at the waist of her wide-skirted grey dress.

"Here you are back again at last, then, Master Kit! And not

95

before time, either. Think shame on yourself to let an old woman worry so. One of these fine days, I tell myself, you'll come here and find me dead in my bed —" She stopped abruptly as she noticed the girl's presence.

"Mistress Mason, here is Margaret who has known me since the moment I was born. She rules this house, and puts up with me like a saint. Margaret, this lady is to be our guest for tonight. Will you show her to her chamber and see that she wants for nothing?" To Deborah, he added: "Shall you be satisfied if we sup at eight o'clock?"

"Perfectly, thank you. And – please, when may I see John Strong?"

"One moment. Margaret, do you know where John Strong is? Here is the young mistress of whom he has talked so much."

"Well, there now!" Margaret's expression of somewhat dubious curiosity was transformed into one of beaming welcome. "And if that isn't downright vexing! There's me sending him off not ten minutes since to the great house to fetch back that silver porringer my lady Penelope had of us last month. All the fine folks have gone away back to London but her ladyship never thought to send me back my basin. Not that that's anything to wonder at, with her head so full of nothing but those frippery young sparks as are for ever hanging on her skirts!" She shook her head sadly. "Aye, poor Master John! I always said —"

"Now then, Margaret. You let your tongue run away with you. Don't worry about your manservant, Mistress Mason. I will see to it that he knows you are here."

"Thank you. You are very kind."

"I shall see you later, then."

And Deborah followed Margaret upstairs.

When she came down again at the appointed hour, all trace of fatigue had vanished from her face.

Margaret could not have been kinder. There had been jugs of hot water brought by two giggling maidservants, a big basin to wash in, soap that smelled of orris root, and white towels to dry herself on. Then had come a tray of little hot cakes and ale cold from the cellar. Evidently the housekeeper had long practice in restoring weary travellers.

Left to herself, Deborah enjoyed a leisurely wash. She had, of course, no proper change of dress with her but, rummaging in the night bag which Jane had insisted on giving her before she left Lichfield, she did find a clean lace collar to replace her dusty and much-crumpled ruff. Continuing her investigations into the bag, Deborah found her eyes filling with unexpected tears. Oh, Jane! Dear, dear Jane! There was a soft blue bedgown, a small package containing needles and thread, a tiny bottle of scent, three embroidered kerchiefs, some different coloured ribbons and, right at the very bottom, a minuscule looking-glass, an ebony-handled hairbrush and a silver mesh purse. How like Jane to take so much thought for another when — No! This would never do. Taking out the things she needed at the moment, Deborah shut the bag and firmly put it from her. This evening she owed to Lord Belstone and what would he think if he saw her with a puffy face and reddened eyes? She sniffed hard once and then applied herself to putting scent on her neck and wrists and untangling her bedraggled, windblown curls.

As she came towards him, Kit Belstone, no mean connoisseur of female charms, was aware as he rose from his chair to greet her of a ravishing vision of unaffected youth and beauty. Her hair, confined now by a plain band, hung in shining waves of red-gold on her shoulders and her cheeks glowed with health.

He had changed and she took note instinctively of the silver lace at his neck and wrists, the green velvet trunk hose, which he wore very short in the French fashion, the silver-threaded garters which showed off his long, well-muscled legs, and the amethyst buckles on his shoes.

"No one looking at you, Mistress, would ever think that you had several hours on horseback behind you."

Deborah found herself blushing. This was the first time in her life that she had ever been alone with a man in such circumstances, beneath his roof, and she was suddenly very conscious of his physical presence close to her. She began to wish very much that she had not after all accepted his invitation. Innocently, if she had thought at all, she had expected that he would have a wife who would be here to welcome her, but this did not appear to be the case. She had observed the table set with only two places. It seemed that the gentleman was a bachelor without even a mother or sister to act as chaperon. There was Margaret, of course, whose respectable appearance was reassuring, but still . . .

As though divining her uneasiness, he broke off what he was

saying to lead her to the table where the light from three branches of candles fell cheerfully on a lavish selection of steaming, savoury-smelling dishes.

"We must not let our food get cold. Are you hungry? I know I am."

"Yes, indeed, my lord," Deborah agreed politely. In fact, she would willingly have forgone the entire meal and could very readily have fled the house upon the instant had she only dared. However, a bowl of hot broth liberally spiced with cloves enabled her to take heart a little.

"Could you fancy some of this powdered beef? Or – no, you must taste the sweetbreads. Margaret cooks them to a recipe of her own and I promise you that you'll not find her equal anywhere in England." He laughed as he poured out more beer into the pewter pots and Deborah laughed with him.

"That," he said quietly, "is the first time I have heard you laugh. It suits you, you know."

The next course consisted of some roasted quails, a squab pie and a sirloin of beef, cooked to perfection, with a sharp sauce spiced with ginger, a salad and an excellent plum tart.

Deborah pushed back her plate.

"No, thank you, my lord. Those marchpanes look delicious but I couldn't eat another mouthful. My compliments to Margaret. It was a wonderful meal."

She was almost relaxed now, her eyes bright and shining.

They had left the table and drawn their chairs close to the bright fire, crackling with sweet-scented herbs to drive away the lingering smell of food. A bottle of wine stood between them together with glasses of precious Venetian crystal. Deborah leaned back, watching idly as her host drew contentedly on his long clay pipe.

"Does tobacco truly possess all the virtues that men claim for it? In London, they say all kinds of things: that it can cure colds, comfort the heart, reduce a fever. There are even those who have it that its use can restore deaf men to hearing, and that it will clear a cough as if by magic."

Kit Belstone laughed. "That I can't tell you, having never had occasion to try it as a remedy. I'm as strong as a horse. There's certainly a good deal of talk along those lines, I agree, but all the same —" He wagged the stem of his pipe at Deborah for emphasis. "There are others who hold a different opinion, dismal fellows who go about declaiming that it makes men blind, eats up the brain, destroys the lungs and I know not what taradiddles else. Personally, whether it be a sovereign cure-all or an instrument of the devil, I take it for my own pleasure and no other reason."

He got up and took from a shelf a small box ornamented on the lid with a gilded trefoil. This, he opened and presented the fine powder which it contained to the girl.

"Would you like to try it? This is a particularly pleasant mixture made up for me by an apothecary in Cheapside who is a real artist in such matters. No? Quite sure? Yet, as I dare say you know, many of our ladies claim to enjoy it – if only in imitation of our dear Queen, God bless her, who is a notorious taker. Oh, this tobacco has us all by the ears, masters and men."

"And that puts me in mind, my lord. Is it not time that John Strong should be here? If I am to leave early in the morning . . ."

"Do not be too impatient. It is some fifteen miles to the great house from here. But never fear. One of my people has gone after him and when he hears that you are come I'll warrant the fellow rides his horse into the ground to reach you."

"How kind you have been to him. I —"

"Do you really wish to prove your gratitude? Well then, I'll tell you what you can do." He grinned at her with mischief in his eyes and settled back in his seat. "Explain yourself, my charming guest. Let me hear something of you, and then I'll cry quits."

This was what she had been dreading ever since their departure from Lichfield, but what could she tell him? She had been racking her brains for possible answers all the way but without coming to any decision. For how much did he know already, or rather how much had Jane said? That was the crucial point.

She sipped at the sweet, heavy Candy wine and wriggled herself into a more comfortable position.

"I am afraid you are going to be very disappointed, sir," she told him lightly. "My life has not been very exciting. I am an orphan, without brother or sister, and I live in London with my aunt who brought me up."

"Let's have no prevarication, if you please. I am not in the least interested in your family, past or present. It is your propensity for getting yourself into impossible situations I find fascinating, as you very well know. Come now, tell me honestly how a girl of your age comes to be roaming the highways without an escort."

"Jane did not tell you?"

He gave a shout of laughter.

"Ah, that's what's on your mind, is it not? Your pretty show of innocence was not altogether convincing, you know. But it would not be very gallant of me, I agree, to let you involve yourself in some shocking tissue of lies, for which, if I remember rightly, you show a marked talent. The truth is that Lady Babington told me, while we were putting that old fool Trockton to bed, that you were in the Queen's service and that it was for this reason that Anthony had felt obliged to detain you at Lichfield. There, you see? I conceal nothing from you. Suppose that you return the compliment?"

To gain time, Deborah picked up her glass once more.

So he did know. She had been very wise to test him first instead of launching into some complicated rigmarole which could only have made her look extremely foolish. But, that being so, it was vital to ensure his silence, while as for revealing anything further . . .

"Since you know so much, my lord," she began with dignity, "you will understand that there is little more I can tell you. You are, I am quite sure, too much her Majesty's loyal subject to ask me to betray the trust with which she has honoured me."

He was laughing again, once more gently mocking.

"Aquit me, Mistress, I beg, of any wish to pry into state secrets you prefer to withhold! You misunderstand me. All I wish is to hear a little of yourself and how you come to be in this employment."

She offered him an apologetic little smile.

"I am truly sorry, my lord, but the two are so closely linked that much as I should like —"

"Let be, let be!" he interrupted her. " 'Sdeath! To look at you, one would take me for a most churlish wretch! All things considered, a touch of mystery becomes you well enough. In God's name, keep it and let's talk of something else."

"Thank you, my lord. I should much prefer it. You are very good – and yet there is still one favour I would ask you."

"Name it, and if it lies within my power —"

"It is a small thing for you, but it matters a great deal to me, and to her Majesty's service. My lord, will you give me your word that none of this shall go beyond ourselves?"

He half rose. "You have it. On my honour as a gentleman. It is the least I can do to win forgiveness for my importunity. And now, if you are satisfied, we shall leave the subject. There are plenty of others to choose from, by far more amusing."

The hours after that passed almost without Deborah's noticing. Little by little, Lord Belstone's caustic wit and bursts of spontaneous gaiety made her forget Lichfield, the terrible events of the morning and the troubles which lay ahead. His manner was perfect, not a word or a gesture out of place, with no hint of the thing that she had feared to begin with. As a result, her own constraint had flown and she found herself chatting in a relaxed, easy way as she might have done to an old friend, sharing his laughter and enjoying this brief moment's respite.

It was not until much later that she glanced up in surprise to find that the servants had all retired to bed, taking away most of the lights. A single stand of candles, heavy with fallen wax, shed its amber light around them.

Suddenly conscious of the silence that had fallen on the house, she got to her feet.

"It is very late," she said, smiling. "I must thank you for a truly wonderful evening and bid you good night. I have a long journey tomorrow."

"I am a wretch to have kept you up so late. My excuse must be that in the company of a lovely woman it is all too easy for a man to forget himself."

He had taken her hand in his. He lifted it to his lips and then stood, still holding it, with his eyes on Deborah's face. There was a glow in his look which she had not seen there before. He released her hand. She stepped back.

"My lord, I —"

The words remained unspoken. Lord Belstone's arms were round her and his mouth locked possessively on hers. She felt herself bent backwards by the strong pressure of his hands on her shoulders.

It was not in the least like David's tentative lovemaking. This was the embrace of a mature man, hard and precise, a man of wide experience accustomed to take what he wanted.

She struggled but he took no notice of her efforts, his hot lips pressed to hers, bruising her with his strength. The buttons of his doublet dug into her chest and she was aware of the insistent pressure of his thighs. Slowly, aided by the scents of leather and ambergris about him, she succumbed to this new kind of madness. She trembled. She was hot and cold. Her mind dissolved before the tingling impulses of her flesh. Place, time, the man holding her, even her own self ceased to exist for her. In their place sprang up a flame, fierce, wild and primitive, burning out fear, modesty and shame. Gone now was innocence, gone the chaste and virtuous maid. In her stead, a different and unknown Deborah, her mind a blank and her senses on fire, who clung to the man's body and demanded his kisses.

He lifted her and she lay in his arms, eyes closed, her mouth still fast on his, while he bore her upstairs and felt his way to a door and opened it. Inside the room, he laid her carefully down on the bed, then turned to close the door and light a candle.

When he returned and began to undress her, she made no move to stop him. Her full, white breasts, their nipples hard and pointed, invited him. Swiftly shedding his own clothes, he came to lie beside her.

The sight of his face close to hers frightened her because she did not recognize it, full of a queer, concentrated passion. She put up her hands to push him away, to fight off the crushing weight on her limbs, and she tried to bring her legs together but his knee was in the way and already it was too late. There was a spasm of agonizing pain and she screamed aloud.

"Sweetheart, I'm sorry. How could I guess that you were still a maid? There was such freedom in your manner, you seemed so familiar with all the uses of the court, I naturally supposed . . . God's life, but it is difficult to believe that no man yet has found the way to teach that glorious body how to love! Dear heart, look at me."

Deborah's face remained buried in the pillow, scarcely listening to what he said. It was not, as he imagined, a belated modesty which kept her there but rather an incomprehensible feeling of disappointment. Was this what love was? This stupid, painful business? The respectable figure of Mistress Tucker hovered incongruously in her mind's eye. Her poor aunt was quite right: it was not worth all the frills it was decked out in! What had made her give herself to this man? Why had she done it? Why? Deborah burst into tears.

"Come now. Dry those pretty eyes. It does not suit you to cry. Or would you be the kind of foolish wench that saves herself for some boor of a husband years older than herself?" The frown left his eyes as he added with great gentleness: "You are so full of life and joy, Deborah. You must not throw it away."

He had drawn her close and was stroking her tangled curls and kissing away the tears from her pale face. Very soon, his expert hands strayed farther, rousing and caressing, while his lips explored the quivering, exquisitely sensitive skin. Deborah was not crying now. A long tremor ran through her body as she felt his hand, warm and knowledgeable, on her thigh. Once again that strange magic took hold of her, blinding her with expectation. She reached up and flung her arms round the lean neck above her.

This time, he did not rush or hurry her, but his movements were tender and sure, seeking her pleasure above all. In a little while, Deborah's body began to move to the same hard, steady rhythm. The motion grew stronger and she made little inarticulate sounds in her throat. Her head turned from side to side, the damp curls streaked across her brow. There was nothing in the world outside this one, unique moment. Sightless and shuddering, she responded to the quickening tempo and the clever, guiding hands bringing her, second by second, nearer to the climax. Suddenly, her body arched as though in the act of receiving some final offering and she uttered a single, hoarse, triumphant cry.

Deborah was sitting on the bank beside the brook, her bare feet dabbling the moving surface of the water and a straw between her teeth.

Around her lay utter peace, only made more profound by the song of the birds and the rippling murmur of the stream as it flowed beneath the motionless willows, their branches hanging heavy in the late August heat.

It seemed as if she was fated to spend her whole time dressed either for travelling or else in country style. Today, it was a popinjay blue kirtle worn over a green holland petticoat with her hair bound in a loose fillet of the same colour which her fancy had led her to stick with two or three of the big white daisies that grew near the stream. This outfit was the best that Margaret had been able to provide, but it was comfortable and Kit had told her that the blue and green suited her perfectly. He had promised to bring back everything she could possibly need the next time he went to London.

Deborah frowned. London was a place she preferred not to think of. London meant the Queen and Aunt Tucker, both of whom had the power to turn her knees to water when she thought of them. It was true that she had not agreed immediately when Kit had suggested that she should remain at Gilford for a while longer, but her hesitation had not endured for very long. The Queen's anger would be the same, with or without the difference of a few days, as would her verdict on the unexplained delay and the inevitable penalty: an ignominious return to obscurity. So surely it was best to take advantage of this beautiful thing that had happened? Strengthened in this irrefutable logic by Kit's amorous entreaties, Deborah had stayed. The few days had lengthened out into weeks: three weeks now since they had first become lovers and the more time passed the less she thought of returning. Who ever turned their back on paradise of their own free will?

She hugged herself and gave a little, happy sigh. There were times when it seemed that her heart must burst apart under the pressure of too much happiness. Kit was so . . . She wrinkled her pretty nose with the effort of finding the right word to describe her lover but could think of nothing strong enough to do him justice. He was unique, that was all: the ideal companion for every waking moment.

They would set out early in the morning, while the mist was still on the ground, riding knee to knee in pursuit of fox or hare, unless, as it might happen, they lingered joyously in Kit's great bed. They ate enormously of the delicious meals which came from Margaret's kitchen, walked together for miles at a time through the woods with the dogs lolloping madly round their tracks, expeditions from which Deborah came home bearing great armfuls of wild flowers and baskets filled with hips and barberries. In the evening, she and Kit would sit together in the great hall, where a small, bright fire burned in the hearth to keep off the creeping chill that could invade the big room even so early in the year. Kit's servant, Sam, sat on the stairs picking out soft airs on his lute while they talked on and on, Deborah in what had become her favourite place, propped up by cushions on the broad settle, Kit next to her, with a jug of ale conveniently to hand. Sometimes their talk turned on grave maters: literature, politics and philosophy. At others they laughed until they cried or sang catches and madrigals to Sam's accompaniment. Now and then, they played cards. Kit taught her and she showed an amazing aptitude.

Then, in the midst of all such simple pleasures, there would come the moment when their eyes would meet and she would read in his suddenly glowing look the promise of the more disturbing joys to come. For, inexperienced as she was, she did not know that she had been granted the inestimable boon of having, as her first lover, a man of manifold and subtle arts, so that her own deeply sensual nature would meet him eagerly in every new delight he taught her. With him, she had no false modesty, no reserves: she loved him, she was his to do with what he would. She could never tire of hearing his voice, of the feel of his supple, fine-grained skin and his man's smell, compounded of orris and ambergris, or of the touch of his body and the joy it gave her. She loved him, oh, how she loved him! When at last he slept, she would often let the candle gutter as she watched him, all hers in his sleep. He lay there, abandoned and vulnerable, and she would put her face close to his and kiss his black hair softly and murmur any number of foolish things into his ear which she would never dare say to his face.

For, oddly enough, if the physical relations between them were wholly free from constraint, there was a marked reticence when it came to describing their feelings. On Deborah's side, this was partly due to timidity. Kit, without doubt, was very much in love but although he demonstrated it at every moment of the day, he had never said so in so many words and the girl's own instinctive pride forbade her to broach the subject first. There was a streak of reserve in his nature which her sensitive spirit was quick to recognize. On more than one occasion a word, a certain look on his face, a faint line drawn between his brows, warned Deborah that she was trespassing on private ground, fenced round with a careful barrier she must not try to pass. Then she would bite back her question, or gloss it over with another, or else change the subject altogether, recounting, perhaps, a piece of rich gossip that Aunt Tucker had picked up from court, at which they could laugh together.

Slowly, a little at a time, she had told him much about her childhood. It was one thing to be politely negative to a stranger you never expected to see in your life again, but quite another to shut up like an oyster to the man you loved and with whom you shared each minute of your day and night. So he had heard about Aunt Jane and about Fleet Street, but however much she might extol the generosity of the Queen, not one word had she said about her plans, and she had insisted that the mission to Chartley had been one of no importance. It was the wisest course, even though Kit had little use for the court and its doings. That was something she had very soon discovered.

"I'll tell you what Whitehall is, sweeting. It's a circus, for ever indulging in the same pointless tricks and driven by sordid intrigue and money-grubbing and unspeakable hypocrisy. I promise you, I visit it as little as I can. I go only for my friend Essex's sake. You have heard of him? He has caused some stir, I believe, though better not to speak of it, perhaps. There are times when his ambitions make me fear for him. He is too rash, too fiery, too impulsive to carry them through successfully. Yet for all that, he is a delightful lad, a fine scholar, brave as a lion and ever loyal to his friends. I have known him from a child almost — He is only nineteen even now, while your loving servant, dear heart, is an old man of close on thirty. We have hunted together. With his house at Chartley, he is often in these parts, but our friendship really dates from last year, from the campaign in the Low Countries in which we were both serving under the Earl of Leicester who is step-father to Essex. You must have seen our gallant Robert, whom the Queen so favours?" Kit chuckled hugely. "The favours would seem to run in the family."

A number of sea ventures, glimpsed briefly through a few words let fall by Margaret, fighting in Scotland and on the Continent, the occasional retreat to Gilford, punctuated by protracted visits to Essex House or to the houses of various other friends, this seemed to have been his life, and a pleasant and luxurious one it was, to judge from the magnificence of his wardrobe and his stables and the visible wealth of possessions that littered his house.

"You know," he said to her one morning as they lay in bed, still lazy with love, "you know, money for its own sake, and the paraphernalia of pomp and circumstance that goes with it, seems to me a waste of time."

She was lying flat on her face, listening, while he had hoisted himself on to the edge of the bed and sat there, idly twisting a lock of her hair round his finger in a way that had grown familiar to her.

"But when it comes to spending it," he went on. "Why, then there's nothing like it! Life is all too short, you learn that with the years, and it seems to me that we commit a crime against our Creator if we do not make every minute as perfect as we can with the means we have. There is pleasure to be got from so many things, though few of us enough are able to grasp them. Take war, for instance. Is there any occupation more rewarding to the man of sense and spirit? Yet there are those who cry out against it and fear it." He grinned. "But I forget that war is not popular with ladies. Very well, there are other things, luxuries of every kind, pleasures whose delicacy you learn to appreciate: the sight of a rare book and the passion to possess it . . . the taste of a delicious meal . . . the bouquet of a fine wine . . . the contemplation of beauty . . . so many things. And not the least of them" – again that sideways glance of mischief at Deborah – "not the least of them, my darling, are those whose marvellous virtues I have already had the pleasure of introducing to your notice." Here he bent and implanted a neat kiss in the small of Deborah's back.

Nor did he appear to nourish any great interest in politics.

"Odd's death, let princes shoulder the cares of state. They are born to it. It is enough for me to manage my own life, I promise you," he said, his carefree, infectious laugh ringing out. "Oh, don't let it worry you. I may be a selfish rogue but I can still love our dear old England and serve her Majesty as well as the next man. But though the Queen may have my life's blood any day she cares to ask for it, my thoughts are still my own and not to be tampered with by any Secretary of State. Not that I've anything against Cecil or Walsingham personally, you understand. They are both remarkable men and their activities do great service to the realm, but I prefer to stand aside like a sensible man. That way I feel more at ease with myself. A man who covets power, Deborah, must be prepared to trample on so many of his finer feelings that in the end he may have nothing left of the only things which seem to me worth keeping in this world: self-respect, freedom and friendship."

Friendship. Dear, kind Kit had shown how strong and loyal his friendship could be.

Deborah stopped chewing her straw, feeling her throat tighten and tears prick at her eyes. Poor Jane. What was happening to her? And Sir Anthony . . . and David? So many questions, and all without an answer. Kit had used all his influence to try and find out something but without success. The whole affair had been wrapped in total silence, and not one scrap of information was forthcoming. No, there had been one thing. A servant sent to Lichfield had found the house empty and closed up, but whether Jane had finally fled or whether she had been apprehended, none could say. Now, today, Kit had gone to Gilford Castle to call on his brother and sister-in-law who had arrived there from London last night. Perhaps, she thought, they might have some fresh news.

Deborah wiped her wet cheeks and got up, shaking out her skirt. Her ear had caught the sound of hoofbeats and her eye followed the sound to where two horsemen had just come into sight around the smooth green shoulder of the hill. She could see Kit's broad-brimmed black hat in front, while behind John Strong's red hair shone in the sun.

Waving, she sped across the grass to meet them.

As she went, she remembered again John's joy at finding her at Gilford, and the flood of questions she had been hard put to it to answer – not to mention the smacking and most unrespectful kiss with which he had greeted her. Since then, uncharacteristically for him, he had not uttered a word about when they might be leaving, or made any mention of their return to London.

Big John was living like a pig in clover, bursting with health, absorbed into the life of the house, made much of by Margaret, whom he adored, and proclaiming to anyone who cared to listen that this country was almost a match for his native Yorkshire and that a man must be Bedlam mad voluntarily to live in any town. As to the future, clearly he was leaving all that to Deborah.

And what of the future? Deborah, too, was unwilling to think of it. All her good sense and ambition, her brilliant hopes had melted in an instant before the powerful enchantment of Lord Belstone's smile. Yet, now and then, some dying spasm of lucidity would clutch at her brain, and a kind of panic take hold of her. Great heavens! How could she have done this to the Queen? And to her aunt? And was she not perhaps, even now, by remaining at Gilford, forfeiting what little credit she might have had left with the Queen? As quickly as possible, she would thrust such thoughts away from her and return, determinedly, to her cosy dream.

She was seventeen years old and terribly in love, and with the single-mindedness of those who are both young and in love, she wanted, against all sense and reason, to believe that this blissful time could last for ever.

XI

Here comes the bride!

The village street was gay with garlands and strewn flowers, sweet herbs and green broom covered the muddy ground underfoot, and the wedding procession wound its colourful, chattering way to the church. Among the guests, surrounded by respectful attentions, Kit and Deborah strolled arm in arm.

"How the country people seem to love you," she whispered in his ear as they drifted along in time to various injunctions to "raise a cheer now for 'is lordship".

"They are good fellows all, and they like us to take an interest in them. In the ordinary way, a duty of this kind should fall to my brother but, since the mere idea of rubbing shoulders with the tenantry is anathema to him, I do what I can."

A fat man in a buff jerkin with a sprig of mint thrust through the button-hole came up to engage Kit in a lengthy discussion regarding the enclosure of a certain piece of land and Deborah, for whom the subject held no interest, soon turned her attention to the remainder of the procession.

It was led by the bride, Rose, a pretty, plump, rosy-cheeked damsel, as proud as a peacock in her orange tawny kirtle and red petticoat with a spray of rosemary pinned to her bosom. Behind, came the musicians with their fifes and serpents all adorned with red and yellow streamers of ribbon, and around them danced a laughing crowd of girls swinging delightful garlands of cornstalks, cunningly plaited and gilded. Jack, the bridegroom, was a blushing youth in a russet cloak three times too big for him, supported in his ordeal by practically every unmarried male in the parish. The rest of the procession was made up of the wedding guests, family and friends, all decked out in their finest clothes, with the inevitable escort of excited, shouting children.

When they reached the church, the wedding party paused and formed a semi-circle outside the door. Two girls darted forward, giggling but graceful, and disappeared inside the church porch, whence they emerged a moment later bearing, with becoming gravity now, a cup filled with some dark beverage which they offered to the bride and groom in turn.

"What is it? What are they drinking?"

Deborah, clinging to Kit's arm, craned her neck to obtain a better view.

"Only wine. It's a tradition hereabouts." He bent a little and murmured in her ear: "A heavily spiced wine to put heart into them for their labours to come." He chuckled, his moustache tickling her cheek. "Nay, you must not blush. Becoming it may be, but you'll have the village wondering what I'm telling you. They can't take their eyes off you as it is. You don't want to set them all by the ears?" Stepping back a little, he added: "Did I tell you how lovely you are in that dress?"

She pressed his fingers gratefully, her other hand stealing to the transparent folds of the tiffany scarf of palest green veiling her breast. The dress was beautiful.

Kit had ordered it from London three weeks before and it had been made up and dispatched in the carrier's wagon as far as Coventry. From there it had been brought to Gilford only yesterday by a messenger sent especially to collect it: a remarkable achievement in terms of speed. And it was exquisite! So beautiful that Deborah, lifting the lid of the box with fingers trembling with impatience, had found the breath stopped in her chest from pure awe. Picture a sumptuous white satin embroidered all over with a design of great, white daisies, at the centre of each a glittering gold bead, and the skirts spread wide over an immense wheel farthingale of the latest and most extravagant kind!

"The very newest fashion," Kit had assured her triumphantly. "Do you think I should have sent for something more suited to a young, unmarried girl? With a bum roll, for instance? I confess I could not bring myself to do it. They seemed so drab it was a sin to think of them in the same breath with you."

It was true that the bodice was cut daringly low. Aunt Tucker would have had a fit to see her niece in such a garment. But Aunt Tucker was many miles away and Deborah, pirouetting excitedly in front of the glass which Margaret was holding for her, her cheeks on fire and her hair flying, was determined to wear the new dress as soon as possible.

She had dragged herself away from the mirror at last and begun eagerly unwrapping, one by one, the scented packages done up in pearl-grey velvet which lined the bottom of the trunk. There was the scarf, and a pair of green gloves to match, a caul of gold mesh for her hair, silk stockings – her first pair, she thought, stroking the delicate, flesh-coloured knitted stuff. There was a pair of gold-fringed garters, too, and a pair of dainty white kid shoes. Last of all, she uncovered a delicious ostrich fan, also in green, and a satin mask to match the dress.

"Oh!"

Forgetting all about the presence of the servant, and regardless even of the rigidly busked stomacher that confined the top half of her body, Deborah flung her arms ecstatically round her lover's neck.

"Oh, Kit, darling! Is all this really for me? Oh, it is too much, I can't —"

"Gently there, gently, you little devil! You're choking me . . . No, no need to thank me. It is enough that you are pleased."

He held her off a little, his two hands clasping her lightly round the waist. "You'll have every man at your feet at little Rose's wedding tomorrow. But then —" He was smiling, a teasing little spark in his eyes. "Well, after that, I think that you had better put all this finery away, perhaps. It's not exactly the ideal dress for harvesting . . . Why, Mistress Deborah! Surely you aren't going to cry like a baby? . . . There, there, sweetheart . . . I promise you that you shall have all the admiration you want."

She was recalling all this now, as she entered the church at his side and she felt suddenly dizzy with the glorious, twofold pleasure of knowing herself both beautiful and beloved.

Then Jack and Rose, united in the bonds of holy matrimony, stepped out from the church porch to a general round of greetings and applause. There were the usual kisses all round and a shower of rice and flowers to bring them luck. Jack had lost his embarrassment. His face redder than ever, he was hugging his little wife close to him planting hilarious, smacking kisses all over the face turned smiling up to his.

All at once, Deborah felt furiously isolated in the midst of that merry crowd. Her mouth quivered a little as she looked at the young couple and she found herself envying them passionately. For them, everything was so simple, so straightforward. In a little while, they would be put to bed amid a general atmosphere of parental blessings, and after that they would have children. Nothing would come to break the even tenor of their lives: no problems, no barriers. Oh

God, if only she were standing there at the church door in their place, with her hand in Kit's!

She blinked away the tears and looked down. Surely she was happy as she was? Did she mean to poison her happiness by dreaming of the impossible? With an effort, she turned back to the newly-wedded pair and forced herself to look at them dispassionately. Fool, she told herself. How could she compare Kit to this clodpole all got up in his Sunday best! What had she in common with that poor child whose prettiness would soon melt away, like butter in the sun, under the burden of domestic chores and babies? Did she really want to turn into a drudge with a horde of children clinging to her skirts with nothing to look forward to but a beating from a drunken husband on Saturday nights? No, a thousand times no! What she wanted was to be herself for as long as he wanted her.

But how long would that be? Deborah had a sudden sensation of fighting for air. How would it all end? Kit had not said a word. What would become of her when the vague length of time she had envisaged had passed? She stood rooted to the spot, overcome by a mixture of doubt and fear. Everything was suddenly horribly clear to her. What a fool she had been! A month before there might still have been time to hurry to Whitehall and win the Queen's forgiveness. Kit could have arranged to see her in London. She could have explained it to him: he would have understood. Instead, like an idiot, she had thought of nothing but the worst that could happen: of the Queen's anger and the parting with Kit, and now it was too late . . .

"Deborah! Are you coming, sweet? You are waited for."

She shivered and looked up to meet Kit's glowing eyes and feel the warmth of him by her side and the touch of his hand on hers. A surge of fierce, ungovernable joy welled up in her, sweeping away her fears. No, she had been right, after all. He was here, and she loved him. What did anything else, past or to come, matter beside that? Nothing and no one could ever take away her present happiness.

Covering her thoughts with a smile, she slipped her arm gladly through his.

Back at Gilford, Kit went straight to the stables to see to one of the dogs which had got a thorn badly lodged in its paw. Deborah was in the great chamber, her arms filled with autumn damask roses given to her by one of the farmers' wives.

The flowers were thirsty and she was just setting down a big pewter jug of water on the long chest that stood between the two windows facing the front of the house preparatory to arranging her flowers in it, when she paused, attracted by an unusual amount of noise outside. So far, there had been no visitors to interrupt their enchanted solitude. Who could it be? Driven by curiosity, she made her way quietly over to the left-hand window, which stood open, and stood in the shadow of the curtain, looking out.

There were three people on horseback drawn up before the door.

The two men, Deborah decided at once, were unimportant, servants merely, and all her attention was given to the lady who was a little in front of them. That she was a person of the highest rank was beyond a doubt. A little dark, high-crowned hat trimmed with a blue band tagged with diamonds was perched impudently on a neat head of close blonde curls, so pale as to be almost white, which perfectly set off a pair of forget-me-not blue eyes and a delicate rose-petal skin of transparent fairness. She was regarding the front door with a degree of impatience and slapping her riding-cane lightly against the smooth stuff of a kirtle which had clearly been most carefully selected to echo the precise shade of her eyes.

"Penelope, my dear! This is a pleasant surprise! What do you here?"

Kit had emerged from the stables and was striding forward to meet her.

Deborah pressed herself against the window-frame. Her heart was beating a little faster, as it always did when she caught sight of him unexpectedly. He was so handsome, standing there in the sunshine, bareheaded, with his black curls all on end and his shirt ties all undone, revealing the strongly muscled chest. There was a smile on his carefree, arrogant face and he looked up at his visitor with a cool, faintly insolent detachment that had more than a touch of mockery about it.

"I've come to give you a severe scold, you naughty man," she answered in a lisping, childish voice from her lofty perch. "No, no. I won't come inside. I am in a great hurry, I'll have you know. I shall give you five minutes and then I must be on my way."

She let go of the reins and he caught her round the waist, lifting her as lightly as a feather. She clung to him for a moment longer than was strictly necessary; a good deal longer, Deborah thought, considering them austerely from her window. Then the visitor

113

twirled gracefully about and took Kit's arm, with a small, ecstatic sigh.

"You are so strong!" she said. "Poor, dear John, now, is far too fat to pay me such attentions."

"There are plenty more delighted to oblige," was his curt comment. "I don't imagine, my dear sister-in-law, that you have come fifteen miles merely to make comparisons between me and my brother. You know John. He is what he is, and has at least the merit of giving in to all your whims, which is more than I should do."

"Sweet heavens! What have I done to be answered so roughly? Is that how you win all your lady friends? Which reminds me, it was on the subject of lady friends that I came to talk to you."

Seeing him thus, chatting easily with a pretty woman on his arm, Deborah was aware of a whole host of new and unpalatable ideas jostling for possession of her mind. In her innocence, she had never thought of him with any other woman than herself. Beads of sweat started down her spine and her hand, clutching the curtain, was shaking slightly.

"How have I offended you?" Kit was asking.

"I am coming to it." The painted lips pouted a little. "You have not been to the castle once since your first call, the day after we arrived. It is not being very nice to your brother — or very polite to me."

"You know quite well, Penelope, that your friends do not amuse me. Nor do I think you have had much leisure there to miss me."

"You must not talk like that." She cast him a roguish glance which made Deborah itch to slap her. "You know how fond John is of you, and how much I am your true friend . . . Besides, to be quite honest with you, I have asked the Earl of Crampton's daughter, Mary. You must remember her. A perfectly delicious dark girl, very vivacious. You seemed to find her very much to your liking at Lady Warwick's in June, and so I thought . . ."

She had released her hold on his arm and now swung round, bending her long, white neck to look up into his face. They were standing quite close to the window now and it was impossible for Deborah to miss hearing what they said.

"I will be quite frank with you, Kit. It is time you thought of marriage. If I have told you so once, I must have said it a hundred times. You are thirty now, you know, and it will not do to plead youth any longer. You cannot spend your whole life flitting from one love to another. As it is" — her laughter was a knowing little

114

tinkle – "why, Priscilla bids me carry you her most tender, loving kisses, Cynthia is counting the days until you return to London, and as for Lady Lynes, well! I don't know what you've done to the poor woman but she swears she'll tear your eyes out the next time she sees you." Another little crow of laughter. "But we were talking about Mary. A delightful girl, with Tudor blood in her veins, too, and more to the point, since the death of her brothers, she is the old man's sole heir. Good God, what more do you want?"

"I'm not saying the Lady Mary isn't by all accounts a most desirable match, but I'm an incorrigible bachelor and intend to remain one. For goodness' sake, Penelope, stop looking like a wet week. It doesn't go with your outfit. I give you my word I will come and see you, but do stop dangling eligible wives in front of me. You should surely know by now that I'm not interested."

Her small, gloved hand closed like a vice on his wrist.

"Are you sure it is not because you are so much occupied with the creature you've been hiding here these past few weeks?"

"Well, well. So you know about that, do you?"

"Does it surprise you? Things get about, my dear. And our people will talk – especially since you so rarely admit a woman to your den."

"That will do." Kit's voice hardened suddenly. "My private life is my own affair. Do not oblige me to be rude to you."

"But this girl . . ." Penelope pursued, without appearing to heed the warning. "You will not do anything silly, Kit, will you? We worry about you, John and I —"

"I think, Penelope, that you have gone far enough. I am asking you for the last time to keep your nose out of my business. Your own family should afford you scope enough for your . . . solicitude. We will leave it there, if you please, before I find myself compelled to tell you a few highly unpleasant home truths. I should not like to be forced to hurt you."

"Oh, you are intolerable!" she retorted. "You may go to the devil for all I care!"

She almost pushed past him and, ignoring the hand which he held out to her amiably enough, she scrambled into the saddle, with the assistance of her somewhat startled grooms, and was gone in an angry swirl of sky-blue skirts.

"Plague take the woman," Kit muttered to himself and, turning, was about to re-enter the house when he was brought up short by the sight of Deborah standing stiffly watching him.

115

"Oh, you were there, were you? That delightful creature is the Marchioness of Gilford. And, with all due respect to my brother, there does not exist a stupider, more ill-natured woman – but what is it? You are quite white. You have not let Penelope's nonsense upset you?"

When Deborah said nothing, Kit swung his body through the window and went to her, tilting her chin up with one hand.

"Now then, what's the matter?" he asked gently.

"Nothing, Kit. Nothing at all. It's been a long day and I'm tired, that's all." She forced a smile. "Don't worry about me."

"Don't tell tales to me. I know you too well. There's something on your mind. Out with it."

"Well . . ." She hesitated. "You see, ever since I have been here we have been quite alone . . . I have never given a thought to the rest of your life. And now I find that I know almost nothing about you."

He laughed and hugged her to him.

"Are you jealous? I swear you have no cause. Penelope's cronies are all the same kind of heartless dolls that she is herself. They are nothing but high-class whores. Nothing like you. As for Crampton's daughter, she has . . . certain attractions. I should be lying if I told you otherwise. But you need not worry. She means nothing to me . . . and besides . . ." He broke off, glanced penetratingly at the beautiful face beside him and then abandoned his light-hearted tone.

"Oh, well . . . now that we have begun, I can see that I had better go on with it. Come and sit down."

His arm round her waist, he led Deborah over to the familiar settle, saw her comfortably installed with cushions at her back and himself stood before her.

"I owe you an explanation, Deborah. You are not a child and I should hate you to suffer from any tiresome illusions. I have not the slightest inclination towards matrimony, either with Mary or with anyone else. Why? Because I will not become one of those men who waste their whole lives sitting by their own firesides, while their wives rule them and sap all their strength. Yet, desiring above all things to be free to follow my own fancies, it seems to me unjust to expect my wife to conform to standards to which I cannot keep myself. So, since I lack the temperament to be either slave or cuckold, I have determined to remain a bachelor."

He sat down by Deborah and took both her hands in his.

"Perhaps I ought to have told you all this before? I am sorry, sweeting. Are you angry with me?"

There was the faintest little sigh as she bravely lifted up the head which she had kept lowered throughout Kit's speech.

"No, Kit. Not angry. You must not think that. I have no claim except to love you, and to hope that you love me a little in return. That – that is all I ask," she said, with a catch in her voice.

His clasp on her hands tightened.

"I would not for the world have made you unhappy, my heart. And yet I cannot, in honour, promise what I know I can't perform. One day, I shall leave you. It is in my nature. But, if you will have it so, there can be much happiness for us both before that time comes." His arm was round her shoulders, possessively. " 'Sblood! I am not in the way of making a display of my feelings, and yet at this moment I want you to know. . . . I've had my passing fancies, like any normal man, and very agreeable some of them were, by God! But they have never meant anything more to me than physical satisfaction. You have given me something different, Deborah. A combination of innocence and passion, a spontaneity that is a continuing delight and a quick, intelligent mind. It adds up to the kind of charm that is rare in women. My sweet love, the days I spend with you are as precious to me as the nights." He smiled. "And that, believe me, is no small compliment. It is not one I have ever uttered before. Nor have I ever felt the kind of tenderness I feel for you."

The last words were spoken in a low, hurried tone, like a confession. His fingers were kneading the satin skirts of her dress, his breathing had grown quick and shallow and, carried away by the warmth and sincerity of his words, she was no longer capable of resisting the eager pleading of his eyes.

Much later, when the crumpled satin dress lay at the foot of the bed and she was lying in a state of divine bliss with her small nose pressed into the crook of Kit's arm, he whispered softly: "No more gloomy thoughts, sweetheart?"

For answer, she pressed her lips against his skin. Only a little while before, it had seemed to her that she was poised above the abyss but now, with her lover's arms about her, she scarcely remembered it.

Even so, their conversation lingered in her mind and as her senses returned, so she was soon to lose her frail happiness.

XII

On September 21st, Kit returned from London after being absent for five days.

As soon as Deborah set eyes on him, she knew that he had bad news. He had lost his habitual careless look and seemed to have acquired an unaccustomed seriousness. Oh God, she thought, when was the last time she had seen him with that grim face and those lightless eyes? Something clutched at her heart and she remembered. It had been at Lichfield.

He drew her rapidly indoors.

"I have some bad news, darling. Sit here, close by me. What I have to tell you is a long and painful story."

"Kit! What has happened? What have you heard? Is it about Jane?"

"Indirectly, yes. It is Babington." He went on quickly, ignoring Deborah's low cry of terror. "It is all over with him. He was arrested at the beginning of August – we suspected as much at Lichfield – along with one of his friends, a man named Savage, tried in secret on a charge of high treason and condemned. Yesterday . . . yesterday six of them suffered a traitor's death in London. Today will be the turn of six more. Yes, I know, my love. I know, but hush, you mustn't cry."

"It's horrible! Poor Jane! And – and David . . . Lord Ashbury, I mean, was he one of . . ." She could not finish the sentence for the tears which were choking her.

"No. He was not on the list. I dare say he may have got away to the Low Countries. I could hear nothing of Lady Babington, either. Poor soul, drawn into that conspiracy . . . For you do not know it all. I have found out every detail of the business now, and it was very much more dangerous and involved than we ever imagined. When I think that Anthony — My God, he must have been as mad as Bedlam ever to have dabbled in such a plot!"

Deborah looked up, surprised by the note of suppressed violence in his voice.

118

"What —?"

"Well, the broad lines of it were like this. Babington, with ten of his friends, was planning to rescue Mary Stuart." As Deborah made as if to speak, he went on: "Yes, that much you know already. But you, like me, were ignorant of the rest. At the same time, six men were to ride to London and assassinate Elizabeth."

"Oh no! But this is hideous! And to think that I was fool enough to pity the traitor!" Anger had dried Deborah's tears for her.

"You are very young still, Deborah, and very impulsive. I wish I could switch my feelings as fast. Unfortunately, I can't."

He had risen and was pacing nervously to and fro.

"Oh, I detest their object with all my heart. I need hardly tell you that. And I doubt if the poor dupe ever gave a thought to the consequences if it had succeeded . . . another civil war and all the other miseries that damned Scotswoman trails after her wherever she goes. And yet – how can I make you understand? I know that he had to suffer death, justly and necessarily, and yet as a man and as a soldier I cannot help feeling some admiration for that kind of pure, disinterested courage. He did not want money, or honours. He was rich, noble, respected, married to the woman of his choice. He had everything to make life pleasant – and it was only his beliefs and his religious faith and a kind of splendid innocence which drew him head foremost into the trap which Walsingham had laid."

"Walsingham! What is this? I don't understand. What trap?"

At the mention of Walsingham's name, Deborah had risen also. She had not forgotten her own interview with the Secretary of State, or the ambush he had arranged for her in the woods near Coventry.

"Yes. That's the other side of this grisly tale," Kit went on. "I had it from Essex and I trust you not to reveal it to a living soul. So far, only a few members of the Privy Council know of it, Cecil being one, of course, and even they are still wondering whether the Queen knew. But it's a long story. You'd better sit down.

"Walsingham is no fool and he's a realist above all. He has known for a long time that the only way to make the Queen's throne absolutely safe was to compromise Mary Stuart beyond redemption. She is the fly in the ointment, here and on the Continent. But he had to go about it very cautiously indeed. The case against her had to be sufficiently watertight to convince the courts of Europe of its utter legality. The old fox knew that there was one way, and only one, to get the Stuart wholly at his mercy and that was to implicate her in a plot to kill the Queen. He waited. He was very patient.

"Then he discovered through his spies that a gentleman by the name of Babington was planning to rescue the Queen of Scots. This was his chance. He sent his own *agents provocateurs* to insinuate themselves into Babington's confidence and, by passing themselves off as ardent Catholics, persuade him that with a little daring, which would only add to the attractions of the plan, he might be able to present Mary Stuart with her freedom and the English crown at one and the same time.

"On Walsingham's orders, the discipline at Chartley was relaxed a little and a means of communication between Mary and the conspirators established. They did not know, of course, that every one of their letters was being decoded and read by one of Walsingham's agents before it reached its destination." Kit paused for a moment.

"Your suspicions were quite justified, Deborah, as it turns out. The younger Goodgraves played a despicable part in all this. It was he who removed the letters from the casks and handed them first to the authorities, who paid him well enough for it."

Seeing that she was about to speak, he held up his hand and resumed his story.

"All this apparent carelessness and the reading of the letters was carried out with one object and only one: to obtain written proof of Mary Stuart's complicity in the plot to murder the Queen. Walsingham's spies in the Catholic plot were busy urging Babington to write to her explaining all the details of his plan in order to gain her written assent. It was a fatal mistake, of course. She hesitated at first when she read the letter, but it can't have been easy to resist so much chivalrous young adoration. It was that generous, romantic side to her nature that Walsingham was banking on and she did not disappoint him. On the seventeenth of July, she sent her answer: complete agreement to all Babington's proposals. That letter is damning. She has signed her own death warrant.

"Walsingham has all the proof he needs now. He'll wait a little, like a card player with all the cards in his hand, and then — Well, you know the rest," Kit finished.

"It's Machiavellian!" breathed Deborah.

"It is indeed. But you must not forget that it was done for England's sake." He looked at her with a weary expression. "And yet it is not easy to judge. If you look at the facts objectively, wasn't Anthony, traitor though you have rightly called him, trying, for all his hateful plans, to do the same? To him, and those like him, our Queen Elizabeth is a usurper who stands in the way of the restoration of their faith." He sighed. "And now what is he? A martyr to the Catholics. A vile traitor to us. It seems to me he was merely a victim, the victim of his own lunatic actions, of Mary of Scotland and of Walsingham."

He put his hand on Deborah's and presed it lightly. "So don't you think perhaps, that we who had the chance to know the nobility of his nature owe him some compassion?"

"Yes," Deborah said softly at last. "Yes, you are right. Poor boy. And poor, poor Jane. My heart aches for her . . . and for Lord Ashbury. Tell me, how do you think it came about that he was able to escape?"

"They rounded up the leaders of the plot first. Probably, he was not important and was allowed to slip through the net."

"Thank heaven! He is so quiet, so gentle. How could anyone imagine him as a murderer? But what about that horrible Thomas?" Deborah spat out the name with loathing. "And the Scottish Queen. What is to happen to her, do you know, Kit?"

"She has been moved to Fotheringhay Castle. Her trial is to begin on October 14. I don't suppose the rest will take long. The Queen will not save her this time, although she has shown herself far too indulgent to the ungrateful creature in the past."

It was then that something clicked in Deborah's brain and she bit back a startled exclamation.

The letter! The letter which she had carried to Mary Stuart. Its contents were still clear in her memory, and the conclusion was inescapable. Her Grace had known what was in the wind and, unknown to anyone, she had made one last charitable attempt to warn her cousin. Hence the precautions in case Walsingham should hear of it. Great heavens! It was like Elizabeth, that streak of unexpected generosity!

She glanced at Kit but he was sitting slumped dejectedly on a stool, his head in his hands. He had noticed nothing. She got up quietly and drifted uneasily about the room, finishing up by the window where she leaned her head against the glass and abruptly, in total silence, she let go of her grief and cried.

The thought of the Queen made her want to cry so often these days. After all that she had done for her, what must her Grace think! That she was an ingrate, inevitably. Unless she had decided she was dead, killed by some papist in the conclusion of the plot. The idea revived her a little. In her present position it was far better so. Let them think her dead! At least it would preserve her in the

Queen's good opinion. Yet, when she thought about it, it was not really her fault. It had not been her decision to go to Chartley, much less to Lichfield. Yes, that was all very well, but how were these arguments to be conveyed to the Queen, or even to her poor aunt?

Deborah sniffed hard and dried her eyes. It would do no good to mope, or to torment herself with trying to determine her precise degree of guilt. There was nothing to be done about it now.

She turned away from the window and, going up to Kit, laid her hand gently on his shoulder.

XIII

Slowly, one by one, the grey silken trails of the night mist pulled apart and vanished. A faint pinkness began to show above the distant hills and grey-white light filtered through the trees and crept in at the window.

Kit was standing, his long legs already encased in high, leather boots, doing up the final buttons of his hunting coat. His eyes were on Deborah who was sitting up in bed watching him as he dressed. The candlelight touched her plaited hair and yellow velvet ribands, lying demurely on her simple white holland chemise with the sarcanet trimmings at the neck.

She was an enchanting picture, smiling at him through the deep fringe of her lashes.

"Three days, sweeting, that is all," he told her cheerfully. "I could hardly refuse, after all. Without these drives, you can't imagine how much damage the confounded beasts can do."

He had been invited to join in a hunt after some of the county's few remaining wolves which was being organized by the aged Baron Feltingham who had been a great friend of his father's.

"Don't worry about me," she assured him. "I'll stay at home and be good." If there was a touch of bitterness in her voice, he did not detect it.

Just then, there was a tap on the door. Kit went to it, listened to what his servant had to say and said something in answer. Then he turned back to Deborah.

"There are two men here who insist on seeing me. They will not give their names. I'd better go and find out what it is about. I'll be back to say good-bye to you."

When he had gone, Deborah let out a great sigh. She felt not the least interest in their visitors but the thought that Kit was going away again depressed her unutterably. She tried to be sensible. She knew that he could not possibly take her with him, and yet she longed to go. More and more, recently, she had been conscious that her relationship with Kit was an irregular one. A host of small things had occurred to remind her and to take away a little of her joy in being with him. It was not Kit's fault that she had placed herself in this equivocal position. He had warned her. She had only herself to blame.

When she was able to examine her feelings with anything like detachment, she had to acknowledge that she was growing more attached to him with every day that passed, and the future filled her with dread. Good heavens, what would she do when Kit left her to go back to the wars, as one day he would, if he had not already tired of her before? A ruined girl, without name or fortune, all she could hope for was to find employment as a menial in some great house. At best, she supposed, her cultivated manners might win her a position as companion to some rich tradesman's wife, for she had humbly to admit to herself that her excellent education was now her one remaining asset.

On the other hand, even if she could summon up the courage to leave Gilford, it could hardly do her much good at this stage.

She could not imagine herself facing her aunt and submitting patiently to her questions and upbraiding. She had gone over that possibility in her mind a hundred times and rejected it. Still less could she picture herself before the Queen. It gave her gooseflesh only to think of what a welcome would await her there. On the whole, she thought, she must bury her shame in decent obscurity. It was when she had arrived at this point of hopelessness that love always came to whisper insidiously that she was a fool to waste her time in worrying about the future. Surely the present was enough? Then, her resolution weakened by Kit's kisses, she would resign herself passively to fate.

"Guess who our unnamed visitors were, sweetheart! Some of Babington's friends."

Kit's voice roused her from her thoughts.

"No, really? Do you know them?"

"Not from Adam. Anthony and I were together a great deal as boys but I have seen less of him, or his friends, in these last years. Partly because I had some inkling where his mind was tending. And also because his friends did not attract me."

"Are you sure these men are what they claim to be?"

"Not a doubt of it. The elder never opened his mouth but the younger gave me proof enough. They wanted me to hide them here today. Of course, that was out of the question, but for Anthony's sake I gave them fresh horses. Now they may go to the devil. That's all. Now I must be off."

"Jane? Had they any news of her?"

"No, none – or so they said."

"Oh. I had hoped . . ." Deborah's voice died away in a sigh. "Tell me, have these men gone?"

"Not yet. Margaret is preparing a meal for them. I am not in the habit of sending folk away empty when they come to seek my help, however undesirable they may be. Don't worry. They'll go as soon as they've eaten. Sam and John Strong are keeping an eye on them."

He sat down on the edge of the bed and drew her to him.

"I shall miss you, sweeting. I'll not be long. I promise."

"Come back soon, my darling," she whispered as he kissed her. "Oh, come back soon!"

Neither she nor he could know that it was to be many months before they met again.

She was alone. What, she wondered, was she to do for three days? At first, whenever Kit was away, she found a thousand things to do to fill the gap. She rode out on horseback to explore the country round, accompanied, invariably, by the dogs who naturally took her to their master's favourite haunts. She denuded the trees to bring back great armfuls of greenery for the house and sat for hours on end combing her hair and smiling to herself at the thought of his delight when he came home to find the hall and their bedchamber transformed into leafy bowers, with herself as fresh and neat as could be with some new trick of doing her hair for him to notice. But today her heart was not in it.

She stayed where she was for a while, thinking of nothing in particular, and when she did get up it was listlessly, without enthusiasm.

When she came to pick up the water jug, she found that it was nearly empty and she was on the point of calling for a servant to refill it when she remembered the two strangers. If they were still in the house, there was no point in attracting their attention. Slipping Jane's bedgown over her chemise, she opened the door and peered out.

She listened to the familiar noises of the house, hoping to hear Margaret's quiet footsteps or the cheerful patter of the young maids' feet. After a moment, she became aware of people talking below, and she started suddenly and, hugging her gown more tightly round her, stepped noiselesly out. It seemed impossible, but she could have sworn . . . that accent . . . She tiptoed forward, then turned quickly and retraced her steps, more cautiously still. Back in her own room, she closed the door with infinite precautions, and then collapsed on the bed, her legs turned to water. She would have known that voice among thousands. It was Perez.

It did not take her long to recover her self-command, for her hatred of the Spaniard was a good deal stronger than her fear. Besides, she asked herself, what could he do to her now? Nothing! A fierce satisfaction welled up in her. He was a hunted man, one who would soon be caught and made to suffer the punishment he deserved. Deborah frowned a little. It had occurred to her to wonder what he was doing to be still in the neighbourhood. Logically, if he had escaped capture, he should have been in Scotland or overseas long before this. It was odd, to say the least.

Silently, holding her hands over her breast to still the beating of her heart, she tiptoed out again into the gallery from which she could gain a good view of the hall and follow the sounds of their conversation rising from below. Crouching in the shadow of the balustrade, she held her breath and peered over, every sense straining.

It was Perez. He was, she observed with no compassion whatsoever, in a deplorable state. His clothes hung in rags, his beard was untrimmed and his sunken face had an unhealthy, yellowish pallor. He appeared, however, to have lost none of his old air of command. He was seated at the table, his elbows propped on either side of his untouched plate, balefully watching his companion, a bull-necked individual whom Deborah had never seen before, working his way solidly through the mountain of food before him with an obvious and audible relish.

"Do you have that clear, Ned?" Perez was saying sharply, as though striving to impress upon the young man facing him an oft-repeated lesson. "If I am caught, it is vital that you should forget nothing."

"All right. I've got it," the other said sullenly. He belched loudly and continued tearing with his teeth at the mutton bone clutched in one greasy hand.

Perez slammed his fist down on the table.

"Stop cramming yourself with food for an instant, you beef-witted clown! One would think the only thing in the world that matters is that you should get your bellyful. Madre di Dios! Try using your brain for once!" He paused for a moment before going on in a more reasonable tone: "Now, say it over for me again just once, like a good fellow. It will set my mind at rest, and there is nothing to fear from these blockish servants."

Mentally thanking providence that she had learned enough Spanish to follow what was being said, Deborah settled down to listen.

"Oh, well, if I must . . ."

Ned laid aside his bone reluctantly and sprawled across the table, the hanging sleeves of his jerkin trailing in the food, in an effort to bring his mind to bear.

"I'll go through it all once, quickly, and after that, with your permission, I'll get on with my meat. The master of the house may not have been exactly delighted to see us but, by God, he knows how to feed! This is the best meal I've eaten for a long time."

He, too, spoke Spanish but with a villainous accent which, with his ruddy complexion, marked him as English.

"Get on with it, man."

Perez's fingers were beating a tattoo on the table.

"Just because you've no stomach for your food, you needn't think – oh, all right. Here we go, then." His tone changed hastily as he caught the look on his companion's face. "If we're separated by any chance, we're to meet at the sign of the Three-Headed-Dog – queer name, that – in Blackfriars."

"You will wait for me," Perez continued for him, "until tomorrow night and no later. Is that understood? I am counting on you. After that, you will pass on my instructions to Basilio, who should be there with the rest. Very well. Go on. What are those instructions?"

Ned numbered them solemnly on his fingers. "Item one, get hold of boatmen's clothes. Item two, hire a boat and on Friday, with or without you, row upriver as far as the village of Isleworth, just before you get to Richmond. Three, lose ourselves in the crowd and wait for the Usurper to arrive."

"Yes, she will halt there to receive a loyal address from the mayor." Perez laughed unpleasantly. "If all goes well for us, by heaven, the good man will find himself pronouncing her funeral oration! So, that will do. Basilio will see to the rest. He has never yet missed his mark."

The Spaniard's lips parted for an instant in a bloodless grin.

127

Then, his face as expressionless as ever, he was murmuring as though to himself: "Queen Mary's trial opens on the fourteenth. We must act before then. Heaven cannot desert us now . . ." He glanced up. "We must go. Have you done eating? I wish we could have travelled by night but you were right not to insist. Lord Belstone was anxious to be rid of us . . ."

Deborah had heard enough. All but crawling on hands and knees, she backed carefully away from her point of vantage. Once safely back in the bedchamber, she sank down on the bed.

Foul traitors! Their devilish purpose was quite clear now. After the failure of their first plan they must have hatched this second scheme hastily as a last resort. As far as she had been able to gather, they meant to take advantage of the royal household's move to Richmond to provide them with an opportunity to kill the Queen. Merciful God! The girl's hands writhed together in anguish. Her Majesty took so little thought for herself. She loved to mingle with the crowds. She took such pride in the trust she had in her people. As these villains doubtless were well aware. One shot from a well-aimed musket or petronel and . . .

Deborah shivered violently at the thought. She sprang to her feet. At all costs, these monsters must be stopped, the Queen must be warned! All her courage and vigour rose suddenly to the surface. Faced with the prospect of an immediate peril, all the indolence of the last months vanished like smoke. What were her own private woes in comparison with . . . The Queen's many kindnesses, her boisterous good fellowship, even her full-blooded oaths came back to Deborah with a commanding urgency. She gave herself a shake. There must be something she could do. The Queen must be saved.

She paced the room for a while, deep in thought, and then, going to the window, opened it and leaned out.

Below was a cobbled yard. Away to the left of it, beyond the well-head with its sprawling canopy of late red damask roses, a whistling stable boy was standing by the heads of a pair of ready-saddled horses.

"Tom!" she called.

The lad looked up.

"Leave those horses and run and tell John Strong to come up to me at once."

She shut the window and taking Kit's small writing-desk over to the bed settled herself comfortably, sharpened a quill and began to write rapidly.

By the time John's knock sounded on the door, she was folding the sheet.

"Come in."

"You asked for me, Miss Deb?"

"Yes. I want you to saddle a horse and ride to London."

"But I thought – eh, that is, I mean . . ." Surprise and dismay were written all over John's honest face.

"No. Our holiday is over, John," Deborah said briefly.

"You mean – we're leaving Gilford? Just like that?"

Deborah had already opened her mouth to say no when the idea struck her. John Strong's words had shown her suddenly, and she told herself that she was a fool not to have thought of it before: she held in her hand the perfect chance to reinstate herself with the Queen. No one was going to care how long she had been away if she turned up again bearing this information. John had unwittingly pointed out to her what she had to do. She must go to London herself. But when, oh when would she return?

She pressed both hands tightly together at her breast as though to crush the pain in her heart. She felt suddenly as if she were rushing headlong down a precipice. She fixed her eyes determinedly on one spot on the wall, a small black dot that might have been a spider, and clung to it desperately as it wavered up and down, swelled to enormous size and loomed before her burning gaze. Soon she ceased to be able to see it at all, only a dim blur, fast dissolving into a watery nothing. Furiously, she squeezed her eyelids tight. It was no use deceiving herself. If she left now, she would not come back.

But Kit? How could she give him up, of her own will? How find the strength to live without his kisses?

Reaching blindly for a handkerchief, she told herself firmly that she was not a child. He had told her so. And he had told her, too, that one day he would leave her. Well then? Surely it was better to be the first to go? All it needed was a little willpower . . . a little pride . . . A chance like this would never come again. She could not afford to let it pass for the sake of a foolish, sentimental whim. Sooner or later . . . he had been quite frank about it.

Deborah set her teeth and, squaring her shoulders, looked up to where John was still standing disconsolately before her holding the letter, waiting for her to speak. He was shifting unhappily from foot to foot, and his broad face was such a picture of misery that he might have been about to burst into tears. She put out her hand.

"Give me the letter, John. I have changed my mind. And do cheer up! Even the best things in life must have an end, you know?"

She took the paper and tore it slowly into fragments. Then she got up and, laying her hand on his arm, said: "There are things I must tell you, John. You have been with me now for seven years. Can I trust you absolutely and completely?"

"Eh, Miss Deb! D'y'need to ask? You know I'd do anything . . ."

"You're a good fellow, John. I knew I could count on you," Deborah said. Yet even she was surprised by the naked devotion she saw in honest John's face. "Listen. We have not much time. You saw the two men who came this morning? I overheard some of their conversation and – well, the long and short of it is they are dangerous traitors conspiring to take the Queen's life." She was aware of his stupefied expression as, without stopping to explain further, she went on to outline her plan and give her orders.

John was to be ready to follow the two men when they left. He would have no difficulty there, she assured him, because they would be forced to spare their horses, since they would not dare to visit posting houses. However, if he should happen to lose them, he was to go straight to the inn at Blackfriars, where he would continue to watch until the constables or other of the Queen's people arrived. Meanwhile, she herself would ride direct to Whitehall.

"Are you quite sure you understand all that?" she asked anxiously. "They must not give us the slip. Not on any account, is that clear? If you do well, the Queen shall hear of it."

"Don't you worry, Miss Deb," John said stoutly, throwing out his chest a little. "I'll not let the scoundrels out o' my sight."

"Yes, and that reminds me. If they spot you and it comes to a fight, don't hesitate to kill." She smiled faintly. "Even two to one, you should have the upper hand. They are both of them pretty exhausted."

"That's all right, Miss Deb. I've not let you down yet, have I? Besides, I've a proper respect for my own skin. But —" Big John hesitated, reddening: "Saving your presence, Miss Deb, what of his lordship? Won't you wait until he comes home?"

"No. There is no time. And it is best as it is." The last words were uttered in an undertone as she felt the tears pricking her eyes once more. Then she gave a small sigh and continued in a firmer voice: "That is not all, John. There is one more thing. If my aunt should ask you, as she is bound to do, I forbid you, do you hear, I forbid you to say a single word about our being here. It is too complicated to explain now," she went on quickly, with more than a shade of embarrassment, "but I have my own reasons for wishing Lord Belstone's name to be kept out of this."

John scratched his head, perplexed.

"Aye, but I'll need to say summat," he objected. "Not that I'd wish to speak against your aunt, but Mistress Tucker's never one to stand a back answer. Happen she'd take a cudgel to me."

"Oh wait . . . I'm thinking . . ."

Deborah paced furiously about the room, her tongue caught between her teeth.

"Look, you need a story no one can possibly check. So we can't pretend you were at Chartley with me." She came to a halt in front of John. "I think I've got it. You must say that I left you at an inn before we got to Chartley, so as to be less conspicuous. That explains why we were not together. Now, as to the rest . . . On the way home, we were set on by thieves in the forest and robbed and – and left for dead! That's common enough. No one will suspect anything odd in it. And then . . . then . . . yes, some charcoal burners found us and took us in —"

"And your aunt will want to know what hindered us from letting her know."

Deborah grinned.

"Ah, but you forget that you were unconscious and I was suffering from shock . . . No one knew who we were, so what could they do? To say nothing of our being quite penniless, of course . . . No, you can take it from me that that will do. Where was I? Oh yes, so we stayed there until we had recovered a little — By the way, do try not to look so horribly healthy. Can't you wear a bandage or something? To make them sorry for you? As I was saying, as soon as you were able to travel, we made our way on foot to the nearest proper village – a frightful journey, it took us several days. The important thing, you see, is to gain time. And there we were lucky because the lord of the manor took pity on us and provided us with horses — That's particularly important because we'll have to explain his lordship's horses somehow. We could hardly pass them off as plough horses. Well, what do you think of it?" She pushed back a stray lock of hair from her forehead and added quickly: "Oh, it's a bit thin when you come to look closely, I know, although I do seem to remember something rather similar happened last year to two City merchants with their servants who were attacked on the Nottingham road. They turned up again three months later after everybody had given them up for dead and started in on the inheritance! And I know the Queen. She'll jump on the news I bring her and forget about everything else."

She broke off and indicated the jug of wine which stood, with a silver cup beside it, on a chest, where it had been put for Kit to break his fast before he set out for the chase.

"Pour me a cup of wine, will you please, John. I'm thirsty after that."

She drank it off at a gulp and coughed. A little colour returned to her pale cheeks.

"Good. But we mustn't forget the most important part. It was at an inn near Coventry today that quite by chance we overheard what these men were planning. I mean I overheard it, because it was all in Spanish. Above all, don't ruin things by saying more than you need. That's the broad outline settled, anyway and by the time we get there tonight there'll be such a fuss that no one will think to ask us anything else, and by tomorrow —" There was a slight catch in her voice as she said the word. "By tomorrow we shall have had time to work out the details. Now, are you quite sure you have that straight? Go over it again to see."

Meekly, his brow creased with the effort, John Strong repeated his young mistress's story.

"Very good," she said at last with relief. "And if Walsingham's men question you too closely, just pretend to be stupid. Tell them you are my servant and I will deal with them. But stick to your guns, won't you? Don't forget that the future for both of us depends on you." She clapped him on the shoulder in comradely fashion. "Go now, John. We'll meet again in London."

Left alone, Deborah turned her back resolutely on her grief. Now was no time to be emotional and, her decision once made, she was eager to be gone from Gilford as soon as possible.

She washed sketchily with the little water left in the bottom of the jug, tied back her hair in a neat coil and got out her riding-dress. Her movements all this time were those of an automaton and she avoided letting her eyes dwell on the objects around her. Her saddle-bag came out of the chest and was refilled, one by one, with the things that Jane had given her: chemises, hairbrush, the empty scent bottle, her bedgown . . . Deborah's fingers strayed for an instant to the wonderful dress of white satin with the embroidery of ox-eye daisies . . . Oh, God, how happy and carefree she had been . . .

Withdrawing her hand firmly, she told herself not to be a fool. It

132

was clearly impossible to take the dress with her, and in any case, she was determined to take away none of Kit's presents. She was going away and therefore had no further right to any of his love gifts. One thing only she could not bring herself to part from, and that was the splendid topaz ring which he had brought her from London. Let her keep one token at least in remembrance of him. God! Oh God! Deborah clung to the bed curtains, overwhelmed by a kind of vertigo. She could not cry, but stayed there, gasping and wretched, half choking with the weight of unshed tears. Almost, she abandoned all her plans and preparations, left the bag unpacked, her willpower gone . . . but no, she managed to force her trembling fingers from their hold and, reeling like a wounded deer, went to the writing-desk once more. She wrote only a few brief words of farewell, she had no strength for more.

"My darling, forgive me for leaving you like this. I have thought about it and it is the best way. Thank you for all that you have given me. Your own Deborah."

From outside, came a cheerful clatter of hooves upon the cobbles. A dog, Ajax perhaps, or Nero, barked. Deborah peeped cautiously through the window.

Perez and the red-faced youth were crossing the yard. Deborah waited for a moment and before long a third figure rode out after them and disappeared in the same direction. Picking up her bag, she turned and made for the door, and left the room quickly, without looking back.

Downstairs, she went straight to the kitchens. They were filled with the rich, plummy smell of damson jam which plopped darkly to itself in the big copper preserving pan. A cauldron of water was boiling merrily and on the table was a great heap of raw vegetables, scrupulously prepared. Margaret was sitting nearby.

Her sleeves were rolled up over her scrawny arms and her apron spread wide over her lap, while a cloud of feathers flew about her as she went to work on some unfortunate fowl. She looked up, her sharp eyes immediately taking in the bag that Deborah was carrying.

"Mistress Deborah! You're never leaving us? Why? What's the matter?"

"Nothing, good Margaret. Nothing you could understand. I am going to London." She laid the letter on the table at the old woman's elbow. "I want you to give that to his lordship the day after to-morrow."

Margaret studied her pale face with keen suspicion.

"You wouldn't go and do anything silly now, would you? Are you sure I can't help?" She put down the bird and wiped her hands on her apron. "Will you stop and let me get you a bite to eat now?"

"No, no. I'm not in the least hungry, really."

Deborah bent and brushed the old woman's lined cheek, at the same time slipping a few coins into her lap.

"There. Take care of your master for me."

Then, cutting short Margaret's exclamations, she made haste to the stables.

She sought no help in saddling Sarah, the sorrel mare she usually rode. "Easy, my beauty," she murmured softly as she adjusted the bit. "Easy. You are luckier than I am. You will be coming back again as soon as I can find a groom to bring you."

A few minutes later, she was already under the trees.

It was late in the evening before Deborah came in sight of the palace of Whitehall, and she was half-dead with nervous exhaustion and sheer physical fatigue. She reined poor Sarah to a walk. The horse was hardly in any better state than herself. Her sides were flecked with foam and many times on the road Deborah had felt that she would collapse under her. It was only by the most judicious use of her spurs and her voice that she had been able to keep her on her feet to the end of that gruelling journey.

Turning down King Street, Deborah made her way directly into the kitchen court. It was there, in one of the adjoining wings, that Mistress Tucker, by the Queen's favour, had her comfortable lodging.

It was not a grand apartment. There were no rich silks, no Flemish tapestries, but instead homely embroideries and one or two pieces of ancient, blackened oak furniture, acquired from the break-up of some wealthy household. The floor was polished until it shone, so that visitors were required to put on felt overshoes to walk on it at all. It was, in fact, the product of a lifetime's work in this world, scrupulously and lovingly amassed to form an appropriate background for entry into the next.

Deborah dismounted outside. A serving man in livery passed by whistling, but stopped and turned round at the sight of her appearance. Long wisps of hair trailed from under her hat, her skirts were heavy with mud and there was such a haggard glitter in her eyes that he came forward to see what he could do.

Thankfully, she handed him her reins and tottered up the few steps to the door. It opened with a push and she found herself face to face with a startled servant.

"Is Mistress Tucker at home?"

"No, ma'am. At this time of day she's at the palace."

"Very well. Send for her. Tell her it is very urgent. A matter of life and death. Say that Mistress Mason says so. Ask her to come here at once. And if you dawdle on the way, you'll hear something from your mistress."

"Yes, ma'am. At once, ma'am." Clearly the girl was only too anxious to escape from the presence of this alarming and masterful visitor.

Deborah sank into the only chair in the room which boasted a cushion: Mistress Tucker's own, it would appear. A quarter of an hour or so later, the door was flung open.

"Abominable child! Thank heaven you are safe!" Mistress Tucker sailed into the room and bore down on her niece like an oncoming galleon. "Whatever happened to you? I have been half dead with worry!"

Deborah was conscious of the stirrings of remorse but she asked herself how she could have set her aunt's mind at rest, even secretly. She could guess only too easily that, wherever she might have been, Mistress Tucker's first and only thought would have been to fetch her back into the nest as fast as possible.

"I'm truly sorry, Aunt, to have caused you so much trouble and anxiety," she said meekly. "I'll tell you all about it – but just now there is not a moment to lose. I must see the Queen."

"The Queen!" Mistress Tucker's plump cheeks positively quivered with indignation. "How dare you so much as speak her name! See her Majesty! Whatever next! Have you the least idea of what a barley-broth you have made of things here?" She snorted angrily. "If you want the truth, I don't see how I'm going to get you out of it. Her Majesty can't bear to hear your name so much as mentioned and indeed I hardly dare go near her myself. And now you stand there, all smiles and impudence, and dare to tell me —"

"Yes, yes. I dare say," Deborah broke in at last. "I've already told you, Aunt, I'll explain everything. But I must see her, at all costs. Listen."

She proceeded to relate the substance of Perez's plot, to a background of repeated exclamations of shock and horror from Mistress Tucker.

"So you see, Aunt," she finished, "I can't possibly wait until tomorrow."

"Wait a moment. Let me think . . ." Mistress Tucker's eyebrows rose and fell in a mighty effort of concentration.

"To my mind," she said at last, "the best thing will be for me to see the Queen myself. There's a reception being put on tonight for the French ambassador, but no matter for that. I can slip a word to her by one of the serving fellows. She'll arrange it, never fear. But if you see Her Majesty, she'll fly into one of her tempers before you can so much as open your mouth. You know her: she'll have you torn into little pieces! She might even dismiss you unheard. But if she hears of this conspiracy from me first, she'll be so pleased with you that her anger will be all forgotten, *I* know."

Adding a mental note to the effect that this way she herself would also be saved much unwelcome explanation, Deborah agreed modestly that it would indeed be best. Then she leaned back in her chair and closed her eyes in utter exhaustion.

"Why, you poor child!" Mistress Tucker exclaimed, her displeasure wholly gone. "Just look at the state you're in, and me without even the time to see to you properly."

Her normally rather cold eyes were bright with triumph and she stroked Deborah's tousled curls with a kind of awkward, unpractised tenderness.

"You had better not be found here, child. There might be questions asked. I'll have Janet go with you to Fleet Street."

"As you wish." Deborah pressed her hands to her eyes. "I can do no more. Oh, don't forget to tell Her Majesty that John Strong is keeping watch on the tavern!"

"Yes, yes, I will, dear. Don't you worry about anything." She wrapped herself in a big, black frieze cloak and fastened it with a silver brooch. "Good, now I'll be off. You shall tell me all the rest tomorrow."

She deposited a rapid peck on her niece's cheek and left.

Deborah gazed round her vaguely. She was back again in her own room in Fleet Street. Janet had been busy and the bed was made up with clean sheets and clean pink counterpane, the curtains drawn. Here was the well-polished work table with its load of books and beside it, catching the gleam of candlelight, the pretty brass inlaid writing-desk which her aunt had given her on her fifteenth birthday, the only piece of furniture in the whole house, Deborah reflected wryly, which was actually her own.

She moved slowly to the window and raised the curtain, then let it fall again. Outside the uneven procession of dark rooftops marched away in the night. Farther down the street, a dim, moving lantern showed the presence of the watch. It was a long way from the quiet trees and the line of moonlit hills. She stripped off her hat and riding-dress and her shift and left them lying where they fell. She would not wear those clothes again. All that was over now . . .

Casting herself face downwards on the bed, Deborah lay with her face buried in the pillow, her naked shoulders heaving convulsively, and cried her heart out.

XIV

The Queen's antechamber.

To think that it was only three months ago that she had sat on this same stool, her fingers fiddling restlessly with her plum-coloured gown while she waited, as she was doing now, for her aunt to summon her. Deborah smiled faintly, with a kind of affectionate contempt for that earlier, timid and inexperienced self. A mere three months, and how much had changed in her life! She realized suddenly, with her new assurance, how much she had grown up since . . . She felt like an old woman.

It was ten days now since her return to London and her information had been acted on with complete success. The tavern at Blackfriars had been surrounded and Perez and his confederates captured by Walsingham's men. After that, there had been the usual routine of torture, confession, trial, sentence and execution. The last had taken place the day before yesterday. Deborah permitted herself the pious hope that the Spaniard was now roasting in hell. Only Basilio had inexplicably slipped through the net but although this had vexed her a good deal at the time she had soon ceased to think of it.

Punishments and rewards. John Strong, blushing pridefully, had received a full purse as a personal present from the Queen, in addition to the less publicized thanks of his young mistress for holding his tongue and sticking so faithfully to the story she had concocted out of her fruitful imagination. In other respects, all had been as Deborah had foreseen. Mistress Tucker, basking in success, had swallowed whatever they chose to say without a blink. Far from casting any doubts on their veracity, she had actually offered to carry the story to the Queen herself, thereby relieving her niece of a great weight of apprehension.

Not, of course, that she had anything to reproach herself for, but even so it would surely have been foolhardy to attempt to explain to Elizabeth why she had not broken her word and escaped from Lichfield. Nor would it have been easy to make Her Majesty understand her affection for Jane, and for David, and the feelings of respect and gratitude which had bound her to her oath. It would probably be enough to give her aunt palpitations and the Queen an apoplectic fit! Certainly neither of them would ever forgive her. No, the best thing was to be quiet and do her best to forget.

Forget! It was what she had been trying to do every day. But there was another recent memory which she knew was too strong, too dear and too painful ever to be forgotten. How could she not think of Kit? He was always present in her mind and she even found a perverse pleasure in probing the wound. She was for ever recalling his careless affection, his mocking laugh and the countless unimportant little loving actions which had gone to make up the richness of their days. As for the nights, it was her body, broken to the regimen of love, which now reminded her, with a fierce and merciless importunity, of what she desired and no longer had. She knew, none better, that she must fight against it, but how? For the present, she could perceive no remedy.

On the day after Perez's arrest, the Queen had left, as arranged, for Richmond. She had returned last evening and a brief communication had arrived in Fleet Street informing Deborah that she was to be granted an audience today. Deborah herself had not been permitted to see the letter and she was much intrigued by her aunt's exasperating air of complacency which was coupled with a mysterious silence concerning the precise nature of the contents.

Relations between aunt and niece had undergone considerable alteration. Mistress Tucker's strictness had given place to a mixture of indulgence of and patient understanding for the moodiness and sudden bouts of depression which Deborah seemed to have brought back from her travels. In fact, she was dazzled by her niece's success, by her intelligence, her grace and dignity, and by her beauty which, by some mysterious alchemy, appeared actually to have grown during her absence. It was as if she recognized in her heart that her own role as counsellor was coming to an end, that Deborah had gone beyond her, and she confined herself to cosseting her capricious appetite and surrounding her with small comforts. Once only did she venture to ask a question, concerning the great topaz which burned on the third finger of her right hand and from which she was never parted. Her only answer was a storm of sobs and a precipitate exit from the room.

Deborah was remembering this, turning the ring pensively on her finger, when the door opposite to her opened and Mistress Tucker's coifed head beckoned in the lighted opening. Deborah stood up.

This time they passed through the Queen's bedchamber and on to the closet which was her private sanctum.

Elizabeth was there, seated before a delicate ebony table subtly inlaid with silver of Italian workmanship. A mirror in a heavy silver frame hung against the wall above. The table itself was at present cluttered with a formidable assortment of toilet articles : brushes, combs, pins, perfumes, sweet oils and pieces of false hair; the stock-in-trade of the perspiring person presently engaged in the arduous task of dressing the Queen's head. This undertaking was not made any easier by her Majesty's own occupation, which consisted of rummaging in the jewel casket on her knees, drawing out her fine, white hands dripping with precious ornaments, pendants, pins and brooches, all heavily encrusted with gems. She was continually leaning forward to try the effect of these in the glass, turning round to address one or other of her ladies, waving her arms, shouting, swearing and giving vent to great, joyous bursts of open-throated laughter.

It was in the midst of all this that she caught sight of Deborah, standing motionless by the door, and instantly, with a word and a snap of her fingers, she had dismissed them all.

"Come hither to me, child."

Deborah obeyed and moving forward sank into a graceful, practised curtsy.

"You have done us great service, Mistress Deborah, and God's death, I am not one of those rulers who accept the proofs of loyalty and then, the danger past, forget to reward the donor. Bring me my casket, Tucker."

This casket proved to be a gilded box, with silver-gilt fastenings. The Queen opened it, revealing an interior lined with lavender-coloured velvet and divided into a series of small pigeon-holes. In each of these, arranged with a perfect symmetry and subtlety that was an art in itself, were rings, dozens and dozens of rings: pearls, diamonds, rubies, emeralds, sapphires, their magnificence of colour, shape and workmanship giving to Deborah's dazzled eyes an impression of a fairy cavern filled with dancing fires. Each had its history, but whether the tale it told was of a city's grateful appreciation of a royal visit, or of the gift of one of the myriad ambassadors who presented themselves and their credentials at her court, each one was in its way a tribute to the extraordinary power of Elizabeth's personality. The Queen's love of jewels was well known.

She was busy now examining each small case with a critical eye,

140

rejecting as she went. At last, she picked up a tiny box, covered in worn, black leather, which lay right at the bottom of the casket. This, she opened and presented to the girl who all this time had remained kneeling at her feet.

"This is for you," she said. "I have no time for your flibberti-gibbet maids who care for nothing but the size of a jewel. I warrant, though, that you, like me, care more for what is behind it." She paused, and when she resumed speaking there was a suggestion of nostalgia in her voice.

"This ring, for me, is a memory of my youth. I wore it when my sister Mary sent me a prisoner to the Tower and, wearing it, I learned, step by step, to fight the hard battle of life . . . You will learn, child, that for each one of us there are times when it is hard to find our way. It is my hope that at such times this ring will remind you of your queen and may help you to find courage and endurance, for you are a gallant child and I like you well."

It was a speech that contained all of Elizabeth's essential charm and astuteness. Unable to bring herself to part with a more costly jewel, she had seen how to gloss over the meanness of the gift and, at the same time, by choosing the right words to go with it had actually conferred upon it a value beyond price. The ring itself was a plain gold band adorned with a single pearl, engraved on the inner side with the letter E.

Still kneeling, Deborah placed the ring dazedly on her finger.

"How can I thank Your Majesty? This ring shall never leave me and I shall be Your Majesty's most true and loyal servant while I live."

"God's death, that was well said!" The Queen smiled, revealing blackened teeth. "And yet you shall have more to thank me for. I have a greater favour for you yet. How say you to a husband, child? And one in a much higher place than by your condition alone you could deserve."

Deborah's heart seemed to stand still.

"The man I have in mind for you," the Queen went on, "is a peer of this realm, Roger Durham, Earl of Norland, a widower without children. He has not yet been told of this but," with a languid wave of one white hand, "he will accept it, never fear. He has good reason." She smiled faintly at the girl's flabbergasted expression. "And since I would not have you deceived, I shall tell you his reason.

"Four years ago, the Earl was implicated in a papist plot – yes, another one, you see. He was arrested and arraigned before his peers

141

on charges of high treason but on examination it was found that nothing could be proved against him and his life was spared. Since then, at my pleasure, he has been living in retirement in the north. As I well know, he will go to any lengths to procure his return to court, even marriage with one whom he cannot regard as his equal. Our dear subject Roger has a horror of country life. This, then, is what I shall propose: let him once marry you and he shall be free to return to London. I warrant you there will be no objections on his side. As to yourself, I doubt not you will know how to value my offer. You are without birth or fortune and the husband I would give you is noble, rich and not old. God's death, you'd be a fool to hesitate!" The last words were uttered with a touch of impatience as, instead of the outburst of grateful thanks which she had evidently expected, the Queen became aware that Deborah had been growing progressively whiter as this plan was presented to her.

"Your Majesty is too kind," the girl stammered at last. "But this is so unexpected, I can scarcely believe . . ."

"True," Elizabeth admitted, somewhat mollified. "I dare say it may come as something of a surprise. You may have until tomorrow to bring me your consent. Also, it has seemed best to us, in order to spare the Earl's feelings, to conceal your relationship to Tucker. You will continue to be merely an orphan of good family, living in Fleet Street. In addition, so that you shall not go to your husband altogether penniless, I have arranged for you to receive a small pension."

"Your Majesty does me —"

"Tut, child. The labourer is worthy of his hire and I dare swear you have guessed already that there is more behind this than simply my wish to reward you for your zeal in my service."

Elizabeth was silent for a moment, her fingers occupied in a kind of cat's cradle with a long gold chain that had lain forgotten in her lap. At last, she looked up.

"For the sake of our own safety and that of the realm, no hothead of that kind can be let go unwatched. Norland here, under my hand, seems to me by far less dangerous than Norland growling like a bear in his northern fastness. Also, he must have no excuse to feel a grievance. And that, child, is where you may do good. A clever woman, sharing a man's bed and board, may have many opportunities to forestall what might otherwise become an unsafe rashness. Moreover" – and here the Queen's eye brightened with a gleam of mischief – "it does not displease me to introduce a young bride to my court who, without prior family claims, may be trusted to keep

142

me informed of what is being said there. Go now, and weigh well what I have said to you. Decide for yourself whether you are fit for this task."

The lined face had already turned away from Deborah. A bell jangled and the Queen's loud voice was added to it, summoning back her ladies to continue the all-important business of selecting the adornments of majesty for the evening's audiences.

Forgotten, Deborah withdrew.

Not for the life of her, could she have recalled the way that she and John Strong took back to Fleet Street that day. At last, however, she was free to retire to her own chamber, alone, away from prying eyes and there, lying on her bed in her favourite position, with both hands linked behind her head, to try and bring her thoughts into some kind of order. The Queen, the Earl of Norland, Kit . . . all these were dancing an infernal galliard in her head without, it seemed, allowing her to form a single coherent idea.

Rolling over on to her stomach, she put out an arm and groped underneath the bed, raising herself at the same time on the other elbow. She had taken the precaution, on her return, of abstracting a bottle of sack from the buttery and now she took a generous swig at it. The wine did her good. She propped herself up straight and started to think.

She had come, she knew instinctively, to a major turning-point in her life, one of the crossroads which await each one of us and from which there can be no turning aside. Left or right? Two roads were open before her and there was still time to choose one or the other: the first leading up to honour, the second down into obscurity. The choice appeared an easy one, put like that, yet Deborah began frantically weighing the pros and cons.

If she accepted this offer it would be to have all her girlhood's dreams come true. It would raise her out of the crowd of common people and set her among the great to enjoy all the pleasures, of wealth and influence which belonged so naturally to the rich and were as inexorably denied to the poor. As for the Earl of Norland . . . Deborah shrugged. She had never seen him but that hardly mattered. How many daughters of respectable families were permitted to choose their husbands for themselves in any case? He or another . . . With one exception, all men were much the same to her, and she had acquired sufficient confidence in her own charms to have

143

very few doubts of her ability to make this northern hermit of the Queen's forget that this marriage had ever been forced on him.

If, on the other hand, she were to refuse, the Queen's favours would be at an end. That much had been made very clear to her. It was either this or a return to the menial life without the prospect of any future escape. Deborah nibbled thoughtfully at her thumbnail. The Queen's final words troubled her slightly, even so. What was being suggested to her was in fact no more and no less than the distasteful role of a spy. Oh, well . . . time enough to make up her mind on that issue when she met the Earl. As for court gossip, if the Queen's courtiers were knaves or fools enough to talk against Her Majesty, then she, Deborah, would be doing no more than her duty in reporting the fact.

Strange, she thought suddenly, puzzled by something her memory had thrown up. The Queen had said not a word concerning Mary Stuart. In the agitation of the moment, she had not remarked it but perhaps, after all, it was as well. No doubt the Queen had heard all that she wished to know about the audience at Chartley from Mistress Tucker and so much had happened since that the affair had no doubt ceased to be of any interest – except to Deborah herself. She wished to God that she had never set foot in Chartley, she wished that she had never . . .

The endless argument proceeding in her mind began again.

Looking at the matter in its coldest light, there seemed to be no reason on earth why she should not leap at this wonderful chance which she was being offered. Then, if that were so, why had her hands, clutching the sheet, turned icy cold? Why was there this tightness in her throat and this dreadful feeling of oppression? She knew only too well why, but until now she had managed to leave out of her mental debate the one serious objection to the Earl of Norland. She let out a little groan and her head turned restlessly on the pillow so that her hair came unplaited and lay in tumbled coils about her face.

Kit! Kit! My love! If she were to marry it would mean giving up whatever infinitesimal glimmer of hope still lurked in her most secret heart. Never again would she have the right to dream about the gentle passion of his lips on hers, never again know the joy of being with him. Never. Why, oh why, when he himself had said that what he felt for her was something he had felt for no other woman, why had he not bound her to him? She would not have interfered with his freedom. She would have asked nothing of him but the

144

right, now and then, to gorge herself with his kisses. She would have waited for him, faithful, smiling, surrounded by her family of handsome, blackhaired children, their children . . . Kit's children. A dumb cry of pain seemed to rise up from her very bowels.

She sat up suddenly and put her hand slowly to her cheek, an expression of shock in her eyes. Was it, perhaps, for that very reason that he had not married her? Oh God, she was certain now it must be that! He could not bring himself to tell her plainly, that was all. He would have thought that she was grown enough to know without being told of the gulf that separated them. Lord Christopher Belstone, a younger son of the Marquis of Gilford, could not afford to marry into anything but a noble family.

She was crying openly now.

How could she have been so green as not to see what was staring her in the face? For a mistress, merely, she had been perfect, of course: docile and loving as any heart could desire. But as for taking it any further than that – oh, no! His lordship must not, as that insufferable Penelope had reminded him, do anything silly, anything that might risk a blot on the Gilford escutcheon! Anger welled up in Deborah, slowly getting the better of her grief, turning it to a fierce and thoroughly aggressive mood. Well, since that was how things stood, she would show these stiff-rumped lords that her quality was as good as theirs. Her blood might not be as blue, but she did not think herself inferior for that.

Deborah put up her chin. The tears still shone on her cheeks but her eyes were dry and bright and resolute. She would be Countess of Norland.

The die·was cast. Fate, enigmatic under its glittering mask of promises, had seized hold of Deborah and was thrusting her, still quivering with bitter disappointment, along the way which had been marked out for her for all time. It stretched ahead of her, a broad way, paved with shining gold and leading, step by step, up to the very heights and topmost pinnacles, and yet, beware, for the sides are steep and rugged, and bordering them a bottomless abyss where the slightest false step could prove fatal, while beneath the deceptive glister of the gold the way is strewn with deadly snares.

PART TWO

The Marriage

XV

The snowflakes whirled past the window and subsided delicately on to the ground where their brief butterfly dance was ended in the yellowish slush that filled the street. Vague, fleeting figures appeared and disappeared, wading ankle-deep through the ordure-laden mire. Even the horses struggled forward with difficulty, barded with snow and muddied to the girths, throwing up showers of filth, while the crack of whips and the curses of those around penetrated into the room.

London, at the beginning of January, was a grey and dismal place.

Sighing heavily, Deborah turned her back on the window and huddled up to the fire, thanking heaven for a good old-fashioned blaze of logs and none of your new, fashionable coal-burning hearths.

She pulled up a stool and sat within the circle of warmth, taking care to arrange the wide skirts of her tub-shaped French farthingale of branched murrey velvet so as not to crush them. The tight, busked bodice and rigid stomacher descending to a point some inches below her waist, emphasized the slenderness of her body, as did the immense trunk sleeves, hugely distended with wire and bombast at the shoulder and cuffed in tightly at the wrist with sable. The low, square neck revealed the swelling of her breasts and the space between it and the great wired lace collar which stood up behind her head was filled in with a triple row of milky pearls. Her lovely hair was drawn back high off her face, encircled by two gold billiments, and diamond pendants hung from her ears.

She was waiting now for John Strong to escort her to Whitehall and as she sat her eyes rested on the rich cloak of sables lying negligently over the bed. It was a gift or, more accurately, a loan from the Earl. The cloak, like the jewels she wore, had belonged to the first Countess of Norland. He had been generous in that respect, although the words with which he had accompanied the presentation had robbed it of all grace.

"Madam," he had informed her, with the coldness which he

invariably used when speaking to her. "You will appreciate, of course, that I can scarcely take much pride in our union. Nevertheless, seeing that you bear my name, I should wish that your appearance at least may do me no dishonour. You will therefore be good enough to inform me of the sum which you will require for your dress. As to your jewels, those of my late wife should, I think, suffice."

Deborah sighed again. She had been married little more than a month but already she had given up any hope of winning the earl's affections nor, to be quite honest, did she retain the slightest wish to do so.

Three days after her audience with the Queen, a messenger had departed northwards, and a week after that the Earl of Norland had made his reappearance in the capital, followed by his servants, horses, dogs and baggage wagons in quantity.

His first concern on arrival, after greeting his sovereign, had been to open up and put in order the fine house belonging to his family in Drury Lane, not far from the Strand.

It was an old house, built at some time during the preceding century, and impressive in its way. The stone façade, extending in its total length over a distance of some hundred yards, was adorned with half a dozen pointed gables, each embellished with an amount of admirable decorative work. Already, at the time of his first marriage, the Earl had instituted all kinds of improvements to bring it up to date. Large, square-leaded windows had been opened up in the walls on a quite extravagant scale, chimneys had been erected to all the principal rooms and the old-fashioned furnishing replaced with more comfortable and convenient pieces. At the back of the house was a garden laid out in the Italian style, and also the stable and kennel buildings.

In the protracted absence of the master, the house had been inhabited only by the rats and other vermin, so that it stood in need of a good deal of renovation and repair. Dust and damp were everywhere but the Earl, who was a perfect old woman where his comfort was concerned, so harried the cohorts of masons, slaters, carpenters, joiners, tapestry repairers, painters, gardeners and other workpeople who descended on it that within five weeks of his arrival Norland House was ready to receive its new countess.

On the wedding day itself, the Earl had intimated briefly to his bride that, for their mutual convenience, they would each occupy their own, entirely separate apartments.

"I have always regarded with abhorrence this passion on the part of the human race for crowding itself together like a litter of puppies. Thank heaven, we are no longer forced to live in disagreeable and insanitary proximity to our servants and life is beginning to acquire a few of the comforts of a decent privacy. Let us take advantage of them."

Deborah's suite comprised her bedchamber, a small closet and her wardrobe. The ceilings of all three rooms were coffered with ornamental plasterwork and the rooms themselves, considering their functions, were reasonably spacious and well-lit.

Handsome curtains of bright green damask paned with gold adorned the bedchamber, the great canopied bedstead was inlaid with ivory and there were three stools covered with crimson velvet also fringed with gold. A needle-work hanging covered the arched doorway leading into the closet where the honey-coloured woodwork formed a background for an armchair of Arras point and a charming little French desk, both of which were reflected in an absurdly pretty gilt Venetian mirror on the wall. Strewings of fresh herbs, mint and rosemary and lavender, were made every day to perfume the room and keep it sweet.

It was only fair to admit that the Earl had treated her well and Deborah could not fault the courtesy of his manners to her. Given the circumstances of her entry into Norland House, indeed, she could not reasonably ask for more. And yet it was his very courtesy, the frigid politeness with which it seemed he was determined to treat her on all occasions, that chilled Deborah to the soul. There was nothing about him of the boisterous, loud-mouthed provincial Deborah had half-expected, with a face like underdone beef and a voracious appetite for quarrelling. Instead, there was this cold, sophisticated and impervious creature and more than once she caught herself thinking a trifle wistfully of that earlier image. Faced with a hot-tempered bully who would have told her straight out what was in his mind, she might perhaps have found the chink in his armour. Unhappily, Norland's contempt and dislike of her were invariably concealed behind a surface of calm good manners before which, as she well knew, she was powerless.

Not that he was indifferent to her charms: he was not. But during these brief exchanges, Deborah was visited by the unpleasant sensation of being no more than a wax doll in his hands, a soulless object to be used merely, with the indifference due to the fleeting instrument of his pleasure. He came to her this way every night to exercise his conjugal rights and the only good word she could find to say about his fumbling advances was that they were at least brief. Clearly, he had no intention of wasting his time in amorous dalliance but came straight to the point, regardless of his partner's feelings. No doubt he was of the opinion that these should be sufficiently gratified in ministering to the satisfaction of his.

These transient visits left Deborah with a deep disgust for both him and herself. Just as Kit's lovemaking had seemed to her the summit of all that was pure and noble in human actions, so did her husband's bony, passionless embraces sicken and degrade her until it needed all her fortitude to endure them.

She had not, in accepting the Queen's proposal, thought much about that side of the contract. In fact, it had scarcely crossed her mind at any time. It was not in the general way a thing one did think of to any great extent. Passionate love was not to be expected inside marriage, there was even something (surely?), a trifle vulgar in the very idea. Leave that to shepherds and shepherdesses. Marriage ought to be based on principles of sound common sense and mutual self-interest. That was the way to found a family. It was practical, too. The union once consummated, the husband was able to return by tacit agreement to his mistresses while his wife sought solace with some discreet admirer . . . All in all, then, she could not complain. Her lot was the common one. The only trouble was that she had anticipated the normal way of things and taken a lover first and the husband after. Not being in any sense an innocent in love, she was only too aware of what was lacking in her relations with the Earl. Yet what could she do? Nothing, except submit with the best grace she could manage: which meant grit her teeth, stiffen her sinews and count the seconds.

What was he like, this man she had married? He was forty-seven years old and tall and thin with grizzled hair. His complexion was sallow and his almost lashless eyes a hard, slate grey. His long, horse face appeared still longer by reason of the length of his nose and the only thing about his countenance that seemed truly alive was his moist, red mouth, framed between drooping moustaches and a short, grizzled beard. To set against this unalluring picture, it was necessary to grant him a distinguished, even a graceful carriage reinforced by an unerring taste in all matters of fashion and a strong sense of his own importance.

Roger Durham, Earl of Norland, came of a powerful Catholic family in the north of England which had never become altogether reconciled to the existence of the Church of England. The reign of Mary Tudor had allowed them to return to what was, for them, the true faith. The old earl, Andrew, died of the plague in 1556, together with his wife, his eldest son and two daughters, leaving the younger son, Roger, sole heir to all his vast estates north of the Trent.

The accession of Elizabeth in 1558 had brought the young man, then aged nineteen, hot-foot to London to take his oath to the new sovereign. Coming fresh from his ancestral dales where he had led an almost monastic existence all his life, the gaiety and luxury of the capital, the beauty and freedom of its women went straight to the young man's head. He had intended to remain for a few weeks, instead he stayed indefinitely, abandoning the care of his estates to his steward. Once a year he would make a brief foray into the north to deal with his affairs and pocket his revenues, which were considerable and derived from the fact that, however poor in a general agricultural sense, his land was ideal country for sheep which, thanks to the ever-increasing demands of the wool trade, were a certain source of wealth.

At the age of thirty-five, he contracted an advantageous marriage but the death of his wife, a colourless creature who had suffered from persistent ill-health, in 1581 had left him without either children or regret. A year later, his name was mentioned in connection with a minor papist conspiracy but since, in the opinion of his peers, his involvement was due more to the known religious sympathies of his family than to any depth of personal conviction, he was released but on condition that he left London.

To Roger, this meant the loss of everything he cared for and he did not recover from it. The blow destroyed the cheerful and amiable side of his nature for ever.

Four years passed, four years of deadly boredom and consuming bitterness in which the better part of his time was spent bewailing, to those companions who could be induced to share his horrible exile, the happiness which he had so foolishly cast away.

The Queen's proposal came in time to pluck him from his misery and for two days he remained closeted in his chamber fighting a desperate battle with his family pride. Assisted by the unrelieved gloom of a north country November and his own passionate longing to go back to London, he was not long in succumbing to temptation. Nevertheless, he never forgave Elizabeth or the new Countess of Norland for demonstrating to him what he had become: a man capable of sacrificing even his own pride for the sake of this world's pleasures.

Nor, he discovered to his surprise, were the pleasures quite the same as they had been before his exile. He no longer felt entirely at his ease in London. The faces had changed and so, he found, had he, while the new crowd of younger men who tended to revolve round the volatile Earl of Essex found little response in his embittered nature. For the most part, therefore, Deborah was left to go to court by herself, while he remained at home, content for the moment with the quiet and comforts of Norland House, the company of his dogs and endless conversations with friends of earlier days, or indulging his melancholy with the flattery of a ready court of hangers-on.

Deborah started from her reverie. A white-capped maidservant stood before her.

"Begging your pardon, my lady —" Oh, the thrill that ran through Deborah every time she heard herself so addressed! "I did knock, my lady, but —"

"I did not hear you. What is it, child?"

"A message from Master Strong, my lady. He says to tell you that there's trouble with the coach, my lady, on account of the weather, it is, and he begs you to excuse him a while longer."

"Tell him to hurry, then. I can't spend the whole day sitting here."

"Yes, my lady. I'll tell him that."

"And send up some more fuel for the fire, will you? It's freezing in here."

The girl departed with a bobbing curtsy and the whisk of a white apron.

Fretting at the delay, Deborah went to the window and, scraping away some of the rime that covered it, peered out at the sky. It was still snowing. Oh, well, she could scarcely ride to Whitehall in this dress in any case, she told herself. She would just have to wait for the coach.

At the thought of the coach, Deborah's face was illumined by a sudden smile of pure joy. It was a beautiful vehicle: not one of the Earl's heavy, travelling coaches but a dear little two-seater ordered especially for her, for her own exclusive use. It was all lined within with crimson velvet, with leather curtains fringed with gold beads and four white ostrich plumes waving impudently from the roof.

She wandered back to the fire and sat down again, wondering what on earth there was to do in this unfriendly, silent house.

Except for her own rooms, which had grown pleasantly familiar, the rest of the house remained hostile territory. She felt out of place there, and unwanted, as if she were some unknown and unwelcome guest rather than the mistress of the house. She frowned. Take Fletcher the steward for instance. The way he looked at her sometimes, you'd think that he knew everything about her, from where she was born to the number of shifts she had before she set foot in Norland House! He was respectful enough to all outward appearance, even obsequious, but not once had he ever asked her opinion or consulted her on anything to do with the management of the house. Everything of that kind was referred directly to the Earl and, smiling with polite contempt at her few, tentative efforts to impose her will, he persisted in treating her simply as a passing guest. She had grown used to it now and almost ceased to care. Let him manage things as he liked. She would not be the one to deprive him of his charge. Nor would she allow his arrogance to disturb her. She had John Strong whom she had brought with her to the house and who followed her everywhere, his ruddy face beaming with affection, consoling her a thousand times over for the many pin-pricks which her self-esteem was forced to endure in the course of every day.

Still, what was she to do to occupy herself?

Suddenly, an idea came to her. The previous day had seen the installation of her husband's great new bedstead, a magnificent piece of furniture which, it appeared, had cost the truly enormous sum of eleven hundred and fifty pounds. At dinner, the Earl, being in a communicative mood, had deigned to enlarge upon its manifold wonders, speaking with a connoisseur's appreciation of its carved oak frame, its double valance of blue silk, its gold laced curtains and counterpane of rich embroidery. There had been a good deal more in the same vein but at the time Deborah had not paid much attention, her mind being taken up with thoughts of her own new dress. Now, however, that she had nothing else to do and had exhausted the resources of her mirror, it occurred to her that she would like to see this marvel.

Rising, she cast the sable cloak about her and left the room.

After passing through a maze of rooms and stairways, she came to a broad gallery, lighted at intervals by cressets fastened to the wall. This was her husband's private domain.

She passed a number of people of the household, all of whom turned to look at her. She could feel their eyes boring curiously into her back and divine their unspoken disapproval. Her ladyship, she

155

seemed to hear them thinking, had no business to be in this part of the house. She was conscious of a slight twinge of uneasiness but banished it at once. After all, the Earl had not forbidden her the place in so many words. At this time of day, she knew, he was generally to be found visiting the kennels, so she ran no risk of disturbing him.

She walked quickly through the wide antechamber and found herself in a panelled room containing a large table on which stood a model of the terrestrial globe, bound in brass. Facing her were well-stocked bookshelves and she paused for a moment before them, gazing in awe and wonder at the gorgeous covers. One or two of them she lifted down, with immense care, and let her fingers play briefly over the jewelled locks. Then she saw a door and pushed it open. It led into a narrow, cupboard-like space beyond which was another door. Unhesitatingly, Deborah opened it and stopped dead, a startled cry on her lips.

It was, as she had supposed, her husband's bedchamber, but she had been very far from expecting the sight which met her eyes there.

A female form, her skirts bundled up as high as her waist was lying back across the bed while half on top of her, his own clothes in disarray, was Deborah's husband, actively engaged.

At the sound of Deborah's voice, he scrambled upright, fumbling for his points, and rounded on his wife who, choking with disgust, had already turned to flee.

"How now, madam!" he exclaimed, laying hold of her arm. "How dared you enter my apartments without my leave?" His habitual calm seemed to have deserted him for the moment. Deborah shook herself free.

"Let me go! I wonder, sir, that you dare use that tone with me! Your own conduct appears to render it singularly inappropriate."

"Madam —"

"One word more, my lord, and I am going. That there should be jealousy between us is, of course, unthinkable and so I trust you not to misinterpret what I have to say. Your conduct, I thank God, is your own affair. You might, however, have the good manners to indulge yourself elsewhere than under this roof."

The Earl's eyes darkened with anger.

"I'll have you know, my lady, that I am master under this roof and I intend to remain so. By God, madam, you have a rare nerve! Do you forget by what commerce you came here?"

"I am not likely to forget, but I would remind you that you entered into that arrangement of your own free will. Honour it, then, and treat me with respect!"

He put his hand to his eyes. "I think," he said, making a visible effort at self-control, "that we had better leave the matter there. We shall understand one another better in future if you will be content to live on terms of mutual understanding and refrain from involving yourself in my affairs. Please go now."

"Gladly. I have seen and heard enough. Yet, first, allow me to give you a piece of advice."

"I beg your pardon?"

"If I were you, I should take more care in my choice of a partner." She indicated the woman by the bed, now crouching fearfully against the curtains, sobbing hysterically into her hands. "That pigeon-livered creature is not like to afford you great entertainment. You should find one with some red blood in her veins."

She almost sauntered from the room, with a sardonic smile that revealed her small, white teeth.

The Earl stood looking after her, his eyes remaining fixed on the closed door and his expression set in a look of implacable detestation.

"One day," he ground into his beard, "one day you will regret that."

"Brute! Vile, filthy swine!" Deborah ran out of words to describe her ignoble spouse. She was choking with rage.

It was not that she minded greatly that he was unfaithful to her. She only wished he would spend all his time chasing after such strumpets: then he might leave her in peace. But here, in their own house, within sight and sound of everyone! To humilate her so! It was too much! Pressing one hand to her heaving bosom, she reached out blindly with the other and snatching a silver comfit box off the table beside her, hurled it furiously across the room.

The gesture, and the clatter made by the box and its far-flung contents, helped to calm her and she found that she knew, quite suddenly, what she had to do.

Surely, she would be the world's greatest ninny if she did not pay him back in his own coin. She had received offers enough in the past month, offers from young and personable men of wit and charm who were disposed to wrangle on their knees over her favours. Good heavens, she was a fool to keep faith with that lecher! To say nothing of the benefit that she herself would derive from it. Her breasts ached for a man's hands to caress them. Her whole body yearned for love. She was sleeping badly, pecked at her food and was altogether in such a state of nervous irritation that very soon her looks were bound to suffer. It was no use thinking of the past now, she told herself, squaring her shoulders. The past was dead. And, as if it could blot out the memory, Deborah began hurriedly to pass under review all the good-looking young men she knew who at a single word from her would . . . But which one should it be? It did not take her long to choose. Indeed, it was as if the choice had been already made long before.

Deborah smiled, with an involuntary quiver of her full lips, as she thought of the agreeable surprise that lay in store for James Randolph.

XVI

The time was not much after noon but already the rooms of White-hall palace were humming with people.

Underneath the fine, moulded ceilings, through the great rooms hung with purple and cloth of gold and silver, behind the screens covered with Flemish needlework, knots of courtiers formed and reformed with talk and laughter. It was still too early for any gaming tables to have been set up and no one had yet begun to play on the lute, the viols or the virginals. This was the time for pleasant conversation, and for the gossip, scandal and intrigue which were the very life blood of the court. It was not until the Queen herself appeared in the Presence Chamber that the revels of the day would really begin, for Her Majesty's vigour and stamina were such that only the youngest and most energetic could keep up with her as she danced on into the small hours of the morning.

Two ladies, their throats, wrists and fingers glittering with gems, sat talking together on a window-seat.

"Dearest Penelope, have you any news of your husband's brother?" inquired the first, an attractive brunette in a dress of jade green·satin which set off to perfection her creamy skin and large green eyes.

"Yes, we found a letter waiting when we reached home yesterday." The second woman answered abstractedly and her eyes strayed continually to the far end of the gallery, as if she were looking for someone.

"Kit sends his best love, my dear, and I believe —"

She broke off suddenly.

"Tell me, Cynthia, who is that young woman over there, standing just by that pillar talking to Raleigh and Lord Duncan? I don't think I know her."

"No, of course . . . you must have been away. Well, my dear, *that* is the new Lady Norland."

"What! I did hear, now I come to think of it, that the Earl had returned to us but have heard nothing of his marriage. Hey ho, that's what I like about London! It is so full of surprises." She shook her light curls vigorously. "Well, go on. Tell me all about it. Who is she, this child?"

"I'm afraid you will be disappointed, my love." Cynthia's perfect cupid's bow lips pursed in scornful disapproval. "She is a perfect nobody. No background whatsoever!"

"No! Good heavens, who'd ever have thought a Norland would marry beneath him! Tell me more!"

"Well, if you ask me, it comes of his being stuck away there in the north with no one but frightful shepherdesses all smelling of sheep! He probably fell for the first reasonably clean-looking girl that came his way! And I don't suppose she exactly put him off, poor old fool." She tinkled merrily.

"My dear, I simply can't get over it!"

"One thing I can tell you," Cynthia went on. "When the Earl brought her to court, our dear Gloriana was unusually affable. I shouldn't wonder if the creature's father doesn't turn out to be some merchant or other that Her Majesty wished to oblige."

"You may well be right. It's impossible to tell who anybody is nowadays. I tell you, by the time our children are grown up there won't be a single really good family left," Penelope said disgustedly, at the same time eyeing the subject of their discussion with a brooding expression.

"Hmm, she'll do, though," she added thoughtfully, not without a hint of regret. "Although, to be honest, I can't help thinking that particular shade of hair a trifle vulgar. Still, I dare say the men may like it. They have the oddest tastes."

"Like it? I should just think they do!" Cynthia retorted acidly. "Every man in the room is hot for her!"

"And?"

"That's just it. No one knows. If our dear Earl has horns, she manages it so well that no one can see them. But don't let it worry you, sweetheart. It won't be long, I'm sure, before we've plenty to talk about." The painted lids drooped, concealing the gleam in her eyes. "Aren't you expecting the honourable James Randolph?"

"Yes, yes I sent him a note this morning. After two months without a sight of me, I dare say the poor angel will have quite pined away." She gave a little giggle and added in an undertone: "Strictly between ourselves, I've missed him, too. Not that he's any great shakes to look at, not like Raleigh – or Kit." This last accompanied by a shrewd glance at her friend. "But dear James is such a lively companion, it quite raises my spirits just to be with him. And, my dear, when it comes to making love . . . !" Penelope leaned and whispered in Cynthia's ear and the two women gurgled with laughter, wriggling and letting out little shrieks, like a pair of excited schoolgirls. All at once, Penelope emitted a delighted crow.

"Here he comes!"

A good-looking young man had just entered the gallery. He was dressed with a good deal of magnificence in a doublet of white damask flourished with pearls. His hair was a warm light brown streaked here and there with gold, and the impudent upward tilt of the nose which adorned his pleasant, friendly face was echoed in the extravagant curl of his moustache. Making his way up the room with a purposeful air, exchanging absent-minded greetings to left and right as he came, he passed Penelope without a pause and forged on, straight to where the Countess of Norland was standing. She turned and held out her hand to him, smiling brilliantly, and the fervour with which he bore it to his lips made the lovely Penelope fairly gnash her teeth with rage.

Uttering an inarticulate sound, she sprang up from her seat and hurried after him.

"Why, James my dear," she cooed, her tiny, white hand plucking at his sleeve. "Have you forgotten your old friends? Surely not?"

The young man turned. "Penelope! This is a charming surprise. I did not see you there. Behold me overcome with confusion." He did not sound it.

"Your eyes, I think, were all for this lady," Penelope said, with an edge in her voice, eyeing Deborah.

Seizing the opportunity to avoid further recriminations, Randolph said quickly: "Allow me to introduce the Countess of Norland. Lady Norland, the Marchioness of Gilford."

The two ladies exchanged frigid greetings.

Penelope! Kit's brother's wife! Deborah had recognized her instantly and but for James and the unavoidable strait-jacket of good manners, she would have turned on her heel and walked away. At the same time, it seemed a pity she was debarred from revealing herself to the odious Penelope as the "creature" of whom she had spoken so slightingly to Kit. She saw herself again, standing in the window at Gilford, listening to that waspish voice dripping its poison, and experienced the same impulse to tear those wired curls and slap the painted face.

161

"What have you done with poor old John?" James Randolph was asking in a tone whose joviality sounded somewhat forced.

"Oh, he's well enough. Our stay in Kent has done him the world of good. . . . But is that all you have to say to me?" The note of petulance was ill-concealed.

"You will have to hold me excused for the present, Penelope. I have something of great importance to discuss with Lady Norland. Do, pray, forgive us both."

He laid a firm hand on Deborah's arm and made good his escape.

"James dear," Deborah reproached him mildly, as they walked away, "that was not very polite."

Inwardly, she was telling herself that she could have hugged him in front of the whole court for putting Lady Gilford so firmly in her place.

"Don't, please, think I enjoyed being rude to her. If there had been any other way of getting rid of the woman . . ."

"Yet she seemed to be on very familiar terms with you."

Randolph gave a shout of laughter.

"That's nothing to boast of. There's not an able-bodied man in this room who hasn't been familiar with her at some time or other. It's true we had some dalliance together in the autumn but" – he made a comical face – "the flower was too easily gathered to be worth the picking. Nor, I think, shall I be betraying any great secret if I say that the fair Penelope's glittering promise is not fulfilled in action. Ask Raleigh, Duncan, Worth . . . any one will tell you the same. Anyone, that is, except poor Gilford who still thinks his wife the eighth wonder of the world. Not that he's a bad fellow – far from it, but a flat. His brother now, Lord Christopher . . ."

Catching sight of Deborah's expression and misinterpreting it, James went on: "No, you won't have met him. He rarely comes to London. I don't know him very well myself. But everyone says he's the devil of a fellow, and all the ladies are mad about him . . . Why, what is it? You look quite pale!" His voice was full of concern.

"Nothing . . . it's nothing . . . a slight headache."

No, Deborah was thinking, it was not fair. She had come here to take her mind off Kit, not to be reminded of him. First Penelope, and now James. She had suffered enough on his account and, according to James, she was not alone in that. Well, let him live like a libertine if he liked, or take to wife some great heiress with a face like a cow if that was what he wanted, only let him not come anywhere near her again, that was all she asked.

162

"And I've been boring you to death with my nonsense," James was saying remorsefully. "Come and sit down."

He led her to a secluded window-seat.

"There, sweetheart. Sit there for a minute and rest. What can I say to make you smile again? See, the sun is coming out. Would a visit to the Curtain tempt you? If the weather holds, there may be a play this afternoon."

"Oh, I should like that!"

Deborah's fingers brushed the lace at his wrist and the young man captured them swiftly in his other hand.

"Deborah, do you like me a little?" He was speaking quite seriously for once. "What kind of a spell have you cast on me, you little witch? Ever since the first moment I saw you . . . I can recall it perfectly. It was in this very room. You were leaning on your husband's arm, looking a little shy and like a perfect rose in your white dress. We met. I smiled and you smiled back, and with such freshness in your smile that all at once you made the painted things around you worthless. You were so different, so wonderfully different! God! For your sake I could accomplish anything . . . Tell me, my darling, are you only playing with me, or may I hope that one day . . ."

His arm had slipped about her waist from which Deborah promptly removed it. Picking up the mask and gloves which she had laid on the cushion beside her, she stood up.

"Fie, sir! Why so impatient? Was it you told me a moment ago that a flower too easily culled loses all its savour?"

"God's death! You would not compare yourself to —"

"Yes, but you did say it," she insisted, smiling, and held out her hand. "Come now, do you mean to forget your promise? It is after one and the play, if play there be, will not wait for us. Do you know, I have never yet set foot inside a theatre?"

The Curtain Theatre, now some ten years old, was situated amid the labyrinthine alleys and insalubrious tenements of Shoreditch, which did not prevent it from being, as James explained to Deborah on their way there, a favourite haunt of enterprising young gallants.

The theatre itself proved to be a large, wooden building built around an open central well. Round three sides of this well ran covered galleries furnished with benches for the more fortunate spectators. The rest stood, or sat on stools and benches on the ground below the stage.

The play had already begun as they mounted to their seats. To Deborah, following, James seemed to be entirely in his element

163

among this cheerful throng. He pushed his way through, clapping a man on the shoulder here, pausing to carry a laced glove to his lips there, while everywhere men turned to cast appraising glances at his companion and women stared jealously at her clothes.

Deborah was glad to sit down at last. The effort of making their way through the close-packed gallery with its varied scents of musk and civet and tobacco smoke, as well as the less refined odours emanating largely, but by no means entirely from the groundlings, had made her head swim.

"Are you comfortable here? Or would you prefer to sit somewhere else?"

"No, no, James. This will do very well. Indeed, I don't believe we could find anywhere better. Sit down."

He sat and took her hand again, and held it, wondering whether she would allow him to keep it or not.

Deborah avoided the necessity for a decision by appearing to concentrate all her attention on the stage. This was a large platform jutting out into the central arena from a point immediately opposite to them and on a slightly lower level than their own. It was at present strewn with an assortment of rushes and adorned with a rustic seat and a pair of tree-trunks and a rose bush made out of painted cardboard, the whole clearly intended to represent a woodland scene.

A dialogue was in progress between a boy dressed as a girl in a red dress and a great deal of false hair and a dashing individual in black velvet paned and slashed with yellow satin and gold lace who was apparently endeavouring to woo her/him.

Deborah made an effort to attend to what was going on. To judge from what she had heard so far, the piece seemed to be some kind of tragi-comedy, probably based on an Italian original, full of lust and intrigue. Certainly, it seemed to be holding the attention of the audience which was expressing itself in breathless gasps and wild applause at the end of every speech. But Deborah found it impossible to concentrate. Her ear caught a few words of verse now and then, but otherwise she remained isolated in her own thoughts.

The feel of James's hand enfolding her own had produced in her a slight feeling of uneasiness. Might he not think badly of her for agreeing to come here with him? And wasn't she, perhaps, committing herself rashly by being seen here in his company? After all, they had known one another barely a month, and what did she really know of him? Only what she had picked up at court: that he was the younger son of a Welsh family and had acquired a considerable fortune by speculating in maritime ventures. What ventures, precisely, no one seemed to be able to say. Everyone had a good deal to say, however, as to the way he chose to spend it, especially the women, who would describe his fine house at Charing, his coaches and his magnificent clothes with all the relish of cats at a cream bowl. Good luck to them. It was certainly not his money which had attracted her to James but rather his gentle manners, his light-heartedness and the delicacy with which he had set himself unobtrusively to guide her first insecure steps at court. How could she forget it? If she enjoyed court life now, it was to James that she owed it, for those early days, whatever her grand imaginings beforehand, had been sheer torture. The women with their critical, penetrating eyes and their everlasting questions, so that she had been forced to plead a headache to avoid the searching inquiries into her ancestry, and the men – all charming and delightful, of course, once you had got to know them and a good deal less curious. Less curious, at least, in some directions, but James was about the only one who had not undressed her mentally every time her husband was out of sight. And what would her husband have to say to this little excursion? Well, let him hear of it. It was not a sin to go to the play. And in any case, she was wearing a mask . . . Hastily, she adjusted it. Really, a mask was most convenient. No one could ever be quite sure of recognizing you . . .

"Enjoying yourself?" James whispered in her ear. Turning, she found her cheek all but brushing his and met his frank, worshipping gaze, like a direct answer to the turmoil within.

"Very much," she answered softly, and with a calmer mind, she turned her attention back to the stage.

In fact, the action did not appear to have advanced a great deal, but listening now to the magnificent poetry of it Deborah found herself wondering where the boy-heroine drew the power to utter those glorious speeches. There was such passion and such beauty there that, despite herself, her hand tightened on James's. Now a third person entered, muffled in a dark cape and brandishing a dagger. Stealthily, he crept up on the lovers. There was a moment's breathless anticipation and then the audience began to shout. Deborah, quite unconsciously, was shouting with the best of them. Suddenly, as though roused by the din, the hero turned and, drawing his sword with a splendid gesture that displayed his doublet to full advantage, ran the villain through. Blood flowed, spattering the rose bush in a manner so realistic that it was hard to believe it was only pretence, and the heroine, conquered by this exhibition of bravery, cast herself into the hero's arms.

This happy outcome was greeted with a perfect frenzy of noise, a glorious cacophony of shouts and bangs and whistles. All around Deborah, people were standing up and cheering and stamping their feet in their enthusiasm. She and James, infected by the general atmosphere, were both on their feet, clapping. People below were calling out and exchanging witticisms with the actors on the stage and a shower of objects from flowers to more tangible tokens, descended on them from above.

"Well, how did you like the play?"

They had resumed their seats and Deborah's hand seemed, as naturally, to have resumed its place in his.

"It was terribly exciting at the end," she answered eagerly. "But, James, surely that costume must be very expensive?" She pointed to the principal player, who was now blowing kisses to his still-cheering public.

"It is not he that pays but the manager of the theatre, who is often put to a good deal of anxiety on that score. The actors aren't always willing to put off their finery when the play is done and they borrow the company's properties for their own use." James smiled. "It's a headache for the management, as you can imagine. But don't feel too sorry for them, will you? Although they are not paid a fixed salary, all the members of the company own a share in it, so that they are a great deal better off than their counterparts in other countries. Nor are they the social outcasts they are in France or Spain for example. Either we're more easy-going, or merely grateful for the pleasure they give us, but there are plenty of men of power and influence – Leicester, Raleigh and Oxford are among them – who seek out their society. Look there, now, to the left of the stage. Isn't that Essex?"

Deborah looked and saw a young man in cream-coloured satin slashed with cherry red sitting on a chair placed to one side of the stage. The magnificence of his apparel was enhanced by the diamonds sparkling in his ears and by the rings that clustered thickly on the hand which he put up to stroke his beard as he chatted idly to those about him.

"Yes, it is, but why is he sitting on the stage? Is he going to speak a part?"

James laughed. "No, alas! A seat on the stage itself, you must know, is the height of honour, accorded only to the most favoured patrons. It seems that Essex is favoured in every quarter."

166

The last words, uttered in something of an undertone, were almost lost in the roars of laughter that were now filling the playhouse. These were prompted by the grotesque antics of the fool who was now holding the stage. He was an enormously fat man with a huge, hanging paunch and his slack-jowled face was a mask of concentrated melancholy as he recited some lugubrious lines, dripping with maudlin sentiment but punctuated by such weird caperings and extraordinary grimaces that he had the audience convulsed with mirth. His favourite trick involved whipping out a bunch of teasles from under the short cassock which he wore and pretending to threaten the nearest spectators with it, and their frantic attempts to dodge him all added to the entertainment.

"Enjoying yourself, sweetheart?"

Deborah turned a rapt and glowing face to his.

"Oh, yes! The fool is so funny! I don't know when I last laughed so much. Thank you, James, for bringing me." She wriggled a little closer to him. Now he was dropping passionate kisses on the veined whiteness of her slender wrist, his moustache tickling the sensitive skin. The fool had gone, followed by the whoops and whistles of the crowd, and Deborah was aware instead of the delicate, sweet notes of a song stealing from the alcove at the back of the stage. She sighed contentedly.

After the Earl's coldness and contempt, it was good to feel suddenly that she was precious to someone, a unique and lovely being to be cared for tenderly. Yet was it, perhaps, too much encouragement to permit him so much freedom the first time they were alone together? Would he think the less of her? No, she told herself, surely not. James was not like that. He would not take advantage of her, he would be patient . . . Suddenly, she was conscious of a glow deep inside her, warm and delicious, such as she had not felt for a long time. It came and went, leaving her filled with an exquisite languor. After all, why worry? Why spoil the moment with a host of ifs and buts? Let things take their course. It was what she had made up her mind to do. For the first time since her marriage she had laughed wholeheartedly, had almost succeeded in forgetting the impossible husband she had let them saddle her with. She was here, with soft music in her ears and a handsome, clever young man by her side who gave every evidence that he adored her. Heavens, what more could she ask?

She was sitting in a trance of well-being, her eyes dwelling idly on the sellers of nuts, apples and other tit-bits as they went their

167

rounds amid a good deal of badinage on both sides, when all at once she had the sensation that she was being watched. Drawn, as though by a lover, she leaned forward.

A man was standing down below with his back to the stage and his head tilted back, staring up at her. For a moment their eyes met, then he turned away casually and Deborah did the same. She told herself that the stranger had probably been looking for someone else and yet, she frowned, there was something unpleasant about him, a look in his eyes that made the flesh prickle on your bones. He did not look the kind of man to have friends among the respectable citizens in the galleries. She risked a second glance and gave a faint gasp of relief. He had gone. Then, as her eye automatically completed its sweep of the crowd, she started and shrank back.

"Dearest, what is it?"

She clutched his arm.

"James, look there – to the right of that pillar, there is someone spying on us! The man in the brown coat."

"I can't see anyone. The playhouse is full of men in brown coats."

"Yes, yes," Deborah insisted, on a rising note of hysteria. "By the post, just inside the door. He's watching us, I tell you."

"Hush now, sweeting. I promise you, there's no one taking any notice of us at all. Look for yourself."

Deborah leaned forward cautiously and scanned the space below. The man had disappeared.

"You're right. He has gone. That's strange." She shivered slightly. "From the way he was looking at me, I could have sworn that he knew me."

"No, really, Deborah. You are letting your imagination run away with you . . . unless — Have you any enemies?"

"Not that I know of."

"That settles it, then. Come, has it not occurred to you that the poor man may simply have been spellbound by your charms?"

Deborah forced a smile.

"Perhaps. Oh, I expect you are right and I am foolish."

"Yes, but so adorably foolish that I've caught the infection. I'm feeling delightfully foolish myself."

Reassured, she allowed herself to be lulled by his compliments into soon forgetting the incident.

·   ·   ·   ·   ·

By the time the play was over and they left the theatre, darkness was already falling.

"May I go with you to Whitehall?" Randolph asked as he thrust a way for her through the crowd of beggars, idlers and pickpockets which collected about the playhouses at the end of every performance.

"Of course you may – if you promise to behave yourself."

For answer, he thrust aside John Strong who had jumped down from the box to hold the door and swung himself after her into the coach.

The vehicle moved off slowly through the crowded streets, followed by James's servant, leading his master's horse.

Inside, with the leather curtains drawn across the window openings, silence reigned for a while between the two young people. Both were breathlessly conscious of the sudden intimacy of their surroundings. Then an unusually violent lurch threw Deborah against James. The sable cloak slipped from her shoulders and, clutching it, they found themselves, velvet and satin, in one another's arms.

Feeling her so close to his heart was enough to break down all the young man's remaining self-control. His hands, under the fur, were round her waist, holding her a prisoner in his passionate embrace, and his face was buried in the scented warmth of her breast.

"My darling, for a month now I have thought of nothing but you, night and day. God's death, I can't go on! Only let me love you," he entreated between kisses.

Love . . . Yes, oh yes! So desperate was her need for love that the agony of longing in his eyes awoke an answering passion in her own. It was so good to sink into a man's arms . . . just how good she had almost forgotten. After all, why fight it? Why deny the imperious demands of her body, the fire in her loins, the exquisite mounting agony . . .

Half-fainting, she closed her eyes and abandoned herself to the mastery of his will.

169

XVII

"My darling . . . my beloved!"

Kicking the door shut, he swept her up in his arms, crumpling the heavy silks of her gown, and whirled her into the room, despite her laughing protests.

"Put me down, Sir! Put me down, I say! You'll frighten Psyche."

The little Italian greyhound which had entered at Deborah's heels was bounding around them, yapping furiously.

"No, James, now that's enough!" Deborah said again, half-smothered by his kisses. "These horrid busks are digging into me."

"That's easily remedied, my fair one! And I'll be your tire-woman."

Without putting her down, he carried her straight into the next room and laid her tenderly down on the bed.

Since he would not for the world have compromised her and yet at the same time could not resign himself to the furtive hazards of occasional stolen meetings, James had found a practical solution to their difficulties. It was too dangerous for Deborah to visit his house at Charing Cross. It was too close to Whitehall and the Countess of Norland too familiar a figure in that area. He had therefore set about moving heaven and earth to find suitable rooms elsewhere and, with the good luck which frequently attends those who are prepared to disburse large sums in gold in its pursuit, succeeded almost at once in finding exactly what they needed. This was a set of rooms in one of the large, many windowed houses blossoming into exotic, turreted frontages which had sprung up in the region of St Bartholomew the Great on land confiscated from the Austin Friars in the reign of Henry VIII. The situation was ideal, being sufficiently removed from Drury Lane and Norland House, close to the country on the one hand and yet within convenient distance of St Paul's and the Strand.

He had brought her there in triumph a week ago and they had inspected its wonders together.

It could not have presented a greater contrast to the sombre grandeur of Norland House and although the taste which informed it was perhaps less sure, the general effect was charming in its lightness and gaiety. The sunny rooms glowed with life, with pale golden oak and hangings of yellow velvet paned and wrought with gold, and exquisite light flowery tapestries. Scattered here and there were delicate cabinets, inlaid stools made of precious woods and frivolous ornaments brought from France and Italy. It became their rendezvous for every afternoon.

The habit, once begun, had grown on them. Deborah would dine at home and sit for a while with her husband, listening submissively to such conversation as he cared to favour her with. Then, when he had left her, John Strong would put the horses to and they would be off, not always by the same route and taking care to observe certain precautions, certainly, although praise God curiosity was not among the Earl's many failings. He never asked questions and, indeed, seemed not to notice whether she was there or not. He was not even, strictly speaking, a complaisant husband. It would have been more correct to say that she had simply ceased to exist as far as he was concerned and he had not the slightest interest in how she chose to pass her days. During the hours of night, it was a different matter, although hours was something of a misnomer for the few, grudging minutes he allotted to the exercise of his conjugal rights over her. Nevertheless, she continued, as in duty bound, to receive him into her bed at the hour of his choice and if anything, she thought, he was a shade more conciliating since that epic row in his apartments. Perhaps he feared a complaint from her to the Queen.

Her afternoons were given to James, her evenings to Whitehall and those brief moments of her nights to the Earl. Of her mornings, at least one every week belonged to the Queen who would summon her, by Mistress Tucker who was delighted, poor woman to parade herself in the presence of her grand niece at Norland House, to attend her in her privy apartments during her hour of dressing. There, Deborah would recount the current court gossip of who was in love with whom and other minor intrigues. On the political side, all was comparative calm, except for the repercussions caused by the trial and condemnation of Mary Stuart whose execution, put off from delay to delay, was being eagerly demanded wherever men were gathered together in talk. This, however, was a subject on which Deborah thought it more tactful not to enlarge. Even within a hairsbreadth of the block, the Queen of Scots seemed to possess the power of winding up her Majesty's nerves to a point of irritation exceedingly wearing on her entourage. From time to time, the Queen would make some inquiry concerning the Earl, but Deborah had nothing suspicious to report of his behaviour and she had the sense to profess herself entirely satisfied with his conduct as a husband. She had no reason to suppose her marital difficulties would possess the least interest for the Queen, or for her own aunt. The only person to whom she might have opened her heart was James but it would have seemed to her somehow indecent to go whimpering to him about such intimate matters. No, when they were together it was far better to forget everything in his arms.

What better haven could she have against the battering of her thoughts? Yet it was stronger than her will and now and then a word would slip out to recall her unhappy situation, and then it was all she could do to smile so as not to distress him. James respected her silence and had never questioned her about her past life but often, as she felt his eyes on her, she hated herself for having so little to give him: kisses and a deep loving kindness seemed a small return for the passionate attachment which he manifested at every moment she was with him.

It seemed to be a source of continued wonder and surprise to him that he could ever have won her at all, and there was nothing he would not do for her to show her how much he cared for her. Each day, he met her with some new, costly surprise. At first she had been inclined to scold him but, very soon realizing that he would have been hurt by her rejection of his gifts, she subsided laughingly under the shower of presents.

Psyche, the little Italian greyhound, had been only the first of these. After her had come a brilliantly feathered macaw all the way from America, rare scents from the Indies and jewels innumerable. This last was something he had not been able to deny himself, although, despite the pleasure it gave him, it was a madness since she could not wear them in public, the emerald drops, the bracelet set with rubies and diamonds, the amethyst ring or the other, a sapphire. Instead, she would put them on with him, in the privacy of their own rooms where all his presents stayed, except for Psyche, for whom she could make some excuse at need and who went everywhere with her.

Today, he had another present for her: a rope of twisted pearls fastened with a diamond clasp. It was a princely ornament and she gazed wonderingly at her reflection as she stood before the mirror, twining it into her hair. Then she turned round and danced over to where he lay on the bed, one hand holding the coiled hair in its net of pearls, the other brandishing the long pin with which she was about to anchor it securely into place.

"James, you give me too much. I've told you so before. You should not spoil me like this." Her eyes teased him. "You'll ruin yourself."

James looked up, raising himself on one elbow to see her better.

"You know," he said, "as I know, that of the two of us mine is the greater happiness. But don't concern yourself for the value of these trinkets. I can well afford them – thanks to those dogs of Spain!"

"Of Spain? What do you mean?"

She was staring at him open-mouthed.

"I forgot – you wouldn't know, of course. So few people do know, in fact. I don't make a point of discussing my affairs." His lip curled faintly. "There is little enough to be gained by it. People are eager enough to tell you about their problems but when it comes to listening to yours – it's like a dialogue of the deaf. Unless, that is, they choose to spread about a garbled version of what you have been fool enough to tell them to all and sundry. Silence is golden, just you remember that. Not, of course, that anything like this applies to you."

"Oh, but I would not want to pry —"

He laughed. "Don't worry. There's no skeleton in my cupboard. The only reason why I've not told you more than I have is simply that the subject never happened to crop up." Springing up, he put his arms round her. "Just now, for instance, I can think of better things to do than waste time telling you that the blood in my veins is not of Tudor or Plantagenet but simply of good Welsh farming stock. My grandfather followed our good Queen's grandfather to London and received a peerage from him."

She laughed back at him, pretending to smack his fingers. "James, be serious for once. Sit down and tell me about it."

"All right, I give in. But very briefly, mind. You've no doubt heard of the trade with the American colonists? Our vessels pick up slaves from the coast of Africa and trade them in the teeth of the Spanish authorities for spices and other precious goods, with a little freebooting thrown in on the way home at his Most Catholic Majesty King Philip's expense. Altogether a risky but highly profitable enterprise, and one much in favour with our good Queen."

173

"Yes, I had heard something of the kind. Go on, James. This is thrilling."

"Not so fast, sweetheart. You aren't looking at any kind of heroic privateer, you know. I merely hold some shares in the undertakings, from which I derive a very easy living."

"How long has this been going on?"

"Eight years. I began when I was twenty and – oh, with hardly a penny to bless myself with. I came to London from Wales to seek my fortune and had the good luck to fall in with a prosperous wool merchant who was in the habit of financing numerous enterprises. To him, I entrusted such little money as I had and the first voyage saw it multiplied five times. After a miracle of that kind there was nothing for it but to persevere. Since then, I have extended my activities somewhat and I can't complain of the results. The fortunes that are to be made in England now – by God, you can't imagine it! And this is only the beginning."

Goodness, it must be nice to be a man! Deborah's fingers itched to hear James talking of all the money it seemed possible to make. When she thought how hard it was for her to make ends meet with the two meagre allowances she received from the Queen and from her husband! There she was cudgelling her brains every month how to meet her dressmaker's bills when with a little intelligence and the willingness to take a calculated risk, neither of which qualities she lacked, one had only to reach out and scoop up the money with both hands. That was the position of women for you! Bound for life, slaves to their husbands' will and with no hope of ever escaping from their mortifying bondage. Masculine solidarity would see to that.

"There," James was saying. "Now you know all about the Honourable James Randolph. Are you disappointed that I've no glorious campaigns in the Low Countries or elsewhere to describe to you?" He was smiling but there was a touch of anxiety underlying his words.

"How can you say such things . . . when you know I like you as you are!" Her face clouded. "I can't bear men who talk of nothing but wars."

Her voice had lost its light note and she crept insensibly closer to him.

"Hold me tight, James," she whispered.

．　　　．　　　．　　　．　　　．

When Deborah emerged into the street, her little dog in her arms, it was already dark. She stared about her, trying to make out John Strong. In a moment there was a rumbling of wheels, heralding his arrival from the side street where he had been waiting as usual.

At that moment, Psyche began yapping furiously and struggling in Deborah's hold. She was pointing in the direction of the adjacent house and as Deborah looked, a dark shadow detached itself from the wall, slipped silently round the corner and disappeared. Telling herself that it was probably only a beggar without a licence who had been alarmed in case Psyche's noise should alert the watch, she scolded the little creature softly and climbed quickly into the coach.

They went out a great deal that month. London seemed full of exciting and fascinating things to do and see, packed with hitherto unknown delights.

To begin with, there were the theatres of which Deborah could not have enough. The memory of her first experience was still fresh in her mind. There was Lady Warwick's masque at which she achieved a flattering success as Diana the Huntress, while for simpler pleasures there was the ever-changing spectacle just round the corner at St Paul's where the fine gallants were to be seen parading their wide galligaskins or Venetian hose, their gold lace and enormous ruffs and their strange sugar-loaf hats. James took her everywhere and showed her all the sights the capital could offer.

Deborah did not doubt that by this time the foetid gossip-factory that was the court was producing rumours by the score as to the identity of the young woman who was so often to be seen in James Randolph's company. Nor did she doubt that, despite the mask she was careful always to wear, there were those who had pierced the secret, but she found it hard to make herself believe that this could really matter. She was always perfectly correct in her behaviour and took care to give no ground for scandal, so what could such escapades prove. She was one among a hundred, she knew that now. How many ladies were there who had never allowed a handsome youth to escort them about the town, even with the consent of their husbands . . . even at the price of a stolen kiss or two . . .? It was accepted practice, almost required, in fact. She would have been a fool not to do it. In any case, the only man who might have any cause to complain was the Earl and he . . .

.   .   .   .   .

"Deborah, are you sure your husband has no suspicions? Oughtn't we to be more careful about meeting?"

They had just returned from St Paul's and Deborah paused to slip off her great fox-furred cloak and cast her muff and her mask on to a chest before replying. Then she looked at him and raised her eyebrows with a little smile.

"He? Dear James, whatever makes you think so? I am the last thing on his mind. He cares for nothing but his books and his dogs and the bunch of old toadies that he gathers round him."

James grasped her elbows and looked into her eyes, seeing the quick flash of bitterness in them.

"Tell me, sweet – I know I swore to myself I'd never speak of this to you, but God's blood, whatever made you wed that dotard?"

Deborah freed herself gently and began to strip off her gloves.

"I shall not tell you that, James. It is a matter between the Earl and myself. That is all."

Undeterred by her tight-lipped, almost hostile expression, James persevered, asking with affectionate concern: "But are you happy? Sometimes I think that —"

"Happy?" She uttered a short, dry laugh. "You can see I am. Deliriously happy. My husband goes his way and I go mine. It is common enough."

Happiness, she thought. Could people talk of nothing else? Was there, in fact, any such thing? Life, her own in particular, was such a messy business. Here she was, with the most charming man in the world at her side and yet, however much she tried, she could not manage to fall properly in love with him. Her heart simply refused, as if it had stopped beating the moment she left Gilford and simply refused to function any more. If only she had met James first, instead of Kit! How different everything would have been! He would not have hesitated for an instant about marrying her. He would not have been content to use her for his present pleasure. His only thought would have been to make her happy . . . Then, as her thoughts revolved in the old circuit, she would wonder whether what James gave her were not, after all, a kind of happiness. With him she felt wonderfully safe and cherished, as if she had nothing to do but live. It was selfish of her, perhaps, because there were times when she felt in danger of forgetting how much she owed him.

Impulsively, she let the gloves fall and running after him as he moved a little away from her, a slightly set look on his face, she flung herself into his arms.

176

"James, my darling, forgive me!" she whispered. "I hate to talk about the Earl and it makes me cross. Of course I'm happy – very, very happy. How could I help it when I have you? Let's not talk about my husband. He does not belong here . . . and remember that for the little time each day I spend with him, we have our whole, lovely afternoons together!"

Later on, she was sitting on the edge of the eloquently ravaged bed fastening her stockings while James stood in his shirt near the window, rummaging in a desk.

"I have this for you."

He came back, holding a small silver enamelled box with a raised design on the lid to represent a perfect, fully-opened flower.

"Oh, what a pretty box! James, you are incorrigible. I ought to scold you. How often have I told you . . . What's inside?" she finished eagerly, her curiosity getting the better of her. She held out her hand.

"Poison."

"Poison!"

Deborah snatched her hand away as though she had been stung.

"Is this a joke?"

"By no means," he answered seriously, opening the box. "Each of these pills contains an infinitesimal dose of poison." He shut the box and laid it in Deborah's lap. Then, possessing himself of her hands, he went on: "Promise me that you will take one every morning when you wake. It is an excellent antidote and one I have used myself for a long time. The body gradually grows accustomed to the toxic substance, without suffering the slightest ill effects, yet if ever —"

"Good God! You terrify me!" She was gazing at him humorously and yet impressed, in spite of herself, by his evident seriousness. "Why should I take these precautions?"

"It does no harm to be prepared. Poison is not so uncommon nowadays, and I shall be easier if I know that you are guarded."

"Aren't you being a little melodramatic?"

"Far from it. I'm surprised you should take it so lightly. In God's name, where were you brought up?"

"I was very well brought up," Deborah retorted, nettled. "I know all about poisons, let me tell you. I could reel you off a list of them by heart . . . wait now . . . Praised be the Lord, first cometh King

Arsenic, and after him the Hemlock, Henbane, Opium which certain Authors claim may be grown with great ease whereby ye may have it ever to hand . . . Thorn-apple, Colchicum, Belladonna which causeth them that drink thereof to suffer strange hallucinations, believing themselves transformed into turkeys, elephants, he-goats and other beasts; the Sardoa which hath a joyous sound for it causeth great laughter and grinning and afterwards death; Aconite, Mandragora, Toad's Venom . . ." Deborah came to a halt for lack of breath. "Whew! That's all I can manage! Have I convinced you?"

"Pooh! That's nothing, a mere beginner's list. There are so many more, newer and more virulent – vitriol, mercury, white lead, verdigris, lead filings and such delightful innovations acquired from abroad. As for the methods of administration – they are legion! I don't wish to bore you, or to frighten you unduly, but you can have no idea of the poisoner's ingenuity. The fact is, my sweet, that most people, far from sharing your delightfully trusting nature, surround themselves with precautions, hence the need for all these subtleties. I have a friend who is a constable and, knowing my interest in the subject, he has made me free of his records from time to time." James shook his head. "It's quite incredible, the diabolical things men and women will be up to. Quite apart from the classic method of slipping poison into a dish of spicy food, there are endless variations, some of them still unsuspected to this day. How many who are thought to have died natural deaths would reveal horrid secrets if we only knew . . . fatal perfumes, poisonous candles, clothes impregnated with poisons, even poisoned saddles and bridles! The slightest scratch and —"

Deborah shuddered and uttered an unconvincing laugh.

"Stop! You're making me shiver. You are in a macabre mood today."

"Realistic, that is all. I intend to make old bones and mean to use every means I may to achieve it. It's better to look a peril in the face than turn one's back on it, whether from stupidity, cowardice . . . or simple ignorance, my love."

"Always supposing that the peril exists, which in my case I do not admit. Good God, who could wish me so much harm?"

"Anyone. The woman who today calls herself your best friend."

"I haven't one. So there you are answered."

"Deborah, please don't be silly. It does not become you. It's odd, in some things you seem to have all the experience in the world and yet in others, you are like a child." He ran his finger along the line of her jaw. "We make ourselves enemies all the time, my dear, without even being aware of it, out of jealousy, envy, spite . . . Take yourself, for instance. Is there a woman at court who has not been put in the shade by your beauty? How many of them would be anything but delighted to see you carried off by some unspecified ailment? So come back to earth and take my word for it that a deadly hatred is very easily aroused. And promise me that you will take my remedy every morning. Promise, you little goose, or else —"

She laughed up at him teasingly: "Or else?"

"Or else I shall ravage that carefully dressed head of yours until you cry quits, and then you will have to do it all over again. Now, promise." He was holding her in his arms and shaking her, half angrily and half in jest.

"Very well. I promise. Now let me go."

She slid out of his grasp and ran to the mirror.

"Oh, you wicked rascal! Look at what you've done to me! Now I shall be late and I told them at Norland House I would be back to see to the final packing of my trunks. Had you forgotten, sir, that tomorrow I go to Greenwich as one of the Queen's ladies in waiting?"

"Damn you, don't take that tone with me. I find it quite alarming."

"Oh, it's only for the time being. I told you. Just for two or three days until Lady Anne is recovered from her fall. All the same, Her Majesty does me a great honour. You will come and see me, won't you? Promise?"

"Promise."

He had come to her now and, neatly removing the last of the pins which held her hair in place, he murmured: "But Greenwich may not have many opportunities to offer so, since the damage has been done, why not profit by it?"

XVIII

The weather was unusually mild for the time of year. The view from the palace windows was a delightful one of green lawns sweeping down to the River Thames and a line of sails, white against green, moving slowly upstream.

Deborah sighed. If it were not for this accursed ankle . . .

She had arrived first thing in the morning, prepared to make a holiday of these few days at Greenwich, and enthralled by the exciting prospect of sharing every moment of the Queen's day. Then, just like that, disaster! She had barely alighted from her horse, had not taken more than a step when she had turned her ankle on an unlucky stone and but for John Strong's ready arm would have fallen, right there in the middle of the great court. For a moment, she had been ready to die of shame, but everyone had been very nice about it. Yet the result was sufficiently trying because she had sprained it and must say good-bye to all the dancing and riding she had been looking forward to so eagerly. Even that, though, took second place to the thing that really mattered which was to perform her duties for the Queen. Fortunately, heaven had been kind and she was able to walk: limping grotesquely and with a good deal of pain, it was true, but still, she could walk. Bandaged hurriedly by her maid, she was even capable of standing for an hour on end with the Queen's heavy sable cloak over her arm while Her Majesty was engaged in conversation with the Lord Admiral Howard a few yards away. The mere thought of it was enough to make her faint, and she remembered the relief with which she had heard Her Majesty turn to address her suddenly, in that unfamiliarly ceremonious voice which she reserved for public utterance: "I shall not need your services for the present, my dear Countess. I am sure you must wish to amuse yourself."

Amuse herself! She had gone straight into the first room she came to, pushed a chair behind a tapestry screen and collapsed into it. Rather than hobble about among the other ladies and become the object of their sympathy, whether feigned or real, she preferred to be alone.

Pulling up her skirt, she glared at the offending ankle and began to explore the bandage with caution. Then her fingers were suddenly still.

The door had creaked and the creak was followed by the sound of footsteps. The door closed softly and a voice that Deborah would have known out of a thousand spoke from the other side of the screen.

"A beautiful morning. Come, Davison."

The Queen and her second Secretary, William Davison. Deborah hesitated, wondering whether to show herself. Her Majesty had a horror of illness, in herself or others, and would not be pleased to find her coddling herself in a corner. Meanwhile, Elizabeth's voice continued:

"See how clear and calm it is. I cannot remember when we had so mild a winter. Faith, we shall have good hunting tomorrow. Are these the papers?"

Deborah shrank back in her chair. She had hesitated too long and now it was too late. She ought to have got up at once and revealed her presence, but now it was better to stay hidden. No one would see her in her nook between the window and the screen.

There was a rustle of papers, punctuated at intervals by the rapid scratching of a pen. Then came a pause. There was silence for a while, then: "What's this?"

"The warrant for the death of the Queen of Scots, Your Majesty."

Mary Stuart's death warrant! Deborah held her breath. Ever since the trial at Fotheringhay and the subsequent conviction and sentence passed on Mary, Elizabeth had been putting off and putting off the moment of execution. Parliament, her ministers, her friends and her people had besought her in vain: so far she had persistently refused to sign the warrant.

Again the pen scratched across the paper.

"God's wounds! The world should know that I have signed this against my will. Take it to the Lord Chancellor. Let it be sealed, Davison, with what dispatch you may. Until which time, I would not have it spoken of." There was a moment's pause and then she added quietly: "I would have it done since it must be so, in the great hall at Fotheringhay, not in the court, for it seems to me more fitting thus."

"It shall be as Your Majesty commands."

Deborah heard a cheerful little clatter which, she assumed, indicated that Davison was collecting together his papers and the writing

181

things, pens, ink and sandbox which accompanied him wherever he went.

"Davison."

"Your Majesty?"

"You may tell Walsingham, but use caution." The Queen laughed suddenly. "The grief of it will go near to kill him outright!"

That the Queen could laugh at all at such a moment proved to Deborah that the decision, once taken, had at least removed the burden from her mind. Grieve Walsingham, who had done his utmost to bring the Scots Queen to the block! That was a joke! Why, it was more likely to have the old fox leaping from his bed of sickness, which was real enough. The idea was not altogether a welcome one to Deborah who could not repress a shudder each time she came face to face with him, although his manner to her was one of unswerving courtesy.

The next sound that reached her was the light tap of the Queen's cork heels moving away, echoed by Davison's heavier tread, and she relaxed a little, knowing that she would soon be able to emerge from her hiding-place. She found that she was trembling in every limb with a curious combination of fright and excitement. Fright predominated. Great heavens! Suppose she had been discovered! She dared not picture the Queen's anger or its consequences. The overhearing of state secrets was never very healthy, but such a secret as this!

She listened and realized that the Queen was talking again but this time there was no trace of any amusement in her voice. It was rather a kind of suppressed agitation, the usual precursor of a storm.

"God's death, I am well served by those who would have me sign this warrant. They clamour for her death but would thrust the odium of it on their Queen who does not desire it. And yet I mind me that these precise fellows swore an oath to ease me of this burden, which now they have forgot . . . Well, go, go, Davison. Your ears are deaf, I know. As for your conscience —" The door clicked shut and Deborah heard no more.

Alone, she rubbed her damp palms together and forced herself to wait patiently for a while longer, meanwhile turning over the Queen's words in her mind.

There could be no doubt that a quick and private end would have been better, both for Mary Stuart and for the Queen. God, what must it be like to wait, day after day, for the headsman's axe? Recalling suddenly the Queen of Scotland's sweet smile, Deborah felt a stirring of something like pity. Pity! That woman deserved none. She had caused too much harm, even to her own people. Painfully dismissing the images of Babington and of poor Jane, and the other memories which came flooding in and threatening to choke her with tears, she rose and put aside the screen.

Next day, as every day, the court hunted. On her return, the Queen seemed on edge. Breaking through the milling throng of courtiers, she strode off to her Withdrawing Chamber, signing Deborah to follow her.

"Run, child, and fetch Master Davison to me. I wish to see him at once."

Deborah ran, as fast as her ankle would let her. She had not slept a wink all night, so busy had her brain been with the news which she had overheard, and now the thought of what this fresh order might portend lent wings to her feet. In a very few minutes, she was back with Davison.

The Queen, who was standing at the window, turned as they came in.

"Master Davison, on reflection I would have you put off the sealing of the paper which I gave you yesterday. It is my wish to consult further of that matter before making my decision final."

"I am sorry, Your Majesty, but the warrant was with the Chancellor yesterday. I gathered Your Majesty desired me to act promptly —" Here Davison broke off and glanced meaningfully at Deborah who was standing a little way away pretending as well as she could for the thudding of her heart to be absorbed in an examination of the Queen's embroidery frame.

Elizabeth, however, appeared to have lost interest in the girl's presence and equally in the Secretary's explanations. She was striding up and down swishing her riding cane and muttering under her breath. Then, without warning, she threw aside the cane and left the room without another word.

A week went by and no more was heard of the warrant which the Queen had signed.

Was it still lying on someone's desk awaiting a further indication of the Queen's pleasure, or had it, perhaps, been put away in a drawer until such time as Her Majesty should suffer another change of mind? And what, indeed, had caused that sudden, apparent change of heart? Deborah could hardly sleep for thinking about it.

On the surface, it was as if nothing at all had occurred. The conversation she had involuntarily overheard might never have taken place and even her idiotic sprain had cured itself almost miraculously, in spite of all her gloomy forebodings. Life was a succession of masques and entertainments and the palace rang with laughter and gaiety.

Deborah filled her lungs with the fresh morning air, breathing in the smell of moist earth from the fields. All round her was a sea of horses, black, roan and grey, all steaming and foam-flecked from the chase. It was over now and for Deborah this was the last time. Tomorrow, February the tenth, Lady Anne who was now recovered would return to take up her duties with the Queen while Deborah went back to London, to Norland House and the Earl, but also to James who, the dear boy, had been growing impatient at her prolonged absence.

This final hunt had been a magnificent run. The stag, a splendid ten-pointer, had led them for mile upon mile over impossible country, strewn with mist-shrouded hollows to the final kill. Deborah's fingers tightened on the reins. The white mist, the imperious cry of the hounds, the headlong pursuit through brake and briar had taken her mind back to other such mornings, riding with Kit in the woods of Gilford, far away to the north of here. A pain that was almost physical clutched at her heart as she thought that Kit had made no attempt to find her, to seek an explanation . . . All that love, and all the time she had been no more than a passing interest! Kicking her mare's flank a little harder than she had intended, she rode forward to take her place in the procession.

They rode through the gate into the great court and into the midst of a scene of almost indescribable confusion. People were everywhere, courtiers and servants running in all directions, waving and shouting and calling aloud to one another. Every door was wide open and still more people were pouring out. It was as though an antheap had been disturbed; as though the whole palace had gone mad.

The hunting party rode forward into the court, their horses' hooves ringing on the stones. The Queen was at their head, followed half a length behind by Lords Howard and Essex.

A sudden, unnerving silence fell and out of it a man stepped forward from a group near the door, a man whose clothes were mud-bespattered and who dropped to his knee before the Queen's white palfrey.

Deborah and those around her were too far away to hear what was said but, unable to bear the suspense, she slipped from the saddle and, giving her reins to Lord Duncan, who happened to be the nearest person, made her way swiftly on foot through the press of people and horses.

"What is it?" she asked a serving man standing nearby.

"The Queen of Scots is dead, my lady. God save the Queen!"

"Dead!" Deborah almost choked on the word. "Dead. What do you mean? For the love of God, how?"

She had grasped the man by the sleeve and was shaking him in an effort to get some sense out of him.

"Why, dead, that's all. Her head struck off on the block. The messenger is come straight from Fotheringhay. Four and twenty hours in the saddle! They say the streets of London are like a fair day . . . It's a great day for England, no mistake. If you listen hard you'll hear the bells from here."

But Deborah had heard enough.

So it was all over with Mary Stuart and the bells whose clamour she could hear indeed borne faintly to her ears were sounding the knell of the Catholic cause in England. The people must be lighting bonfires for joy in the streets of London. England could sleep in peace at last, free from the daily fear of an attack on the Queen's life and free from the hideous threat of civil war. Tears welled up in Deborah's eyes. She wanted to laugh and cry at once, anything to express the feeling which threatened to overcome her. Thanks be to God, and to the Queen who in her wisdom – Deborah started suddenly. The Queen! But surely she had declared her intention of rescinding the order?

Her eyes searching the crowd, some of whom had now dismounted and were embracing one another on foot in a frenzy of excitement, Deborah saw that Elizabeth had disappeared. In a moment she had picked up her skirts and was forcing her way through the mêlée, leaving the man she had been talking to staring after her in astonishment. At the door of the Privy Chamber she ran into Mistress Tucker.

"The very person!" was her aunt's greeting as she drew the girl into the room. "You may be able to calm Her Majesty. She's like one possessed – and all through the fault of that Master Davison."

"Davison! Aunt, whatever do you mean?"

"You'll have heard the good news, I dare say? Well, what do you think? It was all done behind Her Grace's back. Not that she hadn't signed the warrant, you understand, but only to have it by her, in reserve, as it were. Then along comes Davison without a by-your-leave and goes and hands it to Lord Burghley and to Walsingham, and they, of course, can't wait to send it off to the Queen of Scots, and the headsman from London along with it. And a good thing too, say I, but Her Majesty's very far from pleased. Sweet Jesus, what a tantrum! You go to her, child. I've done all I can!"

Taking her courage in both hands, Deborah walked through into the Withdrawing Chamber.

The Queen, still in her riding dress, was standing in the middle of the floor. Her face, always pale, was perfectly livid and she was wringing her hands convulsively. Two of her women cowered against the far wall, holding a long, black velvet gown, while scattered on the floor lay the evidence of Elizabeth's rage; the hat trimmed with pheasants' feathers which she had worn that morning, her riding cane, her gloves and her fox-furred cape.

It was cold in the room, despite the sunshine outside, and taking one look at the Queen's fixed, unseeing eyes Deborah bent and picked up the cloak.

"You are cold, Your Majesty. Let me put this round you," she said quietly.

"Green!"

Deborah recoiled before the violence in the Queen's voice and dropped the cloak.

"You bring us green? When our dear sister is no more and while our heart yet weeps for that which cannot be undone?" Striding to where the women still stood by the wall, Elizabeth of England snatched the black gown from their hands and put it on. Then, clutching the heavy folds about her, she began to prowl in circles around the petrified Deborah.

"Thus it is to be betrayed by one's own council! How dared they act without my authority! God's wounds, are they such coxcombs as to go to work behind my back?" The Queen's voice swelled and throbbed with anger, then died away to a long sigh. "It is true, alas, that our cousin's life was perilous to our own, as true as it is that in my place she would not have hesitated . . . Poor princess, her good sense was never strong. God's death, but I have sense in plenty and I know the consequence of this day's work. Once let the world know that a crowned head is not unassailable but may be brought to answer

186

for its crimes before the law and you strike a blow at the divine right and pave the way for future bloody revolution. It is not a thing for which I would be answerable to posterity. What a page of history have my councillors written for me this day! Elizabeth and Mary Stuart have become the executioner and her victim. Yet as God hears me, I have done everything humanly possible to save her, from herself and from her demons of pride, at the risk of my own life, because it was grievous to me that one of her own sex, estate and kin should be consenting to her death. And now our situations are reversed and I her judge am become the accused – accused before generations yet to come of a death I did not desire."

She ceased, as though overcome with grief. And yet, Deborah was left wondering, was it true? Had she really not desired it? She had certainly tried more than once, against all advice, to help her prisoner. The message which Deborah herself had carried to Chartley was proof enough of that. The tears she shed now should be genuine, the compassion of one woman for the misfortunes of another, and yet . . . Scraps of the conversation she had overheard between the Queen and William Davison ran in Deborah's mind: the reference to the place of execution, the hint that some more private way of death should be found. No, there could be no doubt that a part of the Queen's mind, the royal part, had been compelled to desire Mary Stuart's death for the good of the realm. But if that were the case, why this display of magnificent indignation? Davison, Burghley, Walsingham had done no more than anticipate necessity in taking from her shoulders the burden of an inevitable step, acceding to a reluctance which she had made clear to her secretary. Then, why?

It came to her in a flash, the reason why. Now all was clear, neat and logical: the shock, the fury and indignant rage had all been part of a clever performance. There could be no other explanation. It was the performance of a great queen, a brilliant piece of strategy designed to shift the blame from her own person and throw it on to others and so preserve her people. Oh, wonderful princess!

The Queen had paused in her stride and was standing by the window, looking out. When she spoke again it was as though to herself.

"We princes are set on a stage in the sight of all the world; a spot is soon spied in our garments, a blemish quickly noted in our doings. God's wounds, the world shall find none in our mourning robes! We shall defend ourselves against the charge of this death.

187

Send for the ambassador of our cousin of Valois and we shall remind him that France is in no state to make new enemies on so slender an excuse. As for young Master James —" The Queen gave a harsh crack of laughter. "A little gold will make him forget he ever had a mother! Let them all come and we shall show them who is Elizabeth of England."

The tall figure in the black robe stood up proudly, outlined against the bright gold of the sunlight outside the window and Deborah found herself moved suddenly almost to tears by the lonely, pathetic greatness before her.

"God save Your Majesty," she said in a choked voice. "Blessed be His name for giving us so great a queen."

On a sudden impulse of affection she went to the Queen and, kneeling at her feet, carried the hem of the black velvet robe quickly to her lips.

For the first time, the Queen seemed to notice her presence. Her hand patted Deborah's shoulder and she said: "I thank you, child. For your words and for your loyalty which warms my heart. At this moment I know that all my people speak to me through your mouth, to aid and comfort me in this ordeal. Go, now. And tell Tucker to have Davison and Burghley sent for. Our sister is no more but those guilty of her death may not go unpunished."

The momentary gentleness had gone from her voice and anger, like a mask, had resumed possession of a face grown suddenly more lined. And above the black gown, the flaming red wig seemed to mock at grief.

XIX

"Who are you smiling at, sweetheart?" James asked her softly. Deborah laughed.

"Don't be jealous. I was thinking about the Queen. How brilliantly she set down those in Europe who presumed to question our affairs."

She was standing with James and a number of other gentlemen, waiting for the servitors to finish setting up the tables and laying out the cards.

"Yes, by God! Our lioness is worth all the princes of Europe put together! How she routed them! I'd never have imagined she could feel so for the Scottish Queen – and neither could poor Bellièvre. As French ambassador he was left without a word to say! In any case, it's my belief his protest was a mere matter of form. The Valois has his own troubles, without putting himself out to avenge Mary Stuart. As for poor old Burghley – you'd think he should be used to it by now but they say he very nearly cried when she rated him. But it's Davison I'm sorry for. I suppose they'll let him out of the Tower one day but I should think it's the end of his career. No, on the whole, it's Spain that worries me. I think we may hear more from that quarter by and by. Already, there are rumours . . . but come, they are ready for us now."

Whitehall Palace, deserted during the court's absence at Greenwich, was itself again. The Presence Chamber was crowded and although there was no dancing in deference to the Queen's mood, everyone there seemed determined to enjoy themselves and seek whatever entertainment offered. The palace was alive with a colourful surge of silks and satins, ribbons, laces, feathers and jewels, with white bosoms and luxuriant whiskers.

Deborah, smiling graciously on all and sundry, found her glance turn to ice as it alighted on one person. Penelope, Marchioness of Gilford, was conducting a desperate flirtation with a youthful gallant in lemon yellow satin and the two women determinedly ignored one another. Penelope had not yet forgiven her rival for

189

the desertion of her former admirer. Deborah's hatred on the other hand was purely instinctive.

She sat down and James Randolph took his stand behind her.

The game was Primero. Deborah laid down a heap of gold coins and picked up her cards. Seven of spades, the six, the knave and ten of clubs, that would do nicely. Carefully concealing her hand, she glanced round at her opponents.

They were four in number. Facing her on the other side of the table were Diccon and Charles Wilson, the identical twin sons of Sir Robert Wilson. They were as alike in character as in looks, being both blond and brawling, a pair of roaring boys who hunted together and did not care who knew it. It was common knowledge, for example, that little Dorothy Landsmere, the old baron's very youthful wife, who was now wriggling and giggling in her seat with Charles's hand lying carelessly in her lap would end the evening in some quiet corner with Diccon. It was equally certain, too, that in a week or so the child-bride's charming ears would boast a brand new pair of ear-rings in place of the rather meagre garnets which had been her wedding gift from her husband. One orient pearl apiece was the invariable parting present of the Wilson twins.

On Diccon's left was Harry Culham, tall and gangling with a pleasant, ugly face, and facing him, Timothy, Lord Stenway, plump and jaunty in plum-coloured brocade flourished before with diamonds, of whom it was said that each one of his glittering suits represented a portion of his inheritance. Timothy was a comparative newcomer to London where he had quickly acquired a reputation as a frequenter of The Rose, one of the best known inns in the capital. He hazarded vast sums at Primero, got deeply into debt with his tailor and paid for these extravagances by getting into the hands of moneylenders, offering as security the rich Welsh acres which his father had not so far had the good taste to die and leave to his unfettered use. By the time the old man did die, it looked as if there would be precious little left, but for the present he was beaming cheerfully at Deborah and she returned his smile.

She was feeling full of confidence, knowing that she was looking her best in a new dress, copied from a French model, of black velvet and quilted crimson silk, its hanging sleeves tied with ribbon bows and lined with ermine. She felt a tingle of excitement at the back of her neck and looked up to exchange a knowing wink with James as she drew her winnings towards her.

They played together as a team, which was not uncommon

practice: he staked them, she put their luck to the test and then they shared the winnings. Any losses were gallantly borne by the man.

It was now Deborah's turn to deal. She did so with speed and competence, four to each player, and then, in accordance with the rules of the game, laid the knave of hearts on top of the pack before reaching for her cards. As she did so there was a loud burst of laughter from across the room and, glancing up, she saw a bunch of feathered hats advancing through the onlookers gathered round the table. Her mind registered: "Essex and his crowd." The next moment she was deep in the play which this time was definitely going well: four spades, a flush.

A clear, resonant voice spoke at her side.

"Come, let me present you to the Countess of Norland, the most exquisite ornament of the court – after our divine Gloriana, of course. She is cruel, alas, but so enchanting that she will make you her slave, like the rest of us."

Deborah smiled inwardly, thinking how charming Essex could be when he liked. Not that she encouraged him. Oh, by no means. That, it was very clear, was a royal prerogative and a wise woman would take care not to be seen flirting with him. Besides, for all the glamour which surrounded him, there was a hint of instability which put her off. At one moment he would be full of fun and gaiety, ready for any larks; at the next gloomy and depressed. Today, it appeared, was one of his good days.

She laid down her flush calmly and looked up with a smile of triumph. Then she saw him.

His black hair and dark face stood out strongly among the fair heads watching the game. For the space of a breath, their eyes met and a spark of pure amazement sprang up in the newcomer's and as quickly died.

To Deborah, struggling to keep her head and fight off the panic which was threatening to overwhelm her, it seemed as if every person in the room was looking at her and must be able to read in her face what lay between them. Hardly aware of what she was doing, she bowed to Essex and murmured some commonplace remark. Then Essex was speaking again.

"Adorable Countess, permit me to present Lord Christopher Belstone, a gentleman whom I am proud to call my friend. Kit, the Countess of Norland."

"My lord."

He bowed, expressionless.

"I am honoured, Lady Norland." Then, speaking to Essex although his eyes were still on her, he went on: "I confess, you have not misled me. The Countess is indeed ravishing, although not, I dare hope, so unkind as you have made her out to be."

It was not true. It must be some dreadful nightmare. This could not be the same man in whose arms she had known such fathomless bliss, not this stranger with the indifferent, worldly voice and manner! Yet when she offered her hand and felt his lips brush the back of it she knew, from the tremor which ran through her, that this was real.

He exchanged a few words with James and with the Wilson brothers, then, with another bow to her, he said: "I must beg you to excuse me, Lady Norland. I see Lady Gilford beckoning me."

The other players were waiting a shade impatiently for the game to be resumed. Deborah handed her cards to James.

"Be a dear," she said, "and play this hand for me. I am a little tired."

That game ended, James bent over her solicitously.

"What is it, sweeting? You look quite pale. Would you rather I took you home?"

"No, no thank you, James. It's nothing to worry about. Only a slight headache."

Why did he have to question her? Surely he could see, if he loved her, that she had just suffered a terrible emotional shock? Couldn't he tell that she was on the verge of taking hold of the table and upending it in their stupid, grinning faces as they sat there all of them, laughing and joking while she was in despair? She wanted to spit in their faces, she wanted to scream out loud. . . . Couldn't he tell from the trembling of her lips how fierce was her desire to run after Kit and throw herself into his arms? Was he blind? In a second, she was ashamed of herself. Poor James, it was not fair to take it out on him. She glanced sidelong at him, wondering if perhaps he had not, after all, seen more than she gave him credit for. He was usually the keenest of players, yet now he seemed to be paying scant attention to the game. He placed his bets automatically and his eyes were frowning, his mouth set in a grim line.

They sat like that for three more mortal hours. More than once, Deborah was on the point of getting up and leaving but she did not go. Instead, she stayed riveted unwillingly to her seat, outwardly absorbed in the play, inwardly suffering torments because she could not help stealing secret glances at what Kit was doing.

It was not hard to guess what Penelope was pouring into his ears, casting malevolent glances at herself and James all the while. She would leap at the chance to spread a little bit of scandal. But was it revenge that made him look at Lady Aldhurst in that particular way, or just habit? Certainly, whichever it was, it was having its effect on the fair Cynthia. Her black eyes were gleaming and she was bridling and cooing and showing herself off to, Deborah had to admit it, her very best advantage. Trollop! She might as well strip naked while she was about it! It was positively indecent, the way she was ogling him and preening herself like a bitch in season! Now she was giggling and putting both arms round Kit's neck and he had clasped her to him and was kissing her. Deborah dug her nails into her palms. How could he be so base, make such an exhibition of himself before her very eyes? Had he forgotten that she loved him? The fact that it was she who had left him, and the imagined grievances which she had built up afterwards had all vanished from her mind. She was aware of nothing but the pangs of agonizing jealousy. She wanted to fall on that panting hussy and tear off her clothes, to rend that milk-white skin and trample that victoriously smiling face under her feet and, just at that moment, she would willingly have bartered all her hopes of heaven to achieve it.

Instead, she was obliged to smile and look as if she were enjoying herself and reassure James who would keep asking her anxiously every five minutes: "Are you really all right, dearest? You're quite sure? You've only to tell me, you know, and we'll leave at once."

His tender concern very nearly drove her mad.

She hated herself for treating him like this and yet how could she turn round now and tell him: "No, dear. I was lying to you. I am suffering horribly, I have a galloping fever, my heart is thudding, my hands are sweating, my throat feels tight and my knees weak. Thank you for being so concerned about me but there is nothing you can do to help. Shall I tell you the only thing that will cure me? I want that gentleman to make love to me – the one sitting over there in the window flirting madly with Lady Aldhurst." So, as she could not say any of that, she was doing her best to allay his anxiety by loving smiles which seemed to burn her lips.

She relaxed her clenched hands. Kit had got up to go. There was a burst of laughter and farewells and then he was half-way across the room. In a moment he would be gone. Deborah rose, all hesitation gone.

"Wait for me, James. I'll be back in a second."

193

"What's the matter, Deb?"

"Nothing . . . nothing at all." Why couldn't he be quiet? She forced herself to sound unconcerned. "I'm just going to stretch my legs. For heaven's sake pay attention to the game, dear, or I might find myself having to stand half your losses!"

She strolled, without hurrying, to the end of the room and peered into the gallery. It was in semi-darkness and, for the moment, deserted. At the far end, walking with long strides, Kit was almost out of sight. Still at the same regal pace, her silks and velvets billowing gracefully about her, Deborah entered the gallery but no sooner was she sure of being out of sight of the room behind than she bent and whipped off her slippers with their high, cork heels and gathering her skirts in both hands ran in her stockinged feet as fast as she could go.

"My lord!"

He stopped, searching the half-darkness to see who had called.

A second later and she had reached him, breathless and scarcely able to stand, her face clearly visible in a shaft of moonlight from one of the long windows.

"You!"

"Kit, I wanted . . ." She was stammering in her eagerness.

"It does not seem to me, madam, that we have anything to say to one another."

"Oh no, oh, please, don't! I must speak to you," she managed to say, chilled by the coldness in his voice.

"On what subject, pray? Your aged husband, or your youthful lover? I have no possible interest in either. Good night to you, madam."

He had turned to go but she clung to him sobbing. He freed himself but as he plucked her hand from his arm he held it for a moment in his own.

"If I were you, Countess, I should get rid of that topaz. It clashes oddly with your diamonds."

Releasing her, he raised his hat briefly and was gone. Deborah stood with her hand pressed to her cheek as if she had received a blow and watched the darkness of the palace swallow him.

XX

After a sleepless night spent weeping into her pillow to an accompaniment of subdued, mournful howls from Psyche, Deborah made up her mind what she must do.

She got up very early and summoned her maid.

"Run and tell John Strong to have the coach ready. Then come back and dress me," she said tensely. Then she bathed her swollen eyes and after studying herself attentively in her mirror decided that she looked a fright. Black rings round her eyes, a smudged complexion and grey lips: it was dreadful, truly dreadful. Well, that settled it. Much as she loathed the fashionable habit of slapping paint all over one's face, today was an exception. A little cream and powder wouldn't hurt for once. She rummaged among the selection of pots, unopened for the most part, which she kept in her cabinet, rouged her cheeks with care, dabbed on some powder and did a neat repair job on her eyes with a little green paint. Then she coiled up her hair swiftly.

That done, she seated herself at her small desk and taking a sheet of perfumed paper from a cedarwood box, wrote a few lines and sealed them.

Next, with her maid's assistance, she slipped on one of her plainest dresses, a simple crane-coloured fustian trimmed with parchment lace. Pausing only to add a mantle of the same fabric, she pulled the furred hood round her face without a glance in the mirror, snatched up Psyche and ran quickly down the stairs.

John Strong was waiting for her.

"Essex House, and quick as you can, John!"

Seated in the coach, she offered up a silent prayer of thankfulness that it was possible to drive to the Strand. In this drizzling rain, she would have been soaked to the skin if she had tried to ride while to have ordered out her litter would have been a waste of precious time.

She was proud of the litter which was an exceptionally pretty one done up in murrey velvet but she did not in actual fact use it so very

195

often. Litters were slow and eminently respectable and for any normal journey no one active enough to sit a horse or rich enough to own a coach would surely wish to travel in one. No, where a litter was ideal was for a lazy morning's outing with nothing much to do but gaze about one at the throb and bustle of London.

This morning, however, Deborah's purpose was anything but idle. She had, in fact, a quite definite objective: the residence of the young Earl of Essex.

She looked up just in time to see the tall, three-storeyed building come in sight beyond the bare trees of the garden on her left. She leaned out.

"Stop!" she called to John Strong on the box. He pulled up at once and jumped down. Deborah handed him the note she had written earlier.

"Take this and give it to the porter. You are to wait for an answer."

After what seemed to her an endless wait although it was not in reality more than a few minutes, Deborah saw John coming back.

As so often happens when a moment approaches which has been looked forward to with a tense mixture of hope and fear, all her doubts seemed to vanish suddenly. She was going to see him, at last she would be able to explain to him . . . For the umpteenth time, she went over in her mind the contents of the brief note she had sent him:

"My dear Kit, We cannot part like this. I pray you, give John Strong word of where we may meet and whatever time may be convenient to you. Your most loving Deborah."

She had made sure that it was neither tearful nor melodramatic. Men hated that; his kind of man more than any.

She had a moment more of hope and uncertainty to live through. Oh, John, John, you clumsy oaf, can't you move any faster? As quickly as she could she ran through all the comforting thoughts which had occurred to her in the past twelve hours. Good God, it was only natural that he should have greeted her coldly and so she would have known if she had an ounce of common sense in her. After all, it was she who had left him! Had she really any right to expect him to fall at her feet? Even supposing he were that kind of man. She sighed inwardly. As for his rudeness, the hostility in his manner, surely that was the best proof that he still had some feeling for her? Would he have treated her so if she had been nothing more to him than an agreeable interlude? Surely not. He would have been gallant, chatty, inclined to be amused at their meeting again and pleased that his former mistress should be so well established, with a disposition probably to resume kindly relations with her. That was how it was when a man felt nothing for a woman beyond the pleasure to be gained from bedding her. No, she could not be mistaken. Everything in Kit's attitude made it crystal clear that he had lost none of his feeling for her. . . .

John Strong was standing by the door.

"Well?"

"There was no answer, my lady."

"What do you mean, no answer? There must have been an answer! You were mistaken, you dull-witted clown!" She was almost screaming at him.

John Strong stared back at her, red-faced but undeterred.

"Why, as to that, I'm sorry, but when I'm told no, I understand no. Aye, and yon bottle-nosed porter fellow'd no call to come his airs wi'me neither. 'No need for you to call again, my lad,' says he, 'for the door's not to be opened to you. By order of his lordship,' says he! Why, Miss Deb! Whatever is it? Are you ill?"

She did not seem to hear but sat staring fixedly ahead, like one dead. Big John put out his hand and clapped her awkwardly on the shoulder.

"There, there, what is it now? Tell your old John, can't you? Given me a fair old fright, you have. What was in that damned letter to make you like this?"

Still she did not move. The little dog crouched whimpering in her lap.

John gaped at her perplexedly for a moment longer then a look of slow enlightenment came over his face and, as though he had thought of something, he sprang up to the box and returned bearing a flask.

"Here, drink this. There's nowt like a sup to put fresh heart into you."

He put the flask firmly to Deborah's lips and she swallowed, choked and seemed to come to herself again.

"Thank you, John," she said weakly, pushing the flask away. "What would I do without you?" She gave him a pallid smile and put up her hand to stroke Psyche who was now standing on her lap and trying to lick her face.

"Are you sure you're better now?" John asked anxiously.

"Yes, yes . . . I was just a little faint, that's all. I – I haven't slept

197

well. I know what will do me good. Let's go for a long drive – anywhere, no matter where."

Yes, she thought a little bitterly as she watched John's face clear and felt the little dog settle, reassured, on her knee, it is all very well for them. For them everything has gone back to normal and we can all be nice and cosy again. Oh, how easy it would be if one were a tiny dog, sure of one's daily portion of love and affection, with no problems and no heartache!

John was back on the box now. His whip cracked and the coach moved on. Inside, Deborah flung herself down among the cushions and cried.

He had sent her packing, like any whore! Oh God! After all the love there had been between them, the passion and the unforgettable hours they had spent together, for it to end like this, in scornful rejection, a refusal even to see her, the door shut in her face! She felt as if she were going out like a candle, a tiny lamp flickering on the edge of darkness. Her last hope was gone. She had ruined everything. She had lost Kit for the second time and she was bitterly able to estimate now how poor and feeble a thing in comparison was the feeling she had for James.

What was there left to look forward to? Oh, lots of things, no doubt, lots of splendid things that would make most people happy! Hadn't she herself longed eagerly to be rich, titled, a person of note whose beauty and the wealth which set it off would make her the cynosure of all eyes?

She had only to think of Gilford and the halcyon time which she had spent there to realize just how futile, how pointless and unrewarding was the glittering life of the court. It was padded with every luxury that money could buy, with wit and gallantry and foolish laughter, but it was not real life. Well, Penelope, Cynthia and their like might be satisfied to fill their days with superficial praise and short-lived romance, they had pride of birth and vanity of person to sustain them. But was she going to become as they were, passed from hand to hand, the subject of bawdy comments and comparisons, sly innuendos and public discussion? The thought made her shudder, and yet she told herself with revulsion that she might come to it with the rest, while her true self was eroded bit by bit, corrupted with vice until she was no more than any other proclaimed harlot.

Why, why had Kit re-entered her life? Why must he come to trouble the quiet content which James Randolph had given her? In time, who knew, she might have come to feel a real love for him, might have built up for herself a kind of tepid and self-centred happiness between a devoted lover and a husband who was at least bearable. But now! Now that Kit had come back, now that she had lived through that dark night of despair, she could not doubt how unworthy a compromise it was. What had she to give James in return for his adoration? Her kisses, a few indulgent smiles, a little tenderness, but nothing of the fire which consumed her when she only looked at Kit. And was she going to give up that passion, go on trying to break the spell and immerse herself in the tawdry and secondrate, just like that, without a struggle, only bewailing her lot? She snorted. Good God, had she blood in her veins? The Countess of Norland might be a milk-and-water ninny good for nothing but weeping, but surely Deborah Mason had been made of sterner stuff? Why, instead of those timid, measured words, had she not cried her love to him? Had she even told him she still loved him? No! He might have thought that she had run after him in search of a quick kiss, or even to edify him with the story of her success and display her new-won glory for his gaze!

She sat up and wiped her eyes, then blew her nose vigorously and, cradling Psyche in her arms, leaned back and closed her eyes, thinking.

Some moments later, she rapped on the panel.

"John! Stop here — No, over there, by that piece of waste ground, and come down."

There followed a brief but violent jolting, then John Strong appeared in the doorway.

"Aye, m'lady?"

"John, do you know to whom that letter was addressed?"

"Can't say as I do. I'm not much of a reading man."

"You remember Lord Christopher?"

"It's not likely I'd forget his lordship, is it?"

"Well, he's here, in London. That letter was to him."

"Eh? Then I don't rightly see what all the fuss is about, if you'll pardon my saying so. Seemed to me as you and his lordship were . . . well . . ." John broke off uncomfortably.

Deborah sighed. "It would take too long to explain it all, John," she said. "But because I have no secrets from you, I will try. Well, you see, the long and short of it is that Lord Christopher knows all about it . . . the Earl, that is, my husband . . . James . . . you see?" She was stammering incoherently by this time.

John scratched his head, his face scarlet with embarrassment at this revelation.

"I see, Miss Deb," he said vaguely, forgetting as he always did in moments of stress that she was no longer the small girl he had known.

"Now," Deborah went on hurriedly to avoid further explanations, "here's what I want you to do. You will take me home now and then change out of your livery and go back to Essex House, pretending to be an ordinary idler. There are bound to be plenty of people about in the yard and it ought not to be difficult to get hold of one of them. I want you to find out, without appearing to ask too many questions, all about his lordship's habits. I want to know what time he gets up, when he goes out . . . He often stays there and anyone should be able to tell you. But you must be careful, do you understand that?"

"You can rely on me, Miss Deb." John nodded eagerly. Now that he had something definite to do he was beginning to recover his wits. "I'll worm it out of one of them, devil I don't." He winked appallingly. "And at need, there's my little flask, you know, the one I gave you to sup from just now. With that up my sleeve I warrant you I'd make the bishop himself talk."

"You're a rogue, John."

Blushing at this praise, John said: "I can't bear to see you grieve, lass. Besides, I've a soft spot for his lordship meself."

Two days after this, at about eight in the morning, a trim maid-servant, very neat in grey frieze and white linen, tripped past the porter's lodge at Essex House. The porter, a big, beefy individual, broke off the argument he was holding with a group of his cronies to intercept her.

"You there, wench, where d'ye think you're going?"

"To speak to my lord Christopher Belstone, if you'll kindly show me where to go," she answered with a smile.

"I'faith, I'd be glad to show you the way myself, sweetheart," he answered with an oily chuckle. "But not so fast. Tell me first who sent ye?"

"My mistress, my lady of Gilford sent me, with a message for my lord."

"Did she so?" he said, looking at her with sudden attention. "Then you'll be a new waiting woman of hers, eh? Oh, don't take it

200

amiss, girl. Your little face is a sight easier on the eyes than that frump-faced bezom we've had before this."

The maidservant giggled. "Ooh, Master Porter! Now do, please, tell me where to find my lord. My lady stays for me and I shall be scolded."

"Never fret, sweet maid. Here's one will take you. Sam!" He hailed a passing footman. "Take this pretty poppet to Lord Christopher – from my lady Penelope."

"Thank you for your help, Master Porter."

The girl bobbed a laughing curtsy.

"It's a pleasure, my dear." The man's eyes lingered on the youthful figure. "Now, if ever you've a moment to spare, just you come along and see old William, that's my name, William Doggett —"

"Yes, yes, but I must hurry."

The porter watched her trip away after the manservant and spoke gloomily to his sniggering cronies.

"There she goes . . . they're all the same. Fall over backwards for a lord, they would, soon as look at him." He spat delicately on the ground, then cupped his hands round his mouth to call after the footman:

"And no dawdling on the way, you young devil!"

An immense hall, a stone staircase, the famous gallery hung all about with precious tapestries of which all London was talking, a long, dark passage, seemingly endless, then, at last, a minute antechamber and a heavy door. Her guide stopped and knocked.

"Yes?" A man's voice spoke from inside.

"So please you, my lord, there's a woman come from my lady Penelope."

"Let her come in."

She went in and closed the door carefully behind her. Lord Christopher was seated at a table, writing.

"One moment," he said, without looking up.

She leant back against the door, her eyes following his every move.

He finished his letter calmly, reread it, sanded the sheet and blew on it to clear the last grains away before folding it. As he picked up the wax and held it to the lighted candle which stood before him on the table, he said: "There. Just let me set the seal to this and I shall be with you."

He glanced up as he finished speaking and the wax fell from his hand. He sprang to his feet with an oath, pushing back his chair, and strode across the room to stand before her.

"You again! I might have guessed it! Have I not made it clear to you, Deborah, that there is nothing more between us? What is this absurd disguise?"

She stared back at him, her face very pale.

"It was the only way to reach you, since you will persist in running away from me." She moved forward, beseeching. "Oh Kit, why do you treat me like this? Why? It must be some misunderstanding."

"Misunderstanding? I wish you will tell me how that is possible!" he said sardonically. He had his temper under control now and had moved a step back from her.

"Why, your whole attitude . . . everything you have said . . . I know I . . ." She was stammering now, all her self-possession drained away now that he was there, in front of her.

"God's death, my girl!" he broke in cuttingly. "It's time someone told you a few home truths, I think! After that you will oblige me by getting out of my sight and staying out." He laughed shortly. "Not that I imagine you'll want to do much else. No doubt you value fulsome praises above honest truth." He eyed her with contempt. "You have acted ignobly by me, Deborah."

"Let me —"

He raised his hand. "Oh, I am not talking of the Earl of Norland whom you no doubt seduced with your pretty face and your cajoling ways. Or of poor Randolph who was probably an easy prey. I don't give *that* for either of them." He snapped his fingers in her face.

"But Kit, I can explain —"

"Oh no! Spare me, I beg, the sordid details of your amours." The hoarse revulsion in his voice belied the forced lightness of his earlier tone.

Deborah's hand went to her mouth. She stared at him blindly for a moment before she reached out gropingly towards him, as though driven by some instinctive impulse.

"No, insult me if you like, but let me defend myself at least. I – I love you, Kit – I —"

Savagely, he thrust her off and, staggering, she lurched against a cabinet and clung to it to save herself while he advanced on her with clenched fists.

"Are you trying to catch me again with your lies? Do you think I haven't seen right down to the bottom of your tawdry little soul?

202

I let myself be caught once, I admit, by your innocent, simple airs. I thought then you were different, a real woman, and with a man's honesty at heart." He uttered a harsh, grinding laugh. "Now, just between ourselves, you made a fine fool of me, didn't you? Nice and relaxing, a rest cure in the country with a good man thrown in. God's wounds! And a little touch of love where none existed adds a spice, does it not? Then, when you tire of the game, it's hullo, good-bye, and off in search of other entertainment more in keeping with your nature. Money, titles and social chatter!" He paused for breath, glaring at her. "You're nothing but a grubby little hypocrite, Deborah. It is that I can't forgive, shall never be able to forgive. You played with my feelings and now you want to do it again. Well, I'm afraid you have miscalculated there. I am not to be caught twice in that snare! Oh, you need not look so tragic. There are plenty more who will gladly be taken in by you, dear Countess, for the chance to slip between your sheets! Now, please go and leave me in peace."

He was already half-way to the door but Deborah was quicker. She flung herself across it, barring his way, her bosom heaving. He did not pause in his stride and there was an ugly look about his mouth.

"What? Haven't I given you enough to think about? Don't be a fool. Go. What more do you want?" He began to laugh softly, as though he had thought of a new way to hurt her. "Can it be that your fine court gallants do not satisfy you? Is it for that you have come begging at my door? Is there not man among them all to calm your itch? Alack, fair temptress, you will have to pardon me. Today I am not in the vein. Another time, perhaps, when I am more at leisure."

Her palm made contact with his face with a sound like a whip-crack. He caught her arm but she fought free of him and retreated to the other end of the room, her eyes flashing and her nostrils quivering.

"And now, Lord Christopher Belstone, it is my turn to tell you what I think of you!"

She was boiling with all the anger and indignation so long held in check. All that her pride had suffered in the past three days re-volted suddenly. Nothing mattered to her now but to pour out her heart in bitterness, to throw his insults back into his sneering face. So angry was she that if there had been a weapon to hand she would undoubtedly have used it on him.

"I hate you," she snarled. "I hate you! You disgust me! How

203

dare you treat me so? By what right? No" — as she saw him bearing down on her — "no, you shall not throw me out! You shall hear me! You have given me your version of what I did and felt but has your self-centred mind given one thought to your share in it?"

"What nonsense is this? I warn you —"

"Let me speak." She could scarcely get the words out. "Back there, at Gilford, you were the first, weren't you? Whatever else you may pretend, that, at least, you'll not deny! You can't say I cheated you there! That was something you left out of your grand speech, wasn't it? What's one maidenhead more or less to a man of quality like you. It has the charm of novelty, perhaps, but nothing more! Did you ever think what it meant to me? I loved you from that moment. Believe it or not, I don't care! I loved you desperately." Her voice broke. "So desperately that, to save myself from useless suffering, I left you. For what did you offer me in the future?"

His lip curled in a kind of sardonic satisfaction.

"I thought we should come to it! The innocent lamb seduced and seeking honourable amends! So that's what you were after!"

"Judge others by yourself, my lord! Never, as I hope for salvation, never did I think of you in that light!"

There was such a vibrant ring of truth in her voice that he relaxed a little, as though in spite of himself.

"What did you expect me to do?" she asked him. "Wait for you to tire of me and send me packing? Was I to ruin my whole life for the sake of a man who offered me nothing but a few weeks' happiness? How dare you sit in judgement on me! By what right do you throw my husband and my lover in my face? Did you offer me any kind of future, anything at all, with you? Did you even think of anything beyond your own immediate satisfaction? Do you know the tears I shed, the despair I suffered when I married the Earl of Norland? When I broke with the past and tried, in any way I could, to forget you?"

He said nothing but stood staring at her. Her hair was coming down and golden brown curls escaped from underneath the neat white coif and lay on the shoulders of the dark grey dress and on the bosom which rose and fell with her tumultuous breathing. Her face aflame, her eyes blazing, Deborah had never looked more lovely, more desirable.

"Oh, you need not worry. I have said my piece and now I am going," she told him. "I hate you, Lord Christopher, and I never want to have anything more to do with you! Nor would I keep anything that might remind me of your odious conduct. You may take this!" As she spoke she was tugging at the third finger of her left hand with trembling fingers but in spite of all her efforts the topaz ring which never left her by day or night, refused to come off.

"Perhaps I may assist you?" The words were uttered, white-lipped, with a chilling politeness.

"Thank you, my lord." Her head high, her eyes defiant.

He took the hand which she held out to him. Their bodies were almost touching, and suddenly, before she could guess his intention, he was gripping her fiercely between his hands.

"No!" he ejaculated. "No, by God! We are acting like fools!"

She struggled to free herself but he held her fast. He was breathing harshly, his mask of indifference gone, and for the first time since she had known him, she saw his face ravaged by emotion.

"I was lying to you, Deborah," he said in a broken voice. "I do love you. I have never stopped loving you. Twenty times over, after you left Gilford, I was tempted to go after you, to find you and bring you back to me at whatever cost but then I remembered that curt note you wrote to say good-bye and my heart failed me. But then to see you at court, queening it among those whores, the property of another man — several for ought I knew — it drove me mad!"

"Let me go, my lord. It is all over between us. Can't you see that? You have ruined it."

"No, by God! I will not let you go!" He tightened his grip, drawing her to him until her suffering face was a few inches from his own. "I will not give up what is mine, and you are mine, do you hear? No, do not try to deny it. You tremble in my arms. You are mine, Deborah!"

His arms were round her, crushing her, his kiss hard on her mouth. Instinctively, her lips opened to his demand, joy welled up in her until her whole being was one wordless cry of love. The room reeled about them as they came together.

It was late in the morning when the porter saw the neat maid-servant coming back across the court. There were dark rings round her eyes and her step seemed to have lost something of its spring, but her face was radiant.

"What did I say?" he muttered to himself. "It's always them ones get the fun."

205

Deborah smiled at him as she passed the lodge. She felt as if she were walking on air, so that she almost walked into the beggar who crouched by the wall, his head wrapped in filthy rags.

Poor man, she thought, and because she herself was so happy she wanted to give him something. She felt in the purse she carried at her girdle for a coin and as he reached to catch it, his strange head-gear slipped a little. Deborah had the odd feeling that she had seen him before somewhere and she went on her way with a curious sensation of unease. But although she racked her brains for a moment or two, she could not remember where she could have glimpsed that ugly face before. Then, deciding that it was probably not important, that all beggars looked much alike and most of them equally villainous, she dismissed the matter from her mind. After all, she sighed voluptuously, she had Kit to think about.

XXI

The following afternoon, Deborah went to meet James.

The air was soft with the breath of spring. A timid sun was helping to swell the buds and a handful of puffball clouds, like cherubs on a map, blew merrily across an azure sky. It was not, Deborah reflected grimly, exactly the sort of day to choose for an execution.

An executioner, however, was precisely what she felt like, and the victim she was proposing to herself was the innocent James Randolph. Yet what else could she do? Surely the truth was the least she owed him?

She climbed the stairs slowly, feeling her stomach tie itself in knots as she thought of his passion for her, his eager thoughtfulness, and the thousand and one proofs of his devotion. With the heightened sensibility which remained from her experience of the previous day, she could guess, with terrible clarity, the pain she was going to give him. She heaved a sigh, thinking that only yesterday she had been within an ace of finding herself cast into outer darkness, and now she was about to do the same, to inflict the same agony on another. What made it worse, too, was that James was so clearly not expecting it. The day after that unfortunate game of cards, she had sent him a note by John Strong to say that she was "not quite herself" and that he should hear from her when she was better. And now, only this morning, she had appointed him to meet her here, at their usual time.

One flight . . . two flights . . . she knocked.

The door opened at once to reveal James Randolph looking grey and haggard-eyed.

Instead of his usual joyous greeting, he shut the door and followed her into the room in silence. Deborah was conscious of a cowardly feeling of relief that she had not been forced to check any demonstration of affection.

She did not sit but stood, leaning back against the edge of the table, twisting her bronze velvet gloves between her hands.

"James, my dear," she began, but he interrupted. It was the first time he had opened his lips since her arrival.

"Don't you think all that is a trifle unnecessary now?"

"What do you mean?" Her mouth framed the question automatically, while her brain was asking who could have told him. He knew something, that was obvious from his words, his tone . . . She could not help the momentary thought that it would make her task somewhat easier.

"I know everything." He was staring miserably at the ground. "It did not take you long to make a mockery of one who loved you! The first experienced seducer who comes along can bend you to his will! You are like all the rest!"

"James, listen to me!"

"No protests, madam. I was informed just now, by one who knows, of the new *connexion* you have formed." He laughed shortly. "God's life, what a fool I was! I should have known the other night when we sat at cards. You were not the same after he came. A word, a smile, and that was enough to . . ." He smashed his fist against the wainscot. "But let me tell you here and now, it will not end thus! I will not take lightly to a pair of horns! Christopher Belstone may have stolen my mistress but he shall not long enjoy her! This insult will only be answered with blood!" His fingers were already playing with the hilt of his rapier and he was clearly in a state of inordinate excitement.

"James, are you mad? What do you mean to do?" Then as, ignoring her, he strode to the door, she added sharply: "Where are you going?"

"To Essex House. To make that thief explain his conduct. I have stayed too long already but, foolishly, I hoped . . . I know now all I need to know. Your own behaviour speaks loud enough."

She had run to him and was grasping him by the sleeve.

"Stop! Did Lady Gilford tell you this?"

"Yes," he said, arrested for an instant. "What of it?"

"Nothing. Except that that woman hates us and would be glad to do us an ill turn by getting her word in before mine. Oh no," Deborah's voice was weary, "she was not lying to you, but — No, listen!" She clung to him desperately. "Don't go! If you must kill someone to avenge your honour, then kill me. I am the only one to blame!"

"You, Deborah!" In his amazement he had stopped trying to throw her off. "It cannot be! The man took advantage of you, of your youth. I know his reputation too well. But that you should have gone to him of your own will, have been so base, so abandoned —"

"No, James! No, I am none of those things. But I was telling you the truth. It is not like that. Oh, you cannot know what it has cost me to hurt you. To another man, perhaps, I might have said good-bye and thank you, but not to you, my dear, dear friend. There has been too much that was real between us. I owe it to you to explain."

James was standing still now, his gaze torn between the door and Deborah's tear-filled eyes.

"What are you trying to say?" he asked at last, cautiously.

"It is a long story. The Earl was not, as you thought, the first man in my life. There was a time before that when I was deeply in love with Lord Christopher and I – that is, we . . ." She was speaking very slowly now, choosing her words. "We parted. I believed that all hope was gone and so I made up my mind to marriage with the Earl. Then you came, dear James, and I thought that with you I could forget the past but the other night, when I saw Kit – Lord Christopher, I . . ." Her voice died away and she looked at him beseechingly, twisting her hands. "Oh, God, I don't know how to tell you this, James. But you will understand because you love me. I could not help it, James. I could not. I went to him."

He had dropped heavily into a chair, his anger gone, driven out by Deborah's revelations. She herself, bewildered by his silence, remained huddled where she was, her fingers picking mechanically at the seed pearls sewn on her gloves. Suddenly, James looked up.

"My poor Deborah. What you must have suffered!"

No! This was more than she could bear. If he had only abused her, driven her away . . . beaten her, even. She would have felt less remorse. But that he should be so kind . . . She burst into hysterical sobs. James got up quickly.

"For God's sake, don't cry!" he exclaimed and added more quietly, as though to himself: "Now I understand those sudden sadnesses of yours, and the way you never seemed to give all of yourself . . . You never loved me, did you?"

Deborah sniffed, dolefully. "It was not the same," she said at last, very gently. "But you must believe me when I say you made me very, very happy. With you, I learned to know a kind of peace and joyful serenity which I have never felt with anyone else. Oh, James, I —"

He held her hand.

"I would have done anything for you, Deborah. How often, in my heart, have I not cursed your marriage, believing, fool that I was, that only the Earl stood between us and the life I dreamed of for the two of us. To have you for my wife, all to myself at every hour of the day, to love and cherish with all my heart, God's blood, it was a bliss for which I would cheerfully have pledged my immortal soul! Unfortunately, fate has decreed otherwise." He sighed and the glow went out of his eyes. "I have lost everything. I hope that you at least may have better luck. Some men may call me coward for not fighting him, for not risking all on the chance of winning you back. But you need have no fears, my darling. Your happiness is more to me than my own and what I feel for you is too fine a thing to let me stand between you and your true love for another. Just for a moment, you see, I suspected you of yielding to a momentary lure thrown out by him, and that for me was the worst of all . . . To see someone you have placed so high fall like that. . . . It was unbearable, like sacrilege! But a great love, that I can forgive, for it is worthy of you!" His grip tightened on her hand. "Promise me, if ever you should have need of comfort or . . . of anything at all, if ever you are unhappy, only let me know, and I will come to you, for there will never be any other woman for me. Now go, my darling. Leave me."

Suddenly, of the two of them, it was he who was the stronger and from the tears streaming down Deborah's face it might have seemed that it was she who had been made the sacrifice.

"James . . . Oh, how can I say . . ."

"Hush, my dearest. Don't say anything. Here." He fumbled in the sleeve of his doublet, and held out a gilded key. "This is the key to these rooms. Everything here is yours. Do with it what you will. I will never come here again." He took her in his arms.

"Farewell, my sweet. Farewell, my only love."

A brief kiss on her brow and he released her.

"Go, Deborah. In God's name, go quickly!" he said in a low, tortured voice.

For a second, she hesitated, looking at him as he walked hurriedly across the room. Then she ran to him and, raising herself on tiptoe, lightly brushed his lips, then turned and, with one last glance about the room, she turned and fled.

XXII

"Well, we're heading for it this time, my dear. It will be war any moment now."

Deborah winced at the unconcealed satisfaction in Kit's voice as he made this pronouncement. Oh, those damned Spaniards! There was no getting away from them these days. Wherever you went, to Whitehall or St Paul's, no one was talking of anything but King Philip's latest crotchets, of ships and preparations for war. Every man in the kingdom seemed to have appointed himself Lord Admiral and was busy offering conjectures as to the probable landing-place of the Spanish fleet, estimating and even exaggerating the degree of present peril with a confidence bordering on the absurd. Indeed, it was absurd. The Spaniards, plague take them, had not invaded England yet! They were still miles and miles away across the sea, basking in the sun where, if Deborah had her way, they could remain for a while longer yet and allow her to enjoy the little peace and security which she had won so hardly.

She snuggled down farther into bed. It was true that the situation was growing hourly more fraught and she was neither so stupid nor so deaf as to be unaware of it. News was constantly arriving in London which, when you thought about it, was only the more alarming for its apparently reassuring nature. The entire coastline, from Dover to the Lizard, was bristling with watchtowers, one county after another was mustering and training men for its defence and alarming figures were beginning to circulate about the accelerated production of ships and armaments. All these preparations were clear indication that the danger was real. Even so, there was no news that the colossal armada which the King of Spain was assembling in his ports was anywhere near ready. There was plenty of time yet for him to change his mind, to alter what must surely be a formidably taxing plan, even to die, in the full odour of sanctity or for an epidemic to decimate his accursed troops. Why waste the brief and blissful moments to be spent with Kit in useless fears? There was nothing she could do to change things, tied to the Earl as she was, by

211

Her Majesty's command, like a dog in its kennel. Oh, if she had only been a man, now! A man could afford to laugh at the prospect of war, could plunge into it with gusto and enjoyment and meet the enemy face to face. One could understand their enthusiasm even – Deborah glanced sidelong at Kit – yes, even the enthusiasm which was glowing in his eyes at that moment. Suddenly, illogically, she could almost have hated him for it and her feeling was reflected in the tone in which she took him up.

"War? Surely you're being unduly pessimistic? Spain has been growling at us for a long time now, and we've never been at any great pains to curry favour there. Our sending men and money to help the revolt in the Low Countries can't have helped to sweeten Philip precisely, can it now?"

"Especially when that same Philip had just ordered the sequestration of all English possessions in that country, thereby severely damaging our commercial interests. Don't forget that, my child."

"Oh, I'm not forgetting it. Any more than I'm forgetting the rich harvest in gold we've been reaping from the Spanish galleons."

"Impudent dogs! They've come to look on the sea route from the Americas as their own private highway." Kit gave a triumphant crow of laughter. "God's death! We've shown them! I'd not care to venture a guess how many we've pillaged and sunk by now. With good Queen Bess sitting at home disowning her privateers as meek as you please, and all the time filling her coffers at his Most Catholic Majesty's expense! I must say," he added blandly, "you seem to be feeling a decided tenderness for him today!"

"Oh!" Deborah threw back the sheets and sprang at him, her curls flying. "How can you! The King of Spain indeed! When you know I hate him and all his subjects! I wish they may all die a thousand deaths! I was just trying to make you see that in spite of all the pinpricks, nothing has actually happened yet —"

"But it will happen, take my word." He had drawn her into the circle of his arm and was engaged in smoothing down the rebellious curls. "King Philip has had his eye on England for too long. He'll not let pass the splendid opportunity Queen Mary's death has given him. Especially as all hope of bringing England back to Rome from within has died with her. So there you are: *noblesse oblige* and all that. The Pope's champion may safely stand up, with the approval of the Catholic courts of Europe, to pursue a satisfactory combination of duty and self-interest."

"One might have thought he had enough interests, in Spain and

America and the Low Countries, Sardinia and all the rest of his possessions, to keep him happy, without coming here to interfere with us! Yet they say he's not a warlike man but rather cautious and hard working, always with one eye on his desk and the other at his prayers."

Kit gave a shout of laughter. "A worthy picture of a king! But you're right, of course. It must be a hard decision for him to take. He's supposed to have a horror of war – as, indeed, has the Queen's Grace. Perhaps, after all – the religious question apart – they might have dealt well enough together as husband and wife. She has all the Tudor strength and energy and he —"

"Kit! How dare you! Our Queen and – oh!" Deborah was horrified.

"All right, I was only joking . . . Not that the idea didn't appeal to the depressing Philip in his younger days. He was England's king for four years, you know, my love, when he was married to poor Catholic Queen Mary, although you were not born at the time and I was a babe too young to remember."

"Yes, I've heard my aunt talk about it. It seems to have been a sad business for both of them and it didn't do Spain much good since Mary died without producing an heir. Just as well for us, she did."

"And so she was succeeded by her sister, our good Bess," Kit continued triumphantly. "And what must our hopeful widower do but come trotting back, all smiles, ready to play the suitor once again. As if the welcome he got the first time wasn't enough to put him off for life!" He laughed and made a little grimace of disgust. "Well, we'd had our fill of him and his papism, with his white face and his long chin and his fishy eyes, stinking of olive oil and garlic! Once was enough for us so we soon let him understand."

Kit paused and dropping a kiss on the pretty shell-pink ear which had been taking in his words, he added more seriously: "But all that was nearly thirty years ago, beloved. The time for pretty speeches is gone now, the words have turned sour, the abscess is ripe and must be lanced."

Laying Deborah tenderly back among the warm pillows, he slid out of bed and began to pace the room while she followed him with her eyes.

"Lance it, how?"

"Do you really think the Queen's Majesty will sit back while they finish their armada unmolested, under the eyes of a lot of psalm-singing monks who can't wait to get to work here with their torture

213

chambers to rout out Reform. That's how they do things over there, did you know? All done by prayers and processions! Thank God our Bess has other ideas. In her view, God helps those who help themselves. There may not be much money in the coffers just at present but courage, energy and goodwill she has in plenty and asks of us in turn, and thanks to those we have a fleet which I warrant you will deal some shrewd surprises to that fiendish armada – always supposing that it ever puts to sea! The Queen has a pretty plan in mind which may serve to put an end to Spain's pretensions once for all, and do you know, sweetheart, who has been chosen to command this bold attempt? Drake himself!" Kit's eyes were shining.

"Sir Francis?"

"Who else? There can be no other. The greatest privateer of them all! Just ask the Spaniards what they think of him."

"They're frightened to death of him, from what I hear. Don't they call him *El Draque*?"

"The Dragon, that's right. By heaven, there's a man! Do you know, he —"

"Yes, Kit," Deborah broke in hurriedly. "I doubt if there's an Englishman living who does *not* know. But what about this scheme?"

Kit, however, once launched on a subject which was obviously very close to his heart, was impossible to deflect.

"He was born the son of a simple country parson, did you know that? And now he's vice-admiral of the fleet, with fame and fortune beyond all estimation! You were very young then, Deb, but you must remember the excitement when he landed at Plymouth from his voyage round the world?"

"Of course I remember. That was in 1580, wasn't it?"

"Yes. And by God, we'd all but given him up for lost! Three years it had taken him! To circumnavigate the world in a cockleshell and bring it home piled to the gunwales with treasure! A million pounds in gold and jewels, all lifted out of King Philip's ships. It was fantastic! No wonder the Queen knighted him for it."

"Yes, wait a minute, Kit. Didn't she go down to Deptford and go on board the *Golden Hind* for that very purpose? I remember it perfectly. It was one of the most dreadful days of my life." She laughed. "Oh dear, it's odd, isn't it, how silly we can be sometimes? We ruin the best things for the silliest reasons. We went to Deptford, my aunt and I, in the Queen's retinue, and I had on a new dress for the occasion. It was the grandest I had ever worn – I remember it had white satin sleeves embroidered with rosebuds. Well, I tell you, standing there in all the crowd I was in a constant dread that my finery would be soiled and able to think of nothing but the whipping I should get – and I got it, too!"

They both laughed, and Kit said: "Poor baby! All in all, you'd have done better to have watched the ceremony. There was never anything like it before." Warmth kindled in his voice, as he went on: "Nor more richly deserved! Storms, sickness, Spaniards, even mutiny, all overcome by sheer courage and determination, and that sixth sense which Drake seems to have, like a gift from God, for anything to do with the sea."

"Goodness! You talk as if you know him very well?"

"We are good friends," Kit said simply.

"You never told me!"

"When will you get it into your head, my love, that a great many things happened to me in my life before I met you. I couldn't possibly tell you all of them."

It was said very gently but there was the faintest hint of irritation behind the words. Deborah sighed inwardly. She knew only too well what had made her say that. Kit was not a boy! Yet each time she discovered some new facet of his life she felt somehow frustrated. She wanted so badly that there should be no secrets between them. She wanted to know everything he thought and did . . . Kit was speaking again.

"You must have heard of the famous expedition to the West Indies, three years ago?"

Deborah frowned. "Wasn't that something to do with reprisals for Spanish ill-treatment of our merchants at Bilbao?"

"That's right." Kit grinned, "I must say, Deborah, it's a pleasure to talk to you. I can't stand the kind of woman who has nothing in her head but such frippery ideas as the size of her waist and the latest gossip gleaned from her maid. What was I saying? Oh, yes, it caused an uproar and for the first time the Queen came out of her shell and contributed men and arms quite openly. I went as an officer and you may believe me that we went to it with a will. The capture of San Domingo and Cartagena are among my most treasured memories."

How he loved war, and how far from her he seemed suddenly to have grown, Deborah thought.

Kit broke off to go to the table and pour himself a glass of wine.

She saw him every afternoon now, either at some inn or else on the river, on board Essex's luxuriously appointed barge which he had generously placed at Kit's disposal, both secret places where they were unlikely to be observed, for the Earl, alas, could not be forgotten, even in this new-found happiness. In the days of James, Deborah had been inclined to treat the thought of discovery lightly but now she trembled at every moment. On the mere breath of suspicion, her husband would have the right to pack her off to moulder out her life in his gloomy northern fastness and lock her away from Kit for ever. She therefore redoubled her precautions, making John Strong drive them by the most roundabout and improbable routes to the prearranged meeting-place. Not that it seemed she had the least need to take so much trouble, for the Earl continued to treat her with icy indifference. If only she could have done the same! Many women seemed to manage perfectly comfortably to hold the balance between husband and lover. The situation was ordinary enough. Unfortunately, in this case, she was too much in love with the one not to find herself coming increasingly to detest everything connected with the other. Yet what could she do? She lived in a man's world, made by men for men, and a woman's voice counted for nothing. For him, adultery was something to be enjoyed without a second thought, the privilege of his sex, regarded generally with easy indulgence. He was free to rid himself of an inconvenient or distasteful wife by the simple method of sending her away and shutting her up somewhere, while she . . .

Deborah pulled herself together. Why so bitter all of a sudden? Hadn't she the heavenly hours she spent with Kit in recompense for all that?

On the present occasion, their meeting-place was a comfortable inn a little way outside London on the road to Hampton Court. Glancing idly round, Deborah saw the traditional inn chamber which was already becoming familiar: a fair-sized room with solid, well-kept furniture, clean linen curtains to the big bed, freshly strewn herbs on the floor and fragrant nosegays of spring flowers, primroses and hyacinths in pots set here and there. A bright fire burned in the hearth.

A table in the centre of the room was laid with the materials for a lavish meal. Set out on a fringed white cloth were a spiced chicken pie, some venison pasties, a brace of pigeons roasted, two dishes of sweetmeats, a foaming jug of ale and a flask of Canary wine, all awaiting the attention of Kit's hearty appetite.

Each morning, nowadays, he would ride out into the nearby villages to train the men in the use of arms, teaching them the rudiments of military discipline and how to handle a musket and a bill. Afterwards, he would skip dinner and hurry to meet Deborah, making up for the lost meal with a substantial snack later on, which he shared with her.

Just now, she was lying back, naked between the sheets, nibbling at sugared violets and rose petals which she was fishing from a small dish placed within arm's reach. Kit was standing by the table, helping himself to a large slice of pie.

Wearing nothing but the richly laced shirt which he had flung carelessly round his shoulders, he offered to Deborah's besotted eyes the perfect specimen of virile manhood. She thought that she could never tire of looking at that powerful frame, with its beautifully muscled chest, lithe limbs and handsome, arrogant head. As he came back to the bed, she asked him:

"What about the Queen's plan, Kit? Tell me about that. You were so busy talking about Drake that you forgot the most important thing. Oh, I wish to God this horrid war would go away!"

Kit sat down and began running his hand lightly up and down her arm. He seemed suddenly to have grown faintly ill at ease, like a man about to impart some bad news and already dreading the inevitable tears and recriminations it would provoke. Deborah, however, was serenely unaware of it.

"Well," Kit began. "Drake is to sail from Plymouth on the twelfth of this month for Cadiz."

"Cadiz, in Spain? But isn't that where the Spanish fleet is assembling?"

"The greater part of it, yes. And Drake's mission is precisely to destroy as much of it as possible. If the plan is a success, the Queen hopes Philip may abandon the project altogether and the worst will have been avoided."

"Good God! Sailing straight into the dragon's lair! It's bold enough, certainly. But how did you come to learn all this?"

She reached out as she spoke and culled another rose petal from the dish beside her.

"Hm . . . well . . ." His arm about her tightened a little. A sudden pang seemed to strike through Deborah's breast. She dropped the sweetmeat and sat up to look at him.

"Kit! You aren't . . . going?"

"I'm sorry, my dearest. I —" He took a firm hold on himself. "I leave in three days' time to join Drake at Plymouth. Deborah . . . Deborah, my darling, look at me!"

217

But she remained staring obstinately at the wall.

"How long have you known this?" she asked dully.

"Ever since my return to London. I lacked the courage to tell you before this." He had his arms round her. "Come now, sweetheart. Is this the way to spend what little time we have left? I can understand how you feel. Do you think I'm not grieved to leave you behind? But do you blame me for defending my country? Try and be sensible. It is quite a short voyage, you know. I shall soon be back again."

A short voyage! Oh God! How could he be so blind? He called it a short voyage, this bloody expedition which might take months! The time would pass quickly for him, she thought bitterly. He was sailing to adventure, and to glory, while she . . . she would be left alone here to worry herself to death.

"Think, sweetheart. We still have three days left."

She started. That was true. And afterwards, then she would have time enough to cry her heart out. She choked back her sobs. Every single second of these precious minutes must be used to the full. Above all, he must not carry away a picture of her as a sulky, pigeon-livered child! She smiled, a watery, tender smile which trembled on her lips.

"I'll promise to be good, my love. Only let's not talk any more about your going, or all my courage will evaporate."

He clasped her to him without speaking.

A little later, as they were dressing, he said: "Did you know that there was some talk at Whitehall, Deb, that you are not seen there so often?"

"Is there? Yet I've been there twice this week."

"That's as maybe. Apparently you used to be there every night." Kit stroked his beard, his eyes teasing her. "Can it be that the court has fewer attractions for you now that James Randolph is absent?"

"Oh, Kit! Please, no more of that!"

In her agitation she let fall her comb. Kit picked it up and, as he held it out to her, continued:

"Let me tell you the best of it! The rumour is that you prefer to meet him elsewhere. Isn't that ripe?" He gave a shout of laughter.

"Very amusing," Deborah said tartly.

Why did he have to remind her of James — James who was a thousand times more truly the gentleman and who would never have left her to go ranging the seas? Besides, he had recalled her real reason for less frequent attendance at court, which was that it made her feel positively sick to watch him flirting with creatures like Lady Aldhurst and Penelope Gilford's other cronies.

Thinking this, she could not resist adding a rider of her own, glancing at him out of the corners of her eyes to see how he took it.

"Talking of rumours, you should drop a hint to your friend Lady Aldhurst to cool her ardours in a bucket of cold water from time to time or judging by the way she carries on she'll end in a Southwark bawdy-house."

"That's her affair, not mine," Kit answered easily. "By God, what a wench, though! A luscious mouthful if ever there was one – even if not quite to your taste," he added hastily, catching sight of Deborah's expression.

No, she told herself firmly, no questions! Better not to know. What good would it do, in any case? He was quite capable of telling her the truth, laughing over his infidelities as though they were trifles of no importance. He could be like that, cruel and selfish from sheer thoughtlessness, but she loved him, she knew that now, and that was the only thing which mattered.

That was the evening on which Deborah was very nearly the victim of a fatal accident. At the time, she saw nothing in it but an unfortunate coincidence. But she was to remember it later and, putting it together with one or two other things, conclude that it had not been due to mere chance but to active malevolence on someone's part.

She had got into the habit of walking after supper in the garden which lay behind the house. She liked the fresh, evening air with the moist smells that rose from the shrubs and the quiet peace of it all which seemed to wash away her cares.

The small area had been laid out in the Italian style with broad stone steps descending gently from the house, edged with neatly trimmed box hedges and intersected by broad gravelled walks at right angles. At each of these points were set large urns, planted with the flowers appropriate to the season which gave a cheerful note against the more sober greens of the parterres. Here and there loomed up statues of wood or marble or fantastic shapes of clipped trees. Beyond, the ground levelled out into a shaded walk of ancient lime trees bounded by a long honeysuckle hedge which ended in a delightful green lawn overlooking a willow-fringed lily pool. There the pleasure gardens ended. After that there was a patch of waste ground, given up to a tangle of weeds, nettles, docks and brambles, at the far end of which a narrow path led through a thicket of may trees to the stables and kennels, although the grooms and kennel boys not unnaturally preferred the more direct and convenient paved way linking the outbuildings to the east wing of the house.

It was to this path that Deborah made her way when she had escaped at last from the gloomy meal partaken in as much of her husband's company as might be had from opposite ends of a thirty-foot table.

It was not quite dark outside and there was still light enough to see the path. Scents of spring filled the air, of violets and newly mown grass. Now and then bats darted overhead, their high, twittering voices almost inaudible. The thrush was still singing from his chosen perch on a high branch of an ash tree and an occasional pigeon chortled, soft-throated with love. Something small scuttled in the undergrowth. Deborah strolled on, lost in her own unhappy thoughts. Once past the pool, she picked up her skirts and eased herself cautiously through the narrow gap that led to the stables.

This was the time of day when she liked them best, when no one was about – for the grooms and stable lads would all be gathered indoors for their supper – and the stalls were full of the warm, quiet fustiness of animals at rest. Rich, faintly acrid smells of dung and hay tickled her nostrils and the horses, recognizing her, turned gentle, trusting eyes to look at her as she went from one to another, calling them by their names, distributing titbits of apple and march-pane from her pocket and patting the gleaming hide. Last of all, she came to her own mare, Semiramis, the beautiful, high-bred, high-strung chestnut she had brought with her from Fleet Street. Then, with an extra special hug and kiss for her darling, she turned to go.

As she did so the silence was broken by a furious barking. Deborah glanced over her shoulder at the kennels and hurried a little. The great mastiffs with their slavering jaws and hideous fangs, hurling themselves at the bars of their cage, trampling and climbing on one another in their vain attempts to get at her, always filled her with dread. Only the Earl, who actually liked the ferocious beasts, was able to control them and he held the only key to their enclosure, which no member of the household was permitted to enter; an order everyone was very willing to obey since the brutes, trained to fight bulls and bears, would have made mincemeat of any who were fool

220

enough to venture. They were fed on joints of meat stuck through the bars on the ends of pikes.

Shivering, Deborah hugged her shawl tighter and turned quickly to her left along the back of the stables, a long, brick and timber building, roofed with tiles and pierced at intervals along the wall by small windows.

The stable block at Norland House was built round three sides of a courtyard of which the central portion formed part of the outside wall of the grounds. The fourth side, linking the two wings, contained, as well as harness rooms, coach houses and so forth, the great entrance archway, over which was a big, bare attic used by the grooms for repair work. Its inside face was covered with thick creeper, half-concealing the narrow balcony, its stone balustrade ornamented at either end by a massive stone ball, which overhung the gate.

Deborah was standing just beneath one corner of this balcony, her hand stretched out to grasp the handle of the small postern door let into one of the big, wooden gates, when a noise made her look round. She was in time to see a large rat dart out from behind the water trough and run straight towards her. It had probably been disturbed by one of the stable cats and was simply making instinctively for the shelter of the walls, but Deborah had a horror of all rodents, large or small. Clutching her skirts, she leaped back with a gasp of shock out of the creature's path. It was that which saved her, for at that very moment the stone ball on the balustrade above tottered and fell in the exact spot where she had been standing only a second before.

Deborah's scream and the dull thud of the ball's landing came almost simultaneously. She stood, rooted with horror, staring at the crater which the stone had dug in the soft ground. Another second! But for that rat, she would be lying there on the ground with her head smashed to a pulp.

Icy sweat trickled slowly down her spine and she knew, suddenly, that she was about to be very sick. Fleeing blindly, she stumbled as far as the nearest trees and there, bent double, her knees shaking under her, she brought up all her supper.

From the direction of the house came the sound of a door slamming noisily. A moment later, the quiet night was shattered by a confused babble of voices. Very soon a bobbing procession of lights had reached the stable path, striking flashes of bright green from the sombre hedges on either side.

221

The window on the first floor, which had been open a few moments earlier, closed silently.

Two days . . . a few hours . . . then only a few more minutes: the time passed with lightning swiftness and now the idyll was drawing to its end. The barge, moving downstream, had already passed the first outlying houses of London.

Gradually, the clear, reeded waters of the country gave way to a turgid, yellow-brown flow. Now they could hear the cries of the watermen, the cheerful "Eastward Ho!" and "Westward Ho!" which indicated whether the caller was offering passage up or down-stream. A little farther and the gardens and water gates of the great houses along the Strand were almost in sight.

The river was much busier now. The Earl of Essex's barge encountered vessels of all kinds moving hither and thither on the crowded stream: ferry boats, crammed with men and animals, with bales and casks and every conceivable sort of goods; pleasure boats of the wealthy, filled with fair ladies and fine gentlemen, with the music of viols floating sweetly over the water, small rowing boats and even tinier skiffs in which small boys skimmed dangerously, like so many water boatmen. Yet surely nothing on the river was grander than itself: it was even rumoured that the Queen herself was to condescend to travel in it one of these Sundays, to go to hear the sermon at St Paul's. All heads were turned as it went by to gaze with envy at its magnificence.

The poop was freshly gilded, with a narrow black band which made it glitter the brighter by contrast, so that it shone like a jewel in the sun and seemed to draw into itself all the brilliance of the fine April afternoon. The deck was fringed with gold likewise and in the midst of all this gold stood a dainty pavilion made like a great tent of emerald velvet, with more gold ruching, every seam and bunches of white ostrich feathers nodding gracefully at each corner. The rowers, fore and aft, wore silken caps and red woollen sashes a good ten inches broad about their waists.

The interior of the tent, into whose mysteries the curious on-lookers would dearly have loved to penetrate, was almost entirely taken up with a wide, low couch upholstered in the same velvet and standing on a fur rug. Lolling on this couch, soothed by the ripple of the stream, the passengers could easily believe themselves miles away, sailing on the bosom of some enchanted sea, while a hand

222

stretched out to part the curtained walls could bring them back at will to the real world outside.

There were times, though, when the real world had to be faced, whether one liked it or not, and for Deborah and Kit that time had come. In a moment, they must say good-bye.

Kit held her close to him. "A perfect time," he murmured softly.

Yes, Deborah silently agreed, a blessed moment.

Kit being free of military duties for the two days preceding his departure, Deborah had seized on the first excuse which came to her mind to escape from her husband for that time. The Earl had raised no objection to her visiting a – totally imaginary – friend of her childhood, which was on the whole just as well considering it would have taken a ball and chain to keep her from Kit at that moment.

Early the previous morning she had embarked with him for one brief trip. Together, they had been rowed slowly up the river, between banks white with blackthorn in blossom. They had stopped at a small inn beyond Richmond where she had had him all to herself for one whole night.

All the way there and back she had been simply a woman in love, gay and passionate by turns, forcing herself to forget the coming separation, but alas, such happiness was not without its price and now, as the time approached, that price was to be paid. There was no cheating time. She cast one stricken glance at him, asking herself how long it might be before she saw him again.

As though he had divined her thought, he gently pinched her chin.

"You won't have time to forget me, young woman. The moment we've trounced those damned Spaniards, I'll be back again."

She had sworn to be brave, but it was hard to repress the tears which started to her eyes and she could hardly speak for the lump in her throat. All the same, she managed to summon up a smile.

"Take good care of yourself, my darling."

"Never fear! And you, sweetheart, try to be good. I'll warrant you that young coxcomb Randolph will be after you again the moment my back's turned."

"Oh, Kit! How can you!" she exclaimed indignantly.

"All right, only joking." He smiled. "Not but what I'm damned if I wouldn't rather think of you with Norland than surrounded by a horde of eager puppies."

Yes, thought Deborah, no doubt, as far as his own peace of mind was concerned! What should he care for her strained relations with her husband? Tomorrow, he would be deep in his man's life again and, trusting in his mistress's virtue, could devote himself to war with an easy mind. She bit back the retort which sprang to her lips, telling herself that this was not the moment for recriminations.

She was in his arms again and now he drew her gently to her feet, still holding her. All at once, Deborah felt icy cold. God in heaven, there was no more time! Only a few seconds left! The boat was bumping on the jetty. She gave a little moan and clung to Kit.

"My darling . . . oh, my darling!"

"Deborah, be sensible. John Strong is waiting for you." He was hastening their farewells, more deeply stirred than he cared to show.

Once more their lips met. Through a fog, she felt strong hands under her armpits, swinging her up on to the jetty, where she stood swaying a little, hearing Kit's voice say:

"Take good care of her ladyship, John, old lad. I'm trusting her to you. . . . It won't be for long, my heart."

She turned but already he was back on board.

They stood for a long time with their eyes on one another: Kit very upright on the poop, his broad-brimmed black hat in his hand; Deborah among the crowd of idlers on the jetty, scarcely able to make out the dear, vanishing form for the tears which dimmed her eyes.

XXIII

At first sight, the Earl and Countess of Norland, sitting down together for a quiet evening at home, presented a perfect picture of conjugal felicity.

She sat with her head bent over her embroidery, her needle working steadily over the canvas; he, with a silver cup in his hand, seemed to be enjoying a pleasant moment of relaxation. Yet the silence in the room, the speed at which the level in the jug of hippocras declined, even the young wife's steady concentration on her stitchery, all combined to make the atmosphere oppressive.

At last, Deborah pushed away her work, stifling a yawn. She had gone to bed very late the previous night and had not slept a wink and now it seemed to her that she might as well catch up on some sleep as sit here being bored to death. Her husband needed no help from her to drink himself into a stupor, since that appeared to be his intention. It was curious, though, for it was not a habit of his: on the contrary, he was usually inclined to sobriety. Perhaps he had been crossed in love? Well, if that were so, she thought sardonically, he need not come crawling to her for comfort.

She finished rolling her silks in their square of linen and got up.

"Will you excuse me if I go up now?"

"So soon, my dear?" The Earl, roused from his thoughts, looked grey and pinched about the nostrils. "Is my company so repugnant to you? Come now, try a little harder, won't you? I am not in the mood to sit alone." He smiled unpleasantly.

She hesitated. There seemed no point in prolonging this dismal evening and yet, on the other hand, if he really wanted her company for once, it was not easy to refuse.

"Very well," she said, with no very good grace. "If you wish it."

She resumed her seat and the Earl sank back into his thoughts, paying no further attention to her.

Staring into space, her hands now idle in her lap, Deborah slipped into the bitter-sweet world of memory. Tomorrow the *Elizabeth Bonaventure*, with Drake in command, would put to sea with twenty-four of the Queen's ships . . . Tomorrow, Kit would sail from England.

Suddenly, she became aware that the Earl was watching her. Good heavens, was he going to – oh, no! Not today of all days! Feverishly, she began to cudgel her brains for some excuse to shut her door in his face.

Ever since her reconciliation with Kit, she had found it impossible to conquer the revulsion which her husband inspired in her. The mere thought of his bony body touching her own was enough to give her gooseflesh. She had got into the habit of employing every device known to women whose husbands are irksome to them. For one week every month, she claimed to be indisposed, while the remaining three weeks became an unending succession of headaches and every variety of minor ailment which came into her head. The result was that she saw to it that Norland had little opportunity to exercise his conjugal rights, and when, at last, she ran out of lies and excuses and was forced to yield, their brief encounters became a kind of cold battle between the two of them, a hasty attack on his part which she, nauseated, instinctively tried to fight off.

She could not understand it. Far from being repelled by this attitude of his wife's, he continued to press his attentions on her, apparently quite unconscious of the implications of this near-rape. Perhaps the sense of imposing his will on an unwilling partner gave him more satisfaction than a willing abandonment? According to Aunt Tucker, there were men like that. She shrank a little.

He got up and came towards her.

"It grows late. Shall we go up now? I shall be glad to escort you to your chamber."

He gave an ugly laugh and his hand fell heavily on her shoulder. Deborah shook him off and got up quickly.

"Permit me to wish you good night here. I did not sleep well last night and —"

" 'Sdeath, madam! Tired, at your age!" he growled. "Another of your fine excuses! I begin to think, i'faith, you must be wholly frigid."

He walked heavily across to the table and refilled his wine cup while she watched him with contempt from where she stood.

Frigid! There spoke the cuckold husband! Balm for his self-esteem and comfort for his vanity! Did the fool think to shift the blame for his incompetence to her? A knowledge of the stale, flavourless dishes about to be served up was enough to blunt the

226

heartiest appetite! Did he really imagine his scrawny flesh was a
feast to tempt her? Did he think that because she was dead to him,
no other man had power to bring her to life? Didn't he know a
woman might be a block of ice in the arms of a distasteful spouse
and a burning fire in her lover's knowing hands? Was he unaware
of all this, with his arrogant assumption of superiority over her
when, in the last analysis, she owed him nothing – nothing at all?
There had been no place for love in the peculiar bargain struck
between them: a title for her, and for him the right to return to
London. Now they were quits. As for her gowns and the style in
which she lived, hadn't he himself called it so much dust thrown in
the eyes of the world? There had been no kindness as far as she personally was concerned: she had got nothing from him but an implacable coldness which had rebuffed all the efforts she had made at the
beginning to come to terms with him. Well, since that was how it
was, he could keep his obscene, fumbling advances! For a moment,
she almost wished that he might see her swooning in Kit's arms. It
would do him good. She glared back at him.

"Think what you like. Yet, without wishing to offend you, may I
suggest that your wealth may have a good deal to do with the trans-
ports you are evidently accustomed to in your various mistresses. You
might find it amusing to reflect on. Now let me wish you good
night."

He caught up with her at the door and gripping her roughly by
the arm forced her back into the room.

"You shall not get away so lightly," he snarled. "I have had
enough of your snubs."

"Let me go, sir! How dare you!" she exclaimed angrily.

"How dare I exercise my rights, madam? In case you have forgotten I shall have to remind you that I have rights, you know."

"Would you force me?"

"I should be reluctant to, but if you oblige me to. I am in no mood
tonight to listen patiently to your lying excuses," he told her in a
voice which had grown, she noticed, slightly thickened. He had not
released his grip on her arm.

"You're drunk!"

"Very possibly, my dear . . . very possibly. But it only makes you
more desirable."

Deborah was still struggling furiously to free herself when he
plunged his hand unexpectedly into the bosom of her dress. Her
first gasp of shock was succeeded by an impulse of sheer anger and

instantly her toe made violent contact with his shin. The Earl stepped sharply back, releasing her, whereupon Deborah hit him with all her strength.

They glared at one another, like a pair of fighting cats while he rubbed his cheek.

"So that's how it is!" he murmured softly.

"Yes, that is how it is!" she spat back at him. "And let me tell you, I will not tolerate your disgusting manners any longer."

She was so angry now that she had thrown caution to the winds.

"You slut! I'll show you who is master here!"

He made a rush for her, his hand grasped the bunch of ribbons which adorned her stomacher and he wrenched violently. The silken ties parted easily and it came away in his fist, revealing the frilled chemise beneath. She gave him a push which sent him reeling back a pace or two, giving her time to dive for refuge behind a chair, overturning a stool which stood in her way. There was such a ferocious glitter in her husband's eyes that she was beginning to be seriously alarmed.

"Not so sure of yourself now, are you?" he jeered nastily, as he advanced on her. "Come, confess that you are behaving like a spoilt child. Make amends and we'll say no more about it . . . if you are a good girl." His eyes rested lasciviously on her breasts.

"You expect me to apologize to you! You must be mad! Go and sleep off your drink, sir, and let me pass!"

"Not until you have begged my forgiveness, woman!"

He had kicked away the chair and, grasping Deborah by the wrists, was endeavouring to bring her to her knees. By this time he was beside himself with hatred for her and for himself for wanting her, which in turn only served to increase the loathing he felt for her. She struggled wildly but the Earl had the advantage of a man's strength and she was weakening.

Even so, the struggle lasted for a few moments more. The jug of hippocras was knocked flying, to smash on the floor. Wheels of fire revolved in Deborah's brain and she felt as though her heart must burst. She could scarcely breathe. Was he going to succeed in humilating her, after all? No, not if she could help it! With one last effort, she gathered all her strength and, before he could guess her purpose, she had bent swiftly as lightning and bitten him hard on the thumb.

He let out a muffled curse and opened his hands. Deborah ran,

228

staggering to the door, but she had no sooner grasped the handle than he was upon her. Glaring like a madman, eyes wild and hair dishevelled, he raised his doubled fist and hit her hard on the chin.

Deborah's eyes rolled in her head. She turned half round and dropped like a wounded bird.

He stood staring down at her for a moment with a blank expression, stirring the folds of her dress with one foot while he sucked his bleeding thumb.

"The trollop has some fight in her," he muttered. "A real bundle of thorns!"

His lips twisted in a curious smile and suddenly he bent and, lifting her inanimate body in his arms, bore her awkwardly from the room, reeling a little as he went.

Slowly, Deborah came back to consciousness. She was aware of a strange, bitter smell and half opened her eyes, only to close them again. There was something hard pressing into her stomach. She tried to move and found that she could not. Little by little, memory was returning and with it, fresh and horrible, the recollection of the ghastly scene which had taken place between her and her husband. What had happened since? Where was she? She groaned and opened her eyes properly. There was a hand holding a cloth soaked in vinegar bathing her temples.

"Ah, you are come to yourself again, I see," observed an alcoholic voice she recognized as her husband's. She tried to get up.

"Perhaps I ought to warn you," the voice pursued, "that you may spare yourself useless struggles. You are firmly tied. As a further precaution against your venomous tongue, I have also gagged you. You may curse away, I shall not be troubled by it. For once, my dear wife, you are going to submit to my pleasure." He giggled. "I must say, I wish you could see yourself. A most stimulating sight, I do assure you. Forgive me if I seem to digress, but I really do feel rather naughty." He giggled again. "I am no lady's maid and while I think I managed very creditably in getting off all those petticoats and busks and things you women seem to delight in, I also found it an extremely exhilarating experience, and I must confess, my lady, that I allowed myself a few very agreeable liberties with your charming person in the doing of it."

Deborah heard him, sick with horror. She was fully conscious again now and, from the agonies of discomfort she was suffering, was beginning to realize that she was, in the most literal sense of the words, bound hand and foot at the Earl's mercy.

He had stepped back a little way, apparently to gain a better view of his handiwork, and was leaning against the table, eyeing her with cynical satisfaction.

She was quite naked, her body bent over a small stool and retained in that kneeling posture by the fact that her arms, stretched out horizontally at full length, were tied securely to the bedpost. It was, he reflected, a sight to breathe life into a dying man: the bare flesh, veiled in places by loose, honey-coloured hair, the white breasts swinging free, the curved line of the back which rippled with spasmodic tremors . . . He wiped his moist forehead with a trembling hand, congratulating himself at the same time on the happy inspiration which had led him to bind her thighs to the two legs of the stool, thus forcing them apart and presenting her posterior in an exquisitely titillating light. She might rage and struggle as she would, she was condemned to that humiliating posture for as long as it should please him to keep her there. The knots which held her wrists were fast enough and he had not forgotten to fetter her ankles with a rope. Altogether, a most efficient piece of work.

Swaying a little on his feet, he returned to his victim.

"Well, my dear, I trust you are comfortable?" he continued airily. "Here we are, husband and wife alone together in the marital chamber, about to enjoy a little lawful intimacy." He was bending over her now, his hands exploring her throat, her breasts, fingers stroking, kneading, squeezing the pain-hardened nipples. "What are these murmuring sounds I hear? The first moans of pleasure you have ever vouchsafed me, perhaps? Tut tut! You make me think perhaps it needs some pains to bring you on. Fear not, my charmer, you shall have them. And do not glare at me when I am doing my best to please you." He straightened. "You are so like a wooden image whenever I approach you that the full splendours of your person have never been revealed to me until now. Indeed, it was a sin, my lady, to rob your husband of these joys." He was running his hand over her buttocks as he spoke, feeling the round, firmness of them in his palm. "If there is a fault it is, perhaps, that they could do with a little more colour in them, but that is easily remedied." A cruel pinch between finger and thumb followed the words.

"Was that another amorous sound I heard? Pray control yourself, madam." He chuckled drunkenly and lurched over to the bedpost, where he leaned, watching her from the corner of his eye.

"You look a little pale. Can it be that you are beginning to repent your impertinence? I do not care for that look." His hand came to rest heavily on the nape of her neck, forcing her head down. "There, madam. That is how I would have you: humble and submissive. You stand in need of correction, my lady, which I am about to administer. I meant at first only to give you a good beating, but now I have thought of a more original idea." He started to laugh, hiccuping and almost choking. Then, when he had got his breath back, he went on:

"It's an old custom we have in the north. My steward uses it on troublesome serving wenches. You'll not object to the comparison, I'm sure. All women are alike, and you will soon be ready to lick my boots and beg my favour just like them."

He made his way to a chest on which stood a jug of wine, drank and belched indelicately.

"Oh, I know what you're thinking. He's drunk, that's what you're thinking, he doesn't know what he's doing . . . Well, drunk, maybe, but not too drunk to chastise you properly . . ."

While he talked, he had been putting on the heavy black leather glove he used when hawking. Then, flexing his fingers, he picked up a bunch of green, rather hairy-looking foliage which had been lying on the table. This he waved under Deborah's nose.

"It looks a harmless kind of birch to punish your impudence, doesn't it? Well, wait and see."

He began brushing it up and down smoothly over her breasts and throat.

"It tickles, does it? Be patient. In a little while your skin will come up in red weals and then the itching will become intense. Have you guessed the instrument of your punishment? A bunch of nettles, my dear. It will leave no permanent scars, so have no fear, but for a few hours I am afraid that you will find it quite intolerably painful." He fell silent, absorbed in his task.

By now, Deborah's silken skin was becoming disfigured by great, dark red blotches. Her body twitched and she writhed and twisted convulsively within the narrow limits of her bonds. She had reached that limit of horror where the mind seems emptied of all reasoned thought and wanders in a limbo of pain and loathing. She had lost all count of time; there was nothing, no past, no future, only a great fire in which she was being slowly consumed. Lord almighty, have mercy . . . She bit back the prayer, wondering if it were possible to call on God in such a moment. No, this must be what hell was like: to hang in a timeless abyss, licked by flames at the malign will of the

231

fiend appointed for your torment. Oh, to slay the fiend! She would gladly have given her life then and there to take his! But fiends could not be killed. She found that she was weeping and made one furious effort, writhing on the stool, but the cords bit into her flesh and she subsided, choking back a sob.

Abruptly, he cast the nettles to the ground. His face was shining with sweat and there was a small froth of white spittle at the corner of his lips. He tore off his doublet feverishly, then poured a cup of wine and drank it at a draught.

"It's damned hot in here," he muttered, then, aloud, he said: "Well? Has that tickled you enough? Are you itching nicely?" He laughed. "I'll warrant you'd submit even to my advances, you bitch, in return for freedom to scratch yourself! Well, like a good husband, I am willing to perform that service for you myself. I have here some brambles, picked especially for you, which will do the business admirably."

Suiting the action to the words, he set to work, running the thorny sprays over the swollen, shuddering flesh, leaving a striated web of red weals from which the tiny droplets of red blood began to ooze.

Panting, dishevelled and wild-eyed, the Earl stared down at the blood, his face ravaged with desire. Hurling away the thorns, he took a poniard from his belt and, reeling, sliced through the cords holding Deborah's wrists and thighs. Lifting her round the waist, he kicked away the stool and lowered her ungently to the floor. She was breathing painfully and her eyes were closed. Growling like an animal, he threw himself on top of her.

XXIV

She let the mirror slip from her hands, asking herself how, after the abomination of the night before, she could still worry about the pimple on her chin, or the black rings round her eyes and her muddy complexion. Great heavens, why was she still living after such humiliation?

She stirred cautiously and grimaced with pain. Her whole body was one mass of tiny fresh scabs. She felt broken, soiled; waves of nausea rose up from her stomach and waves of burning heat washed up her spine. Every position was an agony, although it was least painful to lie on her stomach, in spite of the soreness of her inflamed chest. She caught herself hoping it would leave no marks and laughed bitterly at herself for being vain enough to worry about her beauty when her pride was in ribbons.

She reached out cautiously and felt about for the cup of water, then drank greedily. She was very thirsty.

Two hours earlier, a cheerful ray of sunshine had found its way through her bedcurtains and dragged her up from her sleep. The Earl must have carried her back to her own room when he had— She clenched her teeth, overcome by a sudden, murderous rage.

The mere thought of the villain was enough to make her forget her hurts. Oh, she would make him pay for his villainy ten times over, she would rend his evil face, roast him over a slow fire, one joint at a time, geld him, eviscerate him . . . Resigning herself, regretfully, to the evident truth that these exquisite prospects might be somewhat difficult of execution, Deborah was none the less determined that the matter should not be allowed to end there. In his drunken rage, he had wholly forgotten his wife's lofty connections. The Queen would not allow her protegée to suffer undefended. They would see how he maintained his grand airs before Elizabeth! That would soon bring him down to earth. Deborah gave a great sigh of revengeful satisfaction.

But where, she wondered, was her aunt?

Her first action on waking had been to send John Strong running

233

to the apothecary for an unguent with which she had managed somehow to anoint herself. It was impossible to send for one of the servants to help since the grapevine which operated on their level would ensure that the affair became the general property of the whole court within the shortest possible space of time. There was nothing like a domestic quarrel to provide the juiciest gossip! So she had kept to her bed and sent the maid away, claiming a chill. Rest and quiet were the best medicines, so let the women take their chattering tongues elsewhere.

Meanwhile, John Strong had been sent off again to the palace to urge Mistress Tucker to come at once. Her niece, who was in general so self-sufficient, felt today in desperate need of some friendly voice to comfort and sympathize. Besides which, it was important that Her Majesty be informed.

The little greyhound, who had been lying curled up on a cushion, sat up and pricked her ears, then rushed to the door, barking. Someone knocked.

Mistress Tucker came in, superbly herself as ever, her coif neatly framing her honest face, her plump chest thrown out, the very image of grim respectability in her black brocaded dress with its short, quilled cloak and white starched ruff. The one light touch to enliven all this sombre garb was the necklace of garnets which had been her niece's new year's gift. She sailed majestically up to the bed.

"What's this John Strong tells me, dear child? You are unwell?"

She bent down to kiss her niece and Deborah stifled a yelp as her aunt touched her sore shoulder.

"Oh, Aunt! If you only knew! I need you so much!" Tears welled from her eyes and she burst into sobs.

"There, there, my love! Don't take on so," Mistress Tucker said, stroking her hair.

"But if you knew . . ." Deborah hiccuped pitifully. "The most dreadful thing has happened — Ouch! Don't touch me!" The last words were almost a scream.

"Gracious me, child! Whatever ails you? Have you sent for a physician? Mercy on us, your forehead's burning hot! I wonder the Earl — Wait, I'll go to him myself." Flustered out of her usual calm, Mistress Tucker was on the point of bustling from the room.

"No! No, for pity's sake, don't leave me! Sit down, and I'll tell you everything . . . The Earl . . . the Earl is a monster!"

"What's that? The Earl a monster! Why, whatever next, child? Have you taken leave of your senses?"

"Well, you see . . . it's like this . . ." It was not, Deborah found, quite so easy to find words, or rather the words were there, jostling one another, fierce and accusing, behind her closed lips. It was simply impossible to utter them, to tell anyone at all of the shame she had endured. She would rather die, she thought, bursting into fresh sobs.

"There, there now . . . Just you tell your aunty." Mistress Tucker had drawn a stool to the bedside and proceeded to make encouraging noises. "Is that the trouble, then? You've had words with your husband, eh?"

"It's much worse than that," Deborah said, plumping for an edited version of the truth. "He beat me! Think of it, Aunt! He beat me!"

She raised her heated face to her aunt's. Her tears had ceased now.

"He'll pay for it, won't he?" she said hotly. "When the Queen hears of it?"

"Hoity toity, child! What a start is this? Would you have me trouble Her Majesty because you've squabbled with your husband? Is that what all this fuss is about? Mercy me!" Mistress Tucker clasped her plump hands to her heart. "You've taken a weight off my mind. I thought you must be really ill."

Deborah stared at her, wide-eyed.

"But, Aunt, it's terrible. Surely you must see how terrible?" she stammered, disconcerted.

"Listen to me, Deborah. You are angry now, and a bit carried away, I don't doubt, but temper was ever a bad counsellor, as you know quite well. Marriage isn't one long honeymoon, you know. Did you think men were always easy to live with? But there, you're very young still," she added indulgently. "If you were as old as I am, you'd have learned that there are plenty of the nobility keep their mistresses quite openly, and worse than that, even. There's many a wife left eating her heart out in the country, forced to countenance her husband's by-blows and in all else shamefully neglected. Confess now, in general the Earl's not such a bad husband? There's many would be glad to be in your place, surrounded by titles and luxury, only to raise your little finger to have a host of servants run to do your bidding." Mistress Tucker sighed. "Ah, if I'd only had your luck. And just for a few words out of turn, a bit of a hasty blow which I dare swear he's sorry for by this time, you'd have the impudence to go running to Her Majesty when she's so bothered by this nasty armada she's got us all at sixes and sevens and I don't know what! A fine return for all her goodness to you, I must say! Whatever next!"

Deborah simply stared at her speechlessly.

"No, my dear, your private affairs are for you to sort out," her aunt went on, in full spate now. "You wouldn't want to prejudice your future by doing something foolish, now, would you? Never forget, Deborah, never forget the trouble we've gone to to make you what you are. Her Majesty'd not be best pleased to hear that you and the Earl were at odds. But there now —" The white ruff quivered nearer. "What was it all about, eh?"

Deborah forced herself back to earth.

"I don't really know how to . . . It's not easy to tell you, Aunt, precisely . . ." Deborah's face was crimson.

"Not another word then!" Mistress Tucker said hastily, with a modest lowering of eyelids. "I know, I went through it all with my poor John. I'm afraid, my poor, poor child, that such things are all part of marriage, and we wretched women must put up with them, at whatever cost to our feelings. It makes you wonder sometimes what it is the men see in it, to be sure, but there, it seems to give them pleasure. Like it or not, giving in to them is the only way to keep them from straying and in a good humour." She cleared her throat and her pursed lips relaxed a little as she went on: "It's not a subject I like to talk about, as you may guess, but try and be a little more, well, a little more accommodating . . . you know what I mean. You'll see, your old aunt is right. The Earl's not a young man. He'll grow fond of you and then – well, who knows what tomorrow may bring? He's no heir from his first marriage, after all, and if you play your cards right, I dare say he'll look after you very nicely in his will." She sighed. "One never thinks about the future at your age. You go on merrily from day to day, but these things should be thought of. It's very well to be a countess, I grant you, but, just between ourselves, it would be nice to know you had a comfortable jointure coming to you, and everyone says that Norland's very, very well-to-do . . . Deborah, are you listening to me?"

"Yes, Aunt. I'm listening."

"There, you're a good girl. Take my advice and you'll find you'll do better," Mistress Tucker continued, well pleased with her diplomacy. "I was frightened for a moment that – well, there's been a lot of talk at court about you and young Mr Randolph – another madcap by what they say. Above all, child, no indiscretions! Remember that: no indiscretions. You can't afford to. Oh, I know, you'll tell me there's plenty of ladies at court does worse. I know it. But they have powerful families behind them, and money can excuse a lot. While you – well, don't let any of those fine gallants turn your head. Never forget, Deborah, that a spotless reputation is God's most precious gift to us women."

"No, Aunt. I won't forget."

Oh, if she would only shut up and stop preaching and go away. Please heaven, make her go away! Soon! To hear her, you'd think she knew all there was to know about it, that a happy marriage held no secrets for her! Huh! But it was just like Aunt Tucker to sing the praises of wedded prostitution and submission, when she was the most managing creature alive! Why, Deborah thought disrespectfully, she had turned her poor John into a drink-sodden wreck and driven him into his grave with her bullying.

She was clenching her fingers in the bedclothes, wondering how much more she could stand, when there was a timid knock at the door. It opened a few inches to reveal a nervous child in an apron who proffered a folded letter.

Advancing to within three steps of the bed, she curtsied and said: "This is for you, my lady."

"Ha?"

"From his lordship, my lady."

Deborah's hand moved, as though to wave her away, but Mistress Tucker was before her and had already taken the note.

"Allow me to hand it to you, my dear," she said regally, dismissing the girl with a nod.

No one at Norland House was aware of the precise relationship between them and Mistress Tucker was generally taken to be some connection of the Countess's.

"There you are again, child, all fire and brimstone! Suppose we read the letter instead."

Deborah slid one hand out from beneath the covers.

"No. Give it to me, please. I'll read it myself." She broke the seal and unfolded the sheet.

"Madam," she read, "I trust you are not too angry with me. Being much in drink, I so far forgot myself, in the presence of your manifold charms, as to lose that degree of control which properly belongs to a gentleman. I can promise you I shall not do so again, but remain your humble servant, Roger Durham, Earl of Norland."

Damn him! She screwed the sheet of paper in her hands.

"Well?" Her aunt was watching her anxiously.

237

"An apology, naturally. That costs little."

"An apology. That's good, that's very good. He's not a bad man at heart." Mistress Tucker was beaming. "Didn't I tell you so? Everything will be all right. Now, my love, let's have a look at these terrible injuries of yours." She smiled. "Confess now, you were more angry than hurt, weren't you? Just let me see and I'll send John Strong —"

"No, no, Aunt!" Deborah pulled the clothes up to her neck. "It's not worth the bother. I put a soothing lotion of sweet almond oil on it myself, and it will soon be better. Isn't it time you were getting back to the palace?"

"Merciful heavens!" Mistress Tucker started. "With all this fuss, I nearly made myself late. Whatever would everyone have thought. It's never happened before, not in more than thirty years." She was putting on her gloves. "Now, promise me you'll be good?"

"Yes, Aunt. Don't worry about me."

"Chance'd be a fine thing!" her aunt snorted. "I'll make you up one of my poultices of herbs and frumenty. It's a recipe I had off a Flemish woman, a carter's wife, and a sovereign balm it is. I'll bring it tomorrow."

A farewell kiss, and Deborah was alone at last. She knew her aunt meant well but it was a relief not to have to listen to her prosing on with the very advice that she least wanted to hear. Poor Aunt Tucker had led such a restricted life, how could she ever understand that her niece had broken through her strict conventions? It had been foolish even to send for her.

Deborah closed her eyes.

A long while later, when she opened them again, something of the light of youth and hope seemed to have gone out of them for ever. The last link with childhood had been broken. She had lost the vague fear which she had always had of Mistress Tucker and with that fear had gone the feeling which drives the young to seek protection and understanding from those who have brought them up, even when they know that no such understanding is possible. She knew now that she was on her own, there was no aunt or anyone else to lean on. She was alone as every person on earth was alone with their own problems, and alone she must face up to her own problems and solve them.

Well, with all the aids which a bounteous Creator had so generously bestowed, she would manage somehow!

For the moment, discretion was definitely the better part of wisdom. Not even for the pleasure of slaying the Earl was she prepared to risk the gallows. It was simply not worth it. And she had no talent for poisoning, which offered a better chance of getting away with it. Besides, she hated the idea of poison: a coward's weapon which did not attract her and which, because it killed in secret, must surely take away half the joy of vengeance. So, she would be meek and gentle with the villain. Oh, not too much! She could not do the impossible! But enough to allow them to resume their normal, joyless relations. But let him beware! She had an excellent memory and too much pride to forget what he had done to her. It would do no harm to let him wait, though . . . She lapsed into thought, wondering how to punish him.

Setting aside straightforward murder, it was not at first sight, altogether easy. But no, if she killed him it would inevitably recoil on her own head, and she was not such a fool, or so tired of life, that she was ready to sacrifice her ambitions and in all probability her neck, in cold blood, for the immediate satisfaction of her pride. What then? A savage smile crossed her face. Patience. Time would tell. A man like the Earl, who was capable under his cold exterior of such madness, would sooner or later put himself in peril . . . some sordid affair with a woman . . . or politics . . . what did it matter? When that day came, she would know how to use it, and then she could trample him underfoot with impunity.

XXV

Deborah tripped lightly down the terrace steps, pausing for a few minutes at the bottom to greet her hostess, Lady Warwick. Then, exchanging smiles and commonplaces with fellow-guests, bestowing cautious kisses on painted cheeks and offering her small hand, in its scented gloves, to right and left as she went, she passed on into the gardens.

They were packed to overflowing with a brilliant throng, pressing about the intricate knot beds, gazing in wonder at the shapes cut out in juniper and box, leaning over the fountains where the water sprang crystal clear from the mouths of grotesque masks, gesticulating and exclaiming over the magnificent marble statues which Lord Warwick had brought from Italy. Everyone, in short, was swarming to look at the hundred and one marvels which amply justified the gardens' fame.

Deborah moved on, graceful, a little remote, her small head proudly erect.

Beyond the great fountain with its basin of coloured stones round which a bevy of ladies in light dresses were giggling and cooing delightedly, she waved gaily to Sir Walter Raleigh.

As he made his way through the crowd towards her, that most elegant of gentlemen made appreciative note of the equal elegance before him. Her dress of apple-green satin with immense padded sleeves was very tight in the bodice and opened in front, over a bell-shaped farthingale, to show a forepart of coral-coloured velvet flourished with gems. Her hood, a ravishing affair of fine gold lace which echoed the cuffs of the same gold at her wrists and the great triple rebato collar, was fastened coquettishly with clusters of diamonds to match the diamonds at her throat and ears. Standing there, resting carelessly in the entrance to a colonnade, with a halo of gold about her, she reminded him suddenly of one of those Italian damsels whose portraits in their rich garments seemed at once delicate and strong, touching in their half-childish dignity which, under the painter's brush, became tinged with a more disturbing, pagan charm.

"God's death, my fair friend," he exclaimed gallantly as he kissed her hand. "Have you bewitched the sun into parting with his monopoly? You are dazzling!"

Deborah smiled. "I thank you for the compliment. Its originality makes it doubly valuable. I've been sated with flattery, good, bad and indifferent, but this is the first time anyone has ever compared me to the sun. All the same, I fear I shall have to disabuse you. I have no pact with the sun – I merely wished to dress in tune with this fine day."

She laid her hand daintily on his proffered arm and they wandered on together, chatting amicably.

Deborah enjoyed his company for a good many reasons, chief of which was that he seemed to take pleasure in hers, and yet their talk remained direct and friendly, with none of the sly insinuations and embarrassing, even vulgar innuendoes she too often met with from other gentlemen about the court. Furthermore, she might as well admit it, Raleigh was a handsome figure of a man with deep, sparkling eyes set in a face whose clear-cut features were enhanced by his short, dark beard. He had a splendid presence, perfect manners, and it was always nice to be with an attractive man, even for nothing more exciting than a chat. Last, but by no means least, it delighted her to watch the jealous faces of the other ladies when he sought her out. Not that there was anything in it, of course. Sir Walter Raleigh was aiming high and cared not who knew it.

He was the younger son of a Devonshire gentleman who had used his daring and military prowess to such good effect that he had won the royal favour. Now, at thirty-five, he was the possessor of a knighthood, lands and titles in England and in Ireland, numerous lucrative patents and monopolies and had this very year been appointed to the sought-after post of Captain of the Guard. Yet even this was not enough for a man of his ambition. With Leicester failing, his heart was set on the vacant place of favourite closest to the Queen. Alas for his hopes. Just recently the Queen's eye had been turning away from him to the daredevil figure of the young Earl of Essex. Raleigh's star seemed to be setting. As a result, it was not safe to mention the Earl's name in his presence and Deborah, who had no wish to become involved in that quarrel, was careful to avoid it. In any case, there were so many other things to talk about.

241

She would never tire of hearing him describe his travels and she questioned him avidly about the strange lands he had visited, their flora and fauna and the natives who lived there. She wanted to know all about the new colony of Virginia, named in honour of the Virgin Queen and about the strange new vegetable called potato which he told her he was planning to grow on his estates in Ireland. But what entertained her most of all was to listen to his witty and humorous account of the way he had succeeded in popularizing the smoking of the tobacco weed at court.

They were still laughing together when Deborah looked about her at the crowded gardens.

"But where is Her Majesty? I have not seen her," she said.

"She is not here. She has already left."

"But I thought she enjoyed Lady Warwick's parties?"

Raleigh frowned. "So she does," he said bitterly. "But she has become so besotted with that frippery fellow, my Lord of Essex, that it seems she would rather spend her time in his company. She had no sooner arrived here than nothing would do for her but to be off again, leaving her retinue behind and with that stripling for almost her sole escort. At fifty-three, to be so enamoured of a youth not yet twenty – plague take him!"

"Hush, my dear friend. Do not talk so loudly."

Raleigh's face cleared a little. "You are right, as usual, Countess," he said. "There's a deal of wisdom behind that pretty face, I know. Besides, I have to admit Her Majesty had reason to leave in haste – the news from Whitehall —"

"What news?"

"It is not yet official. Only a few of us know."

"Oh, tell me! I'll not breathe a word, I promise you." She smiled roguishly at him, shaking her head so that her ear-rings flashed. "Please, Sir Walter? What was it about?"

"A vessel put in at Plymouth yesterday with news from Drake."

"From Drake?"

"Aha, I see you are as excited about the expedition as all the rest of us! Well, it seems to have been a roaring success, although we've not much to go on yet. I gather he sailed straight into Cadiz harbour and sank or burned most of the shipping inside, all with his usual effrontery and without the least damage to his own fleet. It's worthy of the old sea-dog, isn't it?"

Deborah could have flung her arms round Raleigh's neck and kissed him. Thank heaven! The Spaniard had been beaten on his

242

own doorstep, the danger was over, for the time being at least, and Kit safe and sound! It was the most marvellous news.

"Yes," she said simply. "Oh, yes!" Her eyes were shining like stars. At the same time she was thinking fast. "So that means the fleet should be home soon?"

"As to that, I can't say. . . . God's death, don't look so disappointed. If you want to know so very badly I can probably find out for you. I'll let you know."

He raised her fingers to his lips and was gone into the talking, laughing crowd.

Deborah looked round her. Here and there, knots of elderly gentlemen conferred solemnly, their white ruffs bobbing above dark velvet gowns. Ladies kissed and twittered together, tripping hand in hand in groups of three or four, their bright colours and gemmed hair making them look like so many flowers scattered over the green lawns. Among them stalked the men, preening themselves like peacocks in a variety of exotic hose . . .

Oh, those hose! It was nothing, they said, for a man to spend twenty, forty, even a hundred pounds on one pair of breeches. They came in all shapes, from round French hose, made very short, to long Venetians, gartered below the knee with gold or silver lace. Some wore great wide gallyslops down to the knee, others bombasted trunk hose with canions, while all, without exception, were paned and slashed, fringed and embroidered in the most brilliant colours, pearl white, primrose, carnation, gingerline, and the richest fabrics: satins, velvets, damasks and brocades all newly come from the tailor. No wonder the women could not take their eyes off them.

A servant approached her with an offer of refreshments but Deborah shook her head. For some time now she had had little appetite for her meals. She strolled on, turning her back on the long trestle tables set up underneath the trees. The sight of such vast quantities of food made her feel distinctly queasy and she tried to keep from looking at the silver dishes which the serving men were bearing deftly among the guests.

Suddenly, all she wanted was to be alone to enjoy her happiness, away from all these people and their meaningless chatter.

She caught sight of a low, tunnelled arch half-hidden behind trailing ivy and went towards it, laughingly fending off the several gentlemen who, seeing her without Raleigh, immediately swarmed like wasps round a honey pot.

Musicians were playing softly at various points in the gardens

243

and she sighed contentedly. The sweet airs of lutes and viols were in perfect harmony with her mood. She sat down dreamily in the green shade.

This was the first time she had been out, for although her scratches had been more painful and spectacular than deep she had kept to her bed for a week, with John Strong dancing attendance like a mother hen. Rest and continued applications of sweet almond balm had worked wonders and, to her inexpressible relief, no permanent harm seemed to have resulted.

As for the Earl, he had retreated behind a barrier of remote courtesy and had not attempted to approach her since her recovery. This was a new development and a welcome one. Perhaps, after all, he was genuinely sorry for his conduct and prepared to wait patiently for the memory of it to fade. Optimistically, Deborah shrugged that problem away. What did her painful experience with her depressing husband matter when soon, very soon, Kit would be coming home? The war would settle itself and —

She roused herself abruptly from her amorous dream. Heavens! Sir Walter had promised to get more news. What was she doing here when he was probably looking for her at this very moment?

She rose, shaking out her skirts, and paused for a moment at the entrance to the arbour, half-blinded by the light outside. As she stepped out, she almost ran into an elegant gentleman in a doublet of cloth of silver pricked with rubies.

"James!"

"How are you, Deborah?" He took her hand, which she had been too taken aback to think of offering, and kissed it. "I saw you a moment ago, over by the trees, and was coming to inquire after your health."

"I'm very well, James, thank you. And you . . . how are you?" she answered, with a forced gaiety.

"Oh, I'm . . . you know." He waved the matter away, as though it held no interest for him. "I got back from Wales three days ago, and I heard at court that you were ill?"

"Oh, nothing serious. A chill, that's all."

She was plucking nervously at the ostrich feathers of her fan.

There was a short silence.

"Shall we walk?" he said at last, offering his arm.

"Gladly."

This was agony. Both of them so formal, with an awkwardness between them that was almost tangible. Even the touch of her sleeve brushing his was vaguely embarrassing. Deborah could have screamed. To be reduced to this frigid politeness when they had had such fun together was incredible. Yet, though it shocked her to think of it, she could not help remembering that they had lain together, naked in bed, exchanging the kisses and caresses to which she had consented so lightheartedly, and which now rose up to confront her. She racked her brains for something to say but every time she thought of something she found herself swallowing the words for fear of uttering something out of place, some commonplace observation which would remind them of the past which, still so recent, must not be recalled at any cost, as she could see from the strained look on James's face.

She watched him out of the corner of her eye as they walked. He looked so ill! Where was the infectious gaiety which had warmed her heart as soon as she saw him? Poor James. Impulsively, she pressed his arm affectionately.

He looked down at her, their eyes met and, for the fraction of a second, they were very close. He placed his hands over hers.

"Are you happy, my darling?" he murmured softly.

Deborah had just opened her mouth to answer when she caught sight of two exquisite visions coming towards them. One was fair, enveloped in a cloud of rose-pink gauze, the other dark and sensuous, her heavy skirts of gold purl over red swaying provocatively. Drat them! What would those two harpies think, seeing her with James?

At that moment, she heard her name called and turning, saw Raleigh.

"Ah, my dear Countess. I find you at last."

"Oh dear, I am sorry! Have I put you to a dreadful lot of trouble?" James was forgotten and she was gazing earnestly at Raleigh. "When —?"

"I'm sorry to disappoint you but it seems Sir Francis is determined to prolong his stay among our worthy Spanish friends for a little while yet."

"What?"

"Yes. He's captured the haven of Sagres, near the southern tip of the peninsula, and according to the despatches brought by the trading vessel means to use it as a base for ravaging the west coast and interrupting King Philip's sea traffic. I don't think we can expect to see him home for some months yet."

"But — but wasn't he supposed to come straight home when his mission was accomplished?" Deborah asked in a small, stunned voice.

The two women were looking at her curiously. Raleigh bowed a greeting and said to Deborah: "Look, my dear, if you want to know more about it, why not apply to Lady Gilford? Lord Christopher, the Marquis's brother, is with the fleet and I'm sure that she will be able to tell you much more than I can."

The fair Penelope was already squeezing in between Raleigh and Deborah and now she said in honeyed tones: "But of course! I shall be delighted to help you, Countess. As it happens I accompanied Kit to Plymouth, along with my friend Lady Aldhurst, and we had many opportunities of talking with Sir Francis . . . Oh, what a man!" She fluttered her eyelashes coyly. "His manners, my dear, positively brutal! But such *virility* – it seems to go right through one!" She giggled affectedly and went on: "So I can confirm what you have said, Walter. He never meant to stop at Cadiz. Oh dear no! He explained to his officers quite clearly that what he wanted was to harry the Spaniards in their own waters. I'm sure he's nowhere near returning yet."

Cynthia with Kit at Plymouth!

"Now that I think of it," Penelope was continuing, mercilessly, her eyes on Deborah's pale face, "what a pity, Countess, that you were not able to be with us at Plymouth. Those few days before they sailed were altogether magical. Dancing and revels every night . . . such gaiety! The deck of the *Elizabeth Bonaventure* was quite, quite unforgettable. No one could have resisted it. Aren't I right, my love?"

Lady Aldhurst smiled languorously in smug assent.

Damn them both! Deborah put up her chin and surveyed them, a sardonic smile on her lips.

"I thank your ladyship. You have been most kind. Your news was extremely interesting – more so, I must confess, than your accounts of revelry by night. Although I can understand your own enthusiasm, naturally, and yours, Lady Aldhurst," she added smoothly. "When one is no longer so very young, a little darkness is welcome to dispel the wrinkles and restore the illusion of youth. For myself, I prefer the daylight." She curtsied briefly. "Your servant, ladies." Turning to Raleigh she held out her hand: "Thank you for your kind help, my friend . . . James, shall we walk on?"

James had been standing silently in the background. Deborah took his arm firmly and together they resumed their walk.

XXVI

Hands on hips, the wise-woman surveyed the patient extended on the scrubbed wooden table.

Her manner, her white hands and the cultivated accent all belied her simple garb. Some young woman of quality, for sure, who had fallen victim to the wiles of a seducer and now was come in secret to know the worst. The midwife had seen plenty in her time and she knew that they soon lost their proud airs and wept and begged her to help them. Well, it was all profit to her but, Lord, if she didn't think sometimes that it was all wrong! There were poor folk, often with scarcely enough to feed themselves, and yet longing for kids as if it were heaven's greatest gift! She shrugged and, wiping her hands on her dubiously clean apron, embarked none too gently on her examination of the patient.

The room was filled with the smell of stale cabbage, mingled with something else reminiscent of cats. From the other side of a partition came the shrill, triumphant bawling of a new-born baby.

"No doubt about that, me dear," the midwife declared presently. "Another seven months and you'll have a fine, bouncing child."

Instead of the flood of tears she had expected, her patient's face was illumined by a ravishing smile.

"Are you quite sure, Mistress?" she asked, sitting up a little.

"You may rest easy on that score. Thirty years I've been in the trade and if Doll Woodstock tells you you're with child that's what you are! Now, down you get and be off with you, my girl, I've work to do."

Helping with the hooks of her gown, she asked curiously: "So you mean to keep the little one?"

The other woman looked round, startled.

"Of course. What else?"

"Oh, as to that, nothing." The woman spat on the ground. " 'Twas for your own good I asked. I don't like to see unwanted children brought into this world. I could have given you something."

247

"You are very kind, Mistress Woodstock but, contrary to what you seem to believe, the news you have just given me is very welcome."

The older woman shifted a little uncomfortably.

"I'm glad to hear it, I'm sure. It does my heart good to see the little innocents." She tucked back a greasy-looking lock of hair which had fallen from under her coif and then, folding her arms over her massive breasts, she produced a conspiratorial, would-be maternal smile and asked: "Where do you mean to have the little darling? I can make arrangements, if it suits you. I've some nice clean rooms and I'm not one to shoot my mouth off. You'll be in good hands with Mother Woodstock."

"It's very good of you. I appreciate your offer but you need not concern yourself about me, Mistress Woodstock. I have everything I need at home. Good day to you."

The door closed behind her.

"And there's one I'll not be seeing again," Mistress Woodstock muttered crossly. "That's what it is to have a soft heart. It only ruins the business. I'd have done better to hold my peace. Ah, she's all honey sweet, but she's a whore like all the rest of them!"

She tucked up her skirts and, taking out the purse attached by a string around her waist, slipped into it the silver piece which her visitor had left.

Ugh! What a horrible old woman! Deborah made her way down the dingy staircase. She went slowly and cautiously, despite her anxiety to be rid of the place, since the stairs were so steep and slippery with refuse and filth of every kind that every step threatened to be her last. And this, she told herself with a little rush of gladness, was not the moment to go breaking her neck!

Was it fear of malicious gossip, or the wish to keep her secret to herself for a little longer? She had wanted to be quite sure before putting herself in the expert hands of the midwife most often resorted to by women of quality. That would be the confirmation of her condition.

As a result, she had yielded to impulse and, slipping out of Norland House, modestly dressed in one of the gowns she had worn before her marriage, had made her way on foot to the City.

There, she had gone into the first respectable-looking apothecary's shop she saw and asked her question. The big shop was rather dark inside and cluttered from floor to blackened ceiling with an assortment of pots and jars, all labelled with strange Latin names, with bottles of wine and casks and jars of tobacco. The air was thick with wreathing smoke and at the far end a group of young men were gathered round a glowing hearth engaged, under the direction of the apothecary, in learning the difficult art of smoking tobacco through a pipe. Blushing a little under their ogling gaze, which made her feel as if she had come out without her clothes, she obtained the information she desired and finished up in this verminous tenement.

Well, a few moments' unpleasantness was a small price to pay for such news.

She, Deborah was going to have a child – Kit's child. Of that she was quite sure. According to her calculations, her pregnancy must date from the beginning of March and at that time she had been seeing him every day. Thank you, God! she was saying to herself, over and over again, the glad tears starting from her eyes. Never again would she be alone! When her son was born – for it was going to be a son, she was certain. It had to be! Men were always so proud of their sons and Kit would be no exception. Then, when he was born, she would have a small living creature all her own to cherish and protect, another Kit who would never leave her or be unfaithful to her.

She frowned, thinking that she would have to tell the Earl since, although he may have had no part in the conception of this marvellous son-to-be, he was none the less the father in the world's eyes and – it was to be supposed – in his own. It would not be difficult to juggle with a week more or less and in February, after her return from Greenwich, the Earl had pestered her sufficiently to find it convincing. Poor man, so proud of his family, had he thought, when he married her that he might have an heir, and that heir would have bourgeois blood in his veins? Deborah giggled, a little nervously. Well, he would have to get used to the idea. Besides, although he might not know it, he had been lucky. Gilford was as good as Norland any day and she might have got herself with child by a much less satisfactory lover.

She thought for a moment. Tomorrow they were to make the journey to Gladhurst, invited, like most of the court, to the revels which the Baron was holding in honour of the Queen's visit. Bother! If he took it badly, it would spoil all her pleasure in the holiday, but how could she gauge her husband's probable reaction? He was so impenetrable. Very well then. She made up her mind. She would tell him on their return from Gladhurst in three days' time.

In the street, she hugged her shawl about her and slipped through the crowds. Without her heavy court farthingale she felt so light, light as a girl: for a brief moment she was a girl among other girls, with her own, simple happiness.

All at once, as she turned to admire the artistry of a butcher's stall, where a great boar's head sat crowned with bays and rosemary, she caught sight of a man's figure, in a hooded cloak, four or five stalls behind her, apparently shrinking back behind an awning to avoid her notice. That was odd. As she emerged from the apothecary's shop she had almost bumped into that same hood; she was sure that it was the same because of the colour, an indefinable rusty-green, and – yes, she remembered now, she had seen it lurking in the street when she came out of the wise-woman's house. What on earth did it mean? Could this man be following her?

Deborah determined to find out.

She walked on casually as far as the next turning, rounded it and then turned suddenly. The man was still there, a tall fellow, a little bent under the weight of the satchel he carried slung over his shoulder, his unsavoury hood pulled well down over his face. He was walking rather slowly.

She stood for a moment, pretending to have lost her way, while keeping a watch on him out of the corner of her eye. Suddenly, without warning, he opened a door and vanished inside.

Deborah let out a sigh of relief. She had been a fool, after all. The man was simply on his way home: all the rest had been a figment of her own imagination. And yet, she was still not quite happy, not altogether reassured.

The ragged man had reminded her of someone else, but who? Then she remembered. Surely it was the beggar who was often to be found hanging about outside Essex House? She told herself it was impossible. She must be mistaken. A beggar in the city would get nothing but a fine and the wrong end of a stick about his shoulders. Besides, why should he be following her? The Earl? In league with a beggar? It did not make sense. If he had wanted to catch her with a lover, he need not have waited until now. All the same, she made up her mind to be on her guard in future.

XXVII

Gladhurst lay some twenty-five miles from London in the county of Kent. Deborah and the Earl reached it about mid-morning, after setting out at dawn.

The ride had been a pleasant one, over roads lined with fresh, smiling green. The woods and copses they passed were a mass of bluebells or carpeted with white wood anemones all down the long aisles of hazel coppice, furred with young, green leaf, among which the tall oaks still stood up bare and brown, as though waiting until the last possible moment before putting on, almost overnight, their new dress of bright, unexpected yellow. Wheat and barley were a green haze on the fields, and thousands upon thousands of fruit trees spread their pale blossom to the sky.

Deborah's first sight of Gladhurst drew from her a cry of wonder and delight.

It was a proud and splendid house to which the Baron had just finished making extensive alterations and improvements. A first glance showed where the ancient stone keep which formed the central core of the building had been laboriously extended into two wings of red brick with copings of white stone. The effect was clean, straight and serenely dignified. Nevertheless, the architect had been careful to avoid too clinical a regularity by carving every available inch of stone with a plethora of florid decoration. Pilasters framed the tall windows, extravagantly carved marble columns flanked the three monumental entrance porches, the roof was exotically corbelled and corniced and, to crown all, was surmounted by a pair of turrets domed with copper and covered in gilding.

The entrance court was already a scene of milling animation. A great many ladies and gentlemen were on horseback, apparently about to set out for the chase.

The Baron, a man of fifty or thereabouts, short and stout with an appearance of rude health and the ruddy complexion that comes from good living and even better drinking, was bustling round his guests, seconded by a large, bony female with a hearty laugh that revealed a disconcerting array of immensely long, yellow teeth.

"Lady Gladhurst," the Earl informed Deborah briefly. "As for the rest —" His arm embraced them all: "No need to tell you. You know most of them already. Whitehall to Gladhurst is merely from the pigstye to the paddock!"

"My God!" Deborah said, ignoring the last remark. "Where do they put all these people?"

"Anywhere, I suppose. Helter skelter in the attics and distributed amongst the neighbouring gentry. Anywhere there is a spare corner after the Queen has been comfortably installed. Faith, she and her suite alone must take up three-quarters of Gladhurst! However, you need not be alarmed, my dear. Harry is an old friend and knows my horror of makeshift arrangements. He has promised me lodging here at the house. But for that, I should never have put myself out for this circus, as you may well imagine."

The Baron had apparently been as good as his word. They had no sooner dismounted and greeted their hosts than Deborah was escorted to her chamber – or rather, half a chamber divided by a hanging, from the bustle of people moving about on the other side – but still, a place to call her own. She found to her satisfaction that Betty, sent on the day before with the baggage, had already unpacked and laid out her things.

"Don't dawdle too long in front of your mirror," had been the Earl's parting words: "We are to join the hunt."

Putting off her dusty travelling dress, therefore, she slipped hurriedly into the smart orange tawny velvet braided with whey colour which Betty had laid out for her.

It was the first time she had found herself a guest at such a grand occasion. Ever since her marriage political events, the trial and execution of the Queen of Scots, the imminence of war with Spain, had left little room for festivities, and she was looking forward to it with happy anticipation.

She was just finishing tying her laces with fingers that trembled with excitement when a deafening fanfare, accompanied by loud cheers and the distant sound of dogs barking and grooms shouting, made her jump and run to the window.

"Quick, Betty! My hat and gloves! For heaven's sake, child, make haste!"

She was filled with delicious palpitations. Tearing the hat from

252

the girl's hands, she clapped it on top of her curls, gave herself a conspiratorial wink in the mirror and was off.

Everything went off as planned: the chase in the deer forest, the picnic under the elms, and the triumphal return to the house all took place in a joyous, holiday atmosphere which was enhanced by Her Majesty's loud laughter. Thank goodness, the Queen seemed to have recovered her spirits since the success at Cadiz . . . Cadiz . . . Sagres . . . Kit . . .

Deborah jumped. Fool that she was! The Earl was waiting for her and here she was standing daydreaming. She seized her glass and gave her attention to her hair.

She was in her white linen shift, embroidered with arabesques in gold thread, her neck and shoulders bare. A matching waist petticoat was fastened over the tight busks which constricted her waist and pushed up her bosom into voluptuous curves. Beneath the petticoat, her long legs were clad in stockings of flesh-coloured silk with embroidered clocks, fastened above the knee by lace garters with a rosette of black satin, and ended in a pair of dainty gilded slippers.

She lifted her hand to stop the tire-woman who was busy at her back with combs and brushes and a mouth full of pins.

"That is perfect, Betty," she said quickly. "I don't think we need do another thing. What do you say?"

"Oh, I think your ladyship looks lovely," Betty said with enthusiasm, when she had disposed of the pins, gazing worshipfully at her mistress.

Deborah's hair, after infinite brushing and scenting with orris root, had been drawn softly back in gleaming, coppery waves over her ears and caught up behind in a fat, twisted double plait which was then fastened so as to stand up in a charmingly provocative way on top of her head and kept in place by a narrow biliment of rubies and diamonds.

Now to put the finishing touch to the masterpiece with just the lightest use of cosmetics.

"I'll do this myself," she decreed. "All I want you to do is to hold this steady." She handed the mirror to the girl, then fell to studying her face critically.

Hmm . . . no, decidedly no paint on the cheeks – not even if people did talk, as she had heard they did. To the devil with fashion, and with other women! They could go madder day by day if that was what they wanted: dyeing their hair all colours of the rainbow, chopping it short and then making up for the deficiency with hanks of false hair and padding, burying their faces underneath layers of white and red paint. Let them say what they liked, she was not going to submit to such ravages. No, as always, she would keep her own face, daringly smooth and unpainted, and with it the freshness and originality which distinguished her from other women.

This vital question decided, she drew up her stool to the table and selecting a minute brush which she dipped in a few drops of oil of rosemary, rubbed it delicately over her eyebrows, smoothing them into two shining wings. Next, her eyelids were shaded from a cake of green paste whose delicate colouring made a perfect foil for the brilliance of her eyes, After that, her lips were enlivened with the faintest touch of red; then it was time for Betty to hand her the hare's foot with which to powder lightly over her face, neck and shoulders. The finishing touch was a patch, placed triumphantly over her left cheek.

There! That was the trickiest part done! Busked, curled and painted, nothing remained now but the outer portions of her dress and she would be ready for the banquet.

Betty was already bringing the farthingale, the cumbersome cage of whalebone and wire which Deborah had learned stoically to endure.

After the farthingale, came the cushionet, tied round the waist to give the whole structure the right forward tilt, and a further petticoat to soften the hard lines. Then the boned white satin bodice which, since the dress was not designed to be worn with a separate stomacher, had a long, V-shaped front embroidered all over with seed pearls and diamonds, cut low on the breast and descending to well below the waist. Finally, staggering respectfully under the weight of it, Betty inserted her mistress into the heavy overdress of gold brocade and fastened the separate sleeves, also of gold but monstrously puffed and paned with white satin, which started from the point of her shoulders, leaving the greater part of her breast and collar bones bare.

Even so, this was not yet the end.

Climbing on to a stool, Betty began fixing the collar: two gigantic insect wings of transparent gauze, these, too, studded with pearls and diamonds.

Deborah stood stiffly, abandoning herself to Betty's neat fingers while she fretted inwardly, wondering if it would hold. Heavens! What would she look like supposing the whole beastly thing were to collapse about her ears?

"Have you finished? Good. Fetch me the big mirror and let me see."

Yes . . . oh, yes, indeed! It was worth the exorbitant sum which that new French sewing-woman had demanded. Penelope and the rest of them would be ready to die of envy!

She glanced at the bed where lay her tasselled white satin gloves and her fan, a magnificent jewelled fan which had belonged to the first Countess of Norland and had only required to be refreshed with new white satin. There was the miniature glass to hang at her girdle, her handkerchief, also fringed with gold, nothing was missing.

She gave a start and put her hand to her throat.

Goodness! What was she thinking of? In all the excitement she had almost forgotten the jewels.

"Why didn't you tell me?" she grumbled at Betty. "Run, quickly. Fetch the casket. Another minute and I should have gone down like this! A nice fool I should have looked! All London would have been laughing."

She gave a tiny laugh herself as she opened the casket and turned the contents out on to the table. Huge, deep red rubies glowed softly, surrounded by brilliants and matched with oriental pearls as big as marrowfat peas. A triple collar of gems, bracelets, rings, pendants: all the celebrated Norland jewels which the Earl had condescended to disgorge from his safe for the occasion.

"Go and tell his lordship I am ready," she told Betty as she fastened two hanging drops, like perfect, quivering beads of blood, one at either ear.

The banquet had been going on for three hours. On her right, Deborah had Lord Edmonds, a youthful aspirant to fashion who was much occupied playing games with his other neighbour under the table. She was a girlish thirty-five-year-old in a lilac wig to match a dress cut quite indecently low, who was giggling with delight at his attentions. On Deborah's left was Sir Hugh Denford, an exceedingly self-assured, blond gentleman who, once contact was made, had been assiduous in pressing ardent compliments upon her.

Apart from forcing herself to think up polite replies from time to time to his unceasing flow of gallant innuendo, Deborah soon gave up listening with more than half an ear and gave her attention instead to the glittering spectacle before her.

The walls of the Great Chamber were lined with rich tapestries

255

and hangings of silk brocaded with gold and silver thread. Two long tables stood face to face, covered with needlework cloths and spread with vessels of solid silver. These two tables were joined at one end by a dais, where the Queen sat, enthroned beneath a cloth of state, dressed in rich purple and flanked by her maids of honour, Lord and Lady Gladhurst, the Earl of Essex and other noble and honourable gentlemen, among whom were the Lord Chancellor, Sir Christopher Hatton, and Sir Walter Raleigh who was seen to be eyeing Essex in no very friendly fashion.

Deborah's gaze softened as it came to rest on the Queen. Her Majesty was dazzling today! Who would think to see her now, overflowing with the hearty good-fellowship to which she brought the same fierce energy as she did to the gravest problems of state, that underneath that surface coquetry was a brain endowed with the most varied talents, a mind capable of understanding the most difficult sciences, a linguist of distinction, a fine calligrapher, a —

Deborah's silent paean of praise came to an abrupt halt as the viols ceased playing and silence fell. Like herself, the other guests had turned from their chatter or their food to look about them, in the expectation of some pleasant surprise.

Borne on the shoulders of four men, a gigantic pie made its appearance and passing solemnly in procession down the hall between the tables, came to a halt at last before the royal guest.

The lid of the pie was raised and from beneath it appeared a very young page dressed in green velvet with a crown of lilies of the valley on his head. In a small, piping voice, he embarked on a short speech in Latin, then presented a heavy golden goblet to the Queen.

Her Majesty, looking wholly delighted, patted the boy's cheek and accepted the gift. Plunging her fingers into the cup she swore contentedly and drew them out in a rippling mass of dark blue stones which she raised up on high, to thunderous applause.

"God's death! This is an incomparable necklace!" she exclaimed and, turning to Lord Gladhurst, added: "Come, my Harry. Thou knowest right well how to receive thy sovereign. There, let me kiss thee for it!" And suiting the action to the word, she gave the baron a smacking kiss on either cheek.

Lord Gladhurst rose and bowed very low.

"May Your Majesty see in this humble offering an expression of my respectful love," he said.

"Indeed, and that is what I do see in it, Harry mine," the Queen assured him, while her eyes caressed the sapphires. "Believe me when I say that your loyal affection is what most touches my heart . . ." A second's pause and her hand crashed down on the table as she cried in a loud voice: "Ho there! Music ho! Let us have a song to regale us while we turn our minds to this excellent food. I mean to see that honour is done to our host, my lords!"

The servers and waiters began moving to and fro once more, and a constant succession of fresh dishes was brought in, heaped with delicious meats and decorated with superb artistry with mosses and foliage, flowers and fruit.

Yet, whether it was due to excitement or to her condition, Deborah found that she was not hungry. For the look of it, she toyed with some pike mousse, and then, after refusing successively the carp's roes, the hare paté, the sucking pig stuffed with pistachio nuts, a whole gamut of fish and a variety of birds served with their feathers, opted for a portion of burbot stewed in wine and an even smaller helping of kid in sour cream.

"Some salad, fair charmer? I can't vouch for its being over-sustaining, but it does revive a flagging appetite and, faith, yours would seem to need reviving! What will you have? Here is asparagus, or hop shoots, or a trifle of pickled purslane? This lettuce, perhaps?" Sir Hugh proffered the silver basin.

Deborah thanked him and took a leaf or two, thinking as she did so that if her appetite was flagging, Sir Hugh seemed capable of eating for ten, and drinking to match. Heavy, glowing Tokay, fragrant Candy, clary, muscadel and malmsey . . . the servers with their elaborate silver-gilt vessels seemed to be constantly at his elbow.

She took out her handkerchief and dabbed delicately at her forehead. The atmosphere in the hall was almost unbreathable for the heady fumes of baked meats, of fragrant herbs trampled underfoot by the servitors as they passed and, over all, the heat and sweat of human bodies and the reek of the many different perfumes, orris, civet, sandalwood, musk and camphor, which they all used so liberally.

She finished her salad and was promptly captured by Sir Hugh again who seemed bent at all costs on making an impression.

"May I offer you a sweetmeat? Some fruit? Try one of the Hungarian plums – like the kiss of Venus," he added with his mouth full. "And then let me suggest a little of this cinnamon tart and —"

"Thank you, but the choice is really too great." She let her eye roam over the table.

It was dotted with sweetmeat dishes, fragile ostrich eggs mounted in silver, with jellies, gooseberry and black cherry, confections of nuts and oranges, little cakes of honey and almonds coated in caramelized sugar, so many sweets of every kind in fact that it made you feel sick almost to look at them. Deborah stretched out her hand to a huge salver and selected a Sicilian orange with a ruddy, sunshiny skin.

The high chamber was ringing with noisy laughter and with the shriller voices of the ladies. Sir Hugh Denford, who had fallen silent for a few moments, resumed his ardent courtship.

"Alack!" he mourned in tones that were romantically doleful, if rather slurred. "Why am I not a poet that I might call upon the muse to aid me and by singing of your divine charms melt that stony breastplate of indifference which guards the way to your heart?"

"You do not appear to me, sir, to lack eloquence," Deborah murmured slyly. "Your compliments quite overwhelm me, indeed. I wish you would desist." Her smile took the sting from the words.

"Ah, cruel fair! Why so? Have I not the right to think you the most fascinating of women?" he demanded rhetorically, twirling his moustache. "Is it your misfortune to be saddled with a jealous husband or lover?"

"Really, sir! Is that a fair question to ask a lady?" In spite of herself, Deborah's eyes slid to where James Randolph was sitting at the other table, almost directly opposite, hemmed in on either side by a pair of extremely young and attractive ladies who were clearly doing their utmost to impress him with their charms.

Deborah felt a little pang and suppressed it at once. Shameless hussies they might be, but what had that to do with her? James was free. He had a perfect right to let those frippery creatures make a fool of him if he liked . . . besides, she was strangely gratified to observe, he did not look as though he was particularly enjoying himself. He was quite clearly listening with only half an ear to his neighbours' chatter, dropping in a monosyllable here and there which seemed to satisfy them. They were obviously dazzled by the young man's sheer animal magnetism and his dazzling suit of white velvet flourished all over with pearls and turquoises, and also a little piqued, perhaps, by his lack of interest.

He looked up suddenly and, as they had done once or twice before in the course of the meal, they exchanged shy smiles and, as before, Deborah was aware of an unexpected warmth towards him.

"No, do not desert me again," lamented Sir Hugh at her side.

"But tell me, fair unapproachable, who is the handsome youth making sheep's eyes at you?"

"James Randolph, one of Lord Lindley's sons. An old acquaintance."

"Ah ha, is he so? Do you know, fair one, if I were your husband, I should be devilish wary of the honourable James?'

"Good heavens, whatever for?" Deborah's laugh rang slightly false.

"Oh, just a feeling, only a feeling. In any case, it's none of my business. Suppose we dismiss so uninteresting a subject and return to your exquisite self. Don't you know how desperately I long to take you in my arms? We could —"

"Sir Hugh, how could you! In the middle of dinner!" Deborah slapped Denford's roving hand in mock reproof.

"That wasn't what I meant, as you very well know," he protested a little sulkily. "God's death!" he added impulsively: "Where is the fortunate husband of so virtuous a wife?"

Deborah looked round. Where was the Earl?

He was seated at the same table, about a dozen places away and for once he seemed to have shed his gloomy air and was looking almost affable. Deborah could not but acknowledge that he had been behaving very agreeably all day. He had been almost gallant. Was he trying to impress the world with an illusion of domestic bliss, or was he simply enjoying the flattering sense that other men were envying him his wife? When she had entered the room on his arm, to a subdued murmur of applause, he had even gone so far as to remark for her ear alone: "Faith, madam, you are a sensation! Only look around you – that should feed your vanity. All the men look ready to eat you while their charming wives, I dare say, would be glad to tear you into little pieces." He had spoken in his habitual acid tone but it was nevertheless a compliment – the first he had ever paid her. Not that it made the slightest difference to her feelings or in any way altered her resentment against him, but if he meant to adopt a more conciliatory attitude, while still keeping his distance, it was certainly an advance, especially in view of the news she had to give him on their return. She was prepared to make concessions in order to ensure his countenance for the child. Her own account with him could wait. She could be patient. One day, when the right time came, she would move in and pay him back in his own coin. Meanwhile, the wisest course was to temporize for the good of the child.

The child! Her child! She dreamed about him all the time, deriving an exquisite contentment from picturing how he would look, mapping out a future for him that would be free of all the drawback she herself had suffered. What would he be like? Oh, she could see him now: a chubby, dimpled boy with his father's beautiful black hair and bold, caressing eyes. Perhaps, too, he would have Kit's wilful, single-minded nature, but not with her; she would cherish him so. She would find, invent if necessary, some infallible recipe for happiness and, out of the strength of her own experience, she would guide him step by step, showing him the magic and wonder of life, and also its cruel disappointments, so that he would be forearmed and suffer less when the time came. Under her loving care, he would grow into a man, upright, noble and brave. She smiled – a clear, glowing smile which nearly overwhelmed the wretched Sir Hugh – as she thought how miraculous it was that this gentleman of the future was still no more than a small part of her-self, a tiny, secret thing sleeping quietly in her womb. A fierce, animal joy seized her suddenly and shook her from head to foot, so that as she withdrew her hand from Sir Hugh, who had got it again, she looked about her with eyes blurred with thankfulness. Everyone about her seemed all at once extraordinarily kind and friendly, as though a wave of a magic wand had suddenly changed the feminine jealousy, the hypocrisy and self-interest which normally presided over such functions as this into thin air. Intoxicated with innocent daydreams and sheer happiness, she fell into a blissful state where every other face seemed to reflect the joy in her own.

From this beatific state, she was soon roused by a thunderous din coming from outside the house. The windows rattled and the musicians ceased playing, while all the guests, male and female, rose from their seats and with one accord, trampling and clambering over chairs, benches and even the tables in their haste, made their way in a concerted rush to the door to see what was happening, leaving the Great Chamber to the servants and the empty plates.

As they emerged on to the terrace, a fabulous spectacle met their eyes. From the four corners of the garden there rose up a luminous stream of incandescent darts, spiralling up into the darkened sky, then bursting into sprays and coronets and descending fountains of brilliant light, coloured all hues of the rainbow, spangling the heavens with a myriad glorious new stars which floated back to earth like a rain of fire. To add to the spectacle and complete the splendour of it, lamps which had been artfully scattered here and there about the gardens were all simultaneously lighted, shining on the bright green of the leaves, throwing a rosy light on the statues and catching the diamond droplets of the fountains in a sparkling carcanet. Heaven and earth became one in a fairyland of light in this magnificent firework display which Lord Gladhurst had planned as the culmination of the banquet and a foretaste of the revels yet to come.

Half-submerged under a welter of congratulation, he was bowing low before the Queen who, from her grandstand position at the front of the terrace with her intimates around her, was clapping her hands as eagerly as a child.

"May I suggest to Your Majesty the pleasure of a short stroll," the Baron was saying. He took a torch from the attendant at his side. "There are, I believe, some further surprises yet in store."

"Gladly, my Harry." Elizabeth put up her hand to straighten her wig and laughed. "If they are anything like those we have already seen, they shall have my full approval. Come, my lords. Whoso loves us, let him follow."

At the edge of the little lake the joyous procession, led by the Queen, was greeted by an array of boats, cushioned in red velvet, and illumined fore and aft by great bronze lanterns.

The Earl had rejoined Deborah during the firework display and had remained at her side ever since. Now they embarked, obeying the respectful indications of the boatmen, in one of the craft which was already half-filled with a noisy jostling crowd, all singing at the tops of their voices. Almost at once, as the last guest was comfortably settled in place, the miniature fleet put out upon the waters.

At that moment, as though at an awaited signal, the entire middle of the lake was brilliantly illumined, while a triumphal arch rose from beneath the waters in time to the most heavenly music.

"Ah, I would know that sound anywhere!" the Earl exclaimed. "Listen carefully, my dear. You will not often have the chance to hear such beauty. Do you see the young man directing the musicians? It is John Dowland."

"Dowland? The celebrated lutenist?"

"None other. Our host must have held out some strong inducement to him for he is not easy to lure."

The oars were still now and the notes of the lutes came plaintive and tender through the quiet night. The torches made wavering patches of light upon the blackness of the water and lit up the rapt

261

faces of the listeners and the garlands of flowers which adorned the boats.

Then, abruptly, there was silence, a silence broken after a moment or two by the shrill call of a trumpet.

On the opposite bank, immediately facing Elizabeth, a chariot appeared, drawn by six white horses which plunged breast-deep into the water. Their manes were dusted with gold, of gold, too, were the bells and metal of their harness, and gold the loincloth worn by the bearded giant who drove them, standing upright in the car.

"Neptune?" queried Deborah.

"So it would appear . . . and look, there behind him is Amphitrite, his bride," the Earl whispered, pointing to an opulent female clad in sumptuous draperies and surrounded by a trio of damsels in classical robes of sky-blue silk who rode in the back of the chariot. "Yes, and there if I mistake not are her attendant nymphs, the springs, Amymone, Pyrene and Tyro . . . But that's enough mythology. Let's hear what Neptune has to say."

The giant had brought his chariot to a halt in front of the royal barque and, throwing out his massive chest and brandishing his trident in sign of welcome, embarked in a booming voice on an involved and highly complimentary speech the gist of which was that he, Neptune, god of the waters, acknowledged no peer but the one, indisputable Queen of the Seas, the omnipotent Elizabeth of England.

Delighted at this tribute, the Queen applauded warmly.

Neptune then turned his chariot about and placed himself at the head of the flotilla which then resumed its enchanted voyage, accompanied by an ebullient band of naiads and tritons who had emerged as it were miraculously from the waves and engaged in cheerful banter with the passengers in the boats.

Deborah missed nothing. There was so much to see, so much to remember . . . and still it was not yet over. In a little while there would be dancing and tomorrow the grand masque.

She had given a great deal of thought to her costume for the masque, rejecting one idea after another put forward by her sewing-woman. Venus, Minerva, Ceres, Vesta . . . they were all too common, they lacked originality. No, what she wanted was something out of the ordinary, something she could be sure of not coming face to face with ten times over in the course of the evening. Finally, after much hesitation, she had fixed on Aurora, goddess of the dawn. The disguise was perhaps a little daring, but so very, very pretty! She gave a little shiver of delighted anticipation, picturing the semi-transparent tunic delicately shaded from palest pink to orange, nothing but this fragile harmony of gauzy silks, fastened by a gilded cord, with her hair hanging loose and unbound to below her waist and crowned with a wreath of waxen rosebuds. To this studied simplicity would be added a pair of tiny wings made out of curled, white ostrich feathers and a crystal ewer filled with rose petals to symbolize the dew which she would hold out at arm's length to complete her impersonation of the goddess, which she had derived from lengthy but secret researches into her husband's library, having first made certain that he was not in the vicinity.

As for the truly terrifying expense of all this sartorial extravagance, she had compounded for it as far as she could by shameless depredations into the wardrobe of the late countess who, poor soul, would scarcely be the one to blame her. Lying stored useless and unopened in the attics, Deborah had found innumerable chests and coffers stuffed with every kind of fabric: miles and miles of exquisite embroidery, furs, passementeries, gold and silver lace, brocades and trimmings almost beyond description. These Deborah had simply bartered with her sewing-woman in exchange for what she wanted. It had been to the woman's advantage, admittedly, but in that way Deborah was able to acquire a whole variety of clothes without having to ask her husband for a supplement to her allowance. It was bad enough, she thought, having to accept money from him at all.

"Are you coming, my dear?" The Earl's voice sounded in her ear. "We are come ashore."

She rose. The boats had crossed to the far side of the lake and were now coming in, one by one, to land their passengers on a narrow strip of fine white sand that lay just within the opening of a great artificial cavern.

"Take care, my lady," said the oarsman who was helping Deborah out of the boat. "The water is deep hereabouts."

She stepped ashore carefully and looked about her. The cavern, which was divided by an underground stream crossed by a number of little bridges, seemed to be composed of several galleries into which the flood of visitors was disappearing.

"Come, madam. Let us go this way," the Earl said, leading her with a confident step towards one of the galleries.

"Look," Deborah said, "the boats are going away!" She gave a little crow of laughter. "Does Lord Gladhurst expect us to swim back?"

"Never fear," he told her, a little impatiently. "You won't have to soil your dress. It is all arranged. A torchlight procession through the park, with litters for the ladies. Come, a truce to this nonsense. Let us go on."

Jostled by the moving crowd, they soon emerged into a large chamber which, to judge from the admiring cries which rose on all sides, must hold some unusual attraction.

At Deborah's appearance, a number of young men came forward eagerly but at the sight of her husband's unaccommodating figure just behind her they melted away again with equal promptness. She brushed passed Sir Hugh Denford but he did not see her, being too much occupied in flirting with a diminutive dark lady with a face like a painted doll.

At the other end of the chamber, behind a quickset hedge of glittering, bejewelled doublets and gauzy ruffs, Deborah saw the Queen moving away, talking animatedly to Lord Essex, with Raleigh a little way behind. Not very far away, she saw Cynthia and Penelope but after that her attention was caught by the strange, burlesque world around her and she lost all count of faces, familiar and unfamiliar.

Gambolling lightheartedly among the guests, dressed in a strange assortment of tattered finery, with necklaces of glass beads round their necks, a company of mountebanks danced, pirouetted and performed fantastic acrobatic feats on wires stretched high above the stream. To an accompaniment of screams of laughter and excitement, they swung from side to side, their silken rags fluttering, or jumped down to walk familiarly arm in arm with the gentlemen and whisper their impudent jests in the ladies' ears. Nor was this all.

Among them, conscientiously copying their every action, was a second company made up of smaller creatures, shaped like men but with long, silky fur and large ears fringed with black and white hair. Using their paws with as much dexterity as if they had been human hands, and curling their long, prehensile tails, these creatures leaped on to the men's shoulders, poked irreverent hands curiously into the women's bodices and plackets, fingering jewels and lace, then, shaking themselves, leaped down and ran to climb another interesting farthingale, their tiny gnomelike faces wrinkled in such irresistible mischief that Deborah soon had tears of laughter running down her cheeks.

"Oh," she gasped at last. "It's enough to make one die of laughing! Do you know what they are?"

"They are called marmosets – a kind of monkey brought back by our seamen from the new world."

Her gaze still fixed in fascination on the monkeys, Deborah allowed herself to be borne forward by the crowd. All of a sudden she felt a violent push from behind and stumbled forward to encounter only thin air beneath her feet. She tried to draw back, waving her arms instinctively to regain her balance, but impelled by her own impetus she fell forward and, with a cry of terror, plunged into the dark waters below, her heavy brocade dress bearing her to the bottom as surely as a fifty-pound shot.

There was a moment of shocked silence. Then everyone began shouting at once, explaining to everyone else what had happened and saying what ought to be done about the accident, without any-one's making the slightest move to aid the victim. The Earl's voice rose above the rest, calling stridently for a boat to be fetched.

Faces turned towards him pityingly. Poor man, they seemed to say, he has gone out of his mind, and no wonder! All the boats have gone long ago.

All at once, the crowd shuddered apart and a white figure thrust its way through the gaping onlookers and dashed furiously towards the river.

"James Randolph!" The whisper ran from ear to ear and a rustle of pleasure seemed to run through the crowd at this unexpected treat. Every head was craned to catch a sight of James and the Earl.

Randolph already had his doublet off and, following a brief indication from Norland, dived into the water. Everyone held their breath. Seconds passed . . . at last James reappeared, clasping Deborah in his arms, and she was laid down gently on the bank. Her face was blue, her limbs rigid and her shining hair clung like sea-weed about her. She gave every sign of being in a deep coma. James, his teeth chattering and his face contorted by an anguish which he was past attemping to conceal, did his best to revive her. Laying her head very gently to one side, he was attempting to insert his finger into Deborah's mouth to make her spew up the water she had swal-lowed when the Queen's physician, Ruy Lopez, came on the scene, sent by Her Majesty as soon as she had been informed of the accident.

With a gesture of dismissal to the staring bystanders and a quick bow to the Earl, Lopez knelt at Deborah's side, and competently began to pursue the treatment which James had begun. In a few minutes, Deborah choked and vomited large quantities of water. Her chest heaved as she fought for breath.

At last, the doctor sat back on his heels, covered her with James's doublet which was lying on the ground close by, and then got to his feet.

"You need have no fear, my lord. Lady Norland is out of danger," he said in his strong Portuguese accent.

"How can I thank you, Master Lopez?"

"You have nothing to thank me for. It is this gentleman who should deserve your thanks." He looked at James. "But for his prompt and effective action, all my skill would have been powerless." He clapped his hands. "Ho, there! Let a litter be brought, and blankets! With your permission, my lord, I shall supervise the Countess's removal to the house. There remains the fear of a chill."

"I shall be much obliged to you." The Earl brushed his hand across his sweating brow. "My God, what a nightmare! I still cannot think how it can have happened. Perhaps it was the crowd, a sudden dizzy spell . . ."

Ruy Lopez regarded him sympathetically.

"I think that you, too, stand in need of a cordial, my lord. You have had a shock."

"No, no . . . it will pass. I leave the Countess in your hands, Master Physician. I must thank Her Majesty for her concern for my wife." Turning, at last, to James, he added: "I shall hope, sir, one day to have the pleasure of repaying the debt which my family has incurred this day, to you and yours. As long as I live, I shall not forget your action." He put into the words all the warmth of which he was capable.

"You owe me nothing, my lord," James answered coldly and turned on his heel.

It was the day after next when Ruy Lopez made his report to the Earl. Norland was planning to return to London on the following morning and Deborah was to join him by horse litter as soon as her condition allowed.

"I am happy to be able to assure your lordship," the physician began primly, "that there is now no likelihood of harmful consequences. In another week or two, my patient should be completely recovered from the effects of the accident." He paused and coughed. "Unhappily, however, it is with the deepest regret that I must tell your lordship that your hopes of an heir are not at this present time to be fulfilled. The fall, with the shock and its attendant ills, could not, alas, have proved other than fatal to the child."

"The devil! Did I hear you aright?" The Earl's long face had grown even longer with surprise.

"I ask your lordship to forgive me if I have been unintentionally brutal, but I thought . . . your wife had not yet told you?"

"No . . . no, she had said nothing. Nor, to my knowledge, had she consulted . . ." He had started up from his seat and was pacing the room in some agitation. " 'Sdeath! What a damned mischance!"

"Unfortunate, certainly, but not irreparable, God be thanked," Lopez said and smiled reassuringly. "Have no fear, my lord. Everything has been done that should be done, every precaution taken, all the proper purgations employed, and I can promise you safely that — Her ladyship is young and strong. It will not be long before she is ready to bear again. Rest, plenty of care and then a little healthy amusement will soon have our invalid to rights again. I rely on you, my lord, to carry out my prescription."

After the usual polite farewells, the physician withdrew.

Left to himself, the Earl stood for a moment at the window, deep in thought. Outside, it was raining, a small, fine rain which had not been asked to Gladhurst for the Queen's visit but which had come all the same, uninvited and unwanted but sulky and persistent, to trouble the festivities.

Ha! Festivities! The Earl uttered a short, harsh bark of laughter and snatching up the half-full crystal goblet from the table beside him, hurled it viciously to shatter against the wall.

XXVIII

Deborah was sitting perched on the edge of the bed, a white lace wrapper draped about her shoulders, rummaging in the small casket which she held balanced open on her knees. She looked pale and listless.

It was four weeks since her miscarriage of the child and, as Ruy Lopez had forecast, she had made a swift recovery. Nevertheless, although the accident had left no physical ill-effects, it had affected her psychologically more than she cared to admit.

The fact was simple enough: she had lost interest in everything. She had gone to Whitehall and been bored to death. As far as she was concerned, court life seemed to have lost the powerful charm of novelty and inaccessibility, and now that James was no longer there . . . She realized now, just how much he had contributed to her pleasure in it.

When she had had him to escort her, it had been the simplest thing in the world to pass off other men's attempted gallantry with a smile and a jest. Now, it was a very different matter. Hunted like a hart, with every eye alert for the first sign of weakness, she had to be continually on her guard against the most direct proposals and, by her persistent refusals, she was making enemies.

Oh God, how tired she was of their lascivious glances and their greedy eyes. While as for the she-cats that howled about the palace, the less said about them the better! The truth was that she had nothing in common with them, with their simpering faces and their secret contempt, their freedom of manners and the cold war which they were waging continually among themselves. She would gladly have taken refuge at the gaming tables but her pin money, once she had paid her sewing-woman, left her barely enough over to buy scent and a few titbits for Psyche. She could not afford to wager large sums, with the possibility of incurring debts and being obliged to pay the gentleman concerned in kind: oh, no! That was not her style at all.

Then what was there to do? How was she to while away the time,

268

whether it were to be long or short, before she could be with Kit again?

She had resumed her visits to the Queen and on the last occasion, finding Her Majesty in a good humour, had taken advantage of it to beg for something positive to do, some mission or journey which would give her something to think about and a change of scene. But the Queen had been firm. It was at the Earl's side that Deborah could serve her best. In vain, the girl protested that for the moment at least her husband appeared to have no interest in politics. Elizabeth had not relented.

"Child, child! Believe me, I know from experience that there is often more to be feared from an appearance of submission than from a loud and brawling tongue. Sooner or later, it is to be feared, something may happen and when it does, I wish to know."

Deborah had been obliged to resign herself to what for her had become a tedious, humdrum business.

Today, as she had done yesterday and would do tomorrow, she was idling the time away with her memories. One by one, she took them from the box: her souvenirs. There was a tarnished silver medallion which had belonged to her mother. She breathed on it and polished it with her finger. A lion's head shone faintly, surmounted by the Latin motto: *Par pari refertur*. "Tit for tat", she murmured half unconsciously. Her grandfather had given her the medal when she went away to London. She replaced it in the casket with the childish trinkets and the purse which Mary of Scotland had given her. Her fingers closed thoughtfully on the purse. Less than a year ago: it hardly seemed possible. She felt a hundred years away from the innocent young girl who had set out that sunny morning to ride to Chartley. She sighed. What of David, now, and Jane? She had learned, by discreet inquiries, that the young man was in the Low Countries. Poor David, what room was there in that strife-torn land for his honest daydreams? Of Jane there had been no news at all, only an impenetrable wall of silence. Tears sprang to her eyes, and hastily she put the purse back in the casket. She was feeling dismal enough already, she told herself. It would do no good to make herself more miserable still.

She continued her explorations. A tiny linen bag containing a few grains of corn which she had found in her dress on that hilarious night after Rose's wedding: they were supposed to bring good luck. She sighed again. A goosequill with a silver band – that came from Fleet Street. What was here? The key which James had given her.

Deborah stared at it for a moment or two, biting her lip. An idea had come to her suddenly. Instead of sitting here brooding like an old hen, why shouldn't she go out? It would be something to do at least, somewhere to go other than these four walls. For days on end it had been pouring with rain but in the night the weather had changed and now, she threw a glance at the window to make sure, yes, there was brilliant sunshine out there in the street. What was to stop her taking advantage of it? A new sparkle had come into her eyes as she made up her mind. Yes, that was it. A little trip as far as St Bartholomew's was just what she needed. She would go on horse-back, she could ride quietly down to the Strand and along Fleet Street . . . and James? She shrugged, telling herself not to be a fool. He would not go back there and besides, he was away from London, she knew that because she had looked for him at Whitehall for a week without success to thank him for saving her life.

She shut the casket and set it aside, keeping the key in her hand, and sprang up almost eagerly, a touch of colour in her cheeks.

It would do her good to get out of this unfriendly house, even for an hour or two. It might help her to forget the thought which had been lurking uncomfortably at the back of her mind: was her fall an accident, or had someone pushed her? Time and again, she had tried to recreate the scene from memory. Surely she had not dreamed that violent thrust which had sent her reeling forward? Yet there had been such a crowd that it seemed monstrous to accuse anyone of having done it deliberately. Besides, who? The Earl? Why did she always seem to come back to him? She was not even sure, in any case, that he had been beside her at that precise moment. And yet, in her heart, she knew all the time that her uneasiness was growing. The accident . . . that man the other day . . . She shook her head. Ever since her visit to the midwife, she had taken extra care each time she went out – innocent as her outings had been, alas! – and she could have sworn that no one had followed her. Surely that proved it was all in her imagination? Of course it did. She had better take a firm hold on herself. If she stayed here worrying herself ill with groundless fears, she would gain nothing but a ruined complexion.

She bent to stroke the little greyhound who was gazing up at her mistress expectantly and quivering with eagerness at these signs of movement.

"No, my beautiful. Not today," she said, kissing the small, pointed nose. "You wait here like a good girl."

Disappointed, Psyche trotted off to her cushion, dignified reproach in every line of her. Deborah turned her attention to the problem of what to wear.

The day was hot and sticky, almost stormy. Too hot for all her heavy silks. She brightened. Of course, there was the new dress in the Italian style which her sewing-woman had finished only yesterday! It was a lovely summery taffety in a deep mauve colour, worked with white lozenges, with a white sarcenet petticoat, neat, puffed oversleeves and a falling collar: not in the least stiff or pompous but all airy, frivolous and gay.

She dressed herself quickly, without bothering to summon her tire-woman.

A fine scarf of the same mauve colour for her coppery head, a pair of gloves, a last kiss for Psyche and a final glance in the mirror and she was ready.

She skipped down to the stables and had Semiramis saddled for her.

She opened the door and closing it softly behind her, leaned back against it with a beating heart.

A gasp of surprise escaped her lips. The room was bright and shining as a new pin, the furniture dusted and gleaming, the hangings neatly in place and a nosegay of red roses had been placed in a copper bowl as though to welcome her.

She stepped forward, oddly at a loss now that she was here.

She had imagined, somehow, that she was going to find all the furniture hidden underneath a thick layer of dust, with only a vague, blurred reminder of all that had been. And here, instead of the gentle melancholy she had pictured was the past still bright and living before her eyes, warmly alive and surrounding her on every side. It was all just the same, exactly the same as it had always been – even down to the flask of sack upon the table and the pair of silver cups, waiting patiently in case they should be thirsty; all just as if they had parted gaily with a kiss only the night before to meet again on the morrow. Oh, God! She put her hand to her head and stared about her almost fearfully. Every single object in the room seemed to leap up to meet her, a crude reminder of their love affair. That stool over there in the corner: the first time they came here James had tripped over it, roaring with laughter, and brought it to her, clutched in his arms, to show her the glories of the furnishing. It was there,

271

before that mirror, that on another occasion he had taken out, one by one, with a tender, sensual concentration, all the pins which held her hair . . . And that settle, on those furs . . .

Deborah refastened her scarf with decision and turned back to the door. She had been a fool to come.

Suddenly, she stopped dead, her heart thudding tumultuously. Someone was moving about in the next room. Who? A thief? No, she told herself firmly, much more probably one of James's servants, come in to clean. The cared-for look about the place must mean that he was still seeing to its upkeep. . . . She began to tiptoe quietly towards the door.

Suddenly, the inner door behind her creaked. She spun round, dropping her gloves on the floor.

"James!"

"Deborah!"

After their first, simultaneous cry of astonishment, they stood staring speechlessly at one another, like criminals caught in the act. Deborah was the first to recover her self-possession. She moved towards the young man.

"I am so glad to see you, James," she said awkwardly. "I've not seen you at court since Gladhurst and I wanted to —" He stretched out his hand to ward off her thanks.

"No, Deborah, for God's sake, let there be no thanks between us. There is no need."

"Do you think I am so ungrateful as to forget – to – to forget that . . ." Damnation! She was beginning to stammer.

"No, don't, I beg of you," he said almost harshly. Then, in a softer tone, he went on: "But how you frightened us, my dear. Are you quite well now?"

"Oh, yes, perfectly."

Silence fell between them.

"I . . . I was passing by and – and since it was so hot I thought I would come in here for a moment to rest," Deborah managed to say at last. "But . . . you, James? Lord Duncan told me you were away . . ."

He bent to pick up her gloves and laid them on the table.

"Won't you sit down? Now that I have been so lucky as to find you here, stay and talk to me for a while."

He drew a chair forward but remained standing himself, before answering her question with an assumption of carelessness.

"Yes, I have been at Plymouth on business. I came back last night

". . . and . . . well, you know what it is with servants. I had to assure myself that everything was in order here."

There was silence again.

Deborah bit her nails, searching desperately for something to say. She had not liked to refuse him these few minutes but already she was sorry. What good could it possibly do? Here they were shut up together in this room, empty-handed and with nothing to talk about; she sitting bolt upright on her chair, like a lady paying a social call; he pacing up and down frowning, with lines between his brows which had not been there before. It was unbearable: she would have to go . . .

He came to a halt in front of her, looking her straight in the eyes and spoke abruptly:

"For God's sake, Deborah, stop looking so damned guilty! Please. I can't bear it. I won't, do you hear?" His fingers clenched. "Seeing you – whenever I do see you – so humble and tongue-tied and remorseful, it's – oh, God, it's intolerable!" He groaned. "Deborah, what happened was not your fault, or mine. You owe me nothing, my dearest, nothing at all. Far from it. You gave me a great deal of yourself – more, perhaps, than you realized." He groaned once more. "It doesn't matter. It's enough for me that I have something to remember, a few wonderful moments which I would not change for anything in the world, whatever anguish they have cost me." His voice dropped and there was a tremor in it now. "I am going to tell you the truth. I lied to you just now when I said I came here to see if the servants had done their work properly. . . . When you left me, I swore to myself that I would never set foot here again." He shook his head. "It didn't take me long to break that vow. Now, when I am in London, I come here every day and drug myself with the memory of your beauty and your laughter and all the wonder that was mine through you . . ."

"James!"

"No. Don't interrupt. Only a little more and then I'll not trouble you again. I love you, Deborah. Let me tell you that just once more. I love you, my darling, my sweetheart, my beloved, I love you more than anything in the world, more than my life, and far too much for any other woman ever to take your place. But I love you enough to respect your feelings and promise you never more to importune you with mine."

He stood, breathing heavily for a moment and then, quite suddenly, he smiled.

273

"Now that I have got that off my chest, don't you think perhaps we might be friends, just simply friends? We could go out together now and then – to the play, perhaps, or I could see you at Whitehall. We used to have such fun together, do you remember? Won't you try?"

"Yes, James. I'll try."

She had answered quite spontaneously, without a thought, although her voice shook a little. Dear, dear James. Could there be anyone better or more sensitive than he was? She could not believe it. As for the talk their friendship was bound to excite, she did not care. What harm was there in going with James to a play, or in holding his cards in front of a hundred other people? In any case, she felt so much alone, so desperately in need of affection, that she did not care for anything.

"You're sure you won't regret it?" he asked earnestly.

She shook her head. He smiled, looking all at once very young.

"I think we ought to celebrate at once. What do you say to a visit to the *Curtain* – or would you rather a trip into the country? The sun seems to call us – but it is for you to decide."

Deborah hesitated, wondering if it were wise to go into the woods with him alone. She dismissed the thought instantly. James would keep his word and just then she felt her legs itching to escape from London.

"Yes, James. The country. Where shall you take me?"

They walked their horses amicably side by side. They had left the city behind them and after crossing a few fields now found themselves in a winding lane bordered with nut trees. The dusty surface was spattered with cheerful sunshine and Deborah's long scarf fluttered gaily at the whim of the velvety breeze. After the sticky heat of the city, it was wonderful to smell the freshness of the countryside and breath in the green breath of the undergrowth, redolent of moss and damp grasses.

She was humming to herself. For a brief while James's company and the pleasant easiness which was between them had released her from her anxieties. It seemed incredible that only such a short while ago she could have thought life dull and insipid. She felt ridiculously happy, like a child playing truant, with a childish desire to share her happiness and give out the excess of vitality which overflowed her heart.

274

"James, I'll race you!" she said suddenly, her eyes sparkling.

"What about your dress? You'll ruin it?"

"Never mind my dress. Are you ready?"

She tightened her grip on the reins, plucked a hazel twig to use as a whip and was off like a dart, with James in hot pursuit.

In a little while they were among trees, leaping over ditches, dodging tree-trunks and the thickets which stood in their way, slithering down a steep bank, scrambling up a low hillock all dappled with sunshine and scattered with brushwood clumps, to emerge at last in a long aisle of great oaks, accompanying their mad ride with a series of mingled shrieks and laughter as they urged on their mounts. For both of them, the wild race was, perhaps unconsciously, an outlet for their feelings.

There was a rending sound as Deborah's long scarf, which had been gradually unwinding itself, caught on a branch, leaving half of its length suspended from the tree.

"Oh, James, my scarf!" she called back, reining in her speeding mount. "Get it for me, please!"

She halted at last a little way off, breathless and perspiring, her face as red as a poppy.

"Here you are." James rode up, holding out a fistful of torn fabric. "This was all I could get. Oh, Lord, Deb! Your dress!"

She smoothed her whip carelessly over the smudged and stained taffeta, now ripped in a dozen places and showing through to the petticoat beneath, which fortunately had not suffered.

"Oh dear," she said contritely. "I'm afraid it's past repair." Abruptly, she burst out laughing and dropped the tattered fragments of her scarf to the ground. "There. My sewing-woman can make me another — I pay her enough. She should be glad. But what a ride!"

"Shall we sit down for a while?" James said.

They were in a tiny clearing hemmed in by trees and bushes, with shade overhead and thick grass underfoot.

"A good idea. It will rest the horses. See, they are sweating badly."

James took off his cloak and spread it on the ground.

"There, you can sit on that."

They sat. James chewed a piece of grass and Deborah fanned herself idly with a bracken frond which he had plucked for her, while they discussed their ride with animation.

"Look," Deborah broke off what she was saying and pointed.

"Dog roses. Lend me your handkerchief, will you? I want to pick some."

He watched her as she selected the longest stems with their nodding, fragile blooms of palest pink, thinking how her flushed face and the gay colours she was wearing suited her. And yet – James sighed. He sensed that she was not happy. The depression he had been aware of when he first saw her that afternoon and her abrupt change to her present mood of happy excitement showed only too well that, for some reason which he could not fathom, she had lost her balance. It went to his heart to think that he could do nothing to help her, that he had lost her for ever.

He started, hearing her give a small shriek, and rising quickly went over to her.

"What is it?"

"Oh, nothing at all." She was laughing and sucking her thumb. "Only a thorn."

"Did you get it out?"

"Yes, of course. Don't fuss. Look." She was laughing at him, holding out her thumb. "See for yourself."

He took her hand and saw that she was right. It was the veriest scratch. Yet he could not drag his eyes away from the smooth, childish palm which lay so trustingly in his. Almost against his will, he bent and kissed it and, rising, kept it in his. For a long moment they stood thus, looking into one another's eyes, aware of the nostalgic spell that wrapped them round.

"We ought to go back. It grows late," he said at last, uncertainly.

She gave a kind of desperate sob. All at once, her nerves gave way. The infinite depths of tenderness which she read in the young man's eyes suddenly overcame the heroic efforts she had been making all these past weeks. Her wretchedness became abruptly more than she could bear.

With a cry of: "James!" she fell into his arms, and clung to him, sobbing heartbrokenly with her head on his shoulder, her body shaken with convulsive sobs.

"There, there, sweetheart . . . Hush, my darling, please . . ."

Oh how good it was to weep her heart out, to weep away the ache in her breast and listen to his voice murmuring words of comfort in her ear. How good, after all the pains and insults she had suffered, to be cradled here like a lost child that had been found again. How dreadfully she had missed him!

James held her in his arms, smoothing her tangled hair with a

276

gentle hand. He kept a tight hold on himself, in terror lest his own will should give way before the pressure of the young body clinging to his.

She looked up, the tears still wet on her cheeks. Their faces were very close and instinct, stronger than themselves, drew them irresistibly closer. Their lips met and, still clinging together, they sank to the ground.

Neither Deborah nor James was unaware of the precarious nature of the affair which had blossomed again between them, as a result of circumstances.

"Shall I see you tomorrow?" he asked as he rode home with her.

Her eyes met his directly.

"If you really want to, James, although I'm sure it would be better if we stopped this madness here and now. I can make no promises, you understand? I should be wicked if I tried to conceal from you that when the fleet —"

He drew her to him.

"Hush. What happens then can take care of itself. Just be mine for as long as you can. When – when it is over between us, my darling, when that day comes, believe me, I shall still be the most blessed of men."

Thus it came about that she went again, every afternoon, to the house near St Bartholomew the Great. Her conscience told her that she was betraying Kit, but her worser self only said: Perhaps, but no worse than he has done to me.

Was she to wait for him, sitting wretchedly at home with her horrid husband, as he had suggested? Spend two or three months of the year in snatched, furtive embraces and the remainder in agonizing loneliness? When he came back, she would try and make some arrangement but until then, what was the use of hovering miserably between an uncertain future and a host of dead illusions? She had built up so many hopes around the child, her own lovely baby for whom she had dreamed and planned, and with what result? No, the best way was to make the most of the present and let the rest take care of itself. She knew, none better, that she was powerless against the spell which bound her to Kit. For his sake, for him to make her his for ever, she would gladly have left everything: wealth, honour, ambition, everything. Unhappily, he had made no such demands, had asked no sacrifice, especially none that might endanger his own much-cherished freedom, except the sacrifice of waiting faithfully for him and that she no longer felt she possessed either the strength or the will to do. It was not that she would have given herself to any man who came along, she was not a promiscuous woman, but James was . . . different.

James could give her everything that she could have wished to find in Kit. With him, she was not obliged to play the cruel game of wits, the game in which each player cunningly concealed the cards in his or her hand, and the one who loved the most was automatically the loser. Nor with him had she to keep an anxious watch on his moods, or fear his infidelities. No, there was nothing of that kind to fear with James. He offered her an absolute devotion, whole and unalloyed, which was balm to her wounded spirit. She could trust him utterly and with him recapture for a while her old innocence and drop the mask of sophistication which society had imposed. Before their parting, she had regarded him in the light of an agreeable lover; now, as they came together again, this superficial liking had developed into something deeper, into a real affection which, in its way, was also a kind of love.

Was it possible, she asked herself, to love two men at once? At first sight it seemed a hateful treachery to both men, and yet, God knew, she was not cheating, had no wish to cheat, even. There were times when, making herself look this curious situation in the face, she came near to hating herself. Declaiming her love for one man and then swooning into the arms of another: that was a fine way to behave. Who ever heard of a great love like that? It certainly never happened in books. As for life, she did not know. The heroine ought to sit at home, tastefully swathed in a garment of stoical affliction that would earn her universal sympathy while she counted the days, weeks, months – the years, perhaps – which still divided her from her noble warrior lover and cooling her ardours with her own chaste tears. Well, very likely. Only she was not like that. She was no tragic heroine but a living woman with a body and a heart which were not to be ordered at will. It was weak of her, no doubt, but where was the strength of character in waiting passively for a man who was prepared to offer you nothing but kisses in return? If they had only been drawn together by some common bond of thought or action, she would have been equal to anything but alas, it was not so. So why should she deny herself the simple, warmhearted pleasure James could give her when Kit could abandon her for the sake of adventure?

278

Two loves, and both so very different. The one all passion and the other all affection and, for that very reason, both able to co-exist. The fact that one liked pepper did not prevent one liking honey too. On the other hand, was it deceiving Kit to turn to James to satisfy that longing for affection and understanding which, for her, was a constant need, like hunger or thirst, but which, like a typical man, he seemed able to ignore?

Very well, whispered the small voice inside her, now that we are getting to the root of the matter, what about your body? You lend that to both men, do you? No, she did not lend it to Kit. How can you lend someone something when it belongs to them? Merely, since he had no compunction in taking himself off elsewhere, she had borrowed it back during his absence. As for James, he knew how matters stood. She had been honest with him. And where was morality in all this? Oh, it was easy to talk, but she defied anyone in her place, faced with her agony of mind, not to have done the same. Anyone, that was, other than those poor-spirited creatures, too timidly virtuous to do anything at all.

No, she could honestly say to her conscience that she had nothing with which to reproach herself. It was just that she was not quite sure what would happen when Kit did come back. She could not go on dividing herself between the two of them, only would she have the courage, this time, to hurt James so dreadfully as she must? To that question, she could find no answer.

"Oh well," she told herself, with the cynical fatalism which seemed at present to colour all her actions, "we shall see."

XXIX

It was June 26th and Deborah's eighteenth birthday. She had mentioned it once to James, casually in the course of conversation, and he had not forgotten.

Today, when she arrived to meet him, she found the room overflowing with roses, a profusion of astonishing bright-yellow roses, and with a still more princely gift to follow in the shape of a magnificent sable cloak made up of the finest lustrous, silken skins she had ever seen.

Deborah spent a good deal of the afternoon exclaiming rapturously over her presents, parading in her furs before the mirror, despite the heat, and the rest of it in James's arms. At last, however, the clock struck the moment for departure and she was obliged to say good-bye for the time being to both James and the furs.

It was late already and she hurried out to the street, dragging Psyche on the lead. John Strong must be on tenterhooks, she thought, remembering with a conscience that she had told him to come early. Tonight, there was a ball at Whitehall, for the Queen was to leave tomorrow for a stay at Hampton Court.

Emerging from the doorway, she saw the coach standing a few yards away but the driver's seat was empty. As she wondered what it could mean, a small boy ran across the road and stopped in front of her.

"That your carridge?" he asked, as if in answer to her unspoken question, standing with arms akimbo and surveying her impudently.

"Yes, but —"

"Got a message for you, from your driver. Tell 'er ladyship to get in an' I'll not be more'n a minute, that's wot 'e told me."

"Oh. Thank you. Here, take this for your trouble." She fumbled in her purse and tossed him a coin. The boy caught it and was off like a shot.

Deborah smiled to herself. That was John all over, she thought. He had probably gone off to quench his ever-present thirst over a tankard of ale with the porter of one of the houses nearby and in a moment would come running back, puffing and panting and cursing the heat. She tucked Psyche under her arm and stepped into the coach.

The leather curtains were down and for a moment it did not dawn on her what was happening. She felt herself caught round the waist and flung down violently on the seat while a horny hand was clamped over her mouth. More hands were gripping her ankles. She felt the coach begin to move and began to squirm furiously in the grip of her unknown assailants, struggling, scratching, biting. The only sounds were the rattle of the horses' hooves, the curses of her attackers and the frenzied barking of the little greyhound.

"Get rid o' that tyke!" a man's voice growled.

The curtain was drawn back for an instant and a thud and a squeal indicated that Psyche had been flung out brutally on to the cobbles.

The struggle inside the coach was nearing its end. Indeed, there was little that Deborah, hampered as she was by her rigid busks and intractable farthingale, could do against two men evidently experienced in this kind of attack.

One sat astride her legs, immobilizing them with his weight, while the other was engaged in stuffing a malodorous rag adroitly into her mouth, thereby depriving her of all hope of calling for help. After that, it all happened very quickly. In a trice, she was bound hand and foot and tipped unceremoniously on to the floor.

The one who seemed to be the leader then stepped coolly over her and banged on the partition separating them from the coachman's box.

"Bird's trussed, Sam," he called. "Easy with the palfreys now, my coe. Shog on Newgate pace like all's rug within."

As he turned back, his shoulder brushed against the curtain, pushing the greasy hood he wore back from his face, and for a few seconds the light fell directly on his features.

Deborah's eyes widened as much with amazement as with fear as she recalled where she had seen that evil face and beady, stoat-like gaze before. It was the man whose interest had alarmed her once before, at the Curtain with James. She was quite sure of it, but what did he want with her? Into what kind of a trap had she fallen now? The breath ebbed from her body as bewilderment was added to the terror she already felt. Her brain reeled, and she was conscious of nothing but fear and a cold chill which set her shivering from head to foot.

The man sat down heavily and let out a sigh of satisfaction.

"By the horns of old Beelzebub, there's a job well done, my old Matt!" he declared to his companion. "It's a long age I've had it in mind to be even with this mort. She's had me on the hop these months past, the sly jade. I tell you, you need to get up early to keep on her tail. And hoity toity with it! Zounds, you should'a seen her leddyship fig me a farden when I was a-squattin' agin the wall alongside o' Essex House – an 'er standing 'alf a gallows' off from me for fear of soilin' 'er fine duds, the whoreson trull!" He spat expressively, sending a stream of tobacco juice over Deborah's gown.

Choking back her revulsion, she fought to control the pounding of her heart. She knew that she must keep her wits about her. This was the man from the Curtain and also the beggar outside Essex House and, almost certainly therefore, the man who had followed her in the City: they were one and the same, only hidden under the universal beggar's hood which was a more effective disguise than any mask, she had not recognized him. So much for her vaunted caution! Well, this was no time to grizzle over what was done. What mattered was the present. Use your head, my girl, she told herself firmly. Both the months of patient trailing and this present ambush had been too skilfully prepared to be the work of these varlets. Perhaps, by listening to their talk she might glean something. At least it was better than lying here snivelling.

She stiffened, all her good resolutions gone in a flash. The man called Matt had bent down and was fingering the stuff of her skirt with his great paw.

"Ar'n'orson fine duds the'ar'n'all," he mumbled almost unintelligibly. "Git yer dabs on this'n. Downier'n a sow's belly." He pursed his investigations further into Deborah's underskirts, his voice thickening perceptibly as he proceeded. "Cor, I nivver see sich frillies! See 'er netherstocks? Real silk! What kind of a prigman's doxy 've we got 'ere?"

The other man laughed and told him not to be a fool, that all "swell morts" wore such clothes, but they were none the less women for all that.

"That's as may be," Matt growled. "You can say what you like with your big mouth. You won't get a doxy like that lifting up her skirts for the likes of us, eh Scary?"

"Oh, belt up, and quit moaning. You make me sick. God's bones, you shall have her! Not willingly, I don't say that, but you'll have your fun with her – an' so shall I," Scary added with a hoarse, sniggering chuckle that made Deborah's blood run cold.

"Honest? You're not gulling me? Seems to me there's something peevy about this whole job."

"Oh, peg yer tattler, yer bousy hulk! How many times do I have to tell you? We gets the mort, we 'as our bit o' fun with 'er and then we mills 'er quick, see? It's all rug. With the snap the swell coe's promised for the job, we'll live like lords for the rest of our bleedin' lives. Are you with me now?"

"All the way, my bully, all the way! A piece like that for quire birds like us! It don't 'ardly seem real! 'Ere, tell you what —" The fellow's voice was hoarse with anticipation. "What say we start now – just to be friendly, eh?"

"Quiet, bull's pizzle!" Scary retorted. "This is a coach not a bawdy house! Hold your patience a while yet. You'll get your belly-ful — Scary's oath on that. If you ain't satisfied I'll pay your score at Southwark tonight. Now, keep mum."

Matt subsided, grumbling to himself. Silence fell.

Her face pressed against the gritty planks, a sick feeling in her stomach, Deborah fought down her panic.

Above all, she knew she must not cry or faint. There was little enough hope, it seemed that she would escape with her life but at least she knew now what to expect. This was no time to lie snivelling about it – nor had she been trained to do so! Now or never she must remember the lessons she had learned and use them to keep her courage and her wits about her.

Where were they taking her? These men would not be moved by pity, that was sure, but there must be some way of appealing to their cupidity to prevent the worst. Resolutely, she put aside the horrid images which danced before her eyes. If she began to think about what lay in store for her, she would be lost, for this time there was no one but herself to rely on. Kit was at sea and heaven knew where, while James had no way of guessing what had happened. As for poor John Strong, he might be lying unconscious in an alley, might even be dead. And Psyche? No, it was better to forget them all. She would need all her powers to deal with her own plight. After-wards, always supposing there was going to be any afterwards, she could indulge herself with a spectacular bout of hysterics, but not now.

She stifled a groan under her gag. The body of the coach rested directly on the axles and the jolting was almost unbearable. From the pain of her bruised back, Deborah could have thought the wheels were passing over, not under her. She tried to distract herself by puzzling over the question of who could be responsible for this outrage. Who hated her enough to deliver her into the hands of brutes like these? For a moment, her fear was swallowed up in a surge of furious anger. Who was the "swell coe" the men had talked of? The Earl? She rejected the idea instantly, telling herself she must be mad to think of a person of his quality in connection with a hole and corner business like this. Besides, it was not like him. He was the kind of man who preferred to exact his revenge in person, distilling from it the last drop of satisfaction. But if her charming husband were not the culprit, who was to blame for all the suspicious happenings? Deborah racked her brains. Surely this horrible ambush was not unlike the business in the wood near Coventry? Walsingham, then? No, it did not make sense. She had said nothing: he could hold nothing against her. In any event, she was now the wife of a peer of the realm and, to some extent, a person of importance. The minister was far too shrewd to compromise himself without good reason.

No, she decided. No, she could not see . . . Suddenly, as she cudgelled her brains, another name came back to her, from a very long way off, a name that could still make the hairs rise on her neck: Basilio. She asked herself how she could have been such a fool as to forget the man who had been Perez's accomplice and have believed herself safe from him. He must, somehow or other, have found out the part which she had played in foiling the plot against the Queen's life, must have watched her patiently, choosing the moment to avenge his master. Oh God, she thought, it must be him! The scene in the cellar of the Dalridges' house came back to her, clear in every detail: she saw the implacable Perez, the red-hot poker, and an involuntary sob burst from her gagged lips. She was lost and she knew it.

She became aware that the coach was slowing down. A moment later, it stopped with a jerk. Scary put aside the leather flap and sprang down.

"Shove out the goods," he commanded.

While Scary, aided by Matt, was hoisting her on to his back, Deborah gazed about her avidly. She saw a bare and stony wasteland, dotted with a few, scrubby-looking bushes and farther off what looked like woods. Close at hand was a tumbledown hovel one wall of which was blackened as though by fire. Oh, merciful Father in heaven, guard me . . .

Scary kicked open the four rickety planks insecurely nailed

284

together which passed for the door of the shack and entered, followed by Matt, after first telling the driver, the man called Sam, to remain outside and keep watch.

This Sam was a tall, beefy individual, not unlike John Strong in build. Deborah, her head lolling over Scary's shoulder, noticed at once that he was dressed in Norland livery and recognized the very clothes her faithful John had worn. Poor John, she knew then that he must be dead. There was no mistaking the clothes, for only yesterday she had been teasing John about the splendid feather in his cap and now that self-same feather was waving bravely on the impostor's head.

She was not afforded much time to grieve, for already Scary was depositing her roughly on the beaten earth floor of the hut.

"Now then, my beauty," he said.

For a moment, the two men stood looking down at their prisoner. Then, slowly, Matt moved closer.

James Randolph stood leaning on the carved baluster rail, the taste of Deborah's kisses still on his lips, and watched with the eyes of a man in love the tail of a scarlet kirtle flick gracefully down the stairs. It vanished through the arched doorway and the click of high heels died away but still he leaned there, resting dreamily on his elbows, until he was aroused by the sound of distant, furious barking.

He listened, wondering what on earth could be making the little dog so angry. Had Deborah met with any trouble? Of recent days he had seen one or two unsavoury-looking characters hanging about the place. No sooner had the thought crossed his mind than he was speeding down the stairs but by the time he reached the bottom, the noise had stopped and all that he could hear was a faint whimpering. James ran outside and looked about him.

The street was empty except for one coach, Deborah's, which was fast disappearing. James looked more closely.

In the patch of wet mud which came from a building site two houses away from where he stood, a small form was lying.

Psyche. James ran to her.

The little dog was lying still, whimpering softly. James lifted her carefully in his arms, frowning. What could it mean? Something was wrong, certainly. He knew that Deborah would never have left the dog of her own free will.

He did not hesitate. Shouting for the doorkeeper, who came

hurrying out to him, he handed Psyche into the man's keeping, untied his own horse and vaulted into the saddle.

He caught up with the coach as it turned out of Charterhouse Street in the direction of Cambridge Gate. Feeling increasingly sure that something must be wrong, James was about to give Deborah a hail when he caught sight of the driver's face. The man was dressed in the Norland livery, but he was not John Strong. James drew rein and rode on more slowly, being careful to keep a steady distance between himself and the coach. He was thinking fast.

Why the devil, he wondered, was Deborah travelling in quite the opposite direction to Drury Lane, and why this new driver? Had the Earl got wind of their affair and taken his wife by surprise? There seemed to be no other possible explanation. In which case, since he had no means of knowing what course Deborah had adopted, it was best not to show himself just yet. Since he could scarcely leave her while the matter was still in doubt, the wisest thing was to follow at a safe distance until the coach reached its destination, wherever that might be, and then wait and see. He rode on at an even pace, controlling his anxiety as best he could.

It was the time of day at which the market carts were wont to leave London. Those who had sold all their produce were making their way home with much cheerful laughter and cracking of whips, calling out to one another in bantering tones. Others, who had been less fortunate, were driving home their stale and wilting wares in gloomier mood, cursing ineffectually at the hordes of small boys who followed the carts shouting rude remarks and endeavouring to possess themselves by stealth of what a more selective public had disdained to buy.

It was not long before the road became hopelessly jammed.

The trouble started when a pair of oxen harnessed to a heavy wagon suddenly stopped dead, their great bovine eyes fixed placidly on the ground in front of them, and not all the waggoner's oaths and wielding of the goad could persuade them to move on again. Eventually, purple in the face, sweating profusely and swearing even more freely, the wretched man got down from his seat and began to belabour the beasts with his stick.

Instantly, as though it were a signal, every other driver within sight got down as well and came crowding round, ostensibly to help but really to enjoy the show. To them were added a sprinkling of delighted passers-by, a handful of shopkeepers drawn out of doors by the noise and the inevitable crop of shrieking small boys. All of these persons were prodigal of advice and opinion, advanced with the utmost cheerfulness and good humour which in turn was assisted by the tankards which soon began to appear miraculously from the nearby alehouse, until the scene began to look like nothing so much as a public holiday, complete with questing ladies of light morals and lighter fingers and a whole swarm of licensed beggars, thieves and cut-purses.

By the time that James, caught on the wrong side of this jamboree, had succeeded in making his way, cursing, through to the other end of the street, the coach had disappeared.

Scary's hand shot out and checked his companion with authority.

"Wait for it, stock-fish!" he said. "You may have an itch in your cod-piece, but I know what's due to a lady, if you don't. First, we take off her gag, in case she might 'appen to feel like a bit of a chat, see?"

" 'Ere," Matt growled, "what's all this all of a sudden?"

Scary looked at him, then dug his elbow into the other man's ribs.

"You great lubberly guts, don't you know anything? It's time you learned some refinement, as they say at court. 'Asn't it ever crossed your thick 'ead that it adds a bit o' spice to 'ear them scream?"

Chuckling, he bent and ripped the gag from Deborah's mouth. She bit back a moan, unable to take her eyes from her tormentor's face which was thrust close to her own and lay staring with a petrified gaze into the swarthy, scarred features, twisted at that moment into an expression of crude and savage enjoyment.

"Well?" said the sneering voice. "Lost your tongue, eh? Not so 'igh and mighty now, are we?"

He put out a huge, hairy paw and grasped her satin bodice. For a fraction of a second, overcome with shame and sheer rage, Deborah emerged from the state of animal terror which had held her paralysed.

"Let go of me, you beast!" she screamed in disgust and added, very quickly: "I'll make you an offer."

Scary stood up.

"Oho, so my lady's back on her high horse, eh? Where d'ye think you are then? That's a joke, that is."

Deborah looked about her: a floor of beaten earth strewn with nameless refuse, some broken packing-cases a few feet from her

287

head, a bit of an old sack nailed across the window and these two ruffians standing over her, leering. Escape, in these conditions, was clearly fantastic. Her one chance of safety lay in the men's susceptibility to bribery.

"You'll be hanged, of course," she said in the coldest voice she could command. "You're bound to be, sooner or later, I suppose. However, if you let me go, I'll promise you to say nothing – and pay you twice what you are getting."

"Ho, yes! You think so, do you? An' what about 'is nibs, eh? What's he goin' to say when we turn up empty-'anded?"

"With enough money, you could leave London," Deborah said eagerly. "As for your master —" A flicker of hatred shone in her pale face. "If you'll tell me his name, I'll make quite sure he is in no position to do harm to anyone again."

"You leave 'is nibs out of it. Besides, who's to say if we let you go you won't try and serve us the same trick?"

Deborah bit her lip. What had made her say that?

"Right. If that's all you've got to say, you might as well have spared your breath. And us thinking you was goin' to be a sensible wench . . .' He leered toothily. "E'd a' given you a good time, eh, Matt?"

Deborah, too, looked at Matt. What she saw was the same general appearance, the same stinking rags, the seamed and pock-marked face, with a brutal grin that showed a mouthful of broken, blackened stumps. There was one difference, however. Matt's bleary eyes, unlike Scary's, had a shifty, uncertain look. Perhaps with him there might still be a chance.

"What do you say to a hundred pounds?" she said quickly, speaking to him. "Think! A hundred pounds! A fortune!" Encouraged by the spark of interest she caught flickering in his eye, she went on, using every ounce of persuasion she had left.

"It's better than the gallows, anyway, and if you listen to him, that's where you'll end, after a few other treats the hangman keeps in store for rogues of his sort. And what makes you think you'll ever get your share of the money his master's promised him? Don't be a fool. On the one hand, torture and death on the gallows: on the other riches, more riches than you've ever dreamed of." Her voice sharpened, sounding shrill in her own ears. "If you had a grain of sense you wouldn't hesitate. A hundred pounds, and my solemn word of honour, on the Bible, not to give you away if you take me home safe and sound."

The two men had listened to her in a barely-contained silence. Several times Matt seemed about to interrupt but Scary's hand on his shoulder kept him silent. At Deborah's last words, however, an immense and unexplained hilarity overtook them both. Before the eyes of their astonished victim, they began clapping one another on the shoulder, buffeting each other's ribs playfully and clutching at their midriffs as though about to explode in spasms of laughter.

Scary seemed to be the first to recover, wiping the tears of laughter from his eyes and blowing his nose on his coat sleeve.

"Take her home!" he croaked. "That's rich! Another jest like that an' she'll make me die laughing."

"Yes, by God!" Matt echoed, with all the more conviction because he was conscious of a moment's weakening. "Let's not waste more time. I'm going to get to work."

"Not so fast, my old coe." Scary stepped between Matt and the girl. "Who says you first?"

"You said it – in the coach. You'll not go for to bilk me now?" the other growled angrily.

"Stow it. You'll get your chance to tumble 'er to your heart's content. But I say as things'll be done properly, that's all. We'll throw for 'er." He sniggered. "That way no one need be jealous. Winner blazes the trail, as you might say. Is it agreed? Thieves' honour?"

"Thieves' honour."

The two men crouched down and Scary drew a pair of dice from under his cloak.

"Trust me, they aren't loaded."

In spite of this assurance, Matt picked up the dice and weighed them in his hand, studying them carefully before, apparently satisfied, he cast them on the ground.

"Eight," he said.

Scary collected the dice and shook them protractedly between his hands before making his throw. He bent eagerly over the small cubes of bone.

"Eleven!" he declared, triumphantly.

He pocketed the dice and stood up. Deborah watched in fascinated horror as he came towards her. She knew now that nothing on earth could save her, and she gave herself up for lost.

It was not death that she feared but the attendant outrages which the two villains had given her ample leisure to imagine. Mercy, oh Lord, have pity . . . She was no longer even attempting to control the trembling of her limbs. He was coming! There was nothing she could do now, only pray, pray silently, with the desperate incoherence of the dying.

She screamed as Scary took hold of her ankles and dragged her without further ado into the centre of the room.

"Scream away, my dainty," he taunted her. "You'll have good cause."

Taking no further notice of her shrieks, he seized hold of her dress with both hands and began tearing it savagely apart. When it was in ribbons, the underskirt suffered the same fate, leaving Deborah in nothing but her busks and light, Spanish farthingale, which was simply a stuffed petticoat distended by rush hoops growing larger as they neared the ground, and the thin petticoats she wore beneath it.

Still keeping up a running flow of bawdy jokes with Matt, who was standing by, dribbling into his beard with excitement and missing nothing of the spectacle, Scary took the poniard from his belt and in a single practised movement, slit the wicker frame from top to bottom. It opened slowly, like a reluctantly breaking flower, and a foam of lace escaped.

By now, the man was in the grip of a salacious frenzy of desire. With a shaking hand, he grasped the delicate stuff, tearing and rending to get at the flesh beneath.

He stood up, devouring her with greedy eyes as she lay before him, exposed to his lúbricious gaze, the fair, white roundness of her body rendered the more involuntarily provocative by the shudders which convulsed it.

With an oath, he flung off his coat and, without taking his eyes off her, began fumbling at his cod-piece. Ignoring her feeble struggles, he flung himself on her, thrusting at her rigid thighs, while her screams filled the hut.

They were answered almost at once as, with a resounding crash, like the sound of an exploding cannon, the four rickety planks of the door burst asunder.

James Randolph, his hat and doublet gone, burst wild-eyed into the room.

"Deborah! God's blood! What have they done to you?" he cried, his blazing eyes taking in the scene.

Matt darted for his sword but before he could reach it, James's rapier had run him through the body.

"James! For God's sake, look out!"

Scary had risen and, poniard in hand, was lurching towards

James. But he was handicapped by his own clothes. His hose slipped round his ankles and impeded him so that he was no match for James's agility and the murderous intent which drove him. His clumsy thrusts went wide and with a lightning turn of the wrist James's weapon flicked the dagger from his hand and travelled on, unhindered, to his chest. He fell.

"No!" It was Deborah's voice which checked the young man as he was about to deliver the *coup de grâce*. "Don't kill him. I must know who has paid them."

Leaving the injured man groaning on the floor, James ran to her and, slashing the ropes that bound her, clasped her passionately to his heart.

"Darling . . . my darling! Are you all right? These villains have not – not —?"

Deborah burst into strident, hysterical laughter, very dreadful to hear.

"If you mean have they raped me, no. You were in time, thank God." She sat up, rubbing her swollen wrists. "Give me your shirt, James, will you? I am scarcely decent." She laughed again as she put on his shirt, then said: "Now, tell me how you come to be here? And what about the driver?"

"I caught him busy at the door, with his eye pressed to a crack to see what his companions were up to. I left him outside, unconscious. But in God's name, beloved, what does it all mean?"

Curtly, without unnecessary embroidery, but without omitting a single detail, she told him what had happened.

"And now," she finished, "all that remains is to find out who is responsible for this. I shall not rest until he is dead, if it costs me my own life to do it." She jumped up, clenching her fists.

Appalled, James took her gently by the shoulders.

"Deborah, sweetheart, be calm! There is no danger now. I am here. Leave your revenge to me. It is work for a man, not for you."

She shook her head vigorously, her long hair brushing her cheeks.

"No, James. Believe me, I have learned my lesson. I shall not be taken so easily again, and by heaven, I will be revenged! It concerns my private honour!" She passed her hand over her face. "I need a drink. Do you think either of those brutes has a flask on him?"

"Deb, you can't! It's probably full of germs, if they have!"

"Well, in my present state, I don't think I care much. You tie up that scoundrel, and make sure you do it tightly. He has a lot of things to tell us, and I promise you he will," she said, through clenched teeth. "I'm going to search this one in case . . ."

She bent over Matt who was lying crumpled up in a wide pool of blood, like a broken doll, and began gingerly exploring his unsavoury garments. Finding a leather bottle, she drew out the bung and drank from it greedily. It contained a fiery liquor which erupted like a volcano inside her. She began to feel slightly better.

She was dizzy and rather sick but at least the shameful trembling seemed to have stopped. Poor James, how could he be expected to understand that after all that she had gone through, the refinements of modesty had begun to seem a good deal overrated, that nothing mattered to her now, nothing at all, but the destructive fury which consumed her.

She straightened her shoulders, took a deep breath and turned back with a firm step to Scary, James's shirt fluttering round her naked legs.

"Give me your dagger, James," she commanded. "I'll watch him while you go and deal with the driver. Drop him in a ditch somewhere. We don't want him coming round and giving the alarm."

She watched him go. There was no need for him to hear whatever Scary had to say. If this was Basilio's doing, that was not a secret she cared to share with anyone.

She crouched down beside the wounded man.

He was lying propped against one of the broken packing-cases, bound with the lengths of rope which they had used on her. His breathing was harsh and painful and the red stain on his coat was spreading visibly.

"Now, talk," Deborah told him sternly. "You have nothing to lose now and it will save you further pain. Who employed you?"

He only glared at her defiantly and spat. The blob of spittle, stained an ugly red, hit the ground by Deborah's foot. She brought the dagger up close to his face.

"Talk, or I promise you, you'll regret it. You rancid cur! Do you think I'll feel the slightest pity for you? Tell me the name of the man who pays you, or I'll enlarge that hole in your chest for you."

Silence.

Gritting her teeth, she moved the blade downwards.

"I thought I heard someone screaming. Deb, we must —" James broke off and sprang across the room.

292

Deborah was crouched in the far corner, leaning against the wall like a blind person and vomiting in horrible, shuddering spasms.

"Deborah!"

"It's nothing . . . I'm all right . . . For God's sake leave me alone!" she gasped, between bouts of retching.

Automatically, James picked up the dagger, wiped it and, just as automatically, restored it to its sheath.

Deborah turned round at last, white-faced and staring as though she had just seen a vision of hell. There was blood in great splashes all over the front of her shirt.

"Deborah! What is it? Are you hurt?"

"It's nothing, I tell you. For God's sake, don't ask me!"

She drew away from him, wiping her face in silence with the fragment of petticoat which he held out to her, then pushed back her hair wearily.

James gripped her arm.

"My darling – Deborah, listen to me. We must go, quickly. You are not safe here. That damned driver has got away. He may bring more of them down on us."

"All right. Let's go."

"What about him?" James indicated Scary.

"Don't worry about him. He's dead." Then she went on with a rush "Oh, James, it's horrible. I know now who ordered this, who planned it, detail by detail, who organized it all and hired these men . . . Oh, the cur! James, if you only knew!"

"Who?" James's hand went instinctively to the hilt of his sword. "God's death! Tell me! Who?"

"The Earl."

"The Earl!" James repeated, thunderstruck. "A gentleman mixed up in this filthy business? But – why?"

Deborah shrugged. "Need you ask? Jealousy, I imagine. What else?"

"Your husband, jealous? Jealous enough to plan this foulness? Surely not? Does he hold you so dear —?"

"What other reason? Why else should he have had me followed ever since our marriage? Why else should he want to kill me? Oh, it was a neat plan! I was to be strangled and then those men were to leave me on some unfrequented road where I would be found raped and robbed of all my jewels, with the coach nearby, the horses gone and John Strong lying dead beside it." She laughed shakily. "The verdict would have been obvious. With the country-side so full of rogues and vagabonds, no coroner would have hesitated for a moment to put it down to assault by robbers. Everyone would have pitied my husband and that would have been the end of it. Unfortunately for him," she added grimly, "it didn't turn out quite like that and now I am going to make him pay a hundred times over for the nightmare I have lived through today. He shan't get away with it!"

"No," James cried. "Let me! It is my right! I shall do it for you." He took her hand gently. "How do you think I could leave you alone with that – No. I shall take you back to St Bartholomew's, and then I shall go and settle accounts with Norland."

"No, James. Don't argue. We're wasting precious time. I have made up my mind. I want to kill him with my own hands." She lowered her eyelids, avoiding his gaze. "If you knew the humiliations I have endured, day after day, at that man's hands!"

"God's death! And you have never told me! Why not?" He drew her close, in spite of her resistance, moved to the depths by this anguished cry. "The dastard! But I shall —"

She thrust him away and stood back from him.

"You see," she said almost angrily. "You have not understood, even now!" She was shaking him by the arms, her face close to his. "This is my revenge, between him and me!" she cried. "I want him all to myself – to die like a rat. I won't let anyone – anyone . . ."

She hammered his chest with her small fists. James grasped her wrists roughly and shook her.

"That's enough, Deborah! Stop it! Stop it, sweeting!"

Slowly, she became calmer and the wild glare went out of her eyes.

"Look, my darling, don't be a fool. At least give yourself a chance. Have your revenge but for God's sake do it sensibly. Remember you're a woman and —"

Abruptly, Deborah gave way. "Perhaps you're right. But on one condition. We go together. After dark. There is a way in at the back of the stables, we can go that way and take the Earl by surprise." She laughed grimly. "A charming surprise for my dear husband! Now take me from here, James. I can't bear any more."

He held her passionately to him.

"My love, I'd have given my life to have spared you this agony."

Then, lifting her in his arms, he carried her out of the hut towards the coach. Outside, it was growing dark.

XXX

The stable buildings stood out faintly outlined in silvery moonlight. The little side gate leading from the street opened with a mournful creak and two furtive shadows slipped through.

Inside, it was dark and the air was moist and heavy with the smell of hay and sleeping animals.

Deborah, who had been this way many times before and knew it almost by heart, led the way. James followed. They had gone first to the house near St Bartholomew's and while Deborah revived herself with hot soup, James had gone in search of some more adequate clothing for her than her tattered dress. He came back with a skirt and bodice borrowed from one of the maids at Charing Cross and, dressed in this and warmed by the soup, Deborah was able to step boldly forward between the stalls. Concealed in the folds of her skirt, she held the pistol with which she had provided herself before setting out: a handsome weapon inlaid with mother-of-pearl which James had given her not many days previously. She was in desperate haste now to confront the Earl to revel in the shock her appearance would be to him and enjoy his disappointment – for he must think her dead by this time and be already rehearsing his role of sorrowing widower. Well, let the swine make the most of it. He would not have much longer.

After that it all happened very quickly, much more quickly and in a very different fashion from the way she had imagined.

She was aware of a sound like a sigh just behind her followed by the thud of something falling, and she swung round, levelling her pistol. The next thing she felt was an agonizing pain in her wrist. She dropped the gun and fell forward on to something soft and warm. Her wildly groping fingers encountered first straw, then silk, made out the shape of a shoulder and clung to it. "James! What is it? Speak to me!" But he did not speak, only lay face downwards in the midst of the hay, his body unmoving beneath her shaking hands.

"James! Please, my darling, answer me —"

"It is useless to call on your lover, madam. He will not answer you."

Deborah looked up. Through her tears, she saw the black figure detach itself silently from the surrounding darkness and stand before her.

"You!" she exclaimed in horror.

"Myself, in person, my dear Countess." The Earl laughed softly. Coolly wiping his bloodstained dagger, he continued: "I am grieved to be obliged to thwart your charming plans, but you must agree I can hardly be expected to concur in them. Come now, dry your tears. This young fool is not worth them, and they are scarcely decent in front of your husband."

She sprang at him then, supple as a panther, clawing and scratching. He hurled her off.

"Now, Sam!" he cried.

Something heavy and soft descended on her, pulling her backwards, blinded and half-stifled. She felt herself lifted like a straw and fought for air. Then she lost consciousness.

The Earl signed to the man called Sam and the two began kicking aside the bales of straw which covered the floor of the stable. In the centre, a large trapdoor was revealed and, beneath it, a flight of steps, leading downwards. Silently, one after the other, the two men descended, Sam carrying Deborah rolled in a blanket.

She came to herself abruptly as a bucket of water was thrown in her face. She opened her eyes and saw the figure of the Earl, standing before her with a triumphant expression.

Memory came flooding back: Matt, Scary, the hovel . . . James! A sob broke from her. She tried instinctively to spring at him but found that she was unable to move. Each of her wrists was encircled by a metal gyve attached to a short length of chain which was stapled firmly to the wall.

"Where am I?" she cried furiously. "What does this mean?" She rattled her chains while her eyes took in the bare floor, the water oozing from the walls, the narrow, barred doorway. A cellar! A dungeon, rather: it was to a dungeon that he had brought her.

"The perfect setting for the settlement of our little domestic difficulties, shouldn't you say?" the Earl purred smoothly. "But since those are not, perhaps a matter for public discussion, permit me to dismiss this excellent fellow. Here! Now get you gone!"

A man emerged from the shadows on Deborah's right and caught the purse he threw. She saw that it was the false coachman, still wearing John Strong's livery.

"Ah, yes," the Earl murmured. "I see you have not forgotten my faithful servant here. You see, he did not run away as you so foolishly imagined. He overheard your unpleasant little plot and came here to warn me. Tiresomely rash, my dear, but who am I to complain?" He spoke to the man again. "Get rid of the body. I'll join you later."

The man bowed and vanished through the low doorway.

"Now," the Earl continued, "now that we are alone, let us settle our own affairs."

Deborah glared at him, every muscle quivering.

"I have nothing to say to you. Kill me but for God's sake spare me your rhetoric. I know you too well to wish to hear more of your crimes."

"Tut tut. Hard words from such pretty lips. I am going to kill you, it is true, but not until you have heard what I have to say. Let me have the pleasure of telling you a few things about your despised husband." His eyes mocked her. "You little fool, do you think I care a fig for your adulteries? That I am punishing you for your frolics with that young hothead Randolph, or even with your handsome Lord Christopher? You overestimate your importance, my dear. I am disappointed in you. I had thought you more perspicacious. You have a bourgeois preoccupation with affairs of the heart, my dear. Well, I am sorry to have to disillusion you, my poor drab. It is not on account of your loose morals that I am about to kill you. I made up my mind to it long before, to be precise on the very day the Queen's messenger came to me with the proposition." He was walking up and down before her where she stood breathing hard but making no sound.

"I, Earl of Norland, descended from one of the oldest families in England, to be obliged by this usurper to accept a shameful match that had not even the merit of wealth to make it acceptable! My heirs to be tainted with the blood of one who comes from nowhere, with neither glory nor greatness in her ancestry! It could not be! Nevertheless, for reasons of my own, after mature consideration I agreed to the bargain but with the secret proviso, known only to myself without which I could never, do you hear, never have brought myself to marry you. As soon as I could do so without risk to myself, I determined to rid myself of my unwanted spouse, once and for

297

all." He paused and looked at her, his hands clasped behind his back.

"You see, you personally had little to do with it. You or another, it would have been the same."

"You are a monster!" she flung at him fiercely. "And John Strong? What have you done to him?"

"Now, now. There's no need to be abusive. As for your servant, do not disturb yourself. No doubt he is resting quietly in a ditch somewhere. Let us rather continue with our story which I am sure is beginning to interest you." He permitted himself a satisfied smirk. "If you know what patience, what strength of mind it cost me not to give myself away, to play the devoted husband, proud of his young bride in public and to resist the temptation to wring your neck whenever we were private together. By heaven, it was not easy! Yet it was necessary. I needed time, time to study your habits, time to allay suspicion and evolve a plan which should in no way incriminate me."

"But then," Deborah cried involuntarily, "that stone from the stable gate – the one that nearly fell on me – it was your doing?"

He bowed ironically. "Quite right. That day, unfortunately, the luck was with you and I failed. And now that I have begun to confide in you, perhaps I should confess to having tried on you, without your knowledge of course, a powder which a friend brought me back some years ago from Florence. Mixed with the paint you put on your eyelids, it should have had the happiest results – oh, your sufferings would have been very brief, I do assure you – but it seems the virtue must somehow have gone out of it, for it too failed."

James and his pills! But for him . . . Deborah ground her teeth. What did it matter? Now or a few weeks ago, it was all one, and maybe that stealthy, unexpected death might have been kinder.

"And then again at Gladhurst," the Earl was saying calmly. "It was a golden opportunity and but for that damned Randolph the water would have provided me with a permanent release. Still, you did manage to drown the fruits of our union and that alleviated my disappointment considerably. It was a kind of half success, and failing that I might have been obliged to throttle the little peasant at birth."

"I am afraid, then, that it is I who must disillusion you," Deborah retorted with contempt. "As you have been so charmingly frank, it would ill become me to be otherwise. The child was none of yours.

Do you think I derived such joy from our bedding as to desire a child by such a father? I have loathed you for too long, and now I can say it to your face. As a husband, I could endure you if I must, but as a man, my lord, you made me retch!"

She leaned forward, spitting the words out in his face. "Yes, I made you a cuckold, my lord earl, and enjoyed doing it! And however little you pretend to care, if you are honest with yourself you must admit it hurt – even if only your pride — No, hear me out, if you please." Her eyes scorched him. "Afterwards, do with me as you please, but you owe me this." She paused for breath, then went on: "I too was party to a bargain when I married you, but I made it in good faith and kept it, too, to the best of my ability, until the day you shamed me under our own roof and as good as in front of our own servants by taking a *trull* into your bed! I knew how much you wanted to return to London and I thought that since we both stood to gain something we might be able to come to an arrangement and live together in pleasant courtesy. I soon learned my mistake. You met every attempt on my part with an inflexible disdain. Then came the night when you showed me to what depths of infamy you could sink and after that I came to hate you. Until then, I had borne your scrawny body, your pitiful, fumbling attempts at lovemaking. Afterwards they filled me with loathing."

The Earl took a step towards her, his face livid, his hands working, but Deborah was past caring. If she must die, at least she would do so with the satisfaction of having told this arrogant swine precisely how much he disgusted her.

"Oh, yes, I loathed you," she went on, "but that loathing was a small thing in comparison with my feelings towards you now. I curse you, my lord, curse you for —" She got no further. The Earl's fingers had closed about her throat.

Almost at once, however, he released her with an ugly laugh.

" 'Faith, my dear, you nearly made me forget myself with your insolence. I am in no mind to grant you so swift an end. You shall have time to meditate on your sins and your stupidity. It will do you a great deal of good, I'm sure, and no one will come to disturb your reflections, that I can promise you. These cellars lie beneath the stables. It is twenty years since they were last used and they are much too deep for anyone to hear your cries. So enjoy your thoughts. And just before I go, it may cheer you to know what I intend doing with you."

"And what of the Queen? Have you thought of what she will do to you when she hears of my disappearance? I am her protegée do not forget."

"Do you take me for a fool? Can even that heretical Jezebel blame me for what will seem a fatal accident? Such things happen all the time . . . a stone that falls, a drowning, a robbery. No one would think twice. I shall be left in peace to mourn a beloved wife untimely reft from me. In peace to pursue my real objectives safe from your prying ears. The Armada is preparing for the invasion of England. It were well it should find true friends here, ready to drive out the Usurper and prepared at all costs to fight alongside Spain for the restoration of the true faith. Then I shall be revenged for all that red-headed Jezebel has made me suffer!" he concluded violently.

"Murderer and traitor, your crimes will be complete!" Deborah declared.

She felt curiously detached now. The die was cast and she had lost. Nothing could save her. Yet she felt nothing, neither fear nor pain, only a great emptiness from which she was able to look with indifference at the prospect of her end.

"What's that to you?" the Earl retorted harshly. "Those under sentence are not asked to speak. Suppose, instead, we return to what does concern you. Believe me your *accident*" – he lingered nastily on the word – "your accident, I say, will leave no clues. I have had to improvise, of course, but I am pleased with the solution. You see, such a very feminine caprice on your part, and quite against all my strongest injunctions, you were determined to visit the kennels and tonight, with the stupid temerity of youth, you are going, I fear, to venture a little too close . . . I have no need to tell you what those dear creatures can do. The whole household knows of your fondness for walking alone after dark. Thus, when you are missed tomorrow morning and a search is made of the grounds, during which your remains will be discovered, the explanation will be obvious. Who could dispute it?"

Deborah's eyes were glazed with horror.

The Earl paused for a moment to enjoy the effect of his words before continuing: "Take heart. The thing will not be quite as it seems. Whatever opinion you may hold of me, I am not altogether such a bloodthirsty barbarian as to throw you to the dogs alive. Such a notion would be too offensive. No, I shall merely do away with you in here and then leave your body next to the bars. The dogs may be trusted to destroy any compromising evidence. The results will be the same but I trust that you appreciate my mercy." He sneered. "And now, with your permission, I shall take my leave of you. I shall return when the household is asleep and we shall make an end of a union which has irked me from the moment of contracting it. Your servant, madam."

He bowed punctiliously and reached for the torch.

"Wait!"

The Earl turned back to Deborah. Her white face stood out from the dark figure chained to the wall as a pure oval, so white that it might have been carved from alabaster, out of which two huge bright eyes stared unflinchingly.

"I think, sir, that you are grossly mistaken in your own motives for wishing my death. Before I die, I should be glad to set you right," she said, with the utmost politeness. "Your initial impulse may well have been to put an end to an unsuitable alliance but the fury which drives you today is, I think, due to baser but more human motives, motives which are within the reach of lord and commoner alike. Think for your own part! Examine your wounded vanity; remember my reluctance and the lengths to which you were driven by my refusals, remember the hours you must have spent in picturing me happy in the arms of younger, handsomer men, better endowed than yourself. Remember the joys which have enriched our marriage and it will not take you long to realize it is for this, more than anything else, that you desire my death."

He heard her out, set-faced, without even attempting to interrupt.

"I have been your wife and on that point at least, you cannot deceive me. You are not the man you would be thought, my lord, a cold and rigid moralist; you are a slave to your own appetites, and such a man as you are cares more for his virility than for any more . . . elevated considerations. If I had given in meekly to your demands, been hypocrite enough to flatter and make up to you, don't you think you would have changed your mind? How long would it have been before you abandoned your prejudices, preferring the comforts of my body to the vaunted honour of your family which, it seems to me, you have served ill enough? Weigh it well. The answer will provide you with food for thought when you are a widower again. And remember this—" Her voice rose to a throbbing conclusion: "I would far rather die than live subject to you. A few hours with my lovers was worth a whole insipid lifetime at your side!"

She flung back her head in a last gesture of defiance and was silent.

In the Earl's waxen face and ravaged gaze she read an implacable hatred mingled oddly with something like fear.

"By God, you shameless vixen, do you dare to flout me yet!" he spluttered.

Lifting the torch, he stared for a long time at the girl, her lovely face drawn with suffering, the curves of her body made more maddenly voluptuous by the way her wet clothes clung to her. Then, as he flung out of the cellar, his last words came back to her:

"Pray, madam! You have one hour to live!"

XXXI

She was in total darkness. Only the scurrying footsteps of the rats disturbed the silence of that dank, subterranean place. Except for their furtive scratchings, there was nothing but a felted, menacing stillness, a black well.

Deborah's shoulders drooped slowly. Now that she no longer had to make a show, the courage which had been spurred by the Earl's presence was beginning to desert her.

She did not want to die. It was not fair. You could not die at eighteen, with all your beauty and the hot blood coursing in your veins! Eighteen! She had hardly begun to live and now, so soon, when there were still so many fruits untasted, so many joys which now she would never know! And so many others she did know which passed in a bitter procession before her burning eyes; simple pleasures which now seemed beyond all price. The fleeting splendour of a cherry tree dressed in its springtime blossom; the delicate beauty of a rose; the pure, scented air of the countryside and long rides on horseback, drinking in great happy draughts of life. There were so many things she had passed by carelessly, without really seeing, things she had taken for granted, accepting them as a matter of course, and which she now sought desperately to recapture, refusing to allow her thoughts to wander further on down roads of happiness now equally inaccessible but which she sensed her failing spirits could not bear.

No, she must not think of John Strong, with his big, open face and unfailing devotion, nor of little Psyche, her greyhound bitch, whom she had found awaiting her return, more frightened than hurt, and who must be still sitting there on the brocaded counterpane, her pointed muzzle turned hopefully to the door, waiting for her and James . . .

Deborah's head drooped on her breast. Her body shook with painful sobs and suddenly she no longer tried to hold back her tears. What was the use? Now that her last minutes had come and there was no more hope of escape, why not give way to grief? It was the only consolation that was left. Kit! James! She would never see either of them again. The one had gone before her, through her own fault, into that other place towards which she herself was moving with such trepidation. The other was still in this world, to which in an hour she would no longer belong. Kit! All that had been between them, all the wonderful, mad passion they had known, was lost to her for ever. Lost, too, was James's tenderness. She saw him in her mind's eye, could almost think she heard the little, affectionate nothings he had been used to murmur in her ear, and she found herself staring uselessly into the darkness as though she would encounter his gaze and read there all the boundless comfort of their love, the love which had led him to his death.

A whole host of memories wheeled and jostled in her wavering brain: the chase at Gilford, the Curtain, Whitehall, the river and its boats, a mocking smile and a voice saying tenderly: "It won't be for long, my heart." And "It's quite a short voyage, you know. I'll soon be back again." A pair of protective arms around her and another voice, laughing joyously and saying: "Do you like the sables? They are nothing, just a few fripperies, my precious. Don't you know I'd give my life for you?"

She groaned, like an animal in pain.

An icy sweat was running down her spine, between her breasts and dripping from her forehead. There was a clanging and a banging like demented bells in her head and the darkness seemed to be growing blacker, more oppressive, crowding in on her on all sides to swallow her up. All at once, her legs gave way under her and she fell sagging to her knees, her weight hanging from her chained arms like one crucified.

She screamed then, a long, hardly-human shriek which rang horribly through the underground vaults and died away.

"Miss Deb? Miss Deb, are you there?"

In her half-conscious state she was aware of footsteps coming nearer.

"Miss Deb! It's me, John Strong!" the voice persisted.

No, she would not be taken in by it. It was another hallucination, that was all. Unless she was already in the world of ghosts! The thought made her shrink and hold her breath.

"Miss Deb!" The voice was very close.

Could it be? Oh, just and almighty God, give me the strength to answer! She managed to drag herself up.

There was a gleam of light beyond the barred door.

"Here," she croaked, so feebly that it was more a sigh than a call for help.

The door creaked on its rusty hinges.

"Miss Deb! I've found you at last!"

John Strong appeared before her dazed and still incredulous eyes: a white-faced John Strong who stumbled a little as he walked so that he looked a good deal like a ghost, holding a candle at arm's length before him.

"Come here, come . . . closer . . ."

She was touching him feverishly, feeling his hair, his hands, clinging to him . . . No, it was not a ghost. It was indeed her faithful servant, flesh and blood, alive!

"Oh, John, John!" she said over and over again, while waves of joy poured over her and tears of relief ran down her pallid cheeks. "I thought you were dead," she said at last, laughing and crying at once.

"I'll explain later. T'first thing's to have you out o' this." His horrified eyes took in her appearance. "By God, what's come to you?"

She let go of him, wiped her eyes and sniffed.

"Don't worry. I'm all right." She showed him her chains. "The main thing is to get these off."

John bent over the manacles and examined them minutely. He worked on the locks for a moment, bruising her wrists, but looked up, baffled.

"I don't see how, barring we get the keys."

And the Earl would be back at any moment! Terror took hold of her and she could feel herself on the verge of a fresh outburst of tears but she fought down the rising panic.

"Listen," she said, doing her best to gather her wits together. "There is only one thing to do. You must go up to the stables. You are bound to find a file or some pincers or – oh, something, I don't know, in the harness room. These chains are old and rusty. Look, they are barely holding now. With your strength you ought to be able to deal with them. The main thing is to get me free of the wall. We can deal with the manacles afterwards. Go on. Hurry. The Earl may be back at any minute."

"All right, Miss Deb. And don't fret. I'll be right back." With a reassuring smile, he was gone.

Once again the darkness flowed round her and, with the extra agony of hope and fear she now endured, was almost more than Deborah could bear.

How long had John been gone? Surely it should not take him more than a few seconds to run up to the harness room? What was he doing? To think that her life depended on —

Running footsteps broke in on her thoughts. John Strong appeared, brandishing a pair of tools in triumph.

"This ought to do it. With this hammer and these pincers I'll be hanged if I don't do it. Only, you mustn't mind, Miss Deb, I'll be as careful as I can, but I may hurt you a bit."

"Don't worry about me. Not now," she said briefly. "Just get these irons off, that's all I ask."

John set to work.

Every stroke of the hammer seemed to go right through her and her wrists were raw and bleeding and her lips and tongue bitten in her efforts to keep from crying out, but at last her right arm and then her left were free. They were stiff and numb and each wrist was still encircled by a metal ring from which hung a short length of chain, but at least she could get out of this horrible cellar and breathe fresh air once again.

She laid both hands on John's coat and, raising herself on tiptoe, kissed his rough cheek.

"I'll do as much for you one day," she promised.

"Let be, for that, Miss Deb. We're not done yet. We'd best be getting out of here, and fast. Seems to me his lordship means no good to you, so where am I to take you?"

Yes, what was she to do now? Terror gave her only one idea: to escape. But where to, she asked herself anxiously? To her aunt? The Queen? What would happen if she presented herself as a suppliant, an adulterous wife pursued by a justly angry husband? The Earl was a peer of the realm, while she was nothing. His word would outweigh hers, for Deborah knew very well that Elizabeth would not stand for a public scandal.

Her mind raced and, slowly at first, her natural coolness and common sense reasserted themselves. So did her hatred, also. She, Deborah Mason, to be dragged through the mire, dishonoured, her relations with James made public property, discussed and decried through the fault of that accursed brute. She recalled the young man's body lying in the straw, the nightmare of these past hours, all the humiliations she had endured, and told herself contemptuously that she must be both a fool and a coward if she could forget what was owing to this evil man.

"Come," she said decisively. "I know where we are going. You go in front with the candle and light the way."

They passed in silence along the broad, dark, ice-cold passage, off which opened a number of other, identical cells, then mounted a flight of steps to another passage which led in turn to a second, steeper stair closed by a trapdoor at the top. John Strong thrust up the trap and they were in the stables.

"Are you armed?"

"No, by gum! Those rogues had the lot off me. I forgot, though, I've not told you . . ."

Dismissing the subject, Deborah led him with a firm step to the place where she and James had been caught by the Earl. The body had gone.

Hardening her heart against the grief which threatened to overcome her, she knelt down in the straw and began feeling about her, scattering it in all directions, watched by the astonished John.

A big, black horse in the stall opposite observed her with interest.

When at last she stood up, her hair was full of wisps of straw. She put up her left hand to push it back. Her right hand held a long pistol.

"As I thought," she said quietly, half to herself. "He was so sure of himself he didn't even bother to pick up my pistol." She turned to John. "Now leave me," she said. "I want you to go to bed."

"No, that I'll not. You'll not find me going off and letting you bide here alone, not for anything you may say."

"All right then. Come with me. Pull up the trap again. We're going down."

They retraced their steps. When they reached the bottom of the steps, Deborah motioned to John to stop.

"There," she said, indicating a small cellar lying almost opposite to the steps. "We'll wait there . . . Good God! What's this?" She had hold of John's coat where the candlelight gleamed on a dark, brownish stain. "You're hurt?" she exclaimed.

"Nowt for you to fret yourself about. A bit of a knife glanced off my ribs, that's all."

"You should have told me!"

"We were a mite pushed for time. I'll tell you now, in a few words."

Deborah looked round her.

"Come into this corner. Give me the candle."

She blew it out and, keeping one ear cocked for the least sound, prepared to listen to John Strong's story.

"Well, then," John began painstakingly. "I were coming down Furton Street – that's the side street that comes out into Morton Street right opposite the house, you know – well, I were coming down there when out pops this sturdy rogue from a doorway and grabs at the horses. There's never a soul about there in the afternoons. Then at the same time another couple of the rufflers jump me from behind and pull me off the box. Well, I hit the ground fighting mad, as you can guess but . . . eh, there were three of them, you see, Miss Deb, and one o' them pulled a knife on me . . . and that was my lot, I reckon." John sounded almost apologetic. "The rogues would've finished me off for sure but just then the big one, a shifty, coistrel fellow I seem to recall having seen somewhere before, starts bawling out that he could hear the watch coming and they'd best be off before they got taken. Reckon they thought I'd snuffed it any road. And after that, Miss Deb, I'm sorry to say it was the last I knew until I woke up in the dark, mother-naked or nigh on, behind a dung-heap where the damned rapscallions must ha' stowed me."

"My poor John! What did you do then? . . . Shhh!" She gripped his arm, suddenly alert. "No, it was probably nothing but a rat. Go on."

"Well," John continued, "I made my way back to Morton Street, to the house. The porter there's a good fellow. He bound me up and gave me a sup to drink . . . and, by God, I needed it! Then, when I was a bit more like myself he started asking me what all the trouble was about. 'What trouble?' says I, and then he trots out a whole lot of stuff about your little tyke bein' hurt and Mr James dashing off like a madman and then the two of you coming back and going out again not ten minutes since, with you looking 'pale as death' as he said. I thought it pretty strange mysen'. I mean, it's not likely you'd be with Mr James at this hour o'day. So I put on my thinking cap and then it came to me, just like that, where I'd seen that gurt, shifty good-for-nothing rogue before. It were with that husband of yours, his lord-ship, I should say, one Sunday, in Southwark and I thought then —"

"Shhh! Quiet – I believe . . ." They both held their breath.

308

"No," Deborah said at last, disappointed. "It must have been another rat."

John cleared his throat. "Anyways," he said, "what it comes down to is I began to think there must be summat queer goin' on at t'house and I'd best be on my way. So I borrowed the porter's old coat and trotted back quick like. Then when I got into Drury Lane it came over me as Master Fletcher'd like as not show me the door if he caught a sight of me looking like this – you know what a stickler he is, Miss Deb – and besides, I couldn't get that big lout out o' my head somehow and it seemed best to creep in quiet like. So I let mysen' in by the stables and just then what do I see but a candle come up out o' t' floor. Give me a right turn, I can tell you. I ducks down behind t' wall there and who should I see but his lordship, with that long face of his more like bugaboo than ever. I knew then there was summat amiss. These cellars aren't used nowadays. So soon as he was gone, down I came . . . nobbut I were beginning to think I'd guessed wrong when I heard you."

"Oh, dear John." Deborah felt for his hand in the dark. "How clever of you."

"But what happened to you, Miss Deb? And where's Mr James?"

"He's dead," Deborah answered curtly. "His lordship killed him. I'll tell you about it later. Just now I can't —"

Silence fell between them. Suddenly, Deborah put out her hand.

"Listen. I think I heard footsteps. Don't make a sound. And unless something goes wrong, don't interfere!"

Quick, even footsteps sounded overhead, coming steadily nearer.

Deborah's heart began to thud, her breath came quick and shallow, her jaw tightened and she armed herself against all thought of anything but her hatred, clinging to it with her last remaining strength because it was the friend, true, vigilant and unrelenting, which would guide her hand.

She grasped the pistol firmly, checked that it was cocked then, holding the butt firmly against her chest, pointed it in what she hoped was the direction of the trapdoor.

A square of light appeared in the roof of the tunnel.

A pair of fine leather shoes with jewelled ties appeared, feeling their way cautiously down the stone steps. They were followed by two long, thin legs in violet silk hose, gartered below the knee with tassels of silver, trunk hose, velvet paned with satin, black on black. One step . . . two steps . . . and the whole of the Earl's tall figure was visible, outlined against the wall.

Coming down like that, torch in hand, he was a perfect target.

Three steps . . . four steps . . . Deborah moved silently out of her recess. She was standing facing him but, blinded by the glare of his own torch, he could not see her.

"Earl of Norland!" she called in a firm voice.

She saw him start and raise the torch a little, putting his hand to his dagger. Then, quick as a flash, she fired.

The echoes of it reverberated thunderously through the underground caverns. The smell of powder filled the tunnel.

The Earl threw up his arms and the torch flew from his grasp, falling to the ground in a graceful arc. He pressed both hands to his chest, swayed for a moment and then plunged head first.

John sprang forward to seize the torch before it went out and, lifting it above his head, studied the body.

"You made a fair job o' that," he commented. Then, remembering himself, he added formally: "What I mean to say is as his lordship is dead, Miss Deb, beggin' your pardon." Moved by some deep-rooted force of habit, he bent and straightened the body, setting the tumbled lace to rights and brushing the dust with a respectful gesture from the doublet, except for that sinister patch over the heart where it was rent and stained with blood. "Now what do we do?"

Deborah did not hear him. She was staring with a kind of fascinated intensity at the pallid, dead face of her enemy, fixed now in an expression of eternal astonishment, at the dead eyes which would never look contempt at her again, and the body doomed to everlasting impotence.

She was overwhelmed by a strange variety of emotions as she realized, now that it was done, for how long she had been unconsciously and wholeheartedly living for this moment. After the first wave of fierce elation, a wave of perfect certainty seemed to flow gently over her, and a miraculous peace descended. It was well and just. She had acted properly, according to the dictates of honour.

John Strong's voice roused her from her curious absorption.

"Miss Deb," he was saying anxiously. "Miss Deb, are you listening? What are we going to do? Happen you'll not have thought of that?"

He was right. Oh God! He was right. She had won her freedom, her life, but for the living there was the future to consider and necessity demanded that she consider it fast.

"Look in his lordship's pocket," she said, pulling herself together. "He should have the keys to these gyves on him somewhere."

John felt and produced two keys.

"Happen this'll be the one." Retaining the smaller of the two, he dropped the other, a large iron key, without ornament, on a plain brass ring, carelessly to the ground.

Deborah put down the pistol and held out her hands. A click and the first of the heavy irons fell with a clatter, to be closely followed by the second.

As she nursed her raw and bleeding wrists, Deborah was thinking hard. The first thing that had to be done was to get rid of the Earl. If the murder — no, she corrected herself at once, if the execution could be made to look like accident then she would be the one to play the part of the sorrowing widow. But how could it be done? She was walking up and down in feverish thought when her foot struck the other key and she came to a shuddering stop. Light broke in her brain. She knew that other key. It was —

"John, wounded as you are, do you think you could manage to carry his lordship? I'll help all I can but —"

"Now then, Miss Deb. I'll not need anyone's help." He squared his shoulders, wincing a little with the pain it caused him. "It's no measly scratch is going to get me down. So what is it you —"

"This," Deborah said crisply. "Pick up that key. It's the key to the kennel. Oh, don't look at me like that. I've not gone stark mad. Can you think of any better place to put the body? His lordship was so fond of the brutes." She laughed shortly. "But take care and don't go too near the bars. The door is solid oak. Keep well behind it and then tip the body over into the kennel among the dogs. They – they will do the rest. Do you think you can do it?"

John nodded slowly, his expression appalled.

"Just in case you should be overcome with remorse," Deborah said fiercely, "let me tell you this was the charming end his lordship had in mind for me."

"Eh?" John was shaking his head, wholly at a loss. "To think his lordship — Well, happen I can understand you'll not love him overmuch." More firmly, he added: "Trust me, Miss Deb. I'll see to it."

"Thank you, John dear." She looked up at him earnestly. "You are doing me a great service. You shan't find me ungrateful . . . Oh, and the key. You'd better throw that into the kennel as well. You won't forget? His lordship was in the habit of locking himself in with the dogs and if our plan is to succeed, the key must be found

311

with . . . with the . . . I mean, everyone will think the dogs got out of control and turned on their master. Come, we must hurry."

John was already hoisting the corpse on to his shoulders. Deborah took the pistol, the torch, John's candle and the chains, cast a last glance around to make sure nothing had been left and preceded him up the steps.

"You've done enough now, Miss Deb. You go on in," John said when they reached the stable. He was breathing hard and the sweat was pouring down his face.

"No. I'll wait for you."

"Don't be daft, lass. I don't need you."

"Suppose someone sees you?"

"That's just it," her henchman said with decision. "If I'm by mysen' I can get by. It's me drives your coach and happen I've a right to be about the stables if I've a mind. But you, at this time of night and wi' a look like a wet week! Where's your sense?"

"I think you've got enough for both of us," Deborah admitted humbly. "You're quite right, of course. When you've . . . when you've finished, go to bed and whatever anyone asks you, you don't know anything, and you've seen nothing, do you understand?" She laid her hand on his shoulder. "We'll see to that wound of yours properly tomorrow. For tonight, just swab it with spirits and bind it up in clean linen. And . . . John? . . . I want you to know, I'll never forget what you've done today."

Running, crouching, staggering through the alleys, Deborah made her way through the gardens to the house. By the time she slipped through the door from the terrace she was half-fainting, her mind a blank, her legs trembling. Somehow she got to the staircase but it was only an instinctive effort of will that gave her the necessary strength to mount, step by step, resisting the temptation simply to sink down where she was and blot out thought in the sleep of sheer exhaustion.

Feeling her way along the walls, guided by the faint starlight which crept through the long windows, she came at last to her own chamber.

There, all was quiet and a warm harmony, with the familiar scent of orris and the familiar scatter of her belongings. The white sheets and soft mattress beckoned. Ignoring them, Deborah went instead to the window and peered out.

The gardens slept, beautiful and serene, touched here and there with the pale light of the rising moon. Gazing, with unseeing eyes, she waited.

Suddenly, the silence was broken by a piercing clamour, the rabid baying of hounds.

With a sound that was half a groan and half a sigh, Deborah clung for a moment to the hangings, then slithered slowly to the ground, unconscious.

XXXII

There was a violent hammering on the door.

Deborah, revived from her swoon long since by the cool night air, had been expecting it.

At first, she had simply lain where she was, her mind a blank, but the instinct of self-preservation finally overcame her torpor. She told herself that if she stayed here, flat on the floor, fully-clothed in garments that were not even her own and looking like a ghost, she might as well go and give herself up to the public hangman at once. The hangman! The word imprinted itself in fiery letters on her brain and sent her running to her wardrobe. With trembling hands she pulled off the skirt and bodice she was wearing and put them away at the very bottom of a chest, where she could be sure no servant's prying fingers would find them. Then she washed as best she could in cold water, which was all there was, slipped on her night rail over her shift and huddled under the counterpane, waiting to face whatever was to come.

The hammering continued, more urgently.

Deborah got up and drew her bedgown round her suddenly rigid body. With a glance behind her to assure herself that the bed presented that slight, charming appearance of disorder which would bear necessary witness to a quiet night, she gritted her teeth and walked to the door.

She found herself face to face with the steward.

"Fletcher! What does this mean?" she asked coldly. "What do you think you're doing, waking me?"

"My lady . . . my lady . . . it is my lord . . ."

Fletcher, the mighty and unshakeable Fletcher, was white as a sheet, his clothes on all askew, his hair falling over his gaunt face, and his inarticulate and stammering speech exerted an instantly revivifying effect on Deborah. For the first time, she felt that she was the stronger.

"Well?" she said impatiently. "What is it? Tell me, if you please."

314

"It's horrible ... my lord ..."

"Good God! Is the Earl ill?"

"Alas, no, my lady ... a fearful accident ..."

Deborah felt as though a great weight had fallen from her shoulders. If Fletcher, who had been with the Earl for years and years, had accepted the idea that it was an accident, then she was surely safe! She clutched his sleeve.

"An accident! In God's name, Fletcher, tell me!"

"Those damned mastiffs! They must have turned on him."

"No!"

Putting every bit of horror she could manage into the cry, she closed her eyes and swayed perilously. Some slight affliction would create the right impression, and she was not going to faint again. She felt, all at once, oddly detached, quite cool and unconcerned, as though someone else were there speaking her lines and miming her gestures, and she herself was present merely to direct the scene.

Fletcher put out an arm to steady her but she thrust him away, leaning against the wall.

"No, let be. It will pass."

What ought she to do now, she wondered, burst into tears, or start tearing her hair? Neither seemed exactly feasible just then. In any case, she knew that she must not overdo it. Fletcher was not a fool and a display of uncontrollable grief would look even more suspicious than indifference. No, a dignified sorrow, that was the line to take.

She let out a long sigh, drew herself up and laid her hand on the steward's arm.

"Where is my lord, Fletcher? I wish to see him."

"But, my lady —" Fletcher began, then, taking a close look at his mistress, abruptly changed his mind. "Come with me, my lady."

Silently, in single file, they passed along the empty galleries, down the great staircase and across the hall, where the entire household was assembled in a shuffling, awe-struck group which parted to allow a passage to the mistress of the house. John Strong was there, Deborah noted.

The terrace ... the pool ... the pathway ... The farther they went, the more rapidly Deborah felt her strength and confidence oozing away from her. She knew she could not do it. She could not revisit that dreadful scene, face the ghastly reality of it. She could

315

see the stable roof now. Half a dozen times she almost turned and fled but there was Fletcher at her side, watching her dourly, taking note of everything she did. So she walked on with the stiff, unco-ordinated gait of a puppet, her little gilded slippers stumbling on the stones, with a roaring in her ears and her heart pounding like a drum.

They emerged into the open.

The kennel was bathed in the pink light of dawn. All round it stood a guard of grooms and stable boys, armed with long bills.

Fletcher took Deborah's arm and led her slowly to the bars. Through a mist, she saw the hounds ranging up and down, lean, brindled shapes, and, there, in the midst of them, a few fragments of blood-stained linen. That was all.

The bars began to move, swaying, dancing, faster and faster, like an immense cage swinging round and round, while behind the bars the mastiffs' ugly jaws moved to and fro. One of them gave tongue. The sky became black and she collapsed against Fletcher.

After a cordial and a grudging hour's rest, the physician, who was an optimist, opined that my lady was now well enough to face up to her obligations. These, it appeared, were legion. They poured into the hall, overflowed into the withdrawing rooms, and took pos-session of the whole house: a flood of faces, known and unknown, curious, morbid, falsely sympathetic, encroaching on her with their hypocritical condolences.

The next day was the funeral: a few fragments of flesh and bone scraped together and piously enshrined in a massive ebony coffin which was then duly interred with all the requisite degree of cere-mony in the Norland family vault.

On the following Thursday came the official inventory of the deceased's possessions and the reading of the will. This, in the event, proved to be nothing more than the opening paragraphs of a will, containing nothing beyond a few small legacies to various of the late Earl's friends or hangers-on and a number of bequests to old servants. The document was discovered by the coroner who came, as a matter of form, to make the routine inquiry into a violent death, among the Earl's papers in his cabinet. It was obviously incomplete but no amount of research into the dead man's private affairs served to bring to light any more explicit testamentary dis-positions. Since the existing will was also unsigned, and its authenticity guaranteed by nothing more than the handwriting, it was, as the clerk was scrupulous in pointing out, legally null and void and the dowager Countess was under no obligation to observe its provisions. In fact, since the Earl left no descendants, ascendants or any other kinsman, all his lands and properties, including his northern estates and his fine house in London, with all the movables, furnishings, tapestries, jewels, ornaments and other things which it contained, reverted legally and absolutely to his wife.

Deborah heard the news with indifference. What did such a fortune matter to her? The house she loathed; the estates she did not know and in her present state the very thought of figures seemed a herculean task. Nevertheless, she asked the clerk to attend to the bequests mentioned in the will, saying that she naturally intended to comply with her husband's last wishes, whether she had any obligation to or not.

For her own part, all she wanted was to make an end of this ghastly farce, find some quiet corner where she could rest her weary body in peace and hide a face grown tired of making the expected grimaces, displaying the required responses which were farthest from her mind. She wanted time to shut herself up with her grief and weep her aching heart out for James. James! She had only to think of him, to whisper his name, for a flood of bitterness to overwhelm her: his smile which had held such a world of tenderness, the infectious laughter she had loved so much, the warm refuge of his arms ... never, never again! All that youth and ardent life snuffed out in one fatal instant, scattered ... soon to be dust. He had been absorbed, irrevocably, into the infinite, and she had not even the poor satisfaction of knowing what had become of him. Never more! The words beat in her head like a knell, hammered at her chest while she sat, draped decorously in her widow's weeds, accepting the condolences and regrets being offered to his murderer. It had gone on for long enough. It was time she left this accursed house.

She summoned Fletcher and informed him at once of her intention to quit Norland House for an indefinite length of time. She left the household in his care, confident that he had no need of her assistance to manage all supremely well. She would inform him when it was her intention to return, she added in a tone that did not invite comment, but after the dreadful tragedy which had occurred she longed only for peace.

For the last time, she made her way down the stone staircase, crossed the great hall, bowing in stately fashion right and left to the assembled ranks of her household, and then, with John Strong in attendance, stepped out through the front door without looking back, determined never to set foot in Norland House again.

Her objective was the haven of her adolescent years, the small house in Fleet Street which Mistress Tucker, forewarned by John, had hurriedly rehired and provided with all the necessary equipment and personnel. That all this had been done in the space of less than a week was a tribute to that lady's habitual efficiency and energetic management.

There, in her old room, furnished just as it always used to be with the narrow, girlish bed and starched white linen curtains, Deborah's overwrought nerves gave way at last. For a week she lay, alternating between a semi-conscious torpor and bouts of raging fever, fighting against the phantoms of delirium which assailed her.

From time to time her eyes would clear briefly and she would be aware of the vague shape of Mistress Tucker, or of John Strong's worried gaze. Strong hands lifted her and she was aware of a cold spoon against her lips. Dutifully, she swallowed the musty liquid they gave her. The room was full of strangers, men dressed in black who laid cold hands on her burning limbs . . . men in black . . . the trapdoor in the stable . . . the Earl . . . She screamed and a flood of terrified supplications burst from her throat. Her mind wavered once again and she sank back into the abyss of nightmare. The nightmare was always the same: James, standing there, a long way off, with a great wound in his chest and offering her his bloody heart, but as she went towards him, her hands held out to take it, her husband's mutilated body came between them, barring the way, with a pack of ferocious hounds baying over it.

Days passed. Now the physicians were gone and the nightmares growing fewer. The chirurgeon's cuppings and the physicians' remedies, not to mention the charms and talismans placed by Mistress Tucker in every corner of the chamber, had done their work. Convalescence, dull and grey as a fog-bound winter landscape, was setting in.

Then came the morning when Mistress Tucker surged into the room at an hour when she should, in the normal way of things, have been at the palace, with her hood awry and her usual stately calm flown to the winds.

Deborah lay between the sheets, her uncombed hair scattered on the pillow, and stared at her owlishly.

"You must get up, child," her aunt declared, without the least regard for the invalid's enfeebled state. "You are to go and see the Queen this instant."

"Aunt, you can't mean it?" Deborah protested weakly. "Look at me. I can't even walk across the room! In any case, what —?"

"I'm sorry, but you must get up, at once. You're to be at White-hall in two hours from now if I have to drag you there myself. Her Majesty returned from Richmond last night and will grant you an audience. I asked her myself on your behalf."

"In God's name, what is the matter?"

Rousing herself slightly from her apathetic state, Deborah sat up on her elbow and turned a thin, white face to her aunt.

"The matter, you wretched child, is that if you go on mooning there in your bed like a ninnygoose you stand to lose everything you've gained: money, titles, even your life, perhaps!" Mistress Tucker uttered the last words in a low, troubled voice, pressing both hands to her vast bosom.

"What do you mean?"

Deborah was sitting bolt upright now.

Mistress Tucker regarded her earnestly.

"James Randolph was fished out of the Thames by a waterman early this week . . . Oh, let's have no maudlin tears, if you please," she added roughly. "This is no time to be mewling over a lad that's brought us nothing but a peck of trouble, when all's said. Not that I didn't warn you. No, don't interrupt me. I'm not interested in your feelings. All I'm interested in is the talk there's been about the pair of you, and the way it's starting up again. The body's being found so soon after the accident at Norland House has led people to wonder, and there's plenty glad to make the most of it by spreading nasty tales at court." She sighed. "I said nothing at the time because there seemed no point in it, but today it's got serious. Very serious. I've just heard that the coroner's talking of reopening the case." She moved to the bedside and took Deborah's hand in hers.

"I don't want to pry into your secrets, child. I'm only trying to save you, and there's only one way to do that: the Queen. Her Majesty has some affection for you, and some esteem, as she has ever shown. Go to her, throw yourself on her mercy, show her you are blameless in all this, that it is nothing but a pack of nasty lies; place all your new-found wealth and your life at her service and I think she'll listen to you." The wrinkled eyelids creased knowingly. "She can't be grieving overmuch at the loss of a one-time traitor and more than half a papist at that, and the Norland wealth will be a deal more use to England in your grateful hands than it ever was in the Earl's. Now, listen, child. That is what you must say to Her Majesty. Trust me. I know her. She's always known, with that clever brain of hers, how to make the best of any situation, and she's none too fussy about the details. Her conscience is England's good and outside that the ethics can take care of themselves. There, now we'll dress you and put some colour in your cheeks. The Queen can't bear unhealthy-looking folk about her, so we'll use up a whole pot of rouge if we must."

The Queen sat at her writing table. Behind her, a secretary with his arms full of papers was passing them to her one at a time. Elizabeth took them, leafed through them attentively, then dipped her pen in the ink and signed with a flourish before passing on to the next.

This activity had been going on for an hour or more and Deborah, standing by the door, her eyes fixed on her sovereign's august back, felt almost ready to faint from fatigue and anxiety. How was she to interpret this reception? Surely coldness and marked indifference were the first indications of a fall from grace? Moistening her parched lips feverishly, she went over in her mind all that Mistress Tucker had told her, striving hard to embellish the defence which she had put together hastily on her way here from Fleet Street.

It was not that life itself had so much attraction for her, far from it. But there was a vast and terrible gulf between nursing her miseries at home in the comfortable privacy of her own bed and finding herself hauled ignominiously to the scaffold. She imagined the horror, the edge of the axe touching her soft neck . . . Oh, no! No! Please God, not that, she had not deserved that, it would not be fair! In slaying a malefactor, she had done no more than justice, and was he now to have the last word, after all? No, he should not. And sustained by this thought more even than by fear, she fought off her weakness, forgot for a moment that she had been ill, and gathered up her spirit.

At last the Queen laid down her pen, dismissed her secretary and turned to Deborah.

"Well?"

The tone was not encouraging. Well, courage all the same! And above all, no servility, let there be nothing of the beggar: it would only serve to strengthen the Queen's present attitude.

She advanced, bowed low and remained kneeling in a cloud of black veiling.

"I have come to beg Your Majesty's pardon for having, however unintentionally, neglected my duty to Your Majesty. After the tragedy which struck the house of Norland, I was ordered by my physicians to keep to my bed, which effectively prevented me from coming, after my widowhood, to present my humble duty to Your Majesty and to beg you, in grateful recognition of the immense benefits conferred on your servant, to consider as your own the wealth which was my late husband's and which I now dedicate to Your Majesty's service, whenever you care to avail yourself of it, as I do myself and my whole heart which are Your Majesty's to command, now as ever."

Sardonic? Stern? Inscrutable, certainly, Elizabeth's blue eyes looked into hers.

"It does not occur to you that this offer may be a trifle premature?"

Indeed it had occurred: for what would she have to offer if they cut off her head? No, do not forget, you are innocent!

"I am overwhelmed by Your Majesty's kindness," she said adroitly, "but I can assure Your Majesty that my health is quite recovered. Should you so desire, I am ready at this moment to undertake any mission you might wish to name, however daring, that might redound to Your Majesty's greater glory. I and all I have are yours to command."

A formidable buffet almost knocked the breath from her body and the Queen's loud laugh rang out. To Deborah it sounded like heavenly music. Did it mean that she had won? To change the atmosphere of the room, soften Her Majesty's mood, that was the essence.

"God's death! You pert piece! Was there ever such effrontery? I did not have you taught for nothing. There was even something in your fine speeches reminded me of myself when I was a girl, talking away for dear life's sake with terror in my heart and the axe at my elbow." Her face grew serious again. "Come, child. Let's have no more beating about the bush. We both know why you're here. And if you'd not come of yourself I'd have sent for you. This matter must be cleared up. It is inconvenient for me who made you what you are, and as for you – well, that depends . . . A little frankness

321

may help me to pull your chestnuts out of the fire. What was between you and that poor lad Randolph?" The last question was shot out suddenly, with hardly a change of tone.

"James Randolph?" She had been expecting the question. "Friendship, Your Majesty, that is all —" Oh, my darling, forgive me, she prayed inwardly, while outwardly serene her lips continued smoothly: "A friendship of which I thought no harm, any more than of other friendships which enliven Your Majesty's court without in any way disturbing it."

Talking away for dear life's sake, with terror in my heart: that was it precisely.

"Hmm. And what of Norland and Randolph, tell me that?"

"Strictly speaking, nothing, Your Majesty. I can honestly say I never heard them exchange more than a dozen words, and all in perfect courtesy. But my lord was not often at court. His temper was too grave."

"God's death, he were well to stay at home! His Friday face was no great cheer at our revels. They say extremes meet and I think but that he came of a line of papists, your husband might have made a puritan. Go on."

"What can I add that Your Majesty does not already know? I was horrified to learn of Randolph's death but I do not know how it concerns me, or on what these calumnies I hear of are based. I was as good a wife as the Earl a husband. I have nothing with which to reproach myself and I most humbly entreat Your Majesty to make an end of this malicious gossip."

Like a vice, the Queen's hand closed on her shoulder.

"It suits not with our honour as a prince to cover up a crime. Can you swear to your sovereign that on your soul and conscience you have always acted as you ought? Take care, child. God is your judge."

"I swear it."

The answer came instantly, throbbing with sincerity.

For a few seconds more, Elizabeth considered the pale face before her. The eyes did not falter.

"Very well. I believe you." She rang a bell and a man entered.

"Ask Sir Francis Walsingham to come here at once." The Queen turned back to Deborah. "In your own interest, child, these whispers must be stopped immediately. Our excellent Secretary is the person best qualified to do it. He is acquainted with the business and can deal with it promptly."

Stunned and speechless, Deborah felt a cold sweat trickle down her spine. Only a moment before, she had been ready to believe that she had won, and now Walsingham, of all people, was brought into it. Walsingham! A dangerous enemy: those were his very words, she remembered them clearly, when he had threatened her a year ago after she had refused to betray the Queen's confidence to him. He could scarcely have forgotten either that, or the trick she had served him in the wood near Coventry. She dared not think what might happen if he were to persuade the Queen . . .

The door opened and a shadowy figure slid noiselessly into the room.

"Ah, there you are, Walsingham. Come in, my dear man, we have need of you here."

In the same padding silence, he came to the Queen's side. The contrast between the two was striking. In his austere black gown with the inevitable skull-cap framing his pale face, he looked for all the world like some sinister crow while Elizabeth, in white and gold with knots of sapphires flashing in her red hair, glittered like a bird of paradise.

The Queen continued: "You know the Countess of Norland?"

Walsingham bowed. "We are acquainted. How may I serve Your Majesty?"

"I have talked with the Countess, and I have made my decision. There is to be no inquiry and no scandal is to attach to her name, is that clear?"

He sighed, looking a little careworn.

"I should be happy to oblige Your Majesty but the circumstantial evidence . . ."

"What circumstantial evidence?"

Yes, what indeed? What did he mean? What had he dug up? Deborah tried to think clearly. Of the murder, there could be now no trace. Acting on her instructions, John Strong had thrown the pistol, with the bodice and kirtle she had worn, into a bog more than twenty miles from London. John Strong! Good God, suppose he were to be arrested? They would not scruple to rack him until the poor fellow confessed all. Every separate hair on her body seemed to stand on end. The alternation between hope and despair was killing. But what was Walsingham saying now?

"What we have here is a most remarkable coincidence. Two violent deaths occurring in all probability on the same day. Randolph's body was not, unfortunately, in a condition which would enable us to say for certain but he has not been seen by his household since June 26th, which is the date of the Earl of Norland's death. Your Majesty will agree that the coincidence is somewhat disturbing."

"I know that, but coincidence is not proof."

"As Your Majesty says. Nevertheless, when the two men are connected through a woman, then the facts begin to look a little sinister, and Lady Norland had been seen a great deal in young Randolph's company."

"Tush, man! I am seen a great deal in the Earl of Essex's company and would you dare for that to cast aspersions on the conduct of your sovereign?"

Oh, most excellent Queen! That was unanswerable and Walsingham prudently retired, to attack on another front.

"Even so, the accident at Norland House remains a highly suspicious circumstance. Every member of the household said upon being questioned that the Earl was in the habit of entering the kennel every day and that the beasts had never attempted to attack him."

" 'Faith, the Earl must have ceased to charm them, then. Poor Roger, who would be charmed by that long face he brought back from the north? But where is this leading? Even supposing, and mark well, I only say supposing, that gossip is true and there was some quarrel between husband and lover in which they slew each other, even so, in order to incriminate the Countess it would be necessary to prove that at the same time and in two different places she disposed of two separate corpses, and two at a time might be a lot for any woman, shouldn't you say, my dear Walsingham?"

It was almost unbearable to hear that hideous night discussed with such crude levity. Deborah dug her nails into her palms, fighting off the faintness which threatened her, and tried to listen to Walsingham's reply.

"Your Majesty is not unaware of the power of gold. It would not have been difficult for Lady Norland to purchase accomplices."

"God's wounds! You are beginning to try my patience."

The Queen's voice was rising and her eyes darkening with anger.

"I was asked by Your Majesty for my opinion. I have given it," Walsingham answered sharply, stepping back a pace.

"Then change it. That one does not like me. You are getting old, my poor friend. Or else your health is making you crotchety. Either way, I tell you, you are over-zealous and zealous in a cause which does not require it. To speak frankly: the Earl's death is no peril to

324

the realm, as you well know. But to stir up vague, unfounded rumours may do great harm to his widow, innocent though she be. Let it rest there."

He lifted one sallow hand, knotted with rheumatism.

"I do not know if the coroner —"

"What's this? Do I hear you right? Will you be bold enough to insist?" The Queen's wig toppled precariously as her body jerked forward. She clamped one furious hand on it to keep it in its place while with the other she ripped off her embroidered slipper and flung it at Walsingham.

"Let that teach you who is the mistress here and who the man!" she cried.

Deborah huddled in her veils, hardly daring to breathe. Merciful heavens, when Her Majesty was in such a mood there was no knowing where it might not end! She felt as if the floor might open at any moment under her quaking knees, or that something terrible was about to happen to break the sudden, awful silence which had fallen on the room, but nothing happened.

Walsingham, his face expressionless, picked up the slipper, dusted it and replaced it on the foot which the Queen thrust irritably forward. He bowed.

"Your Majesty shall be obeyed," he said smoothly. "The Countess need have no further cause for anxiety."

The look which accompanied this declaration went some way to marring Deborah's relief. Today, she had won, but it was only an armistice imposed by the Queen. One day, she foresaw, she would come face to face with Walsingham again and then the affront she had witnessed was likely to cost her dearly. She dismissed the thought. That was for the future . . . For the present, she blessed the Queen for making it possible for her to sink back into the privacy of her own quiet bed. She asked nothing more.

That was the end of the affair, but it seemed to have used up the last of Deborah's slender reserve of strength. Life in Fleet Street took on a dull and even tenor, pervaded by an over-all gloom.

Watched anxiously by Mistress Tucker and John Strong, Deborah sank each day further into hopelessness and a fierce misery. She grew daily weaker, barred her doors to all visitors and seemed to have no interest in anything. The Earl's man of business came to see her and she politely sent him packing without so much as glancing at the stack of papers he brought. Only Psyche still seemed to have some power over her mistress and she would lie for hours on end with the little dog pressed against her, her head on the pillow and her eyes staring at the ceiling. Not even thoughts of Kit could drag her from her apathy. She had no news of him and sought for none. He was at once too far away and too vividly alive to help her find her way among the dead.

XXXIII

One afternoon, as she was lying limply on her bed letting her thoughts follow their usual joyless course, a maid knocked on the door and then, greatly daring, opened it a crack.

"Excuse me, my lady, but there's a gentleman downstairs asking to see you."

"How many times have I told you, girl, that I am not at home to anyone?" Deborah said impatiently.

"That's what I told him, my lady, but he only laughed and bade me go and tell my mistress that – that —" She frowned with deep concentration. "Yes, that was it: he did not expect to find the banks of our sweet Thames as inhospitable as the shores of Spain. And then he added: 'She'll see me, never fear.'"

Deborah was sitting bolt upright now, the blood racing in her veins.

"Did he give his name?"

"Oh, yes. I forgot. Lord Christopher Belstone, it was, and a fine handsome gentleman he is – begging your pardon, my lady. But —" The girl was gazing at her mistress, round-eyed. Deborah had flung back the covers and leapt out of bed in one swift movement.

"Well, don't just stand there like a post, girl! Come in and help me. Quickly! My gold laced bedgown and my slippers!"

She ran to the mirror. Good God! Was it possible that she could look such a fright? Those ringed eyes, hollow cheeks and that lank, uncared-for hair: the general air of neglect. Why she was positively ugly! Almost an old woman! Horrified, she ran her hands feverishly over her breasts and hips, realizing for the first time that she was nothing but skin and bone, a walking skeleton. How could she ever have let herself go like this? She swung round.

"Hurry, Betty! For heaven's sake make haste! Stir yourself! Fetch pins, my brush! Where is the rouge pot? And my water of jasmine?"

She reviewed herself cautiously in the glass, and decided that she looked a little more presentable. The rouge had all but obliterated the shadows in her face, her hair was bound up in a coquettish green silk riband, there was a sparkle in her eyes. Pulling her gown about her, she whisked out on to the landing and tumbled down the stairs.

He was waiting in the small closet which opened off the hall. He turned at her entrance, his white teeth gleaming in his tanned, pirate's face and she felt her heart stop at the impact of those black eyes.

It was as though a thousand bells had started to ring, as though all the bells in England were pealing out in unison with the sudden tempestuous joy that swept over her. In an instant, grief and anguish were no more; there was only him, standing there looking at her, his hot lips waking her to life once more.

"My darling! Oh, my darling," she murmured over and over, her face pressed deliriously into the crimson velvet of his doublet.

"What joy it is to see you again, sweetheart. The time has dragged without you."

How could she ever have forgotten that voice. It seemed to caress her whole being?

Lifting her gently in his arms, he carried her to a settle and sat with her on his knee, huddled against his chest and gazing up at him worshipfully.

He tilted up her chin.

"Here, let's have a look at you. It seems to me, young woman, that you're very peaky. I heard of your husband's death, but, 'sblood, I never thought you'd grieve overmuch for him."

The affectionate mockery in his eyes faded before the imploring look in hers.

"Oh, my love, never talk of that to me, I beg you. Tell me instead how long have you been home?"

"I reached London this morning, but we dropped anchor at Plymouth a month since, on the twenty-sixth of June. I couldn't see you sooner, or even write to you because we had scurvy aboard. It was that obliged us to sail home, and gave us a good many headaches when it came to paying off the men." He laughed. "All right. Don't worry. I'm free of it, thank God! Why, what is it, my heart?"

The twenty-sixth of June! That dreadful night! Deborah had begun to tremble like a leaf and all the sparkle had vanished, leaving her face suddenly haggard. Kit studied her thoughtfully.

"I think it's high time someone took care of you," he said. "I'll do it myself, 'faith, and soon have you your old, lively self again."

. . . . .

He was as good as his word. Little by little, under his loving care, a love which absence seemed to have ripened and made the more tender, and thanks in no small part to his own lightheartedness and boisterous high spirits, Deborah began to look about her once again and learn to smile once more.

One by one, the clouds which had wrapped her round were blown away, leaving her with a new assurance.

The warm flush returned to her skin and her body responded to the warmth of love. She had survived one terrible crisis and now stretched out her hands with all the desperate urgency of a thwarted child to grasp at this second chance which life was offering her.

Acting on Kit's advice, she summoned Mr Notham and Mr Redford, her husband's men of business, and began at last to inquire into the inheritance which she had hitherto regarded with such supreme indifference. She was staggered when she realized what was involved.

When the handsome annual income derived from the northern estates was added to Norland House and its contents, which thanks to the late Earl's collecting mania were of incalculable value, and to the jewels, and to a substantial capital sum, Deborah could consider herself one of the wealthiest widows in England.

That this was scarcely in accordance with the wishes of the deceased was not to be doubted. The thought of that unfinished will must be making him turn in his grave, but Deborah had not the least scruple in taking advantage of his neglect. Nor was she at all afraid. He, or rather such parts of him as the grooms had been able to recover, was six feet underground and even supposing that a dead man might return at the full moon to haunt his murderer, it was not the kind of activity to be expected of those scattered bones.

Thus Deborah was rich, very rich, through no deliberate intent on her part but by a simple chance of fate, and she began to discover all the pleasures of wealth. Never before had she had any money of her own: always she had been obliged to curtsy and say thank you like a child, either to her aunt, or to the Queen, or to her husband, and been expected to show a properly humble and grateful face. Now, this fortune gave her freedom, and independence. In future, she could spend what she liked without applying to anyone and without fear of criticism. She could indulge her own whims – and all at once she seemed to have a host of them – and gratify those around her, thus enjoying the position of power which had previously been hers only in small measure and at second hand.

Yes, this money was really hers, whether honestly come by or not – and she cared not a whit what the world might say: her conscience was clear. She meant to make the best use of it.

What, she wondered, had the Earl been thinking of to let so much wealth lie idle? Fragments of her conversations with James came back to her. With this threat of an armada in the offing, there could naturally be no question of putting money into ships, but if treasure hunting was temporarily a dead end there was still plenty of profit to be made elsewhere: in the Hampshire glass-making industry, in Cornish tin – Raleigh would be useful there – in the coal mines of Durham, the forges of Sheffield, the cloth trade of Halifax, Wakefield and Leeds. Her brain reeled with the possibilities of it all. How could the Earl have been so shamefully neglectful, or at the least so negative in his attitude to his possessions? It was not a sin she would be guilty of.

Her first step was to ask Mr Redford to prepare a list of the most profitable investments, telling him that she would decide on her return. For her other decision had been to go away with Kit for a month to the lodge at Gilford. John Strong, naturally, was to be of the party. John was now full of smiles, having been promoted to the post of confidential servant, a position carrying heavy but ill-defined responsibilities which enabled him to spend a great deal of his time and the handsome wage which Deborah insisted on paying him, in supporting the numerous ale-shops in the vicinity.

In her thirst for activity, Deborah had put Norland House up for sale and bought instead a fine plot of ground on the river not far from Charing Cross. Warde, who built for Lord Burghley, had been co-opted to draw up the plans for an elegant house, in the most uncompromisingly modern style, and work was proceeding with such speed that John Thorpe, the master-builder, was due to start operations on the structure of the house at any moment.

Another acquisition was the small house in Fleet Street which Deborah settled on her aunt. It would serve her as a temporary home until her own house was finished and after that Mistress Tucker could do with it as she liked.

When all these details were under way, they set out for Gilford. The month passed all too swiftly. They hunted together, side by side, through the rich, autumn-tinted woodlands, veiled day by day in thin, damp-smelling mists, on the track of fox and wild boar. They sat endlessly talking by the hearth while the firelight illumined both their faces with the same tender glow. They made love in the great, scented bed. To Deborah, it was all a delicious reminder of the magical time of their first meeting, with something else added, a new intimacy and a quiet, almost domestic happiness which made it possible for her to hope that one day . . .

On the first day of November, they parted. Kit was returning to Plymouth where the greater part of the fleet lay at anchor under the command of the Lord Admiral Howard of Effingham and Francis Drake.

Winter was coming in with storms and squalls and furious gales and every available officer was wanted to make the most of this enforced truce, supervising the refitting and re-arming of the ships in time for the expected Spanish attack in the spring. Unfortunately, the Cadiz expedition had not altered Philip II's fanatical determination and the Armada, licking its wounds and making good the damage, was still a very real threat. As a result, Kit would be based on Plymouth for an indefinite time to come, perhaps for months, and it had been agreed between them that Deborah should make the journey west to visit him.

Meanwhile, escorted by John Strong and four stout men armed to the teeth, Deborah travelled northwards to acquaint herself with her possessions.

She remained there a fortnight, her teeth chattering with the cold and her spirits borne down by an unvarying prospect of freezing mist. All the same, she returned to London very well satisfied.

She had succeeded, with the aid of facts and figures, in convincing the Earl's steward, Jonathan Woodburn. Not that it had been easy. Woodburn, who turned out to be an elderly man, all beard and eyebrows with a strong, hooked nose emerging belligerently from the undergrowth, had made no bones about letting her know, from the first moment of her arrival, that he did not take kindly to a woman poking her nose into matters which even the late Earl had always left strictly alone. Well, he had learned. Young she might be, but she could add two and two, and better than he, it seemed. Not that this discovery had gone any way towards lessening the old fellow's dislike but it had at least instilled in him a healthy respect for his new mistress and a salutary caution regarding his own perquisites in the future. He would continue to rob her, that was inevitable, but he would keep his depredations to a minimum and that was all she asked. Heaven forfend that she should have to spend the rest of her days in that grim fastness!

When she was back in the cheerful bustle and animation of

London, with its bright lights and excitement, she sighed with relief. She could almost have brought herself to sympathize with the late Earl.

December passed, and January, and February . . .

Deborah spent the Christmas holiday at Fleet Street. Her recent widowhood made public appearances ineligible and she was not disposed to try private visiting. Given her present position in society, nothing could have been easier than to make new female friends but, apart from Jane Babington, she had not yet met a single woman whom she felt she could trust, while she felt nothing but an unmitigated dislike of the titled ladies of her acquaintance, with their heads full of pride, hypocrisy and envy and nothing on their lips but mindless babble or malicious gossip. In any case, she had better things to do with her time than waste it in their company. There were so many interesting things to occupy her.

By this time, she had become a familiar visitor at the premises from which Messrs Notham and Redford conducted their business. Almost every morning, Mr Redford would see her floating gracefully into his room, with Psyche at her heels. She would sink into a chair, casually throwing back her furs, and set herself to learn.

A friendship had sprung up between the two and while the old man talked, the roll of almost legendary names unfolded before Deborah: the Muscovy Company, the Levant Company . . . ships and caravans bringing spices, silks, perfumes and gems from the Orient, the profits of which, with God's help, would earn a fortune for every member of the company . . . market prices . . . financial strategy . . . there were risks in all these things, of course, but the prospects for gain were enough to make your mouth water.

Her afternoons were devoted to the new house going up by the river near Charing Cross.

There she discussed with Warde such details as mouldings, cornices, pilasters, stiles and muntins – the technical terms tripped off her tongue with astonishing ease. The walls were rising slowly but where a detached observer might have seen only a jumble of brick and stone, Deborah beheld an elegant mansion, symmetrical in design and opulent in conception. At night, she visited it in her dreams, secretly at first, inspecting the spacious hall with its carved pillars supporting the massive staircase which rose in eight separate flights, alternating with landings. On the first floor was the High Great Chamber, its lofty plaster frieze delicately outlined in gilding. Penetrating farther, one came to her own private apartments, an idea which Warde, with his wide experience of Italian buildings, had breathed in her ear, an exquisite retreat hung throughout with silk. The entire west wing was taken up with the long gallery, destined to house beneath its magnificent coffered ceiling, the Flemish tapestries and items of valuable furniture which she was keeping from Norland House. The east wing . . . but no! She must not visit the whole house yet, although she supervised each detail in a fever of excitement, planning for the future, engaging the most famous craftsmen. After all, wasn't it her very own house, her home where, one day perhaps, she might live with Kit.

If the truth were told, this was not a matter on which he had given her any very explicit encouragement to hope. A kind of mutual bachelordom seemed to suit him perfectly, always provided, of course, that he was not called upon to share it with anyone else.

"Be good, sweetheart," he had said to her as he left Gilford. "There you are, more beautiful than ever and a highly eligible match for anyone. I'll warrant all the young men will be round you like flies round a honeypot. But let's have no nonsense while I'm away, eh? You belong to me, don't forget, and I'm not one of your easy-going lovers, mark. God's death, I'll not be made a cuckold of by you, so you are fairly warned." Then, as though to mitigate the sternness of his words, he had added teasingly: "And if the fancy takes you to try another bout at wedlock, then beware. A second husband may not prove so complaisant as the first."

She had simply smiled, but the taunt had gone home, bringing the stinging words unspoken to her lips. Surely he must know by now that he was everything to her? That she could think of no man but himself for husband, and was only waiting until the time when his love might be stronger than his desire for freedom?

She made three journeys to Plymouth but cut short her stay each time. Where was the marvellous understanding between them? There was no place for her among these rough seafaring men, united in their common preoccupations, their common hopes and confidence. It was a man's world, where she was only in his way.

Kit could only see her when he was not required for duty and whenever he was free he was usually surrounded by a clutch of friends who could talk of nothing but "those damned Spaniards", or the Duke of Parma, the celebrated Alexander Farnese of whose very name she was by this time most heartily sick, or else about leaks and timbers and tides, all of them captivating subjects, no doubt, but not to be supposed to interest a woman.

Kit, however, seemed blissfully happy in this masculine environment. He would sit, smoking his pipe, wreathed in clouds of smoke, oblivious of her boredom or the longing she had to be alone with him for a little while. He was in his element and made no attempt to cut short the endless talk that went on over pots of ale. And when at last they did find themselves alone, Deborah's pleasure was spoiled by a faint feeling of resentment.

On her last visit, therefore, she came to a decision. She was determined not to destroy what lay between them through her own stupidity. Rather than have to beg a few hours of his company, she preferred to wait for him until he was free to join her in London.

Kit made no objection. Quite the reverse in fact.

"It's a wonderful thing, my love, to possess a mistress as understanding as she is adorable," he exclaimed, clearly relieved that she had finally managed to grasp that a man could not mix business with love.

One morning in February, when she returned from a visit to the Royal Exchange, Betty handed her a note from Mistress Tucker requiring her presence at the palace that very afternoon.

As Deborah made her regulation curtsy, she noticed that the Queen was wearing the splendid collar of emeralds and diamonds which had been her own gift, taken from the Norland family jewels; an unusually gracious gesture. Elizabeth came straight to the point.

"I have a mission for you. Can you arrange to be free for three or four months? It will entail a journey."

A mission! A journey! The news was so sudden and unexpected that all Deborah's powers of self-control were called for to suppress the tumult of her feelings. However, she said only: "Your Majesty has no need to ask. My life is yours to command and a single lifetime can never be enough to prove my gratitude to Your Majesty."

"God's death, methinks your tongue has made some progress in these two years."

The Queen clapped her familiarly on the back but the smile vanished as swiftly as it had appeared, to be replaced by the anxious, brooding look she had worn earlier.

"We are on the brink of war, child," she went on without a pause. "We can lull ourselves with vain hopes no longer. This year it will come."

Deborah heard her in mounting horror. It was not that she

had been unaware of the seriousness of the danger, precisely, but there had been so much talk of war for so long now, one day it was imminent, the next it had withdrawn again, so that she had almost come to think that it would never happen. Yet now, here it was, rising up to confront her out of the Queen's own mouth.

"It will be like no war that we have known," Elizabeth was saying. "But bloodier and more horrible because it will be fought in the name of religion and in that name there is no atrocity that does not become sacred. If the King of Spain achieves his object and if this dear island of ours is invaded, it will be the end of England, and the end of the Reformed Faith. Everything I have fought for for thirty years, peace, prosperity, a unified faith, all those things which make a realm rich and respected will be reduced to ashes . . . I was much about your age, child, when my sister Mary's bonfires blazed throughout this land. What my eyes saw then was an evil which attacked men's souls as well as their bodies. Yet those who suffered for their faith by fire in those days would be multiplied a hundred, nay a thousand times were Spain to triumph now. What I have seen I will not see again!" The Queen drew herself up proudly, eyes flashing and hands clenched. "It is God's will that I should guide this realm of England and keep it safe from peril and from tyranny, to His greater glory. But to do it I shall need the help of all my subjects. I am asking for your help today."

Deborah knelt at her feet, knowing that she would gladly die for such a Queen.

"Whatever Your Majesty commands," she said chokingly.

"Tush, child. Let us have no dramatic scenes if you please. What I need is a cool head. If you are to understand what I require of you, I must first explain our worthy cousin's plans. Indeed, he is so confident of success that he is at no pains to hide them. It seems half Europe knows what he would be at. Know then that the Armada is to set sail on a given date but not to head straight for England. Its first objective will be to effect a junction with the Duke of Parma's forces off Dunkerque. Parma's a first-rate soldier. There's only one thing wrong with him, and that is the fact that he governs the Low Countries for King Philip. The Armada, then, is to act as escort to Parma and his troops and make for the shores of England, always supposing that they ever reach them. They have our gallant ships to reckon with first, and our shrewd Sir Francis, to say nothing of the winds and tides which, as it happens, we have the considerable

335

advantage of knowing a great deal better than they do. But to return to Flanders, which as things stand is the strategic key to the whole campaign, for it is from Flanders that the great enterprise which the Duke is getting under way on King Philip's orders is to set out. Information concerning that enterprise is vital to our defences. Something, we know already, from the spies I have there but many are double agents and the information they provide cannot always be trusted. This is where you come in."

Deborah nearly jumped out of her skin. She? In that country crawling with Spaniards? Good Lord, she'd be caught before she'd gone a step!

"Oh, not to gather information of that kind, never fear," the Queen said quickly. "But we have a good many Englishmen in Flanders, employed by Spain in key positions. They would be in a position to give us valuable information."

"Does Your Majesty refer to those papists who have fled this country and accepting the hospitality of Spain now fight with Spain against us?"

"Tush, child, nothing so devious. You will learn that a pardon may be well given when it buys advantage. Not that I mean to give a pardon to those traitorous dogs who fought against their own countrymen in the Flemish campaign, but there are those among the exiles who, without themselves plotting treason, have been caught up in treason. More precisely, there are a number who, while having the sense to keep from making war on their brother Englishmen, have also, it would seem, lost something of their enthusiasm for the cause which carried them into exile. Towards such persons I am disposed to show clemency, provided, of course, it can be made to pay."

But where, Deborah asked herself, did she come in? She understood less and less and cursed the rigid etiquette which kept her on tenterhooks, obliged to listen meekly without asking questions.

"From the list which my agents in Flanders have provided, I have selected three. Two of these gentlemen are attached to naval bases, while the third has important administrative connections. The three together should give us an excellent cross-section, and with the two-fold merit of providing invaluable first-hand information and at the same time winning back useful men to our own side rather than letting our enemies have the benefit of them. Everything hinges on whether they can be got, and for that I need someone I can trust, who will be adroit enough to overcome their doubts, reawaken their patriotic feelings and assure them of my good faith, with sufficient proof to bear it out, of course."

The Queen's hand came to rest on the girl's shoulder.

"The person I have chosen to carry this offer is yourself. You possess the right qualifications. The fact that the Norlands were papists will serve at need, and who better than a pretty woman to make our quarry long for England, home and beauty, when they must be sick to death of those pasty Flemish women! I tell you, child, this is a venture which demands intelligence and a cool head. Never forget that you will be putting your head into the lion's mouth, with no hope of rescue should you be suspected. Though you've managed well enough for yourself in your own affairs, I'll say that for you." There was the faintest, meaningful emphasis on the words. "And I've a plan prepared which, if you're careful, ought to give you a fair chance of success. Will you go?"

If pride were indeed a sin, Deborah thought, then she was about to commit a walloping big one. This time it was not simply a matter of carrying a letter of no great importance, with a handful of papists and Sir Francis Walsingham set up as bogeymen to fright her. This was a mission that might well prove vital to England, and one which few men would have the courage and resource to carry out. God forgive me, it is the Queen not I who says so, she told herself.

Three little words sprang to mind to dampen her enthusiasm. Where? When? And How? Time enough to glory in her mission when she had earned the credit, and that did not lie close at hand but far away across the sea. Far away from Kit, from England, from all that she held dear and familiar. Suddenly, she felt very small, infinitely small and vulnerable. Good God, surely the whole scheme must be madness? She, Deborah, all by herself, against thousands and thousands of Spaniards? And suppose she failed?

She encountered the Queen's bold, blue, penetrating gaze and felt ashamed, certain Elizabeth had divined her fears. What was her danger compared to the danger to the realm? The Queen had judged her capable of success. Was her own faith to be less?

"Your Majesty must surely know my answer," she said steadily. "What must I do?"

Elizabeth smiled, well satisfied.

"I hoped no less of your loyalty. Look at this paper. The names and addresses of the three men you want are written there."

Primo: Baron de Stretworth, Second-in-Command, Port of Sluys.
Secundo: Lord Wilner, Château de Geyde, Bruges.

Tertio . . .

The paper almost fell from Deborah's hands. Could it be true? Could she have read aright?

Tertio: Lord David Ashbury, acting Captain, Port of Dunkerque.

She lowered her long lashes to hide the tears which sprang to her eyes.

David! Dear David, she would see him again! It seemed to her all at once as though heaven had sent that friendly name to her as a sign of good omen. She would not be wholly alone in Flanders. Now there was one friend there at least.

Her fingers were shaking a little as she refolded the paper.

Two hours later, she was in possession of every detail of the Queen's plan and took her leave. As she tendered her grateful thanks for the mark of royal favour which had chosen her, Elizabeth interrupted:

"By the way, it is understood, I hope, that you will bear the expenses of the journey. My coffers are all but empty. Fortunately the same cannot be said of yours."

A week after this interview, after a final audience at Whitehall, Deborah left London, in accordance with the arrangement she had made with the Queen.

All her affairs were in order. The building operations were left in Warde's capable hands, Psyche entrusted to Aunt Tucker, Kit – well, unfortunately one could not part from a lover in quite the same spirit as from a charming household pet, with a few tears and the selfish assurance of finding him faithful at one's return. To leave Kit, with no hope of hearing any news of him for months on end, and without that last resort, if absence become more than one could bear, of hastening down to Plymouth to be with him, that was a sacrifice indeed. But she had hidden her anguish in affectionate commonplaces and written him a long letter warning him that she would be away for some time. The estate was causing her some anxiety, she wrote and, since in his absence there was nothing to keep her in London, she meant to take advantage of the fine spring weather to see what that rascal of an agent of hers was up to.

In fact, she did go north to her estates, taking John Strong as escort, and stayed there for two dreary, interminable months with nothing but sheep to look at and a parcel of yokels for company.

Then, one evening, the sound of galloping hoofbeats came to disturb her solitude. A message was left and the messenger gone again almost at once.

338

At last, the signal she had been waiting for!

If her stay on the Norland estates had all the appearance of disgrace, this precipitate departure bore an even stronger resemblance to a flight. For so the Queen had planned it.

With only her faithful henchman for escort, Deborah travelled by swift stages southwards, avoiding large towns and the more popular inns. Coming to London, she turned left, avoiding the city, and crossed the river lower down by boat to join the Dartford road, then made her way through the orchard country of Kent in all the glory of breaking apple blossom, on through Rochester to the harbour of Margate.

It was here, having come to a satisfactory agreement with one John Bradford, the skipper of a small sailing vessel, she said good-bye to John Strong.

John was to go back to London while she, Deborah, was about to take the first step into the unknown.

What lay in store for her in the fantastic and yet perilous adventure on which she was embarking? What part would she have to play in the chaos which loomed ahead? She could not tell but she was drawn forward none the less by an eager curiosity stronger than fear. All she knew was that she went for her Queen, for England and for the home she dreamed might one day be hers to share with Kit. She was going for the sake of all the things which in her eyes made life and love worth striving for.

She glanced back once to where John Strong was disappearing round the bend in a white cloud of dust. Then, facing about, she began to run down the narrow lane, hemmed in by whitewashed cottages on either hand, towards the sea, and towards her rendezvous with Spain.